T0191393
KNOT FOR SAIL

A Pirate's Life for Tea

THE TOMES & TEA SERIES

Can't Spell Treason Without Tea

A Pirate's Life for Tea

rebecca thorne

A Pirate's Life for Tea

A Cozy Fantasy Where Love Sets Sail

BRAMBLE

TOR PUBLISHING GROUP / NEW YORK

This is a work of fiction. All of the characters, organizations, and events portrayed in this novel are either products of the author's imagination or are used fictitiously.

A PIRATE'S LIFE FOR TEA

Map by Rebecca Thorne
Chapter ornaments by Amphi
Tip-in illustration by Perci Chen

A Bramble Book
Published by Tom Doherty Associates / Tor Publishing Group
120 Broadway
New York, NY 10271

www.torpublishinggroup.com

Bramble™ is a trademark of Macmillan Publishing Group, LLC.

The Library of Congress Cataloging-in-Publication Data is available upon request.

ISBN 978-1-250-33317-9 (trade paperback)
ISBN 978-1-250-33318-6 (ebook)

Our books may be purchased in bulk for promotional, educational, or business use. Please contact your local bookseller or the Macmillan Corporate and Premium Sales Department at 1-800-221-7945, extension 5442, or by email at MacmillanSpecialMarkets@macmillan.com.

First Bramble Trade Paperback Edition: 2024

Printed in the United States of America

0 9 8 7 6 5 4 3 2 1

To the people who gave me one-star reviews
because the first book "had lesbians."
I doubled the lesbians in this one. Just for you.

Author's Note

Please note that this novel is intended to be the sequel to the first Tomes & Tea novel, *Can't Spell Treason Without Tea*. However, as this quartet is mostly episodic, you can definitely understand and enjoy this book without reading book one.

Content Warnings: violence, oppression, near-death experiences, blood, drowning, brief animal injury.

(This novel is a cozy fantasy. Although my books have higher stakes than other cozies, you are guaranteed a happy ending. This novel is best enjoyed on a quiet night with a fireplace, a beloved pet, and a cup of tea.)

LATHE
OSLOP
DIARN ARLON'S ESTATE
THE MAGICARY
SHEPARA
NEOLOW
KOLL
JALLIN
THE SOUTHERN SEAS
THE ROILING ISLANDS

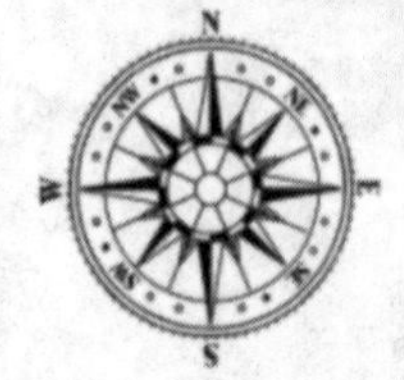

THE REALM

DRAGON COUNTRY
TAWNEY
THE QUEENDOM
ELLIA
THE CAPITAL
RCON
LEONOL

A Pirate's Life for Tea

1

Reyna

There were days when Reyna missed the heart-pounding thrill of guarding a queen.

It wasn't often. She rather loved her quiet life as a tea maker in the small, icy town of Tawney. Loved her friends and their daily drama. Loved the cozy barn-turned-bookstore she'd created with her partner, Kianthe, and the warmth that filled it. Entire days were spent watching the clouds pass. Reyna's biggest concern was how well her baby griffon would take to training that day. Accomplishments came in the form of a quiet kiss or a particularly tasty blend of tea.

But against all odds, Reyna had a certain nostalgia for her old job. Guarding a notoriously vicious queen. Stalking assassins through crowded ballrooms. Hunting down conspirators in back alleys. Besting the most skilled swordsmen in the Queendom in private duels.

Again, it wasn't *often*.

But sometimes.

So, a thrill raced through Reyna as she and her fiancée crested the hill and surveyed the organized chaos of Diarn Arlon's home.

"A ball?" Reyna couldn't keep the intrigue out of her voice. "Diarn Arlon is hosting a *ball* tonight?"

"That would explain why no one but the stable boy was around to greet us." Kianthe crossed her arms. "Gotta admit, I didn't see this coming."

The diarn's riverside estate was massive, spanning an area that could have fit the entire town of Tawney comfortably. But the party was centralized to a manicured lawn beside the powerful Nacean River—Shepara's largest river, so wide the opposite bank was barely visible. A six-piece orchestra filled the nighttime air with gentle swells of music. Torches illuminated a well-stocked buffet table, and square tiles constructed a dance floor over the spongy grass. All of it was visible from their elevated position, where she and Kianthe perched in the shadows of Diarn Arlon's looming hilltop mansion.

But the best part? Constables—Diarn Arlon's private guards—patrolled everywhere. Their black uniforms and silver badges reminded Reyna vividly of her own cohorts, of the days when she and Venne would prowl the edges of Her Excellency's ballrooms clad in crimson and gold.

Her hand drifted to the sword at her hip, and she bounced on her toes. What was Diarn Arlon expecting tonight? Bandits? An assassin, perhaps? She hadn't drawn her weapon for anything other than practice drills in so long.

Beside her, Kianthe bounced for a different reason. "Well, no complaints. By the Stone, that's so much food. Do you think it's free?"

Reyna snorted. "Darling, we've hardly starved up to this point."

"Okay, sure, but homegrown plants only go so far." Kianthe gestured down the hillside. "Look at that spread! Turkey, pork, fish . . . The salmon here is incredible. You have to try it."

"We're here for a reason, Key. We don't have time for—" Reyna paused as movement caught her eye. "—for salmon," she finished lamely.

Down near the riverbank, one of the constables glanced over her shoulder, then slipped into the pine forest that circled the manicured lawn in a dark embrace. The constable vanished in a breath.

Hmm.

"Rain?" Kianthe poked her shoulder, then followed her gaze to the forest. "You have that 'something's wrong' look. What's happening?"

"I don't have a 'something's wrong' look," Reyna replied.

"Sure you do. Your eyebrows twitch, and you start smiling."

Reyna smoothed her expression, but inside her chest warmed. No one else had ever noticed anything like that, not until she started dating Kianthe.

The Arcandor continued, amused now: "You're also the only person I know who smiles at the first sign of trouble." She flipped her dark, shoulder-length hair off her face and casually ignited one palm in flames. "So, who's causing problems tonight? The food can wait."

They'd been dating for years, but Reyna would never get used to seeing a mage just . . . light themself on fire. It was lucky everyone else was near the river—otherwise, they'd definitely be attracting attention.

Reyna squeezed Kianthe's arm, feeling the heat of the flames and trusting she'd never be burned. "First, you are wonderful, and I love you dearly. Second, not everything is a problem."

"Mmm. Sure. But when you get that look, something usually is."

Reyna squinted again at the trees. "It's probably nothing. A constable went into the forest, that's all. It's odd that she'd leave her rotation."

"It *is* odd she'd . . . leaf . . . like that."

Reyna leveled an unamused stare at her fiancée.

Kianthe grinned. "Okay, sorry. Maybe that is her rotation." The mage extinguished her palm by shaking the flames out, like one might after dunking their hand in water. She rocked back on her heels, tugging her cloak tighter around her shoulders as a chill swept off the river. Kianthe didn't love the cold.

"The diarn—is he a diarn or a councilmember?"

"Well, technically he's a diarn who *serves* on the council, but his title will be 'diarn.'"

Reyna nodded, then moved on: "Well, Diarn Arlon has established eight points of focus around the party, and six additional rotations covered by eighteen constables. Seventeen, now." Her thumb rubbed circles over the clay disc on her sword's pommel, the one Kianthe had magicked to cover Queen Tilaine's royal insignia. "Every rotation stays within sight of the grounds. It's possible he'd have more in the woods, but no one else is crossing lines."

Kianthe stared at her.

Reyna quirked an eyebrow. "Something to say, love?"

"You're sexy as hells when you talk like that, and now I'm wondering if I can take *you* off rotation by dragging you into the forest."

It shouldn't have taken Reyna by surprise, but it did. She snorted, then covered her mouth to stifle her laughter. "There are days where I wonder what the Realm would think if they truly knew what the Mage of Ages was like."

"They'd probably think I'm sexy as hells, too." Kianthe grinned, rocking back on her heels. "So, let me guess. You're going to investigate the constable . . . and you're sticking me with the boring job of confronting Arlon about that shipment."

"It's important to cover our bases," Reyna replied steadily. "And I'd hardly be of help with Diarn Arlon. He'll be more receptive to the Arcandor requesting information than an ex-royal guard from the Queendom."

Kianthe set her jaw. Reyna couldn't blame her; they'd encountered that prejudice more than once on their journey through Shepara. The mage's words were clipped. "Not like our countries are at peace, or anything. Not like you don't make the best cup of tea in Shepara *or* the Queendom."

"Ah, yes. A cup of tea. The best way to sway international politics." Reyna winked and started down the hillside. "See you in a bit, darling."

She dove into the forest, casting only a brief glance over her shoulder to see Kianthe trudging down the carefully marked path to the river's edge. A fond smile crossed Reyna's lips. Hopefully Kianthe could stay focused—that was always the question with her fiancée.

Reyna, meanwhile, moved swiftly and silently through the forest, ever alert, years of training resurfacing as easy as breathing. This far north, the pine trees loomed thick and heavy overhead, their boughs swaying in the ever-present wind coming off the massive river. It didn't take long for the orchestra's melody to quiet to a whisper. When Reyna reached the river's shore, she homed in on the subtle *tip-tip-tip* of a constable's footsteps over fallen pine needles.

She was just about to approach when movement on the river caught her eye: an ominous shape moving fast away from the party.

Reyna stepped to the river's edge, boots slipping in soft mud as she craned to see details. It must be a ship, with the smooth way it cruised across the water's surface. But if it used sails, they were black cloth, nearly invisible, and there wasn't a lantern at the bow to signify its presence.

"Excuse me," a sharp voice said behind her.

Reyna whirled, one hand on her sword's hilt.

The constable had found her. With skin the pigment of burnt umber and a uniform of black velvet, she was almost as difficult to see as whatever was drifting downriver. But her tone couldn't be mistaken—it was one Reyna had often used while patrolling.

"Are you a guest of the party?" She also reached for her weapon. Unlike the long, thin blades used by the Queensguard, Diarn Arlon equipped his constables with a shorter sword that curved into a point at the end.

Neither woman unsheathed her sword, but the air was tense with anticipation.

"Something like that," Reyna answered.

The constable frowned at her accent. "You're from the Queendom."

Of course. The constable's tone wasn't shocking—Queen Tilaine had a bad reputation heavily steeped in truth—but considering how many people she'd heard it from, Reyna was getting a bit irritated. After all, she'd separated from that life and was trying to build a new one.

It never seemed to matter.

The constable was still waiting for an answer, so Reyna nodded curtly. "I am. But today, I'm on business with the Arcandor."

"The Arcandor." The constable's tone was deadpan. She didn't remove her hand from her sword. "Last I heard, the Arcandor was in Tawney."

Reyna drew a short breath, focusing on the scent of pine, moss, and wet soil.

"We've come west. Fortunately, the Arcandor isn't tethered to one location." Reyna maintained an amicable disposition, even as sarcasm lurked on the edges of her statement.

The constable frowned. "Hmm. Regardless, weapons aren't allowed at the diarn's ball."

Reyna could respect that. She'd collected many from nobles who thought it appropriate to arrive at the Grand Palace with decorative swords or daggers. But she had no plans to relinquish her own, so she diverted: "I'll remember that when I enter. What is Diarn Arlon celebrating?"

The constable looked like she wanted to push the issue, but she didn't. She shifted in the soft soil of the riverbank, glancing at the full moon through the snarl of pine needles. "He hosts a feast every year on the second full moon of fall. It's meant to evaluate the year's crops and award the highest-performing farmers with bonuses."

"Bonuses?" Reyna's brow furrowed.

"An idea he implemented years ago to encourage the highest yield from his lands. Our barley and wheat exports are the best in the Realm."

Reyna tilted her head in consideration, fingers idly tapping the sheath of her sword. Abundant crops were certainly where Diarn Arlon earned his reputation. Without the rich soil of the Nacean River, Shepara would be facing a food shortage. Even the Queendom, far to the east, purchased his yields in bulk.

Reyna spoke neutrally: "I see."

"You shouldn't be wandering the estate. Come along; I'll escort you back to the party and you can point out the Arcandor." A threat lingered in that statement, like she didn't believe Reyna had arrived with the famous mage. The constable motioned for her to move in front—but her eyes cut to the riverbank only briefly.

Looking for . . . what? That dark shape?

Then Reyna *hadn't* been seeing things.

She opened her mouth to ask—and at that moment, an explosion shattered the air.

The blast shook the forest, sending a smattering of birds screeching into the nighttime sky—a sky suddenly ablaze with orange light. The constable flinched, but Reyna was moving before the echoes had faded, instinct taking over.

Kianthe.

Abandoning the constable, Reyna sprinted through the trees. Fear compounded in her chest as the partygoers' shock faded and their terror grew. Screams and shouts filtered through the crisp air. The constable's footsteps pounded behind her, even as the acrid scent of smoke assaulted them. Reyna covered her nose with her sleeve, ducking past the final line of trees.

"Key," she gasped.

Fire snarled the riverbank, spreading like water from an overturned bucket. The long wooden buffet table was alight, the copious amounts of food igniting fast, too fast. Magic? Or some form of an accelerant?

It hardly mattered now. Heavy smoke and cold dread made it hard to breathe.

To her credit, the constable only hesitated for a moment before leaping into the chaos.

"Evacuate up the hillside. Gather by the mansion," the constable shouted, her commands allowing no argument. People sprinted up the cobblestone path, and she physically shoved those who were too stunned to move. A harpist struggled with his instrument, but the constable hollered, "Leave it," and the man reluctantly obeyed.

The other constables were evacuating in a similar fashion, moving in cohesion as they corralled the guests away from danger.

Reyna ignored them all and ran *toward* the riverbank instead—because if Kianthe was anywhere, it'd be there. She'd just reached the fire's edge, heat washing over her, when the flames lifted off the ground.

This was no simple shift of the wind.

No, this was magical intervention. The flames flowed to a center point and formed a growing, undulating sphere—like the sun had been plucked from the noonday sky with all its brilliance and heat condensed to this new, smaller form. The sphere rose high into the air and dissipated gently, glimmering like stars before vanishing into the night.

Not even the smoke remained. Only the charred wood and scorched earth signified anything had been amiss at all.

In the center of everything, knee-deep in river mud, Kianthe quirked an eyebrow. "Rain, please tell me you weren't about to run into a *literal wall of flame* to save an elemental mage."

Reyna had a lifetime of practice mitigating the physical symptoms of fear, but it didn't stop her pounding heart or the sweat in her palms. She waded into the river, pulled Kianthe into a passionate kiss—just to reassure herself that the mage was here, alive, and safe.

"If I was," she murmured against Kianthe's lips, "it's a testament to how deeply I love you—and how little faith I have in your ability to prioritize in an emergency."

"Touching." Kianthe chuckled, her hands winding around Reyna's waist—and maybe a little lower. She kissed Reyna again, slow and deliberate, and pulled back. "Public displays of affection? Maybe I should almost explode more often."

"You should remember what I said about unnecessary risks." Reyna tapped Kianthe's nose, disentangling herself, smoothing her shirt. "And the punishment that comes with them."

"Punishment, you say." Kianthe's eyes sparkled.

Reyna rolled her eyes and tugged her fiancée out of the mud, squeezing her hand as they reached the riverbank. "Any idea what caused the explosion?"

"Oh, I know this one. I'm going with 'something ignitable.'" Kianthe smirked.

"How insightful. Anything else?"

"Listen, you're the one who loves a good mystery. I'm just wet and cold." Kianthe began magicking the mud and water out of her clothes.

With a sigh, Reyna knelt beside the buffet table, inspecting it visually before feeling around its charred surface. As she ran a finger along the table's underside, an old conversation settled into her mind—something Kianthe had once said during a quiet forest walk near Tawney. *"Did you know? The resin of a ponderous pine can be explosive."*

At the time, Reyna had laughed, rolled her eyes—convinced it was a prank. Those were Kianthe's specialty, after all; no one would dare contradict the Arcandor's knowledge of nature. It was a power her fiancée used liberally, much to Reyna's exasperation. Now she frowned, tapping a sticky substance under the table.

"Someone really doesn't like Diarn Arlon," she commented.

"No shit." Kianthe rolled her eyes. "An all-powerful councilman with more land than any other diarn in Shepara? Whoever would make him a target?"

With the fire gone, the screaming had stopped, but what filled its wake was a steady buzz of chatter—akin to a swarm of angry bees. No one seemed to have been seriously hurt, thanks to the constables' quick response. Of course, that didn't stop the guests' obvious fear and confusion at what had just happened.

Diarn Arlon, flanked by two constables with silver epaulets, stalked down the hillside.

There was no doubt that this was the man they'd come to see. He was about Reyna's height, with a strong build and fierce eyes. He moved like a king, so accustomed to power and privilege that he expected people to move out of his way—and they did, scurrying like mice facing a feral cat. His skin was ruddy, something he'd clearly attempted to hide beneath pale powder. He scanned the constables gathering the crowds, patrolling the forest, or picking through the wreckage of the buffet table.

"Barylea," he bellowed.

"It's Bobbie, sir," the constable flanking Diarn Arlon's left shoulder said quietly.

Diarn Arlon offered him a dirty look. "Someone just ignited my ball, and that's your concern?" He noted Kianthe and said, "Stay put, Arcandor. I'll get to you in a moment. Constable *Bobbie,* report."

The constable who'd confronted Reyna in the woods approached, straightening her uniform in an almost nervous tic. She held her chin high and her shoulders back and didn't look at Reyna or Kianthe.

"The explosion appears to have originated from—"

"I know where it originated, and it wasn't a buffet table. You promised to *fix* this."

Bobbie winced, but kept her eyes glued to an imaginary point just above the diarn's head. In the moonlight, Reyna could see her eyes were a magnificent green, the color of rich moss or deep agate. "Sir, I have no excuses."

Diarn Arlon didn't like that. "Are you going to find this pirate, or do I need to assign someone more experienced to the case? Test me on this, Bobbie, and I'm happy to send you right back to dock duty in Lathe."

Bobbie swallowed, barely perceptible.

"I'll find her," the constable said.

"You have until the new moon. This ridiculous plunderer *will* be brought to justice . . . one way or another." Diarn Arlon waved a hand to dismiss Bobbie, the gesture almost violent. Bobbie saluted sharply, rapping her fist against her silver badge. Her eyes briefly met Reyna's, then Kianthe's, and then she was gone, moving back into the forest with purpose.

So, the constable knew who'd caused the explosion.

A pirate?

Reyna had never dealt with pirates before. She released a long breath, her lips tilting upward in anticipation.

At her side, Kianthe bumped her shoulder. "There's that 'I see trouble' look. Why do I get the feeling that you're going hunting and leaving me to deal with him?"

She wasn't quiet about it. Diarn Arlon straightened indignantly, as if he hadn't dismissed her in a similar fashion mere moments ago. The only reason he hadn't approached them yet was because one of his constables was murmuring in his ear, gesturing at the guests milling near his hilltop mansion.

Reyna refocused on her fiancée. "That was always our arrangement, darling. Divide and conquer, remember?" She pressed two fingers to her lips and whistled sharply. A griffon's screech filled the air, and a quieter one followed. Lilac, Reyna's ill-tempered horse, had been stabled when they arrived at the diarn's estate—but Visk and Ponder preferred the wilderness.

Kianthe pouted. "Okay, but we agreed on that before pirates came into play."

"Key, remember the dragons. And the fiery hells they can bring on our dearest friends if we don't appease them." Reyna squeezed her arm reassuringly. "I saw a ship sailing upriver; I think Visk and I can catch it. It shouldn't take long."

"But—*pirates*."

"You are an international icon. A negotiator of the highest accord, one who has a very important mission here." Reyna smirked. "I'm merely a tea maker; I'll hardly be missed."

Kianthe grumbled under her breath, "Tea makers don't hunt pirates."

Reyna tilted her head, her mind already sailing upriver with that ship. "Curious. The ones from the Queendom do."

A flurry of wings beat the air as their griffons landed in the clearing. Visk—a massive beast with deep brown coloring—chittered, nibbling first Kianthe's hair, then Reyna's tunic. His daughter, Ponder—who was a bit larger than a house cat right now and growing every day—landed on Reyna's shoulder, undoing her meticulous bun as the baby creature scrabbled onto Reyna's head, wings spread for balance.

Diarn Arlon had stopped short, since anyone sensible was cautious about approaching griffons, wild or not.

Reyna pushed Ponder back into the air, then smoothly mounted Visk. Unlike horses, griffons didn't use saddles, but Visk didn't move until Reyna was well situated.

"This hopefully won't take long." Her eyes flashed to Diarn Arlon, and amusement infiltrated her tone. "Enjoy the politics, love."

Kianthe grumbled, stalking petulantly to the diarn.

Meanwhile, Reyna clicked her tongue, and Visk took to the skies.

2

Kianthe

Considering Kianthe almost died today—*and* didn't get to eat anything before the buffet table exploded—Arlon ought to be appreciative of her surprise visit. But contrarily, the diarn looked like he'd swallowed sour wine. It was almost amusing, how the veins on his pasty, powdered forehead throbbed, how his eyes glinted with barely concealed irritation.

Kianthe couldn't help herself. "Arlon. Long time no see. If I'd known your parties were such a blast, I'd have crashed one earlier."

She waited.

"Get it? *Blast*?"

Arlon stopped short, and the red splotches on his cheeks grew. Despite his meticulous appearance, the fine tailoring of his jacket, the careful way he'd greased his hair to cover a bald spot, he was beginning to look out of sorts. Behind him, one of his precious constables pressed his lips into a firm line, trying not to laugh.

"Because of the explosion?"

"Yes, thank you, Arcandor." His response was spoken through gritted teeth, and immensely satisfying. Kianthe would have to remember to tell Reyna that joke later.

Up the hill, the curious and indignant murmurs of his partygoers had grown in volume. Instead of starting a conversation, Arlon simply flicked two fingers. "Follow me." Then he about-faced toward his mansion and told one of his constables: "Get them into the primary ballroom. Restart the music."

The constable nodded curtly and began shouting orders. Slowly, the crowd siphoned into a set of huge double doors on the western side of the house. Kianthe scanned them, but no one seemed hurt. A few other constables jogged past her, already commanding the staff that had appeared to clean the mess by the riverside.

Kianthe raised an eyebrow. By the Stone, he employed a *lot* of people.

Arlon stepped confidently off the cobblestone path, rounding the estate through a secluded trail Kianthe hadn't seen before. It gave her a close-up look at his mansion, a brick-and-wood monstrosity with wide eaves under a sloping roof, accented throughout with thick iron. Expensive by anyone's standards, but ridiculous even compared to the homes of other diarns.

Maybe it was a councilmember thing. All it did was make Kianthe homesick for their cozy bookshop.

Arlon wrenched open an innocuous side door, then gestured for her to step into the dark hallway.

"Is this where you murder me?" she asked innocently.

Arlon's fingers clenched on the iron handle. "Arcandor, if you *please*."

No fun. With a shrug, she strolled inside.

The hallway was tiled from floor to ceiling with intricate mosaics, each depicting Arlon's family's claim to fame: luscious farms along a shockingly vast river. She casually examined a map of the Nacean, where the lands Diarn Arlon managed were tinted blue in direct contrast to the rich green of the rest of Shepara.

Stone damn, he supervised a *huge* section of the river. Everything touching the riverbank from the northernmost town of Lathe to just north of Jallin was tinged blue. Kianthe's brow furrowed.

"Arcandor," Arlon said, recapturing her attention. He'd opened a wooden door into a small study, and now gestured for her to enter.

It was private, merely two armchairs and a heavy wooden desk along the back wall. She deflated a bit; the diarn was rumored to have an excellent collection of books, which were Kianthe's very favorite thing.

"And here I thought you were whisking me to your library. That's the way to a girl's heart, you know."

Diarn Arlon squinted at her, then realized she was actually disappointed. His tone was dismissive. "It's on the other side of the estate, in its own building near the stables. But I'm renovating right now; no public entry."

"Am I considered the public?" Kianthe was not above using her title and status to gain access to the best library outside of Wellia.

"You are when I'm tearing out entire walls. The books are in storage."

Shit. Kianthe crossed her arms, slumping into one of the armchairs by the dark fireplace as constables took position on either side of the door.

Arlon didn't sit. Instead, he loomed over her, scowling fiercely.

"So . . . what's wrong? Other than the fact that you're apparently besieged by pirates." She paused, tilting her head. "How do you know that explosion wasn't caused by bandits or something instead?"

"It wasn't," Arlon said, irritation filtering into his voice. He began to pace, casting occasional angry glances out the window, the riverbank barely visible down the hillside. "And it's not *pirates*. It's 'pirate.' Singular."

"One pirate is causing all these problems?"

Arlon set his jaw, like he didn't want to acknowledge how bad this siege really was.

It was a struggle not to laugh. This wasn't funny; without her magic tonight, that fire could have gotten dangerous, fast. Kianthe knew that.

But there was something about how *one pirate* was setting Arlon off. Arlon, who was renowned for being composed on the council, the contemplative diarn who assessed first and judged only once all evidence was collected.

"One pirate," Kianthe repeated, swiveling in the chair so her legs dangled over the armrest. She conjured a ball of ever-flame, spelling it so it heated but wouldn't burn, and instructed it to hunker down in the hearth. The result was a warm, yellow glow cast over the small room and a soft crackling that filled the quiet space.

An idea occurred to her.

"It's not the Dastardly Pirate Dreggs, is it?"

The eager tone in her voice was unmistakable. She hadn't spoken that name since she was a child. Dreggs and their immense fleet operated in the Southern Seas, enthralling Kianthe until the day she relocated to the Magicary—and tedious lessons overtook the fearsome tales.

Once she became the Arcandor, there was no reason to encounter them. Dreggs may be a terror to honest merchants—but they were a *human* terror. Unless the pirate discovered how to harness a kraken, their reign was outside Kianthe's duties.

Still, she'd always wanted to meet them. They were supposed to be dashing, charming, able to con an army and romance a damsel with the same breath.

"Stars, no," Arlon snapped, shattering her hopes with two words. "If they entered my range, they'd be arrested on the spot. They know better. No, this is a real, honest danger to the lives of my people." To make that point, he jabbed a finger at the window, presumably referencing the carnage of exploded cakes and demolished turkeys.

"This was an exploding buffet table." Kianthe tried not to sound miffed that he'd gotten her hopes up. She had two copies of *The Dastardly Dreggs* somewhere in their Tawney bookstore: both the memoir version . . . and a fan-made romance one, the latter of which had some raunchy scenes that she and Reyna had *definitely* re-created.

It would have been excellent to get an autograph.

Arlon was oblivious to where her mind had gone. He drew a measured breath. "Arcandor, my family has supervised these lands since before magic woke the dragons. The farmers here supply grain to half of Shepara and a good portion of the Queendom and Leonol. Right now, that food supply is at risk."

Ugh. Business. Kianthe sobered begrudgingly. As much as she'd love to joke around with Arlon—who was notoriously boring at all times—she did have an obligation to the lands of the Realm.

"When you talk like that, it sounds like you're being threatened by a plague, not a pirate. So, enlighten me, councilman. How did one swashbuckler put you in such a state?"

Diarn Arlon went silent. He turned his back to her, taking a glass bottle of amber liquid off the desk, pouring it into a squat tumbler. He didn't offer one to Kianthe—anyone familiar with mages knew that magic and alcohol didn't mix.

He took a long sip and replied, "When the attacks on my ships began, I expected an amateur, easily handled by my constables."

"Bobbie."

"She's taking point, yes. Nearly begged me for the job, and her mother's the sheriff of Lathe. I figured she'd be a good resource on the ground; the people in my smaller towns know her well enough." Now Arlon's expression soured, like he was sucking on a poisonous plant. "It was a mistake, one I'll rectify if she can't produce that damned pirate by the new moon."

Interesting. Reyna had been intrigued by Bobbie, and Reyna's instincts were very rarely wrong. Somewhere in the distance, the muffled music of the orchestra swelled again—the party had restarted without its host.

"The pirate has been sailing circles around my best. Her ship is small, handmade, and fast. The winds on the river vary depending on season and weather, but she seems to know exactly when to sail—and how to hide her ship when my constables are closing in."

"Magic?" Kianthe asked.

"Not sure what kind, if it is," Arlon grumbled. "We do have several mages positioned in key towns where the mountains block the wind; they help get ships through the narrower passes. But they won't hunt a pirate. I've already submitted three formal requests."

Kianthe snorted. "Depends on the mage, and how bored they are."

"Are you volunteering?" Arlon quirked an eyebrow.

Kianthe kept her expression smooth. Inside, she was bouncing with the idea of hunting a pirate. A *pirate*. But it wasn't just about her own personal desires—no, now Kianthe was engaged, and Reyna's opinion held weight. And her fiancée had left her very high-stakes job for a reason.

It wasn't to capture pirates—or rather, one pirate—on the Nacean River.

She could hear Reyna's calm voice now, coaching her through this conversation. *"Stay focused, darling. Ask about the shipment. Find the dragon eggs."*

Kianthe sighed, sinking deeper into the chair. Her legs swung in time with the orchestra's muffled music. "Not me."

Arlon harrumphed, clearly not pleased with that answer. "The attacks have escalated quickly . . . and whoever this pirate is, she's evaded identification. We only suspect she's a woman based on eyewitness accounts."

Well, he'd been right: that couldn't be Dreggs. The pirate captain was so androgynous that perceived gender had no purpose in their tales or exploits. They were simply a statuesque figurehead of their feared southern fleet.

"Has she killed anyone?" Kianthe asked.

"A few bruises, several waterlogged constables, and one sailor with a concussion. But no, no deaths." When he saw Kianthe relax at the admission, he hastily tacked on: "But the cost of her damage is immense."

Until Kianthe moved in with Reyna, she hadn't quite understood the value of money. The Arcandor simply billed everything to the Magicary or offered magical help in exchange for goods. But now she'd spent two seasons watching Reyna carefully budgeting, guiding her to cheaper options, counting their coins.

Still, it was hard to sympathize with Diarn Arlon, swathed in opulence like he was.

"How much gold has she stolen?" Kianthe pushed upright, leaning over her knees on the plush velvet chair.

Arlon set his jaw, using silver tongs to select a shard of ice from the metal bucket beside his liquor. He swirled it into his drink, examining the amber liquid.

Kianthe snorted. "That bad, huh?"

"She hasn't stolen any gold." The answer was clipped, and he glared—first at her, then at the constables by the door. In the flickering firelight of the room's torches and the ever-flame in the hearth, dark shadows had settled over his face.

"Then what's the problem?"

"She's stealing food. Wheat. Barley. Grains of any kind."

Kianthe squinted at him.

Arlon took another begrudging sip of his drink. "She also has an affinity for the tea leaves that ship directly to my estate. And bales of hay. The occasional tome collected for my library. Sometimes liquor, but not as often."

A long silence slipped between them. And then Kianthe started laughing, and laughing, and she didn't stop until Arlon had gone very red. Wiping her eyes, Kianthe gasped, "Okay. Sorry. It's not funny."

One of his constables cracked a smile.

"It's a little funny," Kianthe amended, and pushed off the armchair to stand. "Come on, Arlon. A pirate stealing wheat? And she just . . . what? Sails up and down the Nacean River pillaging your farmers' boats?" Now Kianthe paused, stretching her arms over her head. "Actually, that's a pretty brilliant business model."

Diarn Arlon slammed his tumbler on the desk, splashing liquor over the polished wood. "My people operate on a tight quota. If she keeps seizing their food, we'll have to cut exports. Whether it's along the Nacean, or as far east as the Queendom, people will starve." Cold silence filled the room, and Arlon stepped into Kianthe's space, glaring at her. "Is this still funny to you, Arcandor?"

She met his gaze directly, although now a niggling of fear pricked her mind. Because Tawney, the town they lived in, the town full of friends that now felt like family, the town they were fighting to save from the dragons, bought food from Arlon's farms. She'd have to check with Reyna to know the exact number, but Kianthe wasn't stupid. Tawney was nestled in the harsh, icy tundra. Any produce grown had a very narrow window to be harvested, and it wasn't enough to supply the town all year.

When he said, "people will starve," Kianthe immediately put faces to those words.

She set her jaw. "No one is going to starve."

Elemental magic was worth something, after all.

But Arlon wasn't impressed. "And what are you planning to do? Tether yourself to my lands? Schedule seasonal visits to ensure none of us can survive without your intervention?" At her grim silence, he massaged his brow. "There's one solution, and it's glaringly obvious: we find this pirate and bring her to Wellia for trial. The council will decide her fate. But to track her, I need your communion with the river."

Her magic. The Arcandor possessed enough to stop floods and grow forests, with the right conduits. Here, the ley lines thrummed with energy—and everything alive was speaking to her, a whisper of golden color that spread through the air like a spider's web.

He was right. Unlike the Magicary's other mages, *Kianthe* could track this pirate.

"So, I'll ask again, Arcandor. Will you volunteer?"

Sneaky.

Kianthe scrubbed her face. Reyna wanted to focus on the dragon eggs. That said, she would never stand in the way of Kianthe's duties as the Mage of Ages . . . but who knew how long this interlude would take? Reyna would want to return to their bookshop at some point, probably sooner than later.

But maybe there was a way this all worked together.

"Arlon, I would love to help resolve this, but—I'm afraid we came here with a task of our own."

What started as a simple task—finding the three eggs stolen from dragon country a generation ago—had become a lengthy investigation of shipping manifestos, merchant interviews, and mind-numbing research. As much as Kianthe loved delving into fiction, she wasn't looking forward to spending half a season rummaging through Arlon's extensive records—even if Reyna was.

"But luckily for you, I think there's a happy compromise."

Now Arlon looked suspicious. "Oh?"

Kianthe slipped her hands in the pockets of her cloak, rocking back on her heels. "We need access to your extensive library—and specifically the shipping manifests from your early years as diarn."

She didn't tell him why; she and Reyna had discussed it, and they felt it was smarter to keep the dragon eggs a secret for now. After all, someone had ordered those eggs stolen . . . or at least willingly purchased them after the fact. And right now, the path seemed to lead to Arlon—councilman of Shepara, diarn of the Nacean River.

So, she wasn't surprised when he stiffened. "That is proprietary information. I'm under no obligation to share my records."

"No, of course not." Kianthe strolled back to the armchair, running a finger along the soft fabric. "But it's in the council's interest to keep the Mage of Ages in their good graces. And it sounds like it's in *your* best interests to consider an agreement here."

Arlon didn't respond.

Kianthe leaned against the back of the armchair, crossing her arms, tapping one finger against her elbow. "I'll be blunt. I'll capture your pirate—but in return, I need records from the 741st year of the Realm. I want to know everything that passed through your lands, where they went, and why. Get me that information, and we'll solve your pirate problem."

Arlon stepped away from the desk, running a hand over his thinning hair. For a moment, the only sound was the music of the orchestra, the crackling of the ever-flame.

"I'll produce the records," he finally said. "But I want this done in a timely manner. The temperatures are dropping by the day; there won't be another harvest this year. If this pirate keeps stealing food, we'll have a difficult winter across the Realm."

Kianthe held out a hand, ready to seal the deal. "I'll have the pirate at your estate before the winter solstice, provided you supply those records in the same timeframe."

"Fine." He shook, and his grip was uncomfortably strong.

Business as usual.

3

Reyna

A grudging respect simmered in Reyna's chest as she began to realize that her prey, the pirate's ship, had vanished into the night.

Well, not "vanished"—Reyna was scouring the river by air, and there was only so much a ship could do to outpace a griffon. But even peering over Visk's feathery bulk, squinting at the water glowing in the moonlight, Reyna knew she'd been bested. The river was empty, but it wasn't long before they happened upon a plethora of masts and sails congregating in the bay along the river. Ships—dozens of them. Beyond, Reyna belatedly noticed a set of docks and a small, quiet town.

Hmm. Not a bad tactic.

She nudged Visk lower, and Ponder cheerfully wove through the sails of larger vessels as they scoured the bay. But the decks of the smaller ships were empty, and none had the dark sails she expected.

It would be impossible to tell one ship apart from all the others after a mere glimpse of it through the trees. Reyna thought about landing, prying the dock manager for information, but it was late enough that even they seemed to have gone home for the night.

She ran her fingers over Visk's soft feathers in quiet contemplation, leaning over the griffon's bulk. "I guess we'll go back for the night," she said reluctantly. "No point in paying for a room here when the good diarn has so much space."

It was a brief flight back to Diarn Arlon's mansion, so that town must have been Oslop, the second-most northern town in Shepara. Unless the pirate had business in Lathe, the final stop on the Nacean River, they'd be sailing back in this direction regardless. Although the river diverged into several sections near here; it was still possible they'd miss her.

Granted, she and Kianthe weren't here to hunt a pirate anyway. Her priority had to be the dragon eggs, and for that reason she instructed Visk to land on the newly cleared lawn of Diarn Arlon's estate.

Several members of the staff were emptying the buffet table and cleaning up after the explosion, and they startled when Visk thumped down nearby. Reyna hopped off his back and patted the creature's sturdy neck in appreciation. It had taken her a long time to warm up to Visk; griffons were notoriously fierce, so she didn't blame the cleaning staff for showing caution.

"Sorry," she called to one servant, a man who was literally scootching around the buffet table like it would protect him. "He's friendly. Most of the time."

Visk chittered agreement.

At the worst possible moment, Ponder slammed once again onto Reyna's shoulders, eliciting a few startled yelps from the bystanders. Reyna stiffened as the baby griffon nibbled her hair. By consequence, Ponder pulled out several strands from the windswept bun, which was already a mess after the *last* time she landed on it.

Reyna redirected her beak, pushing hair out of her eyes. "She's in training," she called to the staff, which didn't seem to calm them at all. Most were edging toward the estate, clearly deciding the lawn could be tidied another time.

Excellent impression, here. Cheeks burning, Reyna clicked her tongue, her cue for Ponder to land on the ground.

The baby griffon screeched defiantly, but Visk was having none of that. He nipped his daughter with a sharp beak, then screeched at Ponder, loud enough to leave Reyna's ears ringing.

That was the final straw: the servants, four in total, fled to the mansion. Only one was brave enough to gawk as she followed her companions. Reyna was torn between wanting to shout apologies and feeling indignant on their mounts' behalf.

It wasn't like the griffons had started tearing someone to shreds, for the Gods' sake.

Facing Visk's ire, Ponder chittered, teetering off Reyna's shoulder to glide to the ground. Her wings folded as she hunched under Visk's intense, golden-eyed gaze. This time, she didn't test him: a rare response.

Visk huffed as if to say, *Better.*

The sooner Kianthe found them, the better, it would seem. Reyna dismissed the griffons with a shooing motion. "Visk, you're scaring people. We'll bunk here tonight; stay close, and Kianthe will call for you tomorrow." Her eyes skirted to Ponder, who normally would sleep with them, and then to the mansion with the party still happening within its huge ballroom. "Ponder should probably go with you, too."

Visk shook his body as if to shake off the stress of parenthood. It clearly didn't work, so he turned a sharp eye on Ponder and chirped something.

Ponder reluctantly unfurled her wings and took flight.

Visk bumped Reyna's chest in affection, then followed his daughter into the night sky. They vanished against the inky blackness almost instantly.

Reyna started hiking toward the mansion, but she didn't make it more than a few steps before that constable, Bobbie, emerged from the woods for the second time that night. Reyna paused, watching Bobbie pick leaves out of her tight curls, wipe dirt off her cheeks. She looked utterly defeated, her gaze almost deadened.

"Constable," Reyna called.

The woman stiffened, seen. In a blink, the layers of exhaustion vanished, replaced with the cold armor of professionalism. She pulled her shoulders back, placed a hand on her sword, and lifted her chin: the image of authority.

Cute. Not Queensguard material, but a nice try.

Reyna's lips tilted upward, and she approached with as unthreatening an air as possible. "I'm not trying to intrude. Once my fiancée is done speaking to Diarn Arlon, I'm certain we'll be on our way. But in the meantime, I might be able to help with your investigation. Tracking was a large function of my career as a Queensguard."

Bobbie's fight ebbed out of her shoulders. "There's no investigation. She's gone."

The finality of that statement held defeat that clearly spanned years.

"Just like that? How can she expect to hide on a river?" Reyna frowned. "It's hardly a cunning escape if we can just . . . see her sailing from the shoreline?"

"You'd think," Bobbie said, irritation lacing her words. She seemed to realize it and cleared her throat, proceeding in a more respectful tone. "The Nacean River is the biggest in the Realm. In some areas, it's so wide you can't see the other shoreline unless you sail halfway across. Islands are common. Currents twist upstream, then down, depending on physical landmarks. Add in the fog we get this time of year . . ." Bobbie winced. "Sometimes I get lucky. Most of the time, she's gone before I can get on the water."

Reyna chose her words carefully. "I see. Well, I have reason to believe she docked north of here, in Oslop. Do you think she'd continue to Lathe?"

"Considering she just stole four crates of supplies meant for Diarn Arlon's warehouse, I think she'll be stopping at every major town along the Nacean." A pause, a heaved sigh. The constable touched her wrist as a reflexive gesture—then realized there wasn't anything there and dropped her hand. "No. Serrie—ah, I mean, she won't go to Lathe. She has . . . bad memories there."

How curious.

Bobbie winced, perhaps realizing Reyna caught her slip, and angled toward the mansion with finality. "Thank you for the insight, Miss Reyna. You should return to the party." Her eyes dropped to the sword still strapped to Reyna's hip. "That won't be allowed in the ballroom. Just a fair warning. Do you like crocheted animals?"

The last sentence came and went so fast that Reyna thought she misheard. She did a literal double take, stammering for an answer. "I'm sorry. Do I like *what*?"

"Stuffed animals. Ones that have been crocheted." Bobbie shifted her weight, obviously self-conscious, but she reached into her pocket and pulled out a tiny stuffed whale. It had been painstakingly made—not well, either—with blue yarn, and filled with something fluffy—sheep's wool or cotton, most likely. Two tiny black buttons had been sewn on, almost as an afterthought.

Reyna hesitated to take it, but Bobbie looked so determined that she didn't fight. The whale fit in the palm of her hand. The stitching was messy, and little gaps showed the wool inside, but it had a certain charm.

This was perplexing. Reyna stared at it for longer than necessary. "I . . . I'm afraid I don't understand. Not that I'm not grateful, but . . ." For a moment, she wondered if she'd misread Bobbie's intent—if the constable thought *she* was someone to flirt with.

"It's my stress reliever. Crocheting. But then I wound up with so much of it that . . . well, I like to give it away. Scarves and mittens and hats are useful, but these are fun to make. The kids love them." Bobbie massaged her forehead. "I used to spend my time visiting the diarn's towns, getting to know the locals. Now I'm so busy hunting for the pirate . . . let's just say there are crochet projects *everywhere*."

Reyna stared at her. There actually was a little boy next door to New Leaf Tomes and Tea, Sasua's son, who'd love to play with this. But Reyna was still reeling from the absurdity of this conversation.

Of course, Reyna baked for stress relief. Kianthe read. Everyone had their coping strategies.

Plus, the whale was very cute.

Embarrassment seeped into the constable's tone. "You don't have to keep it. But if you need a scarf or something . . . before you and the Arcandor set off, come find me. I wish you two the best." And with a forced smile, she strolled up the hillside. Her gait was a true performance, rigid and purposeful, but exhaustion echoed in the curve of her shoulders.

Reyna pocketed the whale and followed at a leisurely pace, offering apologetic smiles to the cleaning staff cautiously making their way back to the buffet table. When she crested the hill, with the ballroom to her left and the path to the stables to her right, she found Kianthe.

"*Finally*," the mage grumbled, pushing off a wooden bench etched in gold. "For a minute, I thought you'd abandoned me with Arlon. Politics are exhausting."

"Indeed," Reyna agreed. "Try staying alert during an all-day policy meeting with Queen Tilaine and her lords. It's a special kind of torture."

Kianthe wrinkled her nose, rocking back on her heels. "Ew. I leave if it doesn't pertain to me."

"What privilege."

They shared private smiles, and Kianthe cast a glance at the mansion. They weren't close to the party, but her eyes roamed the people milling through a garden near the ballroom. "Are we joining the festivities tonight, or . . . ?"

"I'd prefer a nice warm bed, but you haven't eaten. I could certainly go for a glass of wine first. I'm very much hoping we'll have time to visit the vineyards north of Jallin."

Jallin was the southernmost town of Shepara, where Kianthe was born. From her stories, it was a marsh town with houses built either on stilts in the gentler waters, or with heavier construction along the river's edge. Reyna had been dropping hints to visit for a while now, but the longer it dragged on, the more convinced she was that Kianthe was avoiding the place.

Which was a bit concerning considering her parents still lived there, and they still had no idea about their engagement.

As predicted, Kianthe waved a hand. "Koll is best for wine, but we don't need to fly there to enjoy it. Arlon will have a few bottles out, I'm sure." She took Reyna's hand and led her toward the ballroom.

As predicted, a constable stopped them both and gestured at Reyna's sword. Kianthe merely flashed a smile and said, "I'm the Arcandor. Going to confiscate my magic, too?"

The poor constable hesitated, and his supervisor, the one with the silver epaulets who'd been flanking the diarn earlier, stepped in. "Diarn Arlon gave strict orders that the Mage of Ages and her companion be allowed inside without stipulations. Rooms are being prepared for you, Arcandor. We hope they're to your liking."

"Thank you," Kianthe said with an air of superiority, and pulled Reyna into the party.

She rolled her eyes, falling in step beside the mage. "You're enjoying this, aren't you?"

"Enjoying the power that comes with my very existence? Absolutely, I am." Kianthe grinned wickedly. "You're hungry, but I'm famished. Let's eat." She headed straight for the tables, which had been stocked with backup dishes of meats, cheeses, breads, and desserts.

Once they'd found a quiet corner to enjoy the music, Kianthe got back to business. She took a bite of broccoli, kept her voice low and amused. "Arlon's going to get us the year's records. Or at least, that's what he promised."

"That's good." Reyna was suspicious of Arlon's cooperation, but they'd both agreed it was the smartest course of action to try this first. She took a sip of wine. Kianthe was right: the diarn did import the finest. This was a crisp, earthen blend with high citrus notes.

"Yep. But in exchange, we have until the winter solstice to find him a pirate."

The perfect opening.

"Any pirate, or . . . ? He really didn't strike me as the type." Reyna never had a sense of humor like this before Kianthe, but she also knew it'd make the mage laugh. The longer they were together, the more Reyna prioritized seeing Kianthe smile—even at the expense of her dignity.

Sure enough, the Arcandor snorted into her water. Reyna felt warm all over.

"Damn it, I should have *said* that to him." Kianthe leaned back in her chair, crossing her arms. "How'd you fare?"

"Lost her in a port of ships. It was very clever." Reyna inclined her head, acknowledging the play. Her eyes roamed the ballroom, the attendees dancing to foreign music, and she felt more disconnected than ever from Tawney and their quiet bookshop. Her fingers trailed against the crocheted whale deep in her pocket and a smile tilted her lips.

Kianthe grunted. "Then I'll ask the river for help, and we'll move forward from there. Shouldn't take long to find her." A pause while Kianthe picked out the fluffy, butter-coated innards of a dinner roll and popped a bite in her mouth. "And good news: we get to pair with the sexy constable for the hunt. Arlon insisted, but hey. I wasn't going to argue."

Reyna almost choked on her wine. "The *sexy* constable? Is there something you want to tell me?"

"Only that if I wasn't such a good, devoted fiancée, you'd have some competition."

Reyna traced the rim of her glass with a finger, putting one hand over Kianthe's on the table. Her partner stilled, and Reyna leaned forward, sultry. "Love, I think you're forgetting that there wouldn't be a competition. There'd be a fight . . . and I'd win."

"Okay. That's sexier." Kianthe tugged at her collar, flashed a nervous grin.

Reyna leaned back in satisfaction, then tugged out the whale for Kianthe's inspection.

As predicted, the mage squealed, scooping it up. She ran her fingers over the soft yarn, cuddled it against her chest. "This is so *cute*! Where did you get this? Can I have one?"

"That one's yours," Reyna said in amusement. "At least until we return to Tawney and I give it to Sasua. Your 'sexy' constable crocheted it. Stress relief, she said. I think this pirate hunt is affecting her more than she's letting on."

"Because the pirate's so cunning?" Kianthe set the whale on the table, tapping its little head resolutely.

The wine warmed Reyna, and the orchestra had finally shifted into a slower melody. It was almost calming. "Not quite. I have reason to believe they've known each other in the past—and have a deeper connection than the diarn realizes."

"Oh, he'd love that." Sarcasm dripped from Kianthe's tone. She left the whale alone to dive back into the food, dipping a piece of seasoned meat into some red sauce. "Arlon sent orders for Bobbie to stay on the premises until we're ready to leave tomorrow. He wanted us to take off tonight, but I told him we needed our beauty sleep."

"*You* need your beauty sleep. I'm well accustomed to sleepless nights," Reyna replied.

Kianthe's grin turned devious. "Whoever might cause that, I wonder?"

Well, she'd walked right into that one.

Reyna sighed, pushing to her feet. Kianthe was mostly done eating now, and the wine was making her tired. "It certainly isn't someone who's had broccoli between her teeth since she started eating."

Kianthe flushed and dug at her teeth with a finger. Reyna laughed, pocketing the whale as an afterthought. Now that food was done, her mind was wandering to other things—things she knew Kianthe would happily entertain.

"Come on. Let's see if you can find all my daggers tonight."

"I'm getting closer! Stop sewing them into your shirt—you know I don't look there once it's off."

Reyna pulled Kianthe into a kiss, basking in her dazed expression. "Darling, I'm counting on it."

4

Bobbie

The river was still empty.

Okay, that wasn't fair. It was actually vibrant—full of wildlife and energy, as always. Redspars flitted between the pine trees, frogs croaked along the riverbank, and the lanternflies were just starting to extinguish their lights as the sun crept over the horizon. The river was covered in thick fog, dense and chilly, glowing burgeoning gold in the morning sun.

Bobbie blinked heavy eyelids, then smacked her cheek to wake herself up further. A few hours' sleep wasn't nearly enough, but Serina wouldn't stop in Oslop long. Her pattern of attack had begun to emerge: she'd sail her stolen goods to Neolow, if Bobbie could place bets.

And so, the constable had hauled herself out of bed, only to spend the dark hours of the morning squinting at the Nacean's gentle current.

Which meant she was fully aware of a smaller vessel sailing south, manned by two constables she recognized. The shorter one, Keets, managed the sails, but Tyal pressed against the boat's railing, his cackle bouncing off the river's surface.

"Well, well. Constable Bobbie, the fearless leader of our piratical hunt." Tyal snorted. "I figured you'd be sailing after her, not wasting your morning admiring the river."

Her irritation surfaced immediately. Over a year training in Wellia alongside him—and his cruel pranks—gave Bobbie all the courage she needed. "And after the incident in Jallin, I figured *you*'d know enough to mind your own business."

At the helm, Keets chuckled. They were one of the only constables who could handle Tyal in larger doses, but their easygoing nature made Bobbie more inclined to like them. "If it makes you feel better, Ty, I enjoyed hauling our boat out of the mud. The fact that it was wedged under a house was just an added challenge."

"Shut up," Tyal snapped.

On the shore, Bobbie smirked.

That only incited Tyal more. Their boat was easing by, enjoying a leisurely pace along this portion of the river, but they were still almost out of range. "A pirate was sighted in Neolow this morning, and the diarn is mobilizing added forces. So sorry that you aren't enough, but don't worry. Backup is here."

That timeline didn't make sense. Bobbie had watched the river for hours after the explosion last night. For Serina to reach Neolow early enough to alert the constables and mobilize new forces, she'd have had to sail all evening. She'd have had to skip Oslop entirely.

Bobbie's perplexed silence made Tyal more smug. He leaned back on the railing, casual now. "That's right. We're about to catch your pirate. But don't worry; I'll make sure to tell Arlon it was all our doing." And he winked at Keets.

Keets merely rolled their eyes.

"Good luck on the river rapids," Bobbie snapped, because she had nothing else to say. "Try not to tip over the waterfall." That fork in the river was clearly labeled, but the threat felt intimidating.

To some extent.

She hoped.

Tyal replied something, but he was too far away to hear now. Their boat faded into the morning fog . . . going, going, gone.

It left Bobbie alone yet again, although now she felt vaguely stupid. If there was a pirate south of here, she needed to investigate—even if her instincts said Serina couldn't *possibly* be that far south right now.

With a frustrated huff, she stomped back up to the barracks. The Arcandor was supposed to meet her there anyway, and she'd have better luck finding Serina with eyes in the sky.

As she walked, her frustration wore off, replaced with an echoing sadness. Arlon's estate really was lovely, and Bobbie desperately wished Serina could be here to see it. Dew had settled over everything, and the air was crisp enough to show her breath. The grounds were alive with staff: everyone from maids to carpenters to landscapers bustled past.

Bobbie could imagine the pair of them working as constables, as partners. Visiting all the towns of the Nacean River, helping farmers and townsfolk, ensuring order and bettering the world. Serina had always wanted to travel. This could have been her chance.

This could have been *their* chance.

And instead, she'd chosen pirating. And now the constables were hunting her, and Bobbie might not be able to intervene.

Emotion formed a lump in her throat, and she swallowed hard to clear it. She wanted to crochet something. Well, first, she wanted to sleep—but *then* she wanted to crochet something. Counting stitches, choosing a proper hook size, making something out of nothing . . . that was calming to her.

Not this.

The barracks were a huge building with an interior courtyard, three levels, and outdoor walkways leading to each room. Bobbie moved automatically up the stairs to her door, stepping aside as a couple other cohorts went about their morning routine. She almost envied them; she hadn't had a proper routine in a season.

Bobbie trudged to her door, stepping around the huge open crates of ancient crochet projects: scarves and hats and cloaks and sweaters and even a bin of toys, all adorned with handwritten signs in her meticulous cursive.

For the community. Please take. Free.

For a moment, humiliation washed over Bobbie, and she considered the crates intensely. It made logical sense that this was a

Good Thing. Offering free crocheted projects to help the constables, their families, other workers on the estate . . . some people really did enjoy her work. Every few days, she'd notice another piece had been claimed, which was nice.

But Tyal made her self-conscious. And the Arcandor's fiancée had seemed stunned when Bobbie had gifted her that whale. Bobbie thought it was cute—one of her best, befitting the future spouse of the Mage of Ages—but maybe it was inappropriate.

Maybe it was weird.

Did this reflect poorly on Diarn Arlon? Did it reflect on Bobbie herself? She tried not to care about what people thought of *her*—she'd only ever had one real friend, and one friend was enough . . . even if they weren't speaking right now. But she wanted to do well at her job. She wanted to impress Arlon, impress the Arcandor.

Maybe terrible crochet projects offered in tacky crates wasn't the way to do that.

But it was too late—already, she heard the Arcandor chatting with her fiancée as they strolled into the courtyard below. Bobbie fumbled with her key, desperately trying to get her door open so she could greet them properly, amicably, as if she'd gotten plenty of sleep and was fully prepared to begin the day.

"—operation," the Arcandor was saying. Her tone sounded stern, but maybe Bobbie was misreading. "I just wonder if the council has any idea that he's built his own army out here."

"They're hardly an army," the Arcandor's partner said.

Bobbie slipped into her room and gently shut the door. Safe, for now. She stepped quickly to the mirror, fluffing her hair, wiping dirt from her hands and arms. Her uniform was almost impeccable, but she plucked lint off it regardless. As she assessed herself, her eyes drifted to a frayed bracelet of twine and tiny beads. It was on careful display, untouched by other objects, but also strategically hidden behind a box of combs, rakes, and hairpins.

Her heart twinged, and she reached for the bracelet.

She'd worn it for years—over a decade, actually—and had only recently removed it when she realized *Serina* was the pirate plaguing the river. A betrayal of the biggest magnitude, attacking Bobbie's employer just to stay busy. It was obvious Serina didn't want much to do with Bobbie, Arlon, or their hometown.

But what if it was just a misunderstanding?

If Bobbie could just *talk* to her . . .

Acting on impulse, Bobbie's fingers wound around the bracelet, her thumb rubbing over familiar twine. The beads used to be blue, but now they'd faded to a pale gray. It was a bit of a struggle to get it over her hand—they'd been preteens when they made these—but it settled nicely over her wrist.

Bobbie contemplated it for a moment, feeling sentimental. And on the heels of it came self-loathing, because there was no place for sentimentality when the most powerful diarn in Shepara had declared Serina public enemy number one.

A knock echoed on the door, and Bobbie swallowed a yelp, hastily pulling her sleeves over the twine bracelet. Without wasting a breath, she sprinted for the door and yanked it open.

The Arcandor was there with her fiancée. But while Bobbie expected the Mage of Ages's absolute focus, she'd apparently lost out to the multitude of crocheted projects awaiting inspection. The Arcandor was hunched beside a crate, digging through little toy animals meant for the children, and she froze like a deer sighted by a predator when Bobbie looked at her.

"Ah—this isn't what it looks like." The Arcandor stuffed two foxes, a raccoon, and a tiny dragon into her pockets.

Her partner sighed. "It's exactly what it looks like, Constable. Tell her now if you don't want half of these items missing."

Bobbie fumbled for a response. "Stars, it's—it's my pleasure." Was her embarrassment as obvious to them as it was to her? "Take what you'd like. At least it'll get some use." The Arcandor grinned at her, and Bobbie straightened, forcing professionalism. Stand how a proper constable would stand. Act like a proper constable would act. This was the *Arcandor.*

"Hi," the most powerful mage of the Realm said.

Say hello, Bobbie's mind hissed.

"Y-You must be the Arcandor. It's a pleasure to meet you. Or do you prefer Mage of Ages?" Bobbie hastily dipped into a bow, then tapped her chest in a militant salute, and with nothing else to do, inclined her head in a nod. Humiliation washed over her in waves at the fumbled greeting. A *handshake* would have been fine.

Probably.

The Arcandor noticed—she must have—but she clearly decided not to comment on it. "Actually, I prefer Kianthe, but no one seems to care about that." She straightened, realized her pockets were stuffed, and began slipping her crocheted score into a satchel at her hip instead. "Formality's a bitch."

Bobbie was startled into a laugh.

Meanwhile, the Arcandor—ah, Kianthe's—partner had chosen a dark blue scarf from one crate, wrapping it around her neck. "You said you do this for stress relief?" She frowned, running her fingers along the embarrassingly uneven stitching. "Should we be worried?"

Shit.

Bobbie was good at her job. She *had* to be good at her job, to impress Serina, to impress her mother back in Lathe, to impress Diarn Arlon. So, she clasped her hands behind her back, the picture of a perfect constable. "You have nothing to be concerned about, ma'am. I am more than capable of keeping the pirate under control once we find her."

"'Reyna' will do. And I'm more concerned about you falling asleep at the saddle than a pirate attacking me."

Were the bags under her eyes that obvious? She probably should have gotten some more sleep, but there was still so much to do. Bobbie fumbled to reassure while still sounding halfway competent. "There is a reason Diarn Arlon allowed me to take point on this search. I assure you, I'm fully capable. In fact, if we're ready to head out, I can meet you at the stables."

"I *guess* we can go," Kianthe said, rifling through the hats now. She found one with a pom-pom at the top and tugged it over her hair with a wide grin. It fit perfectly, but Reyna covered her mouth to stifle laughter. Kianthe raised an eyebrow. "What? I think it's great."

"It's perfect," Reyna said.

She sounded like she was lying, and Bobbie couldn't even protest. In hindsight, that pom-pom *was* ridiculous. Some of the kids liked them, but adults? The *Arcandor*—?

"I have nicer hats—" Bobbie started to say.

Reyna glanced at her, calculating, and held up a hand. "Ah, no, Bobbie. I wasn't lying—it truly is perfect for her. These are absolutely wonderful." To further her point, she rifled through the crate and found a matching scarf, winding it lovingly around Kianthe's neck. To emphasize, she pressed a kiss to Kianthe's cheek. "You look beautiful."

"Aww," Kianthe replied, but her cheeks had tinged red.

Warmth spread through Bobbie's chest. If Reyna said she wasn't lying, then she really did like Bobbie's crocheted projects. Which meant Bobbie hadn't embarrassed herself after all.

Satisfied, she tied her sword to her hip. "I have a few more things to pack before we go." A pause, where she averted her gaze from them. "I plan to do what's necessary to capture this pirate. But—if I can just *talk* to her, I think this whole thing can be resolved."

Reyna tucked a few pairs of gloves into her own bag. Her tone felt comforting. "You must care for her, to give her a chance to explain herself before judgment."

"She was my best friend," Bobbie replied without thinking. Shit, *shit*. She clamped her mouth shut, eyes widening. "Ah, I misspoke. I would never be friends with a pirate, especially one who'd put Diarn Arlon's lands and profit at risk."

"Of course not," Reyna agreed good-naturedly.

Move on. Bobbie ducked her head. "I'll get my things. Meet you both at the stables."

She shut the door in their faces.

Inside, she didn't move from the wood. Her head rested on the closed door, and she stared at the ceiling. "Stars above, this is going to be a nightmare." On her wrist, the twine bracelet seemed to burn. She contemplated it for a moment. "Okay, Serrie. I'm coming."

5

Reyna

Bobbie left, which felt final—a dismissal—but Kianthe clearly wasn't ready to abandon these free gifts. She stuffed a few more scarves into her bag. "I got six. How many did you take? Let's see. Matild, Tarly, Gossley. Feo and Wylan will want one. Sigmund and Nurt. Toys for Sasua. This is great."

It was hardly Reyna's concern right now. She started for the staircase, running a gloved hand along the wooden railing in contemplation. "Mmm. That should be fine."

Kianthe jogged to catch up, tossing an arm over her shoulder. The comfort was nice. Reyna tucked into the side of her, which made Kianthe chuckle wryly. "You found a problem, didn't you? You're smiling again."

"Am I?" Reyna drummed her fingers on her sword's pommel, leading Kianthe from the barracks and toward the stables. "There may be a problem. We have a diarn who's absolutely determined to stop this pirate; I'm certain he has a punishment in mind when he meets her. Then, we have a constable working under the diarn's orders to 'capture' this pirate—and there's a very real chance her relationship is deeper than she's expressing. I think she's in love."

"Love?" Kianthe craned to see Reyna's face. "Couldn't they just be old friends?"

"It's possible. Difficult to say until I meet the pirate. But

Bobbie . . ." Reyna paused, her lips quirking upward. "Let's just say she sounds a lot like me years ago, wrestling with duty over emotion. It's no wonder she's stressed."

As they walked, the sun peeked through the clouds, casting them in brilliant light. The fog on the river, far downhill, was already burning off, but the air still held a chill. Kianthe casually ignited a flame to keep them toasty. "Hang on. Did I stress you out?"

"Mmm. The situation was stressful: the illicit romance, the clear clash between my career and the life I desired. Once we left for New Leaf and resolved everything with Queen Tilaine last summer . . . no. I haven't been stressed in a while."

"Good," Kianthe said with finality.

Reyna extricated herself from Kianthe's hold, instead looping their arms together. She raised her fingers to the flame in Kianthe's palm, stealing some warmth. "I'll be interested to see how this plays out, but . . . depending on how this pirate reacts to us, I may have some plans to enact."

"Right. Right." Based on the way Kianthe arranged her expression into six different emotions, she'd noticed *none* of those clues. Unsurprising; she'd been distracted with the crocheted projects.

Reyna chuckled, amused. "It's just a theory. But if it does work that way, can you do me a favor?"

"Anything, as long as it doesn't put you in mortal peril. That stresses *me* out."

Reyna snorted. "I'll do my very best to avoid 'mortal peril.' But I want you to stay close to Bobbie for a time, keep her company. Based on my own experiences, I believe she'll respond well to you."

Kianthe hesitated. "Are you setting me up with the sexy constable? I was joking, Rain."

"Gods, no," Reyna exclaimed, swallowing a laugh. "But I do think Bobbie will need your help. And since our quests overlap here, we might as well see if we can leave the world a little better than *we* found it, too." She tapped the pom-pom on Kianthe's new hat.

The mage heaved a sigh. "Why do I feel like we're meddling in something that's none of our business?"

Reyna smiled slyly. "Key, you should know by now. Meddling is my favorite pastime."

They reached the stables shortly after. The area was crowded; many of the guests had spent the night after the ball and were just now retrieving their mounts. This would be fine, except Kianthe decided to prematurely summon Visk and Ponder—the latter of whom was cute enough to draw a crowd of curious partygoers.

Visk took position behind his daughter, wings folded, gaze almost possessive. The few people bold enough to approach a baby griffon hastily backtracked when a full-grown one glared at them.

Ponder screeched indignantly because she loved attention, which sent Visk on a chittering tirade of his own. Reyna supervised this, but quickly realized Diarn Arlon was moving to intercept them.

She nudged Kianthe. "Your favorite person's here."

The mage followed her gaze, heaving a heavy sigh. "Great. More politics. Rich people are the worst."

Reyna snorted, covering her laughter with a cough.

Diarn Arlon didn't notice. He stepped gingerly through the muck near the stables, nodded to a few of his other guests, and stopped in front of them. Or rather, in front of Kianthe, something that didn't escape Reyna's notice.

"Have you connected with Bobbie yet?" he demanded, craning his neck behind them as if the constable had somehow beat them here. "The stablemaster is preparing her horse; there's no time to waste."

Reyna peered into the stables, sighting Lilac beside a beautiful white stallion. A stable boy was checking their hooves for any rocks or debris, and an older woman was hauling a saddle onto Lilac's back.

Kianthe must have realized Diarn Arlon was ignoring Reyna outright, because irritation flashed across her features. She tossed an arm over Reyna's shoulders, pulling her close. "Arlon, you didn't have a formal introduction last night. This is my beautiful bride-to-be, Reyna."

Confident the griffons weren't about to maul anyone, Reyna dipped her head respectfully. "It's a pleasure to make your acquaintance."

Diarn Arlon frowned at her accent. "Queendom. I heard the Arcandor was dating one of Tilaine's personal guards, but I didn't want to believe the rumor." Now he huffed. "I expected better sense from someone wielding enough magic to be considered a deity herself."

It was the absolute wrong thing to say, and Reyna winced—not at the words, which were nothing she didn't expect, but at the way Kianthe warmed with the fervor of an uncontrolled flame.

"Say that again, slower." Kianthe's expression was dark, and overhead clouds gathered slowly, ominously. "Go on."

Diarn Arlon had the decency to look alarmed. "Enough, Arcandor. Don't be childish; you must have realized the image this puts forth in Shepara, in the Magicary. The risk we'll all face if Tilaine finds leverage over you."

The stable hand arrived with Lilac in tow. He took one look at Diarn Arlon's expression and hastily pressed the reins into Reyna's hands, then scurried back to the stables. Her horse stamped her hooves, looking mildly annoyed that she'd been removed from such luxury.

Kianthe didn't take her eyes off the diarn. "Leverage would imply that the queen can manipulate Reyna."

"Or that she can threaten Reyna to manipulate *you*." Arlon crossed his arms.

Well, that fear wasn't unfounded. Queen Tilaine operated an extensive network of spies, which meant that no one was truly safe from her reach. Last summer, Reyna had visited the Queendom's Grand Palace to negotiate for her life, and it was only by sheer luck—and a dash of vanity—that she was successful. So far, Queen Tilaine was content to let her ex-guard play housewife to the most powerful mage alive.

But eventually, that pardon would come with requirements . . . and there'd be five hells to pay if Kianthe refused.

A problem for another day.

Kianthe scowled, dissipating the clouds overhead with a wave. "You're one to talk about manipulation. From the moment I stepped onto your estate, you had a job for me."

"I—"

"Enough." For this rare instance, Reyna used her Guard Voice: the loud, deep tone she'd perfected during her time in service. The word was imbued with authority, designed to make anyone nearby stop and listen.

It worked. Both of them glanced her way. She would never have spoken to a lord this way in the Queendom, but she wasn't a guard anymore. She was the Arcandor's future wife, and she would maintain a confident energy when handling problems. In one smooth motion, Reyna mounted Lilac, utilizing the height difference to gain more control.

Everyone was more confident on horseback.

She addressed Diarn Arlon first. "I may be from the Queendom, but do not question where my loyalties lie—and do not assume I'll be so easy to threaten." At this, she laid a hand on her sword, still tethered to her hip.

Kianthe smirked, crossing her arms. Smug, right until the moment Reyna caught her gaze.

"And Kianthe, there is merit to the diarn's words. I appreciate your chivalry, but the Mage of Ages has a duty to every country of the Realm." And Queen Tilaine would gladly keep Kianthe's abilities for herself if she felt she could. Reyna paused, her tone purposefully neutral: "There are many rulers who would use your power for their own agenda."

Diarn Arlon puffed in indignation. "Are you implying—"

"The point," Reyna inserted coolly, "is that catastrophizing what *may* happen is an exercise in futility. Instead, let's focus on our goal of the morning: finding your pirate."

Diarn Arlon set his jaw. "I have reason to believe she's in Neolow.

Bobbie has the badge and paperwork needed to use full authority on my lands. Stay close to her, but at this point, I want the Arcandor taking point on this investigation."

Reyna winced. Perhaps that would be their little secret; Bobbie wouldn't be pleased to hear she'd been unseated.

"All right, then. My first command as lead in this hunt: stop telling us what to do." Kianthe's tone was vitriolic, and she waited for a long moment to see if Diarn Arlon would argue.

Of course, that's when Ponder seized the opportunity to flee her father's stern gaze. She flew onto Reyna's shoulder, which made Lilac whinny and shift her weight nervously. Horses—one of many animals preyed on by griffons in the wild—hated them on principle. Lilac had not been pleased that Reyna added a *second* griffon to their little family unit.

Ponder knew this and gleefully took advantage of it. Even now she leapt off Reyna's shoulder, landing solidly on the horse's flank.

Lilac panicked, bucking with a terrified whinny.

Reyna barely had time to react, fear slicing up her veins. She'd been thrown by Lilac once, and if Visk hadn't intervened it wouldn't have been pretty. Now she grabbed the saddle to steady herself. Meanwhile, Kianthe seized the reins, Visk screeched a warning, and Ponder reluctantly took flight, circling high above.

Lilac stamped her hooves, eyes wide, but calmed down once Ponder was gone.

Diarn Arlon watched the entire exchange with exasperation. But instead of speaking, he just tossed up his hands and stomped back up the road toward his mansion.

"Good riddance," Kianthe muttered.

"What happened? It sounded like a commotion." Bobbie wove through a crowd of curious onlookers, offering a dismissive gesture to get them all back. They dispersed, but they'd certainly have a lot of gossip after this ball.

The constable approached, glancing grimly at the diarn's back as he crested the hill to his mansion. "You didn't anger the diarn, did you?"

Kianthe huffed. "Arlon could be taken down a few pegs. No one in Wellia challenges him, so it's my absolute pleasure to remind him that he's just one man standing before—how did he put it? 'A deity herself'?"

"Don't get any ideas, Key," Reyna said, rolling her eyes. "You're just Kianthe to us."

"Shit. Didn't expect a demotion so fast."

Bobbie glanced between them, their mounts, and the baby griffon circling overhead. Her brows pulled together in worry, but she forced a pathetically bad smile for their benefit. "I'll . . . get my horse. Give me a moment."

Inside the stables, Reyna watched her stuff at least six skeins of yarn into her saddlebags. Amusingly, the constable seemed to have added an accessory to her uniform: on her left hip was her sword, but on the right, she had a leather sheath with three large metal needles, each hooked at the end for crocheting.

"Wonder if she ever mixes those up," Kianthe asked, following Reyna's gaze.

She snorted, flicking her reins to get Lilac moving away from the crowds—and from Visk. "I wouldn't be making jokes about the woman who's single-handedly accessorizing your wardrobe right now." She tugged off Kianthe's new hat as she passed, then tossed it back with a teasing smile.

"Good point." Kianthe fit it over her head again, her wild hair barely contained by the yarn. She mounted Visk. "Come on, Pondie. Follow Mamakie."

Mama Key had become Mamakie at some point, and Reyna couldn't decide if it was endearing or funny. A private smile tilted her lips as Visk spread his wings and leapt into the sky. Ponder followed slower, deviating over the river.

"In a few years, I'll find you the best open pasture in the Realm and you'll have plenty of time to relax," Reyna murmured to Lilac. "How's that sound?"

Lilac puffed dreamily, and she merged with Bobbie's stallion into the stream of people leaving the estate.

❦

The clouds became menacing around noon, and by the midafternoon, it began to rain.

The constable still looked exhausted: deep bags under her eyes, hunched over in her saddle. But her stallion picked through the uneven terrain near the riverbank, undisturbed, as Lilac trotted alongside them.

"The rain will make this fun," Bobbie mumbled, squinting toward the river.

High overhead, Kianthe bent over Visk's side, barely visible through the pine trees. It looked like she was gesturing that she'd scope ahead, but it was difficult to make out her motions through the gloom. Rather than keep up the long-distance charade, Reyna tapped the moonstone strung around her neck. Kianthe had a matching stone, magicked to transmit messages through heat and physical taps.

Go ahead.

And a few moments later, Kianthe tapped a reply: *Okay.*

Bobbie scanned the skies, locating Visk and Kianthe as they picked up speed with Ponder not far behind. Once they were out of sight, she turned to Reyna. "Do you really think she'll find the pirate faster than we can track her?"

"Considering Kianthe can just ask the river for tips, I'd say it's a fair bet."

Bobbie tugged her cloak out of her bag, hunching against the rain. "The river just . . . tells her things." Disbelief slid into her tone. "I didn't think that's how magic worked."

Reyna slipped on her new mittens. They were a deep blue yarn, matching her scarf, and were quite warm. They'd get wet quickly—she'd have to switch to an oiled leather set soon. But for now, they were nice. "Trust me, I was skeptical too. But I've seen it happen enough times to know that there's *some* form of communication happening. Who am I to say she's exaggerating the semantics?"

"That's true," Bobbie agreed.

Silence fell. Their horses stepped single file, with Bobbie leading and Reyna trailing behind. The terrain beside this stretch of river was relatively flat, with ample space between the pines. Deciduous trees were starting to speckle the landscape, vibrant leaves turning yellow in the late fall season. Here, the Nacean branched into several smaller sections as the water delved around the mountains—which made scouting for a ship very difficult. It didn't help that a gloomy fog had yet again rolled over the river, thanks to the rain.

Kianthe, far ahead, would have her work cut out for her, but Reyna was content to ride along the river and chat with the constable.

"I'm curious to know why you're pursuing a pirate on horseback." Reyna broke the silence. "Why didn't Diarn Arlon equip you properly? It's hard to believe he wouldn't have a ship to lend you."

"He owns most of the ships on the Nacean, actually, so he has plenty." The constable glanced over her shoulder, tossing her cloak over her horse's flank. "I'm just not much of a sailor."

"And yet you seem to know this pirate well." A neutral statement.

"Not well. Not anymore." Bobbie's fingers fluttered against the crochet needles, but she set her jaw. "My mother is the sheriff of Lathe. My father stayed home to raise me and my siblings, but none of us had a reason to do more than swim in the river. Serina—ah, the pirate—she had a different upbringing."

Serina.

Not Serrie, then.

The name felt like Bobbie had handed her a piece of gold—and an unspoken request to protect it. Reyna didn't acknowledge the name at all, just tucked this new nugget away and redirected back to Bobbie. That was where the constable seemed most comfortable, anyway.

"I see. It still seems odd that the diarn wouldn't pair you with a sailor under his employ."

Bobbie tugged the hood over her hair to keep it dry. It partially obstructed her face from view. "On this assignment, I requested to work alone."

"To protect the pirate." She purposefully didn't use her name.

It was too much. Bobbie flinched. "I'm not protecting her. But if

I don't take point here, someone else will . . . and at least I'll listen to her excuses." A pause. "Even if they *are* irrational."

"Irrational?"

"Well, yeah." Bobbie clenched her reins a little tighter, scowling. "She always said she wanted to better her community, but here she is stealing from it. I just—I don't know. It doesn't make sense."

"Hmm."

They rode for a while longer, each sitting with their own thoughts. Below the trees, the rain wasn't bad, but in bare patches it pelted Reyna's face with an icy spray. She tugged her own fur-lined hood over her head, patting Lilac's neck as the horse huffed in irritation.

Reyna couldn't blame the creature; she didn't want to be out in this weather either. Her eyes drifted upward, to where Kianthe and Visk had returned and were gliding lazily through the clouds. They stayed low enough to remain in sight, and even from here Reyna could see the protective bubble that ensconced them.

Ponder had given up trying to fly in this weather, and was perched on her father's flank, playing with his lion's tail.

Visk didn't seem to mind.

Bobbie followed her gaze. "So, you're engaged to the Arcandor."

"It's a recent development." Reyna smiled at the memory, thinking of the pinyon pine seed they'd planted along the back patio of their bookshop. She wouldn't expect it to sprout during the frigid Tawnean winter, but Kianthe had spelled the seed—so it was entirely possible they'd come home to see it breaking ground.

Not that Reyna was ready to go home and check just yet. Even riding in the rain, this was everything she'd hoped it would be. The thrill of adventure thrummed in her veins.

"Congratulations." Bobbie paused for a moment, then said hesitantly: "I didn't know the Mage of Ages could get married."

"Well, each one is different. And Kianthe delights in breaking the rules."

Bobbie snorted, but didn't remove her eyes from the river. The rain was picking up; it was getting harder to see, and the river rapids were responding to the wind, crashing against the riverbank and whitecapping in the center of the river.

She seemed distracted, so Reyna seized her chance. "Do you have anyone like that? Or are you more of a solo rider?" The question was curious—Reyna truly couldn't tell yet if Bobbie and Serina had a history, or a *history.*

Bobbie just sighed, massaging her brow. She slowed her horse a bit, checking Kianthe's position over them as their mounts drew even. "I know what you're hoping for, but you're misreading this situation."

Her tone sounded awfully familiar. It *sounded* like Diarn Feo, Tawney's Sheparan lord, speaking about Lord Wylan, the Queendom counterpart. And even though Feo would never admit it, they found reason after reason to spend time with Wylan one-on-one.

"And how am I misreading?" Reyna asked.

"You think Serina and I were—um . . ." She cut off, stammering at the knowing smile on Reyna's face. "We're not. We were just friends. Old friends. Childhood friends, really."

Say "friends" one more time. Reyna mentally rolled her eyes, although her expression remained neutral, pleasant. She took pity on the constable and redirected the conversation. "Then Serina was raised in Lathe as well?"

She tossed the name in as another test.

It worked. Bobbie must be letting her guard down; she didn't even flinch. "For a bit." Bobbie turned so the rain didn't pelt her face, and shivered. "Serina's parents were farmers, but . . . well, they weren't very good at it. Diarn Arlon reclaimed their land when we were thirteen."

Reyna frowned. "That sounds traumatic."

Bobbie hunched over her horse. "I was there the day the constables marched up to their farmhouse. I'll never forget the tears on her face, or how she screamed as her parents packed their belongings." She shuddered, the action completely separate from the cold. "That's why I became a constable. In Lathe, my mother knows everyone. Even when she's delivering bad news, they know it comes with good intentions."

"I'm surprised you didn't want to be a sheriff like her." Reyna raised an eyebrow.

"She's got that job covered. I wanted to fix the constables from the inside out." Bobbie laughed hollowly. "Feels like a kid's dream, now."

Interesting.

Reyna didn't let Bobbie dwell on that. "What happened to Serina after that day?"

"Her family moved south to Jallin; I think her dad is a merchant now. He always loved sailing. That's how Serina learned."

Reyna chuckled. "So, instead of a merchant or a farmer, she became a pirate?" It sounded like something out of one of Kianthe's adventure novels.

"She actually did try to be a farmer first. Two years ago. It went about as well as the first time." Bobbie didn't seem to want to dwell on those memories. "But the pirate thing might be my fault. I gave her a book about the Dastardly Pirate Dreggs when we were little. We'd sneak onto her father's boat and pretend we were pirates on the open ocean."

Childhood friends, indeed. Love took all forms, and Reyna was more convinced than ever that Bobbie loved Serina. Whether it was a romantic love or something more platonic remained to be seen, but a person in love was still prone to doing dangerous things.

Reyna would have to keep an eye on this.

The rain was getting harder now, and they'd found a patch of land where the trees receded. Reyna ducked over Lilac, who stamped her hooves in protest with every step. "Perhaps we should get our horses out of the rain, wait for a bit before continuing? Surely Serina isn't sailing in this."

Bobbie hesitated, squinting at the river as if Serina's little sailboat might magically appear. But the only one who arrived was Kianthe. Visk thumped down beside them, and the rain in their circle immediately stopped. It was like all the drops were veering to avoid hitting them or the horses.

Bobbie held out a hand, testing the magic. "That's a neat trick."

"That'll be on my tombstone. 'Full of neat tricks,'" Kianthe said, spreading her arms wide.

Reyna pinched her brow to ward off a headache. "Mages don't have gravestones, dearest."

"Okay, then. Carve it into the tree that sprouts from my ashes."

"I'd prefer not to carve that anywhere, much less on a tree."

"Killjoy."

Bobbie cleared her throat. "Sorry to interrupt, but—was there any sign of her?"

Kianthe heaved an exasperated sigh. "You aren't going to like it."

The constable straightened, both optimism and dread slipping over her features. "You found her?"

"Well, we weren't far behind." Kianthe rubbed her neck. "She's downriver, but I think she accidentally went off course. She's heading straight for some intense rapids."

"She can sail in rapids," Bobbie said confidently.

"Sure. But I'd like to see her sail when her boat is careening off the waterfall at the *end* of the rapids."

Reyna could have strangled her fiancée. "Key, why aren't you getting her to safety right now?" The Arcandor's impulsive choices were legendary, but Reyna really thought she could prioritize here.

"She's sailing slow; we have time," Kianthe exclaimed, offended. "No one's going to—"

But Bobbie was already gone, kicking her horse into a gallop, mud flying in her wake. Kianthe caught it with a wave of her hand, magic twisting it into dried balls of dirt instead. She let them fall to the ground. "I was *going* to say that no one's going to die, but yeesh. Okay, then."

"I confirmed they're childhood friends," Reyna said, pinching the bridge of her nose in exasperation. "And she's in love, whether she realizes it or not."

"By the Stone, everyone's in love these days, aren't they? I could write a *book* about all the love stories we've encountered since you left the palace." Kianthe rolled her eyes, ignoring the irony of that statement.

Reyna pecked her cheek, then lifted Ponder off Visk's back. The baby griffon was clearly sleepy, because she folded her wings and tucked her head against Reyna's chest. She was warm, and it was very pleasant in the cold weather. "I would love to see you write a book. In the meantime, *please* make sure this isn't the origin of Bobbie's villain story, won't you?"

Kianthe grinned. "Your wish is always my command." And with a dramatic bow, she leapt onto Visk and urged him into the sky again.

Reyna sighed, remounted Lilac, and tucked Ponder inside her cloak. Ponder wouldn't bother Lilac as long as the griffon behaved, and right now she seemed content to be warm and dry. "Come on, Li," Reyna murmured to her horse. "I have a feeling the day's not over yet."

They galloped after Bobbie and Kianthe, with Reyna trying to ignore the growing dread in her chest.

6

Kianthe

If she hadn't *just* learned Bobbie had a long-standing relationship with this pirate, Kianthe would have figured it out by the way they shouted across the river to each other. Serina was a curvy woman with long, wavy brown hair and skin the color of the wheat she'd stolen. Wheat that was now bundled in open-air crates, which the pirate seemed quite intent on protecting.

On the shoreline, thundering along on her horse, Bobbie was clearly not pleased.

Visk drifted above it all, his wings tilting almost idly as he eased through the clouds. Kianthe braced herself against his feathery neck to observe the maybe-lovers' spat happening on the ground.

This was great stuff for her upcoming novel. The book may only be a few moments in the making . . . but if Reyna wanted to read it, Kianthe would oblige. She'd been meaning to try her hand at writing anyway.

Below, Serina was scrambling around her deck, attempting to secure the crates of wheat. It was clear from a griffon's-eye view that the river split unexpectedly and she'd intended to take the *other* side, which looked like a lovely, winding stroll. But either the rain and fog had interfered with her navigation, or the pirate just wasn't paying attention, because she'd missed every posted sign and sailed right into the "certain death" side instead.

Her "ship"—which Kianthe had expected would be a larger vessel, based on the conversations around it—was more of a small fishing boat. It had one sail and seemed to boast a smaller storage area belowdecks, but Serina would be sleeping under the stars on a boat like this.

Which meant it *really* wasn't faring well with these rapids.

And yet, she had the audacity to shout to the constable: "Just because I pillage doesn't mean I'm breaking the law!"

Bent over her horse, Bobbie hollered, "That's *exactly* what it—" She cut herself off, trying a different path. "Never mind. Serina, you have to get to shore."

Kianthe tapped Visk's neck. When she had her griffon's attention, the mage said, "Remember this, buddy. Great shit happening here. Star-crossed lovers. No. Sea-crossed lovers." A pause. "River-crossed lovers. Hmm. It's falling apart, isn't it?"

Visk chirped.

Kianthe opened her mouth to keep musing—and realized too late that Serina was making a very stupid decision.

Instead of riding out the currents with confidence and grace, waiting for the moment that the Arcandor would gently guide her ship to shore, Serina had panicked on hearing the word "waterfall" and spun the helm violently. The result was her small boat twisting sideways on the river, and immediately water washed onto the deck, capsizing the entire thing.

The whole event took less than a few breaths and Kianthe was left staring at the spot where Serina *used* to be sailing.

Suddenly, Kianthe's "no one is going to die" line wasn't so funny.

An anguished scream sliced through the air, and Bobbie yanked her horse's reins so the animal skidded to a stop, spraying mud. She leapt off his back, sprinting toward the riverbank like she was going to dive into the water herself. In the very next breath, a wall of earth pinned her legs, physically trapping her from that suicidal move.

Bobbie might be pissed about that later, but Kianthe couldn't deal with *two* people drowning right now.

"Visk," the mage snapped, but her griffon was already diving toward the waterfall. Kianthe pushed upright on his back, digging her knees into his shoulders to gain as much height as she could. With a violent ripping motion, she physically *pulled* the currents away from each other, slicing the river in half.

Serina's ship was already starting to shatter along the river rocks. The crates were gone . . . and odds were the ship was too. Kianthe may be the most powerful elemental mage—but even the Arcandor couldn't stop an entity like the Nacean River. It was like standing on the sun, trying not to burn.

But there was Serina, pinned between her ship and the water gushing at her from every angle. She seemed to be frozen in a state of panic, eyes wide, choking on water. She was going to die. Stone *damn* it all, if Kianthe blinked for even a second, this woman would die. Kianthe couldn't let that happen—couldn't bear to look Reyna in the eyes if it did.

Panic swelled in her chest, overridden for now by sheer determination. *Not today.* Sweat poured down Kianthe's face as she peeled water away from the pirate, like stripping a very stubborn orange. "Visk," she gasped. "Get her! I'll hold the water."

Visk tried, he really did. He screeched, folding his wings, and angled straight for the raging river. But the rain was too intense; the ship groaned and cracked and even Kianthe commanding the wood to *stay put* couldn't stop the enormous pressure slamming into this boat.

It shifted, knocking Serina farther downriver, and she vanished into the rapids.

Right over the waterfall's edge.

"Visk!" Kianthe screamed.

But her mount wasn't afraid of danger, and griffons were among the most agile creatures in the sky. He dove, slicing between shards of sodden wood and broken crates, and hooked his talons into Serina's clothes.

It wasn't gentle, but it worked.

Kianthe felt like crying in relief. She released the magic holding the river back, and a violent flood cascaded over the waterfall. The Nacean itself seemed irate with the interruption, but Kianthe scowled at it and, deep in the Magicary, the Stone of Seeing pulsed to reinforce her will, quieting the river into normal rapids.

They soared up over the waterfall's lip. Visk beat his wings confidently, peering at his catch . . . but Serina was limp.

Still.

"Find a spot to land," Kianthe ordered.

The griffon chittered agreement and angled to the shoreline. There was a section of dense pine trees, their branches plentiful enough to keep the rain off the ground, yet high enough that Visk could carefully weave between them—at least a little ways in.

He set Serina down, beating his wings fiercely as he landed beside her.

Kianthe leapt off his back. "Get Rain."

The griffon was off without any extra prodding.

Kianthe dropped to Serina's side, pressing a hand to her chest, feeling the water in her lungs. Dangerous, but fixable. Irritation swelled unfairly at this woman, at the casual disregard for her own life, at the position she'd placed Kianthe in with just a few bad decisions.

No time. Drawing a shaky breath, Kianthe hooked her magic into the water, tugging it out of Serina's chest. The pirate coughed harshly, violently, but Kianthe pulled until every drop was expelled.

She was breathing now, but she still wasn't moving.

Long, wheezing breaths passed.

Why wasn't she moving?

"Key," Reyna gasped. She must have been close for Visk to return this fast. She dismounted the griffon—Lilac had probably been tethered somewhere in her haste—and sprinted over. Ponder was close on her heels, trouncing happily and biting Reyna's ankles until Visk nipped her tail. The baby griffon sulked back to the clearing's edge, giving them room.

Reyna crashed to her knees beside Serina. "Is she alive?"

"I—I think so?" Kianthe's voice wobbled, and she refused to get close.

Her fiancée checked the pirate's pulse, her breathing, just like Matild had taught her. "Unconscious."

Reyna rocked back on her heels, turning that calculating gaze to Kianthe instead. And just like always, she *saw* past the bravado, past the shield of her humor. Kianthe's heart pounded, her hands shook, and she couldn't stop remembering the vicious, almost irate pull of the river as it tried to swallow Serina whole.

She couldn't contain her shudder.

Reyna's brow knitted together.

"I'm okay," the mage tried to say.

"It's all right if you aren't." Reyna pushed to her feet, pulled Kianthe into a tight embrace. Reyna's hugs were always like an anchor in a storm—a welcome thing when Kianthe's brain felt like it was spinning out of control.

She should have been faster.

She shouldn't have wasted time updating Reyna and Bobbie.

She shouldn't have joked or flown overhead judging a stupid conversation while the rapids loomed.

She should have just plucked Serina off the boat when she first saw her and been done with—

"Kianthe." Reyna pressed a kiss to her forehead, and the *should-haves* stopped.

"Sorry." Kianthe forced a smile. She was making a concerted effort to control her anxiety, to remember the here and now instead of spiraling into dangerous potential outcomes. And right now, Reyna's body fit against hers like a glove, her hand warm on Kianthe's cheek.

When she said, "You saved her life," it was with such adoration that Kianthe wondered what it would be like to see herself the way Reyna saw her: as a hero, a confident, capable mage. And then that niggling fear slipped in, making her wonder what would happen if the Arcandor *didn't* save someone.

Would Reyna still speak to her like that?

"Her ship is gone." Kianthe clenched her eyes shut. "I tried to save it, but the river swallowed it too fast. I could have stopped it with a bit more time, or—or a stronger ley line."

It wasn't even that the ley line here was *weak;* in fact, so close to the Magicary and the venerated Stone of Seeing, magic thrummed everywhere. But rivers held an ancient power, stronger even than stone . . . and the Nacean was the largest river in the Realm. Controlling it for longer than a few breaths would take immense preparation.

Reyna pulled back, lifting Kianthe's chin. "Let me repeat what's important: Serina is alive. You saved her life." She waited for a few moments, and when Kianthe didn't argue, she turned back to the griffons. Ponder had found a very interesting mushroom at the base of a nearby tree and was testing its strength against her talons.

The talons were winning.

Reyna sighed and turned to Visk instead. "Can you get Bobbie? Bring her here."

The griffon chittered agreement, pointedly glared at Ponder, then prowled through the trees before taking off over the river. The baby griffon watched him go, then went back to her mushroom, sinking her claws into its bulbous shape.

A bitter chill whipped through the air, and Kianthe ignited her hands to keep everyone warm while they waited. She remembered belatedly that Bobbie would still be trapped in her stone shackles and pulled that magic away so the earth crumbled back into the ground. At least now Visk would be able to physically bring her.

While the moments passed, Kianthe's heart began to slow and her hands stopped shaking, but she kept glancing at Serina. Just in case.

As if she sensed the attention, the pirate groaned. Reyna bent back over her, pushing sopping hair off the pirate's face. Serina had round cheeks, thick bangs, and—finally, Kianthe could see them—blue eyes. The color of a stormy ocean, almost gray, but with a hint of deep-sea.

"Y'can't arrest me," Serina mumbled, her voice hoarse from choking on water. She noticed Reyna, blinked heavily, and asked, "Who—" before breaking off into another round of coughing.

She sounded half-dead. Reyna glanced at Kianthe, concern written on her features—for both Serina, and how Kianthe would react to this development. To reassure her, and possibly hide some of Kianthe's own turbulent emotions, the mage mustered up some humor.

Just for Reyna, mind.

"Just once," Kianthe stepped into Serina's line of sight, "I'd like to have a vacation without mortal peril. I don't feel like that's too much to ask."

And bless her, Reyna took the bait, slipping into their normal routine of banter. "Darling, this isn't a vacation." She cast Kianthe a wry smile, one that said, *I see you, and everything's okay,* and tapped Serina's shoulder to regain her focus. "And you should probably learn to sail better."

Shifting the blame, as if this wasn't Kianthe's fault to begin with.

Kianthe both loved and hated that Reyna felt the need to do that.

"T-Thanks," Serina muttered. She blinked, still dazed, clearly fading again. "If you see a mean-looking sheriff, tell her to fuck off."

Kianthe snorted. She couldn't help it.

"I told you *so many times before*. I'm a *constable,* not a sheriff," Bobbie said from the edge of the clearing. She stepped to Serina, but the pirate clearly hadn't heard her—or was ignoring her in the most fabulous fashion. Either way, Serina's eyes were closed yet again, her body lying prone on the hard ground.

Kianthe balled up the flames in her palms, sending them into the trees in tiny flickers of ever-flame. They'd burn, offering light and a gentle warmth, but they wouldn't ignite anything. Not even the few drops that made it past the canopy would extinguish them.

Bobbie knelt beside Reyna, pushing a strand of hair off Serina's face. The motion was so gentle, so intimate, that even Reyna looked away. A fond smile tilted Bobbie's lips, and her green eyes cut back to Reyna and Kianthe.

"Thank you," she said, voice thick.

Kianthe nodded, and for a moment, she didn't feel like a total failure. Reyna took position beside her, squeezing her hand in reassurance.

That was the moment Bobbie seemed to realize what was happening, because she straightened stiffly. The professional constable, private lawman of the diarn's lands, was back in a breath.

Reyna had always worn her Queensguard personality like a second skin, so close to her actual temperament that it took Kianthe two seasons to recognize the difference. With Bobbie, it was like watching a child struggling into a parent's oversized jacket.

Acting at its finest.

Kianthe was beginning to wonder if Bobbie was in the right field.

"Diarn Arlon will want to know we've captured the pirate." The constable pushed to her feet, squinting at the sky, then the river. "The town of Neolow isn't far from here. We'll bunk there for the night, then begin the trek back to his estate tomorrow morning."

"You're still going to turn her in?" Kianthe said incredulously.

"Of course." Bobbie glanced at Serina, regret evident on her features. "She can't just run around breaking the law. Unless you want to fly her back to the diarn tonight?"

While she spoke, Bobbie pulled Serina's limp form into an upright position. The pirate's head fell against her shoulder in what might have been a nice embrace—except for when Bobbie expertly tied Serina's wrists together with a rope.

"Huh. You're awfully good at that. Had a lot of practice?" Kianthe said innocently.

Bobbie nearly choked, fidgeting suddenly with the knots.

Meanwhile, Reyna had her scheming face on again. It was like watching a theater production, carefully coordinated, yet utterly innocent. When she spoke, it was with the exact right amount of exhaustion and amicability.

"I'd prefer a night to recuperate. This day was rather eventful." Reyna yawned—a fake yawn, but Bobbie wouldn't know that—and offered a smile that sent butterflies through Kianthe's stomach. "Darling, if you fly me back to my horse, we can simply meet Bobbie and Serina at Neolow."

"I may need help getting her to my mount—" Bobbie said.

"Nonsense. You wouldn't transport a prisoner before they're conscious, would you?" Reyna crossed her arms, disapproval in her features.

Kianthe nearly snorted.

Bobbie looked uneasy. "Protocol dictates—"

"You have a protocol for *this*?" Reyna gestured at the clearing, the rain, the river. Everything about this situation was off-book, and they all knew it.

The constable clenched her jaw, but laid Serina back down.

"Besides," Reyna said cheerfully, mounting Visk in one swift motion. She patted his back pointedly, and Kianthe obeyed the unspoken command like she was a puppet tied to strings. Reyna continued speaking: "By my understanding, you take pride in your job. How will Diarn Arlon react when you arrive in Neolow alone, toting the very nuisance he sent the *Arcandor* to handle? A promotion may be in your future."

The constable stared at the pirate, tied at her feet. "Y-Yeah. You're right." She didn't sound convinced, but she did push to her feet, digging in her bag for a new hat. This one had two pom-poms for some inexplicable reason, and it was bright orange. Absolutely *not* Kianthe's color, but Bobbie handed it to her anyway. "You lost your other hat."

"I—" Kianthe felt her head and yelped in horror, spinning around the clearing—but sure enough, her old red one with the cute pom-pom was gone. Her eyes landed on the river, barely visible through the trees, and she seethed. "You bastard."

The river's magic pulsed in response, a petulant huff that basically insinuated it was Kianthe's fault for being careless, not *its* fault for sweeping her precious hat away.

"Key, please don't fight the Nacean."

Reyna's smooth voice startled her out of her budding argument. She petulantly tugged the orange one on her head instead. It wasn't as cute, but it was still warm. Once Kianthe was done mourning her last one, it'd be fine, she supposed.

Reyna seemed amused, but she turned away resolutely. "Come along, sweetie," she told Ponder, who was busy ripping the mushroom to shreds. Then she asked Kianthe, "That's not poisonous, is it?"

The mage feigned insult. "Rain. *Really.* Do you think I'd let her play with anything poisonous?"

"I don't know. You have a different level of concern for plants than most of us."

"Well, I can verify that the mushroom isn't too happy to have her attention." Kianthe sniffed. "Pondie. Here, girl!"

The baby griffon chittered, abandoning her mess of mushroom to fly to them. She barely cast a glance at Serina and Bobbie before cruising out over the river. The rain was letting up, but the sun was beginning to set; it'd be dark soon.

Visk followed his daughter, and once they were out of earshot, Kianthe said, "So we're just going to leave them alone tonight?"

"Bobbie is a capable young woman; I'm sure she can start a fire. Besides, Serina will be fine once she rests a bit." Reyna craned over Visk's back as they flew past Bobbie's horse, who'd been tethered under a patch of trees and was happily grazing. Farther upriver, Lilac was in the same situation, and Reyna sighed in relief upon seeing her horse.

Kianthe narrowed her eyes in suspicion. "That's not why you left them alone."

Reyna sniffed. "Diarn Arlon will toss Serina in jail to set an example of her. And that will make their Stars-crossed love story very difficult to pursue."

"River-crossed love story," Kianthe corrected.

Reyna rolled her eyes and went along with it. "Either way, I merely bought them time to work out their differences."

"I think you're reading too many romance novels." Kianthe laughed, winding her arms around Reyna's waist.

Reyna intertwined their fingers, leaning back against the mage. "And who do I have to thank for that?" A pause. "Perhaps we should introduce rope into our evenings on occasion."

A thrill swept through Kianthe, and she struggled to keep her voice level, play it cool. "Ah, sure. Sure. Whatever you want, darling."

Suddenly, Bobbie and Serina were pretty far from her mind.

7

Serina

Serina was *fairly* sure she didn't die on that waterfall.

Okay, halfway sure. Because when she opened her eyes in the late evening to see a crackling fire, a horse grazing nearby, and Bobbie, *Bobbie,* crocheting against a tree, Serina truly thought she'd lost her mind. Bobbie was a sheriff—or a constable—or something, now. Bobbie had gone rogue. *Bobbie* had lost sight of everything, and now she was here, with Serina in her sights instead.

"You're awake," Bobbie said, caution lingering in her tone.

Caution. This was the same person who used to absently braid Serina's hair on sleepovers. Who'd hold the lantern while Serina picked the lock to her parents' barn, just to steal a horse and ride to that special spot north of Lathe and watch the sunrise. Bobbie used to be *everything* to Serina, and now—

Now they were on opposite sides of a war.

Serina pushed herself upright. Her entire body felt heavy and achy, and dark bruises had formed on her upper arms. Her wrists had a faint imprint on them, like she'd been tied at one point—but she wasn't now, so Serina didn't think about it long.

"A griffon snatched me out of the sky. Am I remembering that right?" It sounded stupid.

"That's right," Bobbie replied.

Great. At least Serina's memory wasn't as gnarled as her thoughts right now. She pressed a palm against her forehead, scootching backward until she could rest against another tree. Bobbie stared uncomfortably. Serina had figured she'd grown out of that, but clearly not.

"You're staring again, Bobbie."

It made her flinch. "Ah, sorry." A heavy pause, where she lowered the yarn in her hands. It was yellow, but she had a black ball of yarn beside her too. "Just wanted to make sure you're okay. I was worried."

So blunt. Serina swallowed hard, turning her gaze upward. They were under a thick canopy of trees, but a quick glance toward the river proved that it was raining lightly. The smoke drifted through an almost unnatural hole in the foliage—which showed soft firelight gleaming like lanternflies in the leaves.

Magic. Then a mage had joined them, at least for a time.

They were alone now, though.

"Don't say that," Serina muttered.

Bobbie frowned. "Don't say what? That I was worried?"

"Yes. Don't pretend like we're friends again. Don't pretend like you care." It was childish, unfair, and Serina knew it. But she also couldn't fight the betrayal that lurked in her heart.

"I do care." Bobbie's hand drifted to her wrist, then dropped again. "You scared the shit out of me. Didn't you see the signs to avoid the waterfall? There were a dozen other paths you could have sailed through."

Serina bristled. "I *know* that. You think I don't know how to get south on this river, after my whole family had to move? What, do you think I wanted to destroy the boat my father made when we were kids?" The fucking audacity of this woman, implying that. Even exhausted, even after a traumatic incident, Serina felt ready to fight.

Bobbie stiffened. "I—assume that's sarcasm."

"It is," Serina retorted. "But this isn't. If you hadn't been distracting me, I wouldn't have stayed near the shoreline. This is your fault."

It was cruel, a cheap jab, and Serina knew it. But Bobbie was still in her constable uniform, the exact same uniform she'd worn when she told Serina to forfeit the farm . . . again. If Serina learned one thing about her ex-friend that day, it was that time didn't always heal wounds. Sometimes, they festered.

"I'm not the one who decided to become a *pirate*," Bobbie snapped. "What the hells, Serrie?"

"Don't call me that. Not anymore."

Bobbie set her jaw, even as anguish flashed across her gaze. It made Serina's heart twinge, but there was just . . . no way to fix this. Not now. Maybe not ever. Especially when Bobbie said, "You could do anything, but you decided to be a *pirate*. You're causing a lot of problems for me at work."

Oh, that was rich. "I'm so sorry I'm disrupting your oppression, *Constable*. However will you have the time to evict unsuspecting citizens from their property if you're so busy chasing me along the low seas?" Serina snorted. "Also sarcasm, by the way."

"Thanks, I got it." Bobbie bristled, shoving her yarn into a bag. It almost looked like a stuffed animal. Was that a new hobby she'd picked up? Viviana, Bobbie's mom, used to crochet—Serina supposed it made sense.

How nice that she had the time to pursue a hobby while people were starving.

Bobbie's words were scathing. "The only people I'm evicting are those who aren't using land properly. And they're given a severance; plenty of money to make a new life for themselves. Most transition into better professions, which means we can use their land for people who actually *know* how to farm." A pause, a quiet add-on: "Unlike your family."

"My *family*—" Serina surged to her feet, but it was too much, too fast. She swayed, grabbing the tree trunk for balance as the world swam around her.

Bobbie was at her side in a heartbeat, her hold on Serina's arms steadying, yet gentle. "Serrie! Shit, are you okay? You shouldn't be standing yet."

"Leave my family out of this," Serina said faintly, wrenching away from her. She drew slow breaths, gripping the tree, feeling like she was back under swirls of water. Water crashing over her head, then being viciously ripped apart—

Her eyes drifted to the firelight above them. Unnatural, magical flames. So . . . not a mage then. *The* mage. The Arcandor.

She should be flattered.

Instead, she was just tired and angry. She held Bobbie's gaze, feeling distant, deadened. "My family had that farm for generations. Arlon stole it because we couldn't make quota—and the quota's only risen since then. That 'severance' was barely enough to get me downriver. But you probably didn't even count it, did you?"

"It wasn't my money to count," Bobbie said stiffly.

"Of course not. Perfect Constable Bobbie, just following orders." Serina rolled her eyes. "What the hell happened to you? We played pirates for a reason. We wanted to make the world a better place."

"I am making the world a better place." Bobbie bristled, one hand on the sword at her hip.

Serina followed the motion with her eyes, then pointedly stared at Bobbie again.

The constable hesitated, removing her hand from the pommel of the weapon. "I *am* helping our lands, our people. You might think I'm the bad guy, but I'm out there making sure towns on the river have what they need to survive. Arlon takes a cut, sure, but that's no different than any other governing body. It goes back into the communities—we use it for public services like maintaining the roads between towns or commissioning mages to help ships get upriver."

It all sounded so reasonable. Did Bobbie have any clue what lurked beneath the surface of that speech?

Knowing her, probably not. She was an earnest person. If someone told her the truth, she'd believe it.

Serina set her jaw. "The system isn't as perfect as you think. Arlon is taking too much. He's slowly starving everyone."

"Really?" Bobbie deadpanned. "Then why is Lathe always doing just fine when I visit? My mother has never once complained about a lack of food. Our neighbors are doing just fine."

Serina was quickly losing patience. "I don't have time to point out every single infraction to you, Bobbie. Either you believe me, or you don't—and it's obvious you don't. So, leave me alone, and let's both go our separate ways."

Serina took a step forward—and Bobbie caught her wrists, wrapping them in thick rope before Serina could blink. She wrenched against them, twisting out of Bobbie's grasp, but Bobbie had clearly learned something in the years they'd been apart. Her iron grip settled around Serina's arm instead, muscling her toward the horse.

"What the fuck are you doing?" Serina snarled. "Let me go!"

"Serina of Jallin, formerly of Lathe, pirate of the Nacean River . . . you are under arrest for pillaging, stealing, swashbuckling, and otherwise disrupting public peace." Bobbie's voice sounded expressionless, but even Serina could hear the edge hidden deep beneath the words. "If you fight, you will be met with force."

"Like hells," Serina spat, and twisted on her heels to try and wrench away. Bobbie danced with her. The horse watched dispassionately as they wrestled in the clearing, as they crashed to the ground beside the fire. Serina grunted, writhing under Bobbie's hold, but the constable was unmoving.

She sat over Serina, pinning her arms, then seemed to realize the bruises left by the griffon and readjusted her hold. Under her body, Serina panted, gasping for breath, her vision graying.

"I-If I hadn't just drowned—" she wheezed, "I'd kick your ass."

Against all odds, Bobbie laughed, like she couldn't *believe* this was her life right now. "You could try. Are you going to come quietly?"

Serina scowled, feeling as hot as the fire beside them. "Come on, Bobbie. You know me."

And Bobbie heaved a sigh, like this confirmed every suspicion she had. "Shit, this is going to be a long night."

"Yep."

8

Reyna

Neolow was the second-largest town on the Nacean River, right after Jallin. It was a hillside town nestled at the northern tip of a series of mountain lakes, and it marked the change between the coniferous forests of northern Shepara and more colorful deciduous trees to the south. As such, the hills were swathed in reds and yellows that were undoubtedly vibrant during the day, but seemed dull in the silver moonlight's glow. Reyna was getting tired of arriving in these towns so late, but there really wasn't anything to do about it.

Despite the late hour, the port was a bustling hub of trade, with dozens of larger ships docked and several more arriving or leaving the port. Neolow was on the western side of the river, and Reyna boarded Lilac at a set of stables on the eastern side, where a few buildings had been constructed in a makeshift extension of the town. Visk flew them across, although a ferry sailed between the two ports all night long.

Reyna watched it pass underneath them, a simple boat with a glowing lantern at the bowsprit, and basked in a sudden thrill. "I've never been to Neolow before. Queen Tilaine never felt this place was worth her time." No one to coerce here, after all. No reason for a diplomatic mission so far inland, with such extensive travel times.

"You've been to Jallin," Kianthe remarked.

Reyna shrugged. "Sure, but Jallin is very close to Mercon: just a single day of ocean sailing. It's just . . . exciting. I've heard the lakes here are gorgeous."

"They are. Old glacier lakes, with minerals that make them the most ridiculous shade of turquoise." Kianthe grinned widely, nudging Visk to land on the outskirts of the town. "Maybe we'll take a hike. Have a picnic."

"Darling, we have a job to do." If Bobbie and Serina showed up in a timely manner, which Reyna estimated was about a 73 percent chance.

"There's more to life than our missions." The mage sounded almost petulant. "I thought we could treat this trip as a celebratory vacation. I've been told it's not wise to marry someone I haven't traveled with extensively."

The mention of who Kianthe should marry made Reyna recall Diarn Arlon's words, and a sour pit settled in her gut. She forced a smile. "Well, it is wise to consider your partner carefully. Gods forbid you marry someone who can't handle a crisis."

That wasn't her, Reyna knew. She was excellent at managing problems, excellent at calming Kianthe down, excellent at exploring all angles. But traveling through Shepara, seeing what the Arcandor meant to people on a smaller level—and seeing how they felt about *her*—Reyna wondered if Arlon was right.

She loved Kianthe . . . but nothing was quite that easy when world leaders got involved.

"Stone forbid I marry someone other than *you,*" Kianthe said pointedly.

Reyna laughed, but something below them had caught her eye. Visk circled to land, lowering at a leisurely pace, but Reyna squinted at several constables gathered in a group on the edge of town. In unison, they saluted their leader, a constable with silver epaulets, and started down the southern path out of Neolow.

Hmm.

"Find something interesting?" Kianthe asked.

"Maybe." Reyna didn't elaborate, and Kianthe didn't ask.

Visk soared over a few buildings and picked a nice big dock to touch down on. Reyna hopped off his back, resecuring her sword. As Kianthe dismounted, Reyna kissed her griffon on the head. "Ponder, be good for Visk, okay?"

Ponder was spoiled and enjoyed the occasional night inside—but she was still a griffon, and they preferred to be exploring forests and sleeping under the stars. She chirped, prowled under her father's stomach, and nibbled his feathers. He nuzzled her fondly.

"See you tomorrow, buddy," Kianthe said, and scratched Visk just under his vicious-looking beak. "Don't wait up; something tells me we'll be sleeping in. But if you see Bobbie and Serina, come get us, okay?"

Visk bumped her chest with his head, chirped at Ponder, and they took off toward the western hills.

Reyna turned toward the city, tilting her head. This place had the feel of a quaint tourist town, with shops lining every street and taverns on every corner. Lanterns hung every few feet, offering plenty of firelight. And bonus: the town was bustling. Even at the docks, people were unloading crates and mending sails. A few street vendors hawked late-night meals of fish and meat.

They passed by a group of sailors sharing a drink, and Reyna caught a snippet of their conversation: "—that Dreggs sailed north."

"Come on, what a lie," one replied, shoving the other's shoulder. "Dreggs stays in the Southern Seas."

"My cousin saw the *Painted Death* sailing through Jallin with his own two eyes! Sent me a carrier pigeon yesterday. You saying my cousin's a—"

They passed, and a smile tilted Reyna's lips. Dreggs, hmm? She filed that information away, tucking herself against Kianthe's side as they moseyed farther into town. Reyna's eyes landed on a tiny wooden stand where someone was selling cider, and her mouth watered.

"I bet the apples here are fantastic," she said offhandedly.

Kianthe chuckled, then cheerfully approached the vendor and bought two steaming mugs. She handed one to Reyna, and they sat shoulder to shoulder in a tiny cobblestone square, leaning on the bench as they people-watched.

It was late enough that Reyna felt a bit dazed, but she sipped her cider and leaned against Kianthe. "We should find an inn."

"Later. You should slow down a bit." Kianthe tossed an arm over her shoulders. "How's the cider?"

"Divine. A literal gift from the Gods," Reyna said. A couple passing by glanced her way, and she lowered her voice. "Although perhaps I should keep those beliefs to myself here." Only Queendom citizens worshiped the Gods, after all. In Shepara and Leonol, the primary deity was the Stars above, unless one was a mage.

Kianthe glared at the couple, her entire body warming with magic—like she could ignite anytime. Reyna pulled away.

"Key."

The mage glanced at her, sighed, and cooled off immediately. "Sorry."

"I appreciate that you're trying to protect me," Reyna said, settling back against her. "But we really should discuss a plan for when Her Excellency comes knocking. She's merely biding her time, enjoying the fact that she can flaunt you like a prized pony right now." Reyna sipped her cider, savoring the sweet flavor. It contrasted with the bitterness of her words. "Once she tires of that, she'll start summoning favors, just like Diarn Arlon said."

Silence settled over them, icy as the temperature. In the plaza, warm lamps glowed, but it felt like they'd been cast in darkness.

Kianthe rested her chin on Reyna's head. "You really need to redefine 'relaxation' in your mind. Because this conversation isn't it." She was forcing amusement, but Reyna didn't miss the anxious undertone to her voice.

Reyna *did* need help with that. In Tawney, in their bookstore, she could busy herself with tea, books, and good company. The most stressful part of her day—at least once Queen Tilaine granted her blessing and removed the threat of death for treason—was determining which tea New Leaf Tomes and Tea would feature that week, and what pastries might complement it.

But Reyna would never forget finding Kianthe deep in dragon

country, unconscious, half-frozen, and nearly dead. The way that dragon loomed over her, the fear that raced up Reyna's spine when she realized the extent to which Kianthe would go to protect Tawney, their friends, their shop . . . and Reyna herself.

Things had turned out fine, just fine, but only because Kianthe promised the impossible: a bindment to locate three dragon eggs long since removed from Tawney. The spell was clear: the dragons promised peace if Kianthe returned the eggs, and dangerous consequences would await the Arcandor if she didn't. If this lead wound up being a dead end—if Diarn Arlon didn't have the information they needed—Queen Tilaine would be the least of their worries.

It was hard to turn off that part of Reyna's brain, the side that had spent an entire career calculating the worst-case scenarios . . . and planning ways to stop them.

But Kianthe didn't need that, so she sipped her cider and replied, "Apologies. We'll focus on one thing at a time. First, the dragon eggs, then our marriage, and maybe address Her Excellency in a few years' time."

"Rain." Kianthe sounded pained. She went silent, as if she was deciphering how best to phrase her thoughts. "When you say that kind of thing, I worry that you think Queen Tilaine is your problem—that you're going to handle it alone, the same way you handled her over the summer."

Reyna felt seen. She stiffened involuntarily, then forced herself to relax. It was so minute no one else would have noticed, but Kianthe tightened her grip on Reyna's shoulders, almost like a hug of acknowledgment.

"I knew it," the mage said, disheartened. "Tell me how you're feeling, Reyna."

She was thinking seventeen things at any given point, and parsing them now was difficult. It was late, she was warm against her mage's side, the cider was good, and for once, she didn't really *want* to address it.

But Kianthe had spoken the magic words, and their rule was that they actually said how they felt when prompted. Otherwise, their entire communication style broke down.

"I'm feeling scared," Reyna admitted, exhaustion lacing her tone. "There's no immediate threat, but I'm worried we can't enjoy our married life with Queen Tilaine lurking on the edges of it." She waited, but Kianthe didn't interrupt—that was the other unspoken promise between them. Once the question was asked, the person got to talk until all the feelings were laid bare. "I have a few ideas, but I'm not sure how to go about enacting them just yet. If I tell you what they are, I'm worried I'll get your hopes up—and I highly doubt things will be so easy in real life."

Kianthe perked upright, but stayed silent.

"I'm done." A smile tilted Reyna's lips.

The mage was clearly waiting for it, because she leapt right in: "Easy? Is there an easy way out of this?" She pulled away a bit on the bench, just enough to meet Reyna's gaze. Her dark eyes glimmered with excitement.

And there it was. Reyna sighed, pinching her nose. "It's a low possibility, but I keep recalling something Diarn Feo said to me when we visited Kyaron last summer. They mentioned a Sheparan rumor that Queen Tilaine's mother had another daughter."

Kianthe's expression fell. "I've heard that rumor. It's insubstantial."

"Perhaps."

Now the mage frowned. "You don't think so?"

Reyna stared at her cider, tracing the mug's rim. They'd have to return these to the vendor when they finished, but for now she admired the deep blue glaze, the careful craftsmanship. "Key, my mother vanished for an entire year when I was young—maybe four or five. At the same time, Queen Eren stopped making public appearances: she spent time in her private chambers, or saw audiences only from afar. I didn't even remember until Diarn Feo mentioned the timing."

"By the Stone of Seeing," Kianthe breathed. "There's another heir?"

Confirming it felt like admitting mythical titans roamed the deep seas. Reyna desperately wanted to believe in a secret heir . . . but that meant keeping her expectations in check until all the research was completed. For now, her voice was cautious. "Diarn Feo has volunteered to gather a collection of eyewitness reports and articles written at the time. It's possible I'll explore it next year once we've resolved the dragon egg threat."

"And had our wedding."

"Indeed." Reyna pulled Kianthe in for a quick kiss, a reassurance more than anything. "It's a problem for another time."

Kianthe nodded, but she had a faraway look in her eyes now.

To redirect, Reyna tugged her off the bench. "Come on. Let's check out the town. See if we can find an inn. Speaking of the wedding . . . what are your hopes for it?" She handed their mugs to the vendor as they passed. "Where would you like to get married?"

"At our bookstore," Kianthe replied instantly.

Reyna laughed. "Not Wellia? Or the Magicary? I bet either would put on a grand show for us."

"If we chose to host a wedding in Shepara, Tilaine would throw a fit." Kianthe rolled her eyes. "If we have it in the Capital, the council will throw a fit. The Magicary is just a bunch of stuffy mages. So, I say we forget them all and have a small, intimate wedding with our best friends, and let everyone else deal with the fact that they missed it."

"Bold move. No one's going to be happy with that arrangement."

"Except for us, and we're the ones who matter." Kianthe smirked. "I've already discussed it with Matild. We'll clear out an area in the field south of New Leaf Tomes and Tea, ignite some ever-flame for lighting, let Sigmund and Nurt spread the word so there's no formal invitation to trace back to us. Gossley can . . . I don't know. Do the dishes. Or be lovey-dovey with his girlfriend. And did you know Tarly sings? Matild said he spends his winters practicing with his band."

"His . . . band." Reyna laughed at the idea of their local blacksmith singing in a band, and a pang of homesickness hit her. Even as they walked up the street admiring this strange new town, she would have given anything to be back in Tawney. "I miss them."

"Me too." Kianthe sighed, adjusting her orange hat. It looked ridiculous with her complexion.

Reyna had found an almost identical replacement in Bobbie's community crates that morning, anticipating Kianthe would lose her first one. But it was in Lilac's saddlebag, and she really didn't want to fly back across the river to retrieve it.

Kianthe continued, oblivious to Reyna's thoughts. "I've never been the type to miss anyone but you, but—I don't know. Extended travel isn't as fun anymore."

At that moment, Reyna was inclined to agree.

They chatted amicably as the moon rose higher and they explored the town. Neolow was built on a hillside, which meant the deeper into town they got, the more of the river they could see. The view was stunning: the river was wide enough that the other bank was a mere glowing line of firelight. Neolow's docks spread across the entire riverfront. And instead of smaller ships like she'd found in Oslop, the ships here were ocean-worthy vessels.

Reyna was squinting at a particularly ornate one—thinking it looked oddly like the brigantine she'd heard Diarn Arlon commissioned decades ago—when Kianthe pointed at another, smaller ship.

"See that one?" Kianthe waited for her to hum acknowledgment before continuing. "Designed for a mage on the crew. They only need one sail at the front, and the mage keeps it moving with wind magic while the captain steers."

Reyna studied it. Her eyes were starting to burn from exhaustion, but she didn't want this lovely night with Kianthe to end. "Huh. Is it hard to find a mage for that?"

"Well, all mages can reside in the Magicary—but they're encouraged to explore the world at large, spread magic however they can. I think Harold got his real-world experience on a ship like that one. Must have been eons ago, the old coot."

"*Master* Harold, you mean?" Reyna snorted. Fighting the dragons, and the resulting bindment spell, had nearly killed Kianthe. Of the two mages who'd visited Tawney to offer their magic and help her, Harold was . . . not Reyna's favorite. "And here I thought he'd saved an entire village, to be as arrogant as he was."

Kianthe laughed. "You'd think."

There was a natural lull in the conversation, and Reyna knew if it dragged on, Kianthe would push them toward a room, a bed, and sleep. Desperately clinging to this night, Reyna started a new conversation: "Look over there. That ship looks as nice as Queen Tilaine's personal vessel. I wonder if it's Diarn Arlon's."

The ship in question was trimmed in gold and silver edging and stained a deep mahogany; it boasted two tall masts, a crow's nest, an upper and lower deck, and at least one level belowdecks.

Kianthe squinted at it, whistled. "Maybe. I know he has one to travel the river when needed." Her eyes landed on Reyna again. "I see what you're doing, and it's not going to work. Come on. You're swaying on your feet."

"That's an exaggeration." But Reyna let herself be towed to the inn across the cobblestone street, basking in the warmth. The sun would be rising sooner than she'd like, but this unexpected night in a new town, enjoying Kianthe's company, was a memory Reyna would cherish for years.

As they settled into bed, Reyna snuggled against Kianthe and murmured, "Key—no matter what happens with Queen Tilaine, we'll handle it together, okay?"

"Same with the dragons," Kianthe replied, kissing her. Her lips tasted like apple cider, and Reyna smiled against them. "Now get some sleep, love."

They were both out in moments.

9

Kianthe

The next morning, they enjoyed a nice breakfast at a local restaurant: the specialty here was thick, flaky slices of bread, lightly toasted and topped with melting cheese and an egg. It was divine, rich with flavor, and Kianthe was savoring it when Reyna lightly tapped her arm.

"What?" Kianthe's mouth was stuffed.

"Don't talk with your mouth full," Reyna said in amusement. "Look there." And she took a sip of her tea, gesturing down the street.

Ah. Bobbie and Serina had arrived . . . and Bobbie did *not* look good.

To be fair, Serina didn't seem much better—but that was because she was protesting to the five hells, not because she was injured. The pirate's ankles had been knotted into Bobbie's horse's stirrups, her wrists were tied to a metal ring just below the saddle's horn, and she'd been gagged with a thick cloth. Despite this, she writhed against her restraints, glowered at Bobbie, and shouted at anyone who passed them, her words muffled and furious.

Bobbie led the horse by the reins like a woman condemned. The bags under her eyes were deep and pronounced now, and it seemed like a struggle to pull her shoulders upright and act like the professional constable she was. Whenever someone moved to help Serina, she tapped the silver badge, and they backed away like she'd lit them on fire.

Reyna and Kianthe were seated at a little shop near the docks, basking in the bright sunlight. Reyna shielded her eyes, raising one eyebrow, and said to Kianthe: "Perhaps it was cruel to leave Bobbie alone with Serina. It looks like she had a rough night."

"It's wholly possible we've overestimated their relationship." Kianthe took another messy bite of her thick bread. It somehow managed to be flaky *and* fluffy at the same time, and the yolk soaked into it beautifully. Messy. Delicious. She chewed, swallowed, and added, "Either that, or this is Bobbie's idea of *roping* Serina into something serious."

"Darling."

"Come on? Because of the rope?" Kianthe laughed, spewing crumbs. "That's hilarious, and you know it."

Reyna rolled her eyes, pushing away from the table. "If I'm being honest, it feels like you're tying too hard." And with a sly smile, she strolled across the street to intercept the constable.

Kianthe nearly choked. She stuffed the last of the bread into her mouth, gulped her morning tea—a strong blend of vanilla and cinnamon—and jogged after Reyna. The closer she got, the more obvious it was that Bobbie was about two steps from falling over. She probably hadn't slept the entire night. Maybe the last two nights.

There'd be a lot of stress-crocheting in her future, Kianthe could tell. Suddenly, she felt bad judging the silly orange hat with the two pom-poms. Poor constable was trying her best.

Probably, Kianthe should have just taken Serina back to Arlon and saved everyone some time. Of course, last night had been something special—a glimpse into how she and Reyna would travel as a married couple—and it wasn't something Kianthe would trade for all the magic in the world.

So, yes, she felt bad.

Just not *that* bad.

"Is the gag necessary?" Reyna asked.

On the horse, Serina thrashed, yanking her wrists against the metal ring. Her left hand had been bandaged at some point. Was she injured there? Kianthe couldn't remember. Everything from the river rescue felt like a bad dream.

"Gags are optional by our handbook, but recommended for the problematic criminals," Bobbie intoned, her voice unfeeling.

Serina rolled her eyes in such an exaggerated motion, it seemed like she might fall off the horse. She kicked her leg out, but the stirrup meant she couldn't *quite* connect with Bobbie's backside. The constable stepped away with practiced ease, which spoke volumes about their evening.

Kianthe shouldn't laugh.

She did anyway.

"She could be a mage, with that kind of fire."

"Mmmrhph," Serina replied, which could have been *I know,* or could have been *Fuck you*.

Reyna was more concerned with Bobbie. "Constable, and this is not a statement on your competence . . . but you look like you're about to collapse."

That got Serina's attention. She glanced sharply at Bobbie, squinting at the back of her head. But Bobbie wasn't facing her, and whatever she saw in Bobbie's tight spirals of black hair did nothing to persuade her of that truth. The pirate huffed, yanking again at her hands. Her wrists were starting to rub raw.

"Insomnia," Bobbie muttered, massaging her brow. "Normally, I can power through with a few hours a night. But a certain someone made that difficult."

Serina rolled her eyes.

"I did try a new stuffed toy." Bobbie tugged a small yellow circle out of her pocket. It had white yarn wings and one black stripe, but everything was lopsided on it. The stitches were too loose, and there wasn't enough wool inside to puff it up. It mostly looked like a deflated mess of yarn with black buttons for eyes. Bobbie raised tired eyes, her tone hopeful. "It's a bee."

Reyna stifled a laugh, shifting it into a polite cough. Kianthe patted Bobbie's arm. "I see it. Great job."

Satisfied, Bobbie tucked the monstrosity back in her pocket.

"So, your grand plan of talking her out of this life didn't go well, huh?" Kianthe ventured to ask, gaze cutting to the pirate. Serina scowled around the gag.

Bobbie chose her words carefully. "After several discussions, it became apparent that she needs more persuasion than I can offer in a night. With that option discarded, my duty lies with Diarn Arlon." She tightened her hand on the leather reins. "I merely wanted to inform you both that I've secured a ship to take us north. If you're coming with me, you'll have to board soon."

"And then Serina will be jailed," Reyna said steadily.

"She will answer for her crimes." Bobbie cast a pointed glance at Serina. "But if she comes willingly, the diarn has promised mercy in her sentencing."

It seemed extreme, but no one could deny she'd broken the law. It still didn't sit well with Kianthe, though. She frowned. "Let's take a day and think about this. Arlon doesn't know we've found her yet. We can discuss—"

But Bobbie was clearly at the end of her rope—heh, rope—because she snapped at the words: "With respect, Arcandor, I'm done discussing." She glared at Serina, a bit of fire hitting her emerald eyes now. "You could have gone anywhere. Your father runs a successful business—even that would have been better. But you decided to play farmer, and now you're playing pirate, and I'm fucking *tired*, Serina."

Serina went ramrod straight, glaring at Bobbie with absolute fury—and then she yanked so hard at her bindings that the horse whinnied, shifting his weight uneasily.

Bobbie grabbed the reins, clenched her eyes shut, and drew a breath through her nose. Against Serina's new tirade of muffled racket, she said calmly, "Join us or don't, but the ship is leaving."

With that, she resolutely turned away from them, leading the horse down the cobblestone hillside.

The silence that rang after them felt louder than the pirate's shouting.

Kianthe rubbed the back of her neck. "Ah, Rain? I think we may have miscalculated."

"Hmm." Reyna's tone was suspiciously neutral. "We should go. I worry what might happen if we don't follow them north." And she started after them, taking a far more leisurely pace.

Her casual air made Kianthe uneasy. She trailed after Reyna as they headed for the port. "Love, I can see you plotting."

Reyna pressed a hand to her chest. "Key, I never plot . . ." For a moment, she trailed off, glancing at the people strolling past. Wait, not *people*. One person, clad in a tricorne hat with an absurdly large feather. Their eyes locked for a brief moment. With a smirk, the person tipped their hat and spun on their heels, disappearing into the morning crowd.

Kianthe rubbed her arm, jogging to catch up as Reyna began walking again. "Who was that?"

"I have no idea. I think they were looking at someone else." Reyna breezed past it, waving a hand. "Anyway. *Plotting* implies nefarious intentions. I plan. Sometimes, I strategize."

Well, okay then. The mage almost pointed out that Reyna had no qualms murdering people she viewed as a threat, but they'd had that discussion before and it rarely ended well. Instead, Kianthe sighed, tucking her hands inside her cloak to warm them up. "Okay. What's your plan, then? You wanted me to stay close to Bobbie."

"Indeed, if you don't mind. I'm not confident it'll work out as I imagine, but there's a small chance—very small—that we'll be separated sometime soon." Reyna patted her arm reassuringly. "Only briefly. And in the meantime, please try to mitigate Diarn Arlon's response."

"Mitigate—" Kianthe grimaced. "What are you going to do?"

Reyna smiled brightly. "Me? Absolutely nothing."

And she started whistling, stepping onto the docks with an accomplished bounce to her step.

There were moments—like this one, specifically—where Kianthe felt she should probably intervene. That Reyna was a dangerous person to unleash on the world, and that she should at least warn those involved to give them the best chance.

But then she remembered that controlling Reyna was borderline impossible and sounded like the least fun *ever*, so she decided to trust her future wife and let everyone operate with independent free will.

The boat Bobbie had secured was small, with the diarn's emblem—a pine tree framed by a blocky *A* that looked like a mountain—burned onto the hull. A single mast loomed overhead, its sails waiting to be unfurled. It was barely big enough to fit a few people, much less a horse, but Bobbie walked the stallion up the boat's ramp nonetheless.

"Who's our captain?" Reyna followed them onto the deck.

Bobbie sighed. "Me."

"I thought you said you didn't sail?" Kianthe asked.

"I'll learn. And we'll have you, Arcandor. The river narrows north of Neolow, right before it splits into all those smaller channels. Either we need a mage on board to manipulate the wind, or we'd have to use another option."

Kianthe tested the winds, which agreed to be amicable if she asked. Out of curiosity, she said, "What are the other options?"

"Rowing, being towed from the shoreline, or a sea anchor dropped into an opposing current." Bobbie winced. "The last one requires someone who knows the river exceedingly well—they're expensive to hire. Mages are cheapest and easiest, since they usually just fly back to Neolow on their griffons."

"New job for you, dear," Reyna teased.

Kianthe snorted. "I'll keep it in mind."

Meanwhile, Bobbie moved to slice the rope tying Serina's feet into the stirrups with a serrated knife.

Reyna put a hand on her hip, clearly intrigued. "You're untying her?"

"Protocol. Can't have a prisoner tied to a horse on a boat—if it sinks, that's a death sentence." Bobbie didn't sound happy about it. Of course, her dark attitude wasn't helped when Serina kicked Bobbie's stomach. She yelped, doubling over, and only narrowly missed Serina's boot smashing into her nose.

Kianthe grimaced, unsure whether she should intervene.

"Damn it, Serina, *enough*," the constable snapped, backing away, still slightly hunched in pain.

Serina offered a very lewd gesture with her unbandaged hand.

Reyna stepped between them, putting a hand on Bobbie's arm. The constable tensed, but she offered a reassuring smile. "Sometimes, it's best to delegate a prisoner transfer to someone who hasn't already, ah . . . offended the culprit. Why don't you let me secure her belowdecks while you and Kianthe prep the sails? I'm sure between a mage and a constable, we can get this ship moving."

Bobbie glared at Serina, who glared back. The constable looked like she wanted to either cry or stab someone.

Just as a precaution, Kianthe gently removed the knife from her hand. Bobbie almost gripped it harder, but when she saw it was the Arcandor herself intervening, she loosened her hold. Kianthe clapped her shoulder. "You know that Reyna was a guard in Queen Tilaine's palace. She can handle this."

"Don't kill her," Bobbie said, a bit too forcefully.

Irritation—and a bit of hurt—dashed across Reyna's features, gone before anyone else noticed. Kianthe's brow knitted together, but her fiancée had already moved on: "She will be unharmed when we reach Diarn Arlon. I swear it."

Bobbie scrubbed her face and mumbled, "Okay. I'll come check on her soon." And she stepped toward the mast, fiddling with the ropes there.

As Reyna approached, the pirate lashed out again with her foot. Kianthe almost laughed. That might work on Bobbie—sleep deprived, clearly conflicted—but Reyna sidestepped it as if they were dancing partners. She took the knife Kianthe held and waggled it at Serina. "Listen to me. If you struggle, this will get worse." And something in her voice made Serina pause.

Their eyes met.

And Reyna quirked a smile.

"You better not fall in love with her," Kianthe told them, making it purposefully vague which one she was addressing.

"Darling, please." Reyna rolled her eyes as she stepped to Serina's other side, slicing the rope at the stirrup with one smooth motion. "Go help the poor constable. I'm questioning if she knows how to get this boat out of port without sinking us."

Across the boat, Bobbie was muttering under her breath, looking thoroughly confused as she untied various ropes.

Kianthe raised her hands. "Your wish is my command."

She stepped across the deck, keeping an eye on Reyna as she sliced the final binding on Serina's wrists, then strong-armed her off the horse. Serina was taller and curvier than Reyna and she put up a pointed struggle, but even Kianthe could tell she wasn't *really* fighting. Reyna made it look convincing, though—retying her wrists with a practiced motion, then marching Serina belowdecks.

"I'm still confused about how a Queensguard can be here," Bobbie said after they were gone. "I heard Tilaine kills anyone who tries to leave her service. She isn't still loyal to the Queendom, is she?"

Tilaine had spies everywhere, so Kianthe had to step carefully here. She highly doubted Bobbie was under Tilaine's employ, but any false assumptions would be a stupid, potentially fatal mistake to make. She shrugged, helping Bobbie lower the topsail. "She and Tilaine have struck an agreement. It benefited Her Excellency more to release Reyna from service."

"Because of you."

The heat of irritation rushed along Kianthe's arms. She wanted to say, *No, because Reyna is amazing and she negotiated for her life,* but the truth was, it never would have worked without Kianthe's status as the Arcandor, the Mage of Ages.

So, she begrudgingly said, "Yes. Because of me. But that's not why we're together."

"Sorry." Bobbie tied a rope to a tether at the base of the mast, then stepped back to survey the sail. Already, the boat was starting to pull against the dock. "Your relationship is none of my business. And while we're on the subject, I'd appreciate the same courtesy."

Fair point.

Kianthe mock-saluted, thumping her fist against her chest. "Fine by me."

Bobbie offered a drained smile and trudged to the side of the boat. A swift slice of her knife had the vessel slipping away from the dock—but it almost immediately edged toward the neighboring ship.

"Shit. *Shit.*" Bobbie sprinted for the helm, spinning it. The boom swept across the deck, nearly smashing into Kianthe's head. She narrowly leapt out of the way, and the boat drifted right back toward the dock instead.

Bobbie yelped and tried to overcorrect, and Kianthe got flashbacks of yesterday—the tiny boat being pulled under, Serina vanishing into murky water, the angry pull of water as the Nacean tried to keep her.

"Enough, Bobbie, hang *on,*" Kianthe snapped, and reached into the currents. Unlike the implacable whims of the Nacean River, here the waters were far more amenable to her magic, and she was able to shift them ever so slightly to coax the ship free.

At the helm, Bobbie raised her hands and stepped back, giving Kianthe control.

The Arcandor pulled a bit of wind at the sail, then a bit more, and soon they were free from Neolow. Once they were in the open river, Kianthe lowered her hands. "Okay, now go." Bobbie took hold of the helm again, spinning the massive wheel so the boat angled north.

Kianthe shifted the winds and currents to adjust. Across the river, the sailors of another ship shouted to each other, scrambling to adjust their sails against the sudden change in air. Kianthe winced. "How long until we reach the diarn, again?"

They were sailing past Neolow, out onto the open river now. The stables that housed Lilac were slipping away on the east side of the river, so Reyna's horse was apparently getting another minivacation. Oops.

"A day. Maybe two." Bobbie leaned heavily against the helm, blinking against the bright sunlight. Below them, the boat rocked in an almost soothing fashion. "Stars, I'm tired."

"No shit," Kianthe drawled.

"It didn't look like a bee, did it?"

"Not really, no."

Bobbie heaved a sigh.

The breeze was crisp, but the midmorning sun countered it nicely. The river was clear of fog this morning—everything was fresh and damp after yesterday's rainstorm. The scent of wet leaves and rich soil drifted over the river, and the dramatic hills behind Neolow were painted in reds, yellows, and golds. Kianthe was almost sad to be leaving—she wouldn't have minded a few hikes to see the glacier lakes.

Kianthe realized that Bobbie hadn't said anything in a few moments. A quick glance showed the constable sagging against the helm, eyelids fluttering. Kianthe snapped her fingers. "Much as I love the idea of our captain falling asleep while we sail, I feel like there's a better way to do this. Why don't you go belowdecks and get some rest?"

If other mages pushed boats up the river all day, Kianthe could manage to guide this one for a few hours.

Bobbie snapped to attention, scrubbing her face. "Serina is down there. I can't."

"So is Reyna, and she's delightful company." Kianthe smirked. Bobbie didn't seem persuaded, so the mage continued, "Take a nap on deck, then. Seriously, Bobbie, you won't impress anyone if you face Arlon slurring your words."

But Bobbie squinted at the waterline, then held up a hand. "Hang on."

"Rude."

"Does the river look closer to you?"

Kianthe almost replied something snarky about how they were *on* the river, so this was about as close as it'd get—but immediately swallowed the words. Because Bobbie was right. The water level was rising, inching higher and higher up the boat. Whereas before it was a six-stone drop, now there were maybe three, and that gap was closing fast.

She reached out with magic, and sure enough, water was flooding belowdecks.

"Uh—"

"We're sinking," Bobbie exclaimed, abandoning the helm to lunge down the narrow staircase. Kianthe was right on her heels, leaving just the constable's horse on deck. Below, the small space was flooding fast through a human-sized gap someone had smashed in the hull. How Reyna even *managed* that was beyond Kianthe.

Stone be damned, her fiancée was incredible.

And speaking of, Reyna and Serina were—of course—gone.

Bobbie gaped at the empty space. "H-How—"

Water was filling fast. Kianthe ordered the wood to patch itself, but yet again, the Nacean had sensed weakness and was feeling greedy. Clearly her pom-pom hat wasn't enough for this ridiculous river: water pummeled the weak patch, and it wouldn't be held back by magic for long.

They had to get off this boat.

"We have to go." Kianthe grabbed Bobbie's arm, towing her above deck again. Fear gripped her that Reyna was just . . . gone. But Rain knew how to swim; she'd escaped with a *literal* pirate; and she had warned Kianthe multiple times this might happen.

The mage just hadn't expected this exact scenario.

The stallion was prancing on deck, huffing nervously as the boat began listing sideways. "Hang on," Kianthe shouted. Bobbie sprinted to her horse, and Kianthe took position at the bow of the boat. They were a fair distance from shore, but the current was mild and they were still afloat—at least for a little while.

Kianthe pulled magic from the Nacean River's ley line, and with a burst of air and a careful current, shoved the boat toward the shoreline. The entire vessel lurched under her magic, and sweat trickled down her neck as she calculated how fast they were sinking versus how quickly she could aim them to dry land.

The only bonus here was that wood floated, so at least they wouldn't completely submerge. But that was a small consolation for the horse on board.

Bobbie gripped her mount's reins, keeping him as stable as she could. "It's going to be tight!" Panic tinged her voice.

"That's what she said," Kianthe shouted back.

"Right now?" The boat listed further, and Bobbie's horse whinnied as everyone staggered. Kianthe ripped a wave up to level the boat, and despite all that, Bobbie still managed to look indignant. "Really?"

"I make no apologies." Kianthe grinned wickedly. "Hang on!"

The boat ran aground with a scraping *thud,* and everyone but the horse fell over. The stallion neighed, stomped his hooves, and leapt off the boat in a smooth motion, tail flicking as he trotted away. Bobbie watched him go, then slid off the boat herself and sank to her knees on the gravely shore.

"I can't believe I lost her *again,*" the constable moaned, burying her head in her hands.

Kianthe leapt overboard, released her magic on the river and wind, and breathed a sigh. "At least we're safe—" And she stopped short, squinting downriver.

A gorgeous ship, easily triple the size of the one Bobbie had borrowed, had been moored a short distance from the other ships at the docks of Neolow. Reyna had pointed it out last night, almost casually; Kianthe should have known she'd been scheming—oh, sorry, *strategizing*—even then.

Now, that ship was drifting downstream. For a moment, the motion was so subtle that Kianthe almost missed it . . . but then one sail unfurled in a decisive manner. Two people scrambled around the deck, tying it tight.

Overhead, two griffons—one large, one itty-bitty—circled.

"Um, you may not want this news right now," Kianthe said carefully, stepping to the constable.

Bobbie lifted her head. "What news?" She sounded utterly defeated.

Kianthe winced, rocking back on her heels. "Never mind."

"What is it, Arcandor?" Bobbie pushed to her feet, stumbled a bit, caught herself at the last minute.

"Well, there's . . . ah, there's a chance—a *slight* one, mind—that my fiancée helped your pirate escape. And there's a better chance—still just a chance, but a better one—that they've stolen that ship right there."

Kianthe pointed at it. It was angling south, away from them, heading downriver.

Bobbie stared, jaw gaping.

"That's . . . that's Diarn Arlon's personal vessel. He'd sent it to Neolow for repairs."

The two of them watched in silence as Serina unfurled more sails, as the wind caught, as they careened away. Overhead, Visk and Ponder broke for the hills. The fact that Visk didn't retrieve Kianthe told her that she'd been betrayed by both her fiancée *and* her mount.

If she squinted, she could see Reyna waving cheerfully from the upper deck.

"Damn them to the five hells," Bobbie groaned.

10

Reyna

"I have to admit," Reyna called over the wind, the gentle swell of waves against the ship, and the panicked shouts of sailors left behind in Neolow, "it was remarkably easy to hijack this vessel. I expected more resistance taking the diarn's private ship."

A small part of her was immensely pleased that Serina had agreed to take the ship so quickly. There were six other options in the harbor, but the pirate clearly couldn't resist sticking it to Diarn Arlon.

Which gave Reyna uninterrupted access to the diarn's most mobile hiding spot.

Excellent.

"I know, right?" Serina laughed, perched confidently at the helm. The wind swept her long hair into a frenzy, and she tied it off with a piece of twine from around her wrist. Her bangs couldn't be tamed, but she didn't seem to mind. She spun on her heel, offering a charming wave at the single constable on the pier. "I figured Neolow would have more constables keeping guard."

Reyna chuckled. "I'm fairly sure they were sent on a special assignment yesterday. I saw a group of twenty or thirty of them heading south."

"Bet those sailors weren't happy about that." Serina grinned.

The five sailors who'd just weighed this ship's anchor—

presumably to return it to Diarn Arlon—spluttered at them from the river's surface. Three started swimming to the riverbank, while the other two were treading freezing water in utter disbelief.

It had been surprisingly simple to shove them into the water one by one. Reyna was more skilled in combat, but Serina operated on raw determination and a dash of spontaneity, which proved to be a potent mix.

"We're going to need a real crew for a ship this big, but I can get us to the next town, at least. As long as you help." Serina jogged across the ship, fiddling with the lines on the foremast.

Reyna wrung her own hair out, tying it into a tight bun. The river had been ice-cold, and she shuddered in her wet clothing. Luckily, the exhilaration of theft kept her plenty warm, and the sun was bright today. "Of course. Just give me a moment." Reyna leaned against the aft railing, squinting at the constable's ship farther upriver. As predicted, Kianthe had guided it to shore, and it didn't seem like anyone was hurt.

She waved at Kianthe, and far across the river, the mage waved back. On the shore, Bobbie was hunched over herself in apparent anguish.

"They're okay," Reyna said, pleased. "Well, Key is, at least. I think Bobbie's having a harder time with this turn of events."

Doubt flickered across Serina's face. She winced, then covered it with a firm set of her jaw. "Bobbie will survive. She has her precious job and her crochet needles and her stubborn pride, and that's probably enough to put her to sleep at night." Serina scoffed, tossing her long ponytail over her shoulder. "Here, stay at the helm and keep her steady while I handle the sails."

Reyna took over, and Serina skipped down the staircase to unwind another line, releasing a third sail. This ship had two masts with at least seven huge sails, although some seemed too heavy to lift with one or two people. As a result, Serina was strategic about how she used them, pulling the smaller ones open so the wind could catch them. Reyna kept steady hold of the helm, aiming for the center of the river just in case.

She hadn't realized the Nacean got this wide. Near Oslop, trees and mountains were visible on the opposite side of the river—far away, but still obvious, especially with the islands that created thinner channels between them. Near Neolow, the river narrowed, which was why they'd built a ferry station on the east side for people to cross its width.

Here, even just a little farther south, the Nacean widened to mimic an actual ocean. Already, the banks pulled away, leaving a huge open waterway for them to travel. She admired the sheer distance of it for a few moments—and then noticed a large ship anchored south of Neolow, surrounded by a dense forest.

It was stationary, but something about it prickled her arms, exhilaration catching in her chest. In an instant, she recalled the person who'd winked at her in town—the one with that ostentatious feather in their hat.

Reyna covered her eyes with a hand, barely able to contain her excitement. "Do you think that's the *Painted Death*? The Dastardly Pirate Dreggs's flagship?"

"What?" Serina balked. "It better not be. Dreggs is from the area, but they haven't been back in decades." She joined Reyna at the railing, just for a moment, leaning over it to see the ship better. After a moment, she shrugged. "No red sails. It's probably just a fishing vessel. Great salmon in these parts."

"Hmm." Reyna wasn't convinced.

Serina, meanwhile, had resumed tying off several more lines while Reyna held the helm steady. The pirate called over her shoulder, "Thanks for helping me. If Arlon sank his claws into me, I'm not sure anyone would see me for a while."

"You don't think he'd settle for a fine?" Reyna asked.

"I wonder sometimes if he'd settle for jail."

Those words hung like a noose between them.

Serina breezed forward, her tone too casual. "Why'd you help me, anyway? Aside from the obvious lure of adventure." She moved across the deck like she'd been sailing it every day of her life, but her confidence was belied by the way she avoided eye contact, the forced smile on her lips.

Reyna considered it for a moment, shrugging her cloak off to dry. The sun was warm, but the air was chilly, and she shivered again as the wind hit her damp skin. Swimming back to the docks hadn't been the grandest part of Serina's plan, but it was effective. Reyna took hold of the helm, and underneath her hands, the polished handles were smooth and sturdy.

"Simple. I needed a break from my fiancée's jokes," Reyna teased.

Visk had seemed very confused when she asked him *not* to retrieve Kianthe and Bobbie, and Reyna was lucky the griffon trusted her judgment. She didn't want to make this easier on the constable, and a flying mount was nothing if not timesaving.

Still, it wasn't hard to imagine Kianthe's exasperation as Reyna abandoned her to live out a pirate adventure.

But that adventure warmed her veins, made her feel truly alive for the first time in two seasons. She hadn't felt a thrill like this since hunting an assassin in Queen Tilaine's crowded ballroom. Kianthe found adventure every time she left home—it literally came with her job title—so Reyna didn't feel bad seizing a few moments in the sun herself.

Plus, she now had access to Diarn Arlon's private vessel. And if the documents Feo dug up on the diarn were true, he had any number of hidden compartments on this ship.

She did regret insulting Kianthe's jokes, though.

"That's a lie," she amended. "Key is hilarious. But if I tell her that, she'll be insufferable."

"Okay . . ." Serina grunted, yanking another line. She winced as it rubbed against the bandage on her left hand, but she didn't release her hold. "That still doesn't answer my question. You don't know me. I thought you two were working with Bobbie before this."

Skepticism lined her voice.

It was a valid concern. Reyna had only just met the pirate, but there were underlying influences at play.

So, she answered honestly. "I don't trust Diarn Arlon." Reyna twisted the helm just a bit, just enough to avoid a set of rapids on their left. "And I'm curious to get a second opinion. Ideally from someone who isn't employed by him . . . and that seems difficult to find in his lands."

She'd opened the floodgates. Serina tied off the lines almost angrily, eyes glinting like blue flames as she yanked the knots into submission. "Everyone is employed by him. Literally everyone. It started slowly, with his grandfather making deals with the farmers and merchants and sheriffs: 'Work for me, earn a consistent supply of food and income regardless of how much your lands yield.' But in the contracts, he slipped in clauses that give him control of everything. Not *governance*, like most diarns practice. I'm talking total ownership."

That was exactly how the Queendom operated. Ironic it was being replicated here, considering people in the Realm widely viewed the Queendom as antiquated in its policies and leadership. A monarchy, pressed against the meritocracy of Leonol, or the revered Sheparan council.

It was murderously outdated.

"And that's . . . bad." Reyna kept her voice mild, neutral.

But her accent reminded Serina of just who she was speaking with. The pirate scrunched her face, like she was sorting through intense thoughts. "Look, okay. In the Queendom, your lords own the land, right? But they let their people, their citizens, farm it, and sell what they grow. The lords collect a tax, but otherwise they don't interfere unless there's a problem. Right?"

"Correct," Reyna replied. She'd been a fly on the wall of many meetings where Queen Tilaine gauged tax collection and doled out punishments when lords weren't meeting their quotas.

But for the most part, lords—like Wylan, the Queendom representative of Tawney—were left alone to manage local areas. In turn, the lords left their people alone, unless they were a special kind of vindictive.

Which, unfortunately, some were.

Reyna just didn't expect that kind of thing from Diarn Arlon, who'd seemed sneaky, but mostly harmless until this point.

"Okay, so here, Diarn Arlon owns *all* the land. And the buildings. And the ships, and the livestock, and the crops. And we, as his citizens, are given a salary of his choosing based on what we can produce for his estate."

"That's . . . a curious choice."

"'Curious' is one word for it. So that party, the one where I exploded his precious buffet table?" Serina rolled her eyes in disgust, swiftly scaling a rope ladder to tug a few lines higher up. "That was to announce bonuses—extra coin—for his top earners. Farmers who happen to have very rich soil, or tools to harvest their crops faster. But they're the ones making more money, and the rest of us are barely surviving on the salaries Arlon gives."

Reyna frowned, holding the helm steady. "So, it's not a tax. It's the other way around. He takes everything, then doles out what he feels a town needs."

"Mmm. And he's not tracking birth rates, or droughts, or unusually cold seasons. Some towns are doing great. Some are starving, and he doesn't give two shits about it." Now Serina licked her finger, held it to the wind, and untied another line. A triangle-shaped sail attached to the bowsprit shifted slightly in response. "But," she grunted, tying the line tight in its new location, "if we try to keep some of the food *we* grow to feed our families . . . he calls it 'stealing' and sends his constables to have a chat."

Fury spiked in Reyna's chest, but she reined it in, attempting to be logical about this. It was just one opinion. Still, it was shocking she'd never heard of this before: if this was happening, people had to know about it. Surely Feo, Tawney's cunning diarn, would have mentioned it before sending them west.

"Wouldn't the council intervene if that were the case?" But the second she said it, Reyna knew it wasn't true.

Serina quirked an eyebrow.

"Diarn Arlon is a councilmember." Reyna pinched the bridge of her nose.

"The richest one, in fact. He's the closest thing Shepara has to a king, and no one looks closely at how his people are living." Serina set her jaw. "So, I became a pirate because it's better than starving and better than serving as one of his constable lackeys. And yet, Bobbie calls *me* irrational."

Reyna had been afraid of this. Even in the Queendom, the lord may own the land, but the physical items citizens used to tend it were passed down through generations.

Granted, the Queendom's lands weren't rich to begin with—their main export was stone from various quarries, not crops from a bountiful river. Without Diarn Arlon's supplies, the Queendom would struggle to feed its people.

Queen Tilaine had spent many nights attempting to strong-arm Diarn Arlon and the council into a finalized contract to ensure their food supply. It was only partially successful, and only because the council couldn't be seen causing a humanitarian crisis by refusing.

From high above the deck, Serina squinted upriver. "No one's following us, so that's a pleasant surprise. You can tie off the helm, if you'd like—I think we're clear of any obstructions for a while."

Across the river, another ship was heading north to Neolow, but they couldn't know that this ship had been stolen. Reyna watched it carefully, but it seemed intent on keeping its distance, going about its business.

She tied off the helm as instructed. Her knot was messy, but Serina appeared at her shoulder and said, "Like this—" and retied it in a quick, easy fashion. "Simple and strong, but easy to undo in a hurry."

"Clever," Reyna replied.

Serina nodded at the sword Reyna had left out to dry and smirked. "We all have our talents."

With the helm secured, Serina motioned for Reyna to follow her belowdecks. "Anyway. Enough misery. We've just stolen Diarn Arlon's private vessel. Let's see what the king of Shepara has to offer, hmm?"

Reyna chuckled humorlessly, but that title stuck like a knife in her gut.

She'd have plenty to say to Kianthe the next time they found each other.

In the meantime, she trailed after Serina. The vessel was a brigantine, but it wasn't nearly as large as the ships she'd seen at the Capital's harbor. Still, it was large enough to have a captain's quarters below the helm—accessible through an ornately carved door on the lower deck—and a narrow staircase leading into the ship's belly. There were no cannons; this ship was clearly meant for luxury transportation and little else.

"I'm surprised sailing ships can operate on a river," Reyna said.

Serina swept out her hands, gesturing at the grandeur of the Nacean. "Just *this* river. It's deep enough that ships don't have to worry about running aground, and wide enough that the wind can really pick up speed."

"I imagine there are hazards here we wouldn't see in the open ocean, though." Reyna raised one eyebrow. "Is Diarn Arlon the only reason you decided to stay on the Nacean, rather than telling him to go to hells and traveling south to the Southern Seas?"

"Well, if I told him to go to hells, a lot of people wouldn't eat this winter." Serina stepped down the staircase belowdecks.

It was nearly pitch black in the ship's belly, and both the women had to duck as they descended beneath the captain's quarters. Once they rounded the base of the staircase, a large cargo hold spread before them. Reyna squinted into the darkness, even as Serina fumbled to light the enclosed lantern hanging on a metal peg near the staircase.

"It's big," Reyna remarked.

"Mmm. Bigger than my last ship, anyway." Serina tried to sound optimistic, but her voice hitched.

Reyna glanced at her, sympathy knitting her features. "Was that ship important to you?" Reyna hadn't seen Serina's old one—not in daylight, anyway—but even she knew this ship was bigger and better equipped, comparatively.

Serina struck a match and held it against the wick of the lantern, then closed the lantern's tiny glass door once the flame caught. "My dad built it. We were a family of farmers, but he loved the Nacean. We'd go sailing on that ship whenever he could take the time."

Reyna had never known her father. Her mother, also a Queensguard, raised her, with her uncle stepping in to teach on occasion. The idea of spending day trips with her father was strange.

Bobbie had gone over this, but she wanted to hear Serina's side—so she played ignorant. "Is he still a farmer?"

"No. We lost the land." Serina's bitterness was obvious. She moved past Reyna, clearly done with that conversation.

Reyna let it drop, following dutifully. Together, they explored the areas of the cargo hold: the hammocks that swung over heavy wooden crates, the tiny glass windows at the bow of the ship that brought in a little light, and a trapdoor to the bilge—where water filled during a storm, and could be removed with a specialized pump.

Reyna wrinkled her nose when they found that area. "Smells . . . lovely."

"Like a brisk summer day, right?" Serina joked, letting the door drop shut. Then she plucked a long metal rod hanging on the bulkhead and pried open one of the crates. Inside were a few ornate vases packed with straw. They'd obviously fetch a sum, but Serina groaned as if she'd found dog shit instead.

"Useless," she muttered, resetting the crate's lid.

"You could always resell them."

Serina tossed up her arms. "I'm not in the resale market. I'm in the 'Hey, someone can eat this' market. Arlon may value that kind of thing, but I certainly don't."

Reyna couldn't argue with that. Her eyes scanned the cargo hold one more time, noting several areas to inspect when she had a bit of privacy. Then she blew out the lantern, rehung it near the staircase, and followed Serina to the lower deck.

They explored the captain's quarters next. Although "captain's" quarters was misleading, since this room had obviously been designed for Diarn Arlon, not the captain of his ship. There was a gorgeous rolltop desk, stocked with ink bottles and quills and leather-bound notebooks. A real bed with silk sheets and gold embroidery anchored in the back corner. Long stained-glass windows lined the wall behind it, offering a tinted view of the river. A door on the adjacent wall revealed a small washroom—although it lacked any of the modern upgrades they enjoyed at their home in Tawney.

"This is ridiculous." Serina rolled her eyes. "A trip downriver only takes three or four days. Upriver is a bit longer, but he could still get from Jallin to his estate in a week if the wind is good. But he can't spend that amount of time without a real bed?"

"Are you surprised?"

Serina pinched the bridge of her nose. "Not particularly." She slammed the door shut on that room, shaking her head. "Okay. Next steps. This ship is too much for us to sail alone, especially once the river narrows. What say we take a trip to Koll?"

Reyna laughed. "Sure."

11

Kianthe

It took several hours to reach Neolow's eastern shore again.

Bobbie wanted to ride ahead, but Kianthe was absolutely *not* going to be abandoned—especially by a constable who looked like she could collapse at any moment. She insisted Bobbie ride her horse and get some sleep, and Kianthe led the mount through the wilderness by the riverside.

Sleeping on horseback—or on the back of any mount, really—was difficult, but Bobbie was so exhausted that she slumped over the horse's neck and was dozing in seconds. It looked incredibly uncomfortable, and if Kianthe thought she could get away with it, she'd have stopped and insisted they get some rest.

But Serina was sailing south, and Bobbie was quite clear that they needed to follow.

When they arrived at the stables on the eastern side of the Nacean, Kianthe left Bobbie blinking in the sunlight to check on Lilac—who was, of course, luxuriating in her current vacation. The horse's tail flicked irately as Kianthe patted her flank, and she turned resolutely away from the mage.

"Listen, you may need to step up," Kianthe said. "Since your owner clearly told Visk to make himself scarce."

Lilac leveled an unimpressed stare her way, as if to say, *And how is that my problem?*

Why most of the Realm used horses to travel, Kianthe would never know.

She pinched her brow, contemplating her next course of action, when a commotion outside caught her attention. Kianthe stepped out of the stables to find two constables flanking Bobbie, perched atop stern-looking horses much like hers.

"Guess the investigation isn't going well, is it?" one drawled. He was a taller figure with thin, angular cheekbones, sandy skin, and beady eyes. Everything about him looked like a seagull. "When Diarn Arlon hears about your screwup, he'll have your head. You'll be *lucky* to patrol in Lathe."

"I mean, your mom does work in the sheriff's department. Might be fun." The other constable snickered. This person was shorter, with skin the shade of pine bark and a dazzling smile that oozed insincerity.

Bobbie had been groggy after her nap, but seemed more alert now. She set her jaw, gripping her horse's reins a bit too tightly. Her green eyes flashed. "Bold words, considering she stole that ship right out from under your noses."

The seagull constable's face colored. "She wouldn't have had the chance if you hadn't let her go."

"What does the diarn say about excuses? Come on, Tyal. You literally came down here to capture a pirate. You couldn't have stopped her from getting on that ship?" Bobbie scowled.

"We weren't here for *this* pirate—" Tyal started, then clamped his mouth shut.

Kianthe folded her arms. *Well,* she thought. *This just got interesting.*

Bobbie latched on, as expected. "Wait. Who else is there?"

"If the diarn didn't inform you, you don't need to know." Tyal lifted his chin, clearly basking in the glow of superior knowledge.

And then his companion went and ruined it. "Dreggs is in the area. We believe they're anchored on the western shore, but we're checking the eastern side just to be certain."

"*Keets,*" Tyal hissed.

"She deserves to know." Keets shrugged.

Kianthe, meanwhile, was bouncing in excitement. "Wait, hold up. *Dreggs* might be here? The Dastardly Pirate Dreggs, right across the river?" With a muttered curse, she turned her gaze skyward. "Damn it all, where's my griffon when I need him?"

"Do you think Dreggs is after the river pirate?" Bobbie sounded vaguely panicked now.

Tyal set his jaw, stubbornly silent, but Keets stepped in again. "It's just a rumor so far. It's possible, but more likely, they're poking at Arlon. The pair have a pretty long-standing rivalry." Now Keets gestured at Kianthe. "You're working with the Arcandor. So, maybe we can all fix this."

All three constables turned to look at her.

Kianthe waggled a few fingers.

"The Mage of Ages isn't a contract employee," Bobbie said. "Diarn Arlon made it clear that she operates on her own free will. I doubt pirates are high on her list."

"Actually—" Kianthe saw Bobbie's exasperated expression and cut herself off. "Never mind."

Bobbie gestured at the mounted constables. "Arcandor, allow me to formally introduce you to Tyal and Keets."

"'They' or 'them' pronouns," Keets said, tapping a pin at their lapel. They'd clearly chosen a white paint to make it stand out against the black uniform.

"He/him," Tyal added.

"'She' is fine for me," Kianthe said, even though most people in the Realm already knew. "It's a pleasure . . . and it's flattering, truly, to think that I'm the shining beacon of hope who can solve all your problems. But Bobbie's right; my magic has a broader purpose in life, and helping capture a pirate isn't it."

Keets sighed. "Well. There goes that option."

"We don't need the Arcandor." Tyal brushed Kianthe off just as fast, nudging his horse so he loomed over Bobbie. "We don't even need Arlon's pet constable. Things have changed with the theft of Arlon's ship. Dreggs or no, that vessel must be recovered—and by someone competent enough to manage it."

Bobbie flinched.

Tyal addressed Keets. "While everyone is on the west side chasing rumors, I say we pivot to the problem at hand. If she can't capture that pirate, we'll do it. A great theft requires equal punishment—I'm not above splattering that pirate's blood on its deck."

Keets sighed. "Whatever you say."

And that was the moment Kianthe realized this was turning into a true manhunt—and Reyna had just positioned herself squarely in the center of the target. The mage raised a hand, and a gust of wind swirled around them, a pointed reminder who was in charge.

"All right, simmer down. No one's gutting a pirate. Especially not when my fiancée is also on that ship."

The constables exchanged a glance.

Bobbie slumped, like she'd wanted to keep that detail a secret.

"Then you do have a stake in this game." Tyal leaned over his horse. "Unless you *want* your fiancé drowning in the Nacean before you can reach him. When we storm that ship, accidents could happen—but if you join us and help, we'll make sure he's safe."

"My fiancée is a woman, and I'll thank you for not assuming. And if you think you can catch her unawares, you're dreaming." The air around Kianthe sparked, and her eyes burned like hot coal. "I also don't appreciate the manipulation, so let me be clear. I'm the Mage of fucking Ages. And if you do something stupid and my partner is hurt in the process, Diarn Arlon and Dreggs will be the least of your worries."

The words hung between them, a fatal promise.

Keets broke the silence first, flicking the reins of their horse. "I'm not here to fight the Arcandor. But Tyal is right; if we're accused of losing that ship, we could lose our jobs. And then my family doesn't eat. Apologies, Arcandor, but we're going hunting."

"We'll keep an eye out for your fiancée," Tyal said snidely. His pride was clearly wounded by Kianthe's display. "Nice crochet hook," he added to Bobbie, and it wasn't a compliment.

They nudged their mounts into motion.

Bobbie tugged the reins of her own horse, physically blocking them from leaving. "They are nice crochet hooks; custom made in Wellia, in fact. And you two haven't been dismissed. I'm the higher-ranking officer here. Stand down."

"You're on special assignment." Keets glared.

"And you're interfering." Bobbie pulled her shoulders straight, her emerald eyes narrowed dangerously. "You're only here to find Dreggs. The river pirate is *mine*. If you're bored, feel free to tell Diarn Arlon personally that I'm closing in, and will have her back on his estate before the solstice. If that doesn't suit you, your orders are to return to Neolow and try to keep any other ships from being stolen."

Tyal looked ready to murder. "You think you can stop us?"

Faster than Kianthe could track, Tyal had a sword against his chest. It was thicker than Reyna's, curved to a wicked point, and still lethally dangerous. Behind the blade, Bobbie's expression was deadened, thoroughly done.

"Today," she said, "I have captured and lost the pirate. I've been kicked, bitten, insulted, and attacked. I haven't slept properly in days. The pirate sank my ship and almost killed my horse in the process. And I tried to crochet a bee, which *should have been easy*, and it turned out like this." Now she reached into her pocket and pulled out the misshapen toy, glowering as Tyal and Keets recoiled. She stuffed it back into her pocket and snarled, "I will not—how did you put it? 'Sit idly' while you two ruin my investigation. Cease and desist, Tyal. This is your final warning."

Keets blinked, almost impressed. Tyal reached for his own sword.

Kianthe lit a hand on fire, holding up the flame where they all could see. "Don't test her. She's really upset about that bee." The threat was probably a lot less intimidating in her dual pom-pom hat, but brazen displays of magic usually got the point across.

Keets raised their hands. "We'll go back to Neolow."

Tyal kept silent. He didn't look pleased about the decision.

Another beat passed, and Bobbie sheathed her sword. "Get on with it, then. The ferry boards over there." And she waited while the two constables guided their horses in the opposite direction—north, not south.

Only once they were gone did Kianthe extinguish the flame in her hand. "Your coworkers are assholes."

Bobbie didn't acknowledge that statement. "They backed down now, but they're not going back to Neolow. I suspect they're going straight to Diarn Arlon, to try and twist the story so they aren't at fault. And if Arlon agrees to assign more constables to this hunt, anyone on that ship is at risk." Exhaustion tinged her voice as she gestured at the stables. "Get Reyna's horse. Our timetable just got shorter."

"Oh, good," Kianthe muttered.

They rode hard, which was unpleasant in the best circumstances, but absolutely awful so late at night—especially with the fog that had settled over the forest in an eerie gloom. Lilac kept up with Bobbie's horse, but she clearly hated every second. She tossed her head whenever Kianthe tried to pat her neck, and seemed to purposefully hunt for ways to throw Kianthe off the saddle.

Miserable thing.

"This would be faster with a ship," Kianthe called to Bobbie, who'd set this ridiculous pace. "Easier on the horses, too."

That made Bobbie pat her own horse, running a hand over his mane. "Because a ship worked so well last time." The constable's words were nearly snatched away by the wind. They were following a winding trail near the river's edge. With the fog, it made even *seeing* the river difficult, so Kianthe was careful to keep Lilac angled away from its bank.

"Normally a ship works fine, when someone doesn't smash a hole in its side," Kianthe huffed. "How far is our destination, again? And how sure are you that she'll be there?"

"We're going to Koll. It's the only place Serina can feasibly go—she can't sail a ship that big on her own, not even with Reyna's help. They'll have to find a crew, or steal something smaller. If they opt for the latter, we might still be able to return Arlon's prized ship back to him."

"If I were Serina, I wouldn't return Arlon's ship."

Bobbie's shoulders slumped. "That's what I'm afraid of."

Lilac huffed, leaping over a small dip in the path. On the other side she seemed thoroughly done, because she tossed her head again and slowed to a casual trot. Kianthe tried nudging her into motion again, but she wasn't very skilled with horseback riding, and Lilac just ignored her.

"Uh, Bobbie? Might need to slow down."

The constable glanced back, saw Kianthe and Lilac falling behind, and seemed to contemplate just . . . abandoning them both. But ultimately, her decency won out, because she pulled the reins and slowed her own horse, giving them time to catch up. They continued at a calmer pace that seemed to make Bobbie's skin crawl, based on the way she fidgeted.

It was a direct contrast to Reyna's calm and steady presence. Heaving an exasperated sigh, Kianthe aimed for distraction. "Reyna is convinced you had a crush on Serina, but based on today, I'm questioning that."

Bobbie recoiled like she'd been burned. It was so dramatic that Kianthe checked to make sure she hadn't accidentally ignited a flame somewhere.

The constable cleared her throat, looking pointedly ahead. "We knew each other in school, as kids. That's it."

Kianthe quirked an eyebrow. "That's it, huh?"

"Yes." Long silence passed, and finally Bobbie set her jaw. "She was my best friend. My only friend, if I'm being honest. Being the daughter of the town's beloved sheriff meant they expected me to *be* someone—and most things don't come naturally to me." Absently, she gestured at the orange hat Kianthe was wearing. "I thought two pom-poms would be fun, but seeing it on someone, it just looks ridiculous."

"Gee, thanks," Kianthe said, but she didn't take the hat off. It was warm, after all. "If it makes you feel better, I wasn't a natural at anything, either. I'm still shocked that the Stone of Seeing gave me the Arcandor's power."

Bobbie laughed humorlessly. "Must be nice to be saved by

magic. I just existed as the laughingstock of Lathe, the screwup. But Serina wasn't a prodigy either. Her parents were terrible farmers, and everyone knew it. No one was surprised when Diarn Arlon reclaimed their land."

Huh.

Bobbie tilted her head toward the night sky. The stars weren't as bright with the moon so full, but their light still glimmered on the river. "My parents expected a lot from me. Her parents didn't expect anything from her. I guess we met in the middle."

"And you fell in love." Kianthe smirked wryly. This was a fantastic story for her new book.

"We aren't in love," Bobbie retorted hotly.

Enemies to lovers. Or rather, friends to enemies to lovers. Second-chance romance? Kianthe grinned. These were great.

Bobbie saw the look in her eye and glowered. "We *aren't* in love. We kissed once when we were young, right before her family moved to Jallin, and it was terrible."

"Yes, because teenagers know so much about kissing," Kianthe drawled.

Bobbie ducked her head, kicking her horse into a faster trot. "Okay. Think what you want, but I know what's true."

"Sorry, sorry." Kianthe laughed, urging Lilac to catch up again. "But there must be some unfinished business, or you wouldn't be trying so hard to save her."

"I'm trying to *arrest* her."

Kianthe raised her hands, conceding the point even though she conceded absolutely nothing in her own mind. "Whatever the semantics, something's happening between you two. How did old friends go from kissing goodbye to kicking hello?"

Bobbie rubbed her stomach, as if still feeling Serina's boot. "We were screwups as kids, but . . . well, I got wise. I practiced; I worked my ass off, and I became competent at some things. A decent rider, a decent swordsman, a sheriff in the making. Serina didn't understand. She just wanted to have fun until the day her family sailed south." Bobbie drew a short breath. "She lived in a fantasy world. And she hated the constables for retaking her family land."

"I mean, that's understandable."

"They could have been nicer about it, but . . . I don't know. I distribute scarves to their families. I play with their kids. They're like me, just doing our jobs," Bobbie said.

Kianthe thought that when jobs came with power, they also came with the responsibility to decide how to use it. But she saw what Bobbie meant—even if those constables refused Arlon's order, more would have come to complete the task.

Overhead, owls hooted in the pine trees, and the fog seemed to glow in the moonlight. The magic of this place was so vibrant—yellow strands lacing between the trees as they communicated, lingering in the air like a fine golden mist, trailing along the ground like a sheet of ice. The Nacean was the ultimate ley line, and it wanted her to know it.

They followed the path around a curve in the river, and at the base of a hill, a glimmering town awaited them. It was much smaller than Neolow, closer in size to Oslop, but several ships still shone in its harbor.

Bobbie tugged the reins, stopping her horse, squinting down the path. "Koll. One of the Nacean's vineyard towns." She gestured at the hillside, at the rows of grapevines growing in the distance. "Prepare for drunks."

"I believe they're called connoisseurs, here," Kianthe replied, grinning. "I hope Reyna found wine. Drunk Reyna is my favorite."

"Really?" Bobbie rolled her eyes. "Drunk Serina is a menace." And she clicked her tongue, urging her horse down the hillside.

Kianthe cackled and started after her.

12

Reyna

The wine was *incredible.*

After all the chatter about the vineyards along the southern Nacean River, Reyna expected it to be overblown. She expected bottles of exotic wine that didn't truly taste that different from the stuff Queen Tilaine made near the Capital. But while that wine was dry, almost dense—which matched perfectly with the barren landscape of the Queendom—this was crisp, light, and *sweet.* Reyna had never had sweet wine before.

It felt like she was drinking juice.

"This is divine," she gushed, taking another sip. "Ha. Divine wine. Wine-vine. *Wine-vine!*" She cackled and took another deep gulp, savoring the sugary flavor. Kianthe would be so proud of that pun, because wine grew on vines.

Wait. Wine didn't grow on vines. Grapes grew on vines.

Yes.

From behind a long wooden bar, the bartender lifted his chin. "Is she going to be all right?" he asked Serina, a smile tilting his lips. He was a plump man with ruddy cheeks and bright gray eyes, and he wore an apron embroidered with the words I GO BOTH WAYS above two wineglasses, one with red thread, one with white.

Reyna liked him immediately.

His shop was also delightful. Packed edge to edge with locals and tourists alike, every single space was taken. The tables were standing height, and a small terrace through a set of double doors overlooked the river. The entire place blazed with firelight. Two servers flitted among the crowds, offering platters of cheese or refills.

"What's this called?" Reyna asked, pointing at the small glasses she'd been given. They were itty-bitty, far smaller than a normal pour, but there were enough of them to keep her nice and tipsy. Apparently each glass held a different kind of local wine.

She might never leave this place.

"A tasting flight," the bartender said patiently, casting a pointed glance at Serina.

The pirate patted his hand. "She's fine. Promise. Bobbie would be towing me back to Arlon right now if not for her." Now Serina told Reyna: "Drink up. Anything you like. On me."

"Dangerous offer," Reyna replied, and downed another glass in the flight. "This tastes like nectar. Am I a hummingbird? It feels like I may be a hummingbird. And hummingbirds fly, and this is a flight, so . . ." Reyna giggled in delight.

The bartender snorted. "It's a dessert wine. Paired with chocolate."

"You have chocolate?" Reyna gasped.

Serina grinned and motioned at the bartender. He sighed heavily, making a show of rolling his eyes as he ducked below the bar for a huge chocolate cake. Reyna was literally bouncing as he cut a massive slice for her, then offered a metal fork with very fancy designs on the handle.

The cake was delicious. Rich in all the right ways, but almost too sweet when paired with the dessert wine. She swirled it around her sampler glass, squinting at the sugar clinging to the side as the wine slid down, then took another bite of cake.

In the meantime, Serina lowered her voice, leaning across the bar. "I need a crew, Judd. A navigator, a carpenter, a boatswain. At least three seamen in addition." Reyna opened her mouth to comment on the word "seamen," but Serina held up a hand. "Don't."

Pouting, Reyna went back to her cake.

"Six sailors?" Judd the bartender quirked an eyebrow, leaning on the counter casually. "How big a ship did you get, Serrie?"

This time, the nickname didn't seem to bother her nearly as much. Serina grinned vindictively. "It's not as big as some. But I need to take care of this one. Treat her right. Which means I'll need sailors who are somewhat off their rocker, but anticipating adventure where they can get it."

"I heard tell the diarn's private ship was stolen from Neolow earlier today. Two women pushed several sailors into the river and laughed all the way out of town." A pause. "You heard that rumor?"

"I heard it," Serina replied, drumming her fingers on the counter. "Seems a bit far-fetched—but if it *were* to happen, the folk who did it would have to be awfully bold. And they might need a crew of similar insanity."

Reyna looked between them like she was watching a jousting tournament inside the Capital's stone walls, perched behind Queen Tilaine's throne, waiting to see who'd fall off their horse first. She snickered, and the noise gained Judd's attention. He offered a wry smile and pointed at her empty sampler glasses.

"You pick a favorite?"

"All of them." Then Reyna dissolved into laughter. "Okay, fine. The not-so-dessert wine." She tapped the second-sweetest; not the one like nectar, but the one above it. "You have red wine? I love reds."

"Me too," Judd replied, tapping his apron pointedly. "I think you'll like these. Any preference?" And he retrieved another two bottles from below the bar.

Reyna examined the labels. "You choose."

"Judd. We're on a timetable here."

"With the diarn's ship, I'd imagine so," the bartender drawled. He chose the left bottle, filled a glass for Reyna, then winked when she beamed at him. He seemed to realize Serina was still waiting, because he shook his head. "Serrie, you know I love you and appreciate what you're doing for folks along the river."

Serina leaned against the bar. "Your cousin seemed pretty excited for that shipment of grain. Her horses were thrilled with the hay."

"And I'm grateful. Honest. But you're asking me to find a crew for Diarn Arlon's stolen ship. That vessel will turn every head on the Nacean now—even if the sailors agree to the risk, it's a dangerous game for everyone involved."

Reyna sipped the red wine and felt it tasted more like chocolate than the chocolate cake. She sank into the glass, releasing a satisfied sigh. "What if we change the look of the ship?"

They glanced at her.

She raised her glass. "Well, the problem is that it's too identifiable. So, we either steal another ship, or we make it *less* identifiable."

"Won't fool many," Judd replied. "Most on these waters know that ship."

"But at its core, it's another brigantine." Reyna leaned forward like she was whispering a conspiracy. "We add a black sail, just like your old ship—something we can pull down when we're ready to strike fear, but bundle up when we're hiding in plain sight. We rename it. Sand down the gold trim, replace the stained glass with regular. We can't change the shape, but if we remove those features, it might fool people for as long as we're in town."

The two of them exchanged glances. When Judd didn't immediately protest, Serina's grin grew. She took a swig from her own wineglass, then stole a bite of Reyna's chocolate cake. "Delicious. What do you think, Judd? If it's not Arlon's ship, how hard would it be to staff?"

"Hmm. Not very. Give me a day or two. I think I can get a crew together." Judd tilted his head. "What's the salary?"

Serina told him, and Judd laughed, and laughed, and laughed.

"You could have just said it's too low," Serina said, although her cheeks had colored in embarrassment. "I don't have much else. Shit. Maybe we do need a smaller vessel."

Reyna thought for a moment, then patted Judd's hand. "We have vases. Expensive ones. They'll fetch a sum. I can pretend I brought them from the Grand Palace in the Capital. Unless no one out here wants something from Queen Tilaine." Bitterness infused Reyna's voice now. "Since everyone hates us."

"Items from the queen's collection will sell, no matter what people think of her. It's still a symbol of royalty." Serina slapped the table, then shook Reyna's shoulder happily. "Brilliant. We'll have payment, Judd. Just get a crew together, and keep quiet about it."

Judd sighed. "Your wish is my command."

"As always, it's a pleasure," Serina said, and tossed a few coins on the wooden bar top. "Come on, Reyna. We have some work to do."

They'd been smart enough not to anchor the stolen ship in Koll's harbor—instead, Serina had expertly steered into an inlet barely visible off the Nacean's main path. Dense trees gnarled near the entrance, hiding it from view, but once they anchored, it had been a short walk into town.

Now they traversed the same path, laden with supplies. The moon was bright overhead, and they took turns pulling the cart they'd rented from town. Reyna had stocked many wine bottles in the recesses of the cart, and kept checking to make sure none had broken.

"Matild is going to die when she tastes these," Reyna said, when Serina saw her checking a fifth time.

The pirate snickered. "Is Matild one of your friends back home?"

"Our best friend," Reyna confirmed. "She and her husband welcomed us into town when everyone else was suspicious of what we were doing. They made me want to stay in Tawney, despite the weather and dragon attacks."

"Dragon attacks?" Serina repeated incredulously.

Reyna typically would have minced words, but she was warm and giddy from the wine. "Oh, sure. They burned half the town on a regular basis. We thought they hated that humans had settled so close to dragon country, but then Kianthe found out someone had stolen three of their eggs a generation ago. That's why we're out here."

If she had her wits about her, Reyna wouldn't have revealed their mission to a stranger—but Serina was feeling less and less like one. And frankly, she had insider knowledge of the diarn's lands; that could come in handy later on, depending on the records Diarn Arlon produced.

"You're looking for dragon eggs?" Serina stopped short, eyebrows shooting up. "I mean, shit. I knew the Arcandor would have important business, but I didn't expect . . . well, that."

"If you know where they are, that'd save me an awful lot of time."

Serina snorted. "I can't say I've ever seen a dragon egg or heard mention of one, much less three."

Reyna sighed, picking up her pace again. "Well, worth a shot."

"You should check with Bobbie's mother. She and the other sheriffs keep a close eye on shipments coming in; I think they'd have noticed dragon eggs."

"By our standard, they were very well hidden. It's a tricky search."

"Well, now you're a real pirate, hunting for treasure just like the Dastardly Pirate Dreggs." Serina wiped her forehead with her arm and tapped the wooden handle of the cart. "Your turn." She ducked from behind it, letting Reyna take over.

"Have you ever met Dreggs?" Reyna asked. "We have a biography of them in our shop. Two, actually." A blush spread over her face.

Serina noticed. "The fan-made version? Sexy stuff."

"One of Kianthe's favorites. Still, though—they sound marvelous."

"They're pretty cutthroat, by my father's standards. His ships have been attacked by Dreggs more times than I can count." Serina didn't sound upset about that. In fact, she sounded starry-eyed. "But from what I've heard, they try not to kill anyone. Their reputation is impressive enough now that they just wave their flag and people hand things over."

Reyna tilted her head. "You don't seem to have a bad reputation yourself."

Serina smiled proudly. "Damn straight. I target ships right before the constables take control of a yield. Farmers are supervised loading everything onto the diarn's ships, so he has a record of what they turned in. Then it hits the water, and I steal what I can before the ship reaches Arlon's warehouse. He loses his profit, but everyone's still paid."

"No one fights you on it?"

"At first they did." Serina shrugged, rolling out one of her shoulders. "Now, though, people see me coming and set aside what they can. They know it goes right back to the community."

Reyna laughed. "Talk about a brilliant plan."

"It'll be better once I can hit some bigger targets. Finding ships with crops is getting rarer as the season ends, but there are still families without food." Serina set her jaw. "I'd love to try a heist at his warehouse, but that's bold, even by my standards. It's crawling with constables."

"Hmm. Sounds risky."

The sound of wooden wheels rolling along uneven dirt was constant background noise. They'd packed the cart full of glass panes, cloth for a single black sail, and sanding material. Reyna had secured some black paint and a thick fur brush, with plans to paint the new name on the side of the ship. Her handwriting was excellent, after all.

"Have you thought about what you'd rename the ship?" she asked as the vessel came into view. Right now, the name on the side was as ostentatious as Diarn Arlon was: the *Prestige.*

Serina squinted at it, wrinkling her nose. "My last ship was just called *Lathe's Lumber,* since that's where my dad built it. Let me think on this one for a bit."

"Sure. Something tells me we'll be busy anyway."

They got to work. The ship was too tall to board by ramp, so they had to tie their supplies into a wooden bucket and swim it to the ship. Serina scaled the rope ladder, then crafted a pulley system to haul their supplies on board. It took several trips, and Reyna was freezing by the time they managed it, but eventually everything was locked in place.

Of course, Serina wasn't one to dawdle—they worked hard into the night, sanding gold trim, cutting and sewing the black sail into the right shape and size. Replacing the glass proved to be a pain: the wooden trim holding the glass in place was more stubborn than Reyna had bargained for. Still, she wasn't much help with the sail, so she tackled this job as best she could.

Dawn's light was just beginning to peek over the horizon, filtering through the trees, when Kianthe barged into the room and shouted, "Rain, my dearest, I've come to rescue you from the fearsome pirate!"

Well. That didn't take long.

13

Kianthe

It was incredibly easy to ditch Bobbie in Koll. Mostly because the constable was literally swaying on her feet, so coaxing her into a room at the local inn while Kianthe "continued the search" for their culprits proved shockingly simple.

Searching for Reyna was even easier. All Kianthe had to do was step into the river, and it told her exactly where they'd gone. A few perplexed sailors squinted at her as she hauled herself out of the harbor, and in answer to their unspoken question, she called, "I'm keeping up on *current* events."

She thought it was a funny river pun, but they clearly didn't get it. Tough crowd. With a wave, she magicked the water out of her clothes and strolled off toward the inlet, whistling.

It was well hidden, all things considered. It spoke volumes to Serina's knowledge of the river that she found it at all. The inlet ended in a little stream that made its way through a sparse forest, but it was hidden almost entirely by leaves. Unless someone was really squinting, the masts would look like two more trees.

Kianthe followed a small dirt path right to the water's edge. She smirked at the cart left by the shoreline, at Serina hauling a black sail up the mast. Diarn Arlon was going to be furious when he discovered how she'd defaced his property, but for now, Kianthe was just excited to see Reyna.

"Carry me," she instructed grandly, and stepped onto the water. It did the water-equivalent of sighing, but the Stone's magic made an impressive argument and the water reluctantly solidified to ice under her feet. The current wasn't intense enough to wrench it away, so her footsteps left little patches of ice bobbing in the water. Kianthe strolled right to the ship's edge and hauled herself up the rope ladder left there, acting like she was coming to tea instead of intruding on a pirate's vessel.

"I've arrived!" Kianthe tipped onto the deck and swept her hands out. "Please, hold your applause."

From her spot by the crow's nest, Serina snorted. Her eyes roamed behind Kianthe, squinting out toward town. "Are you alone?"

"For now. Your girlfriend was about to fall over, so I put her to bed. Hopefully this time she actually sleeps."

"My girl—" Serina cut herself off, spluttering. "Listen, I don't date constables. Especially not ones who commandeered my farm. Twice."

"Twice?" Kianthe tilted her head.

Serina hopped into the crow's nest, tying knots swifter than Kianthe could follow. "Well, Bobbie didn't exactly commandeer the farm the first time. We were only thirteen. But the second time, whoo, you should have seen how she marched onto my property. As if a friendly face delivering shit news would make it stink less."

"That's a great line. I'll save it for my future novel." Kianthe crossed her arms. "Would you be so kind as to direct me to my fiancée?"

Serina rolled her eyes and pointed at a door on Kianthe's left. It was carved with very pretty northern designs, more geometrical than the nature-based art of the south. Anticipation racing through her veins, Kianthe shoved the door open and proclaimed, "Rain, my dearest, I've come to rescue you from the fearsome pirate!"

High in the crow's nest, Serina said, "Oh, for the Stars' sake."

At the windows, Reyna offered Kianthe a brilliant smile. "That took a bit longer than I expected. Where's your charge? Surely you didn't lead her right to us?"

"No, no. I put the kid to bed, just like you wanted." Kianthe had no idea if Reyna wanted that, but it was fun to pretend. She strolled into the lavish room and swept Reyna into a hug. Then, as an added flourish, she dipped her low, kissing her deeply in the colored light of the stained-glass windows.

Romantic shit, right there.

Reyna snickered when Kianthe righted her. "My, my. Missed me that much?"

"You're far better company than the constable. She's going through some things." Kianthe squinted at the glass behind her. "What are you doing?"

"Replacing glass. But now that you're here, we can get to work." Reyna patted her arm, then stepped to the door and called, "Serina, we're going to take a few moments of privacy. Is that all right?"

High overhead, Serina sounded exasperated. "Trust me, I won't be bothering you."

Reyna smiled and closed the door. At the windows, Kianthe hesitated. "Here? I mean, I guess we can check 'on a ship' off our list—" She slipped out of her heavy cloak.

"Darling, as attractive as you are, Diarn Arlon's old bedroom is absolutely killing the mood." Reyna squeezed her arm and tugged her toward the wall. "However, an elemental mage would be extremely useful in identifying secret compartments."

"I feel used," Kianthe deadpanned.

Reyna pulled her into a passionate kiss, one that made Kianthe lose track of time for a moment—*several* moments, maybe longer—and sent shivers all the way to her toes. When the ex-Queensguard pulled back, she seemed utterly amused. "You know I'll make it up to you. Now, the compartments?"

It took Kianthe a moment to place herself, and then she muttered a complaint and stomped to the wood. The magic within it pulsed under her hands, spiderwebbing away from her. Chopped wood was much less interesting than a planted tree, where the magic of each intertwined deep belowground with a root system so complex it'd boggle normal minds. Here, the magic was dulled, the wood set in a state of dormancy.

She pressed her magic into it, brightening the dull yellow into brilliant gold. Tiny sprouts began edging away from the hull, growing little leaves.

"Is this why you stole this ship? Because you've caused quite a stir amongst the constables," Kianthe said as her magic prodded around the room.

Reyna watched her work with fascination. Magic always impressed her. "Well, it certainly wasn't to live out a pirate fantasy."

Kianthe shot her an unimpressed look.

"Not *only* to live out a pirate fantasy," Reyna corrected, grinning. "But yes. I don't trust Arlon to hand us incriminating documents. It'd be silly to cease our investigation on his promise alone. Someone ordered those dragon eggs stolen, and this ship was commissioned right around the same time period—it stands to reason that he might have hidden records here."

"Assuming he didn't burn them instead."

Reyna sighed. "I'm not saying it'll be easy, but it's a thread worth pulling."

The wood told her that there were two compartments in this room—one on the underside of the rolltop desk, and one carved under the floorboard beneath the lavish rug. Both glowed with magic, and she relayed the location obediently. Reyna quickly stepped to the desk while Kianthe moved to the rug.

It took a few moments of finagling to get access to the floorboards. The rug was nailed down, and her magic only *barely* extended to metal. She could lift nails, but it took a lot more concentration.

Which meant she was distracted when Reyna, feeling along the underbelly of the desk, said, "Key, you don't feel like I left you behind, do you? When I fled with Serina?"

"Well, you warned me, so . . . no?" Kianthe replied distantly. Then the full implication of Reyna's words hit her, and she paused in her efforts, rocking back on her heels. "Why?"

"I just—" Reyna cut herself off, huffed, and tossed her ice-blond hair over her shoulder. Normally, it was pulled in a loose bun; she must have wanted something more casual for the evening. "I think all this travel has reminded me of my old life. Of the adventure behind it. And I don't want you to think that I'm . . . pining, I suppose . . . for something I don't have anymore."

Kianthe *had* noticed that. It was impossible not to—Reyna was built for motion, and even last summer had a difficult time settling into a more mundane lifestyle. The way she inserted herself into dangerous situations, the way she observed Bobbie and Serina, the way she handled Arlon . . .

"Are you unhappy?" Kianthe asked.

Her fiancée smiled, warm and content. "I'm always happy with you. And I love Tawney, and our bookstore, and our friends. But I don't think I realized how much I missed an active lifestyle until this trip."

"Well, duh."

"Pardon?"

Kianthe snorted. "You train with that sword every day, even though you haven't had to use it in a season. Someone content to sell books and make tea wouldn't do that, Rain."

Reyna glanced at her sword, which was propped by the door. She sighed, poking around one of the desk's drawers. "I suppose that's true. I expected I'd find enjoyment in smaller things, but when life is *all* small things, it's easy to get distracted by the bigger mysteries." At that, she pressed a button inside the drawer, and a *click* echoed across the room.

And almost immediately, a flash of magic blinded Kianthe. Alchemy, bright crimson against the sunshine yellow of her own elemental blend. It slammed into Reyna with all the force of a diving griffon, and she crashed to the ground.

Kianthe was at her side in a breath. "Reyna!"

Her fiancée flashed bloody teeth, then swallowed and grimaced at the taste. "Huh. Should have expected there'd be a protective barrier over his things." She wiped her mouth, and pushed upright, her ash-brown eyes dazed.

Blood smeared on her hand.

Kianthe pulled her into an aggressive hug. "Fuck." She buried her face in Reyna's hair, then drew several breaths to slow her trembling. "Okay, new rule. You wait for me before poking around anything on this ship."

"Key." Reyna laughed against her. "I bit my tongue. That's all."

She massaged her jaw, gently extricated herself, and pushed to her feet as if to demonstrate that she was, indeed, fine. And although she wobbled a bit, she stayed upright. Kianthe still ached to touch her, but that felt ridiculous when she was clearly okay, so the mage forced her hands to her side.

Reyna noticed. Of course she did.

"I won't touch anything else on the ship without you around," she said softly. "I admit, I didn't expect him to have such a defense in his own quarters. But considering how they guarded the dragon eggs in Tawney, the spellwork Feo had to disable, perhaps I should have."

Kianthe drew a trembling breath, then reached out with her magic to test the drawer. She wasn't skilled in alchemy, but she knew enough to identify that a spell was indeed still present on this drawer. Whatever was inside would have to wait until she could get a mage skilled in alchemy to disarm it.

And honestly, Feo was the only person she trusted to tackle this.

"It'll keep smacking you back until we counter it." Kianthe squinted into the drawer, noted the circular spellwork burned on the inside. "I can try burning that symbol off, but depending on how the spell originated, we might just make it worse."

"Leave it, then. I won't touch it for now." Reyna rolled her shoulders, wincing.

Relief slid through Kianthe's veins. "Thank you." She kissed Reyna's forehead, then pulled up the remaining nails on the rug and slid it back, revealing a small latch in the floorboards. A quick inspection proved that there wasn't any alchemy spellwork here—just a normal lock, and one eager to please the Arcandor. All she had to do was glance at it, and it popped open under her magical influence.

Reyna peered over her shoulder as she tugged open the compartment to reveal . . .

"Paperwork."

"Shipping records?" Reyna asked optimistically.

Kianthe sifted through it, then shook her head. "The commission paperwork for this ship. He must have a copy at home, and a copy here to prove ownership."

"Hmm. I'll confiscate that, then," Reyna said, plucking the papers from Kianthe's hand and rolling them in a tight spiral. She tucked that into a fold of her trousers, well hidden by the draping cloth of her shirt.

"Is this a big enough mystery for you?" Kianthe asked before she could help herself.

Reyna paused, studying her. Whatever she saw must not have been comforting, because she tilted her head. "Key, you're my priority. We're obligated to find the dragon eggs, but if investigating this way is going to cause you stress, I'll stop. I don't need to play pirate—we can leave Serina and Bobbie to their lives and ransack Arlon's estate ourselves." She tugged the roll of parchment from her trousers and offered it to the mage. "Just say the word."

Kianthe didn't want that. Reyna had stolen this ship for a reason, and it seemed bigger than investigating Arlon's secrets. The mage scrubbed her face. "No, it's okay. I just . . . didn't expect alchemy here. Those spells can be dangerous."

I don't want you hurt.

Reyna kicked the rug back over the floor compartment, repocketed the scroll of paperwork, then wound her arms around Kianthe's waist. "I'll be careful. I promise. And if my calculations are right, we won't be separated for long." She paused, glancing at the windows and the dark night sky. "Speaking of, how long can you stay here?"

It was a welcome change in the conversation. Kianthe held her close, their bodies pressed together as she mused, "Before Bobbie, the woman who hasn't slept in at least two nights, wakes up? Probably all morning and a bit of the afternoon."

"No, Key." Reyna smirked. "How long before Bobbie, the overly stressed constable who will hunt a pirate to the edge of the Realm, who goes multiple nights without sleep to follow a lead, realizes you're gone?"

Kianthe winced. "Ah. Quite possibly until the sun comes up."

"That's a bit more appropriate. All we'd need is her finding Serina now, when we've just gotten started."

"I'll keep her away from you both." Kianthe was having a hard time mustering up the enthusiasm to leave. Reyna was a warm certainty in her arms, and all she wanted was to curl up in that nice bed together and sleep until midday. "Is Serina going to need a crew for this ship? It seems big for just you two."

Reyna brightened. "We found the greatest bartender. His name is Judd, and he's getting Serina a crew. His wine is exquisite, Key. You truly can't even fathom."

"Considering I've never had a drop of alcohol, that is accurate." Kianthe smirked. "But wine is a big export for this region. I'm sure Arlon makes a fair bit of coin off this town alone."

A dark shadow crossed over Reyna's face. She pulled away, tucked the papers in her trousers once again, and crossed her arms. "Actually, I wanted to ask about that. Did Bobbie say anything to you about how Arlon manages his lands?"

"Nothing I remember." The mage frowned, foreboding prickling along her spine. "Why?"

"Serina tells me that Diarn Arlon *owns* all the land . . . and the tools the farmers use, and the buildings, and the ships, and the crops. The farmers are given salaries, and it's not enough." Reyna's expression was troubled. "People are starving here, but it's not because of Serina."

Kianthe tensed. "I've never heard of that." She wasn't denying it was true—Reyna was rarely wrong. It just took her by surprise. "Sheparan law is that diarns manage the land, but it's owned by the citizens lucky enough to inherit, or rich enough to buy some for themselves. Feo certainly has no claim to our bookstore, after all."

"Lord Wylan does, if you examine Queendom law." Reyna wrinkled her nose. "But he gifted us the land and building, which was unconventional. Regardless, Diarn Arlon's practice seems far closer to Queen Tilaine's rule than the council's."

That sat before them like a sour apple, rotting from the inside.

"Can we do anything about that?" Reyna asked.

"Possibly an intervention, either with the council, or—if things get nasty—the Magicary. But we'd have to prove it with a paper trail. And Arlon isn't just going to hand that over." At that, they both stared at the rolltop desk, at the alchemy spell keeping its contents a secret. Kianthe swallowed a groan. "All I wanted was a vacation."

"We'll get one, love. Just not now." But that excited gleam had overtaken Reyna's eyes again. "One way or another, we need to solve this pirate problem—and rather than hauling in the one person bold enough to stand up to Arlon, I think we should be creative here."

Kianthe sighed. "You always do." And with a final kiss, they parted ways.

Kianthe took the long way back to town, just in case Bobbie was awake and watching the direction she entered. The leisurely stroll through the hillside vineyards was a pleasant way to clear her head—and it meant she was out in the open to see two shapes flying her way. Griffon shapes.

"Visk," Kianthe called, waving her arms.

The griffon screeched hello, landing in the field nearby. Ponder flapped busily alongside him, her mischievous eyes already scanning the vines for something to eat or play with. Kianthe snatched her before she could take off again, snuggling her close, kissing her tiny, feathery head.

"By the Stone, I forgot how cute you are!"

Ponder chittered displeasure, nipping Kianthe and flexing her claws. She could easily break skin, but she'd learned at a far younger age that it hurt the humans—and as much as she threw fits, Ponder never wanted to hurt them. Her beak left light scratches on Kianthe's arm, but it was more for show than anything.

"Oh, sorry." Kianthe laughed, letting Ponder go. "I didn't mean cute. I meant fierce. A vicious beast."

Ponder chirped agreement, puffed up her chest, lion tail swishing.

Standing over her, Visk leveled a look at Kianthe that clearly said, *Uh-huh. Keep telling her that.*

Kianthe scratched under his chin. "Hey, buddy. It could be worse. You could be supervising three of them, like your mate is right now."

Visk shook his entire body, as if to rid himself of the thought.

Kianthe cackled, patting his neck. "I'm glad you found me. We still can't have you lurking around—if Bobbie thinks I can fly again, she'll send me 'searching,' and Reyna isn't ready to be discovered just yet." At Visk's questioning purr, she shrugged. "She's living out her pirate fantasy. It's a lot less kinky than I expected."

Visk stared at her impassively.

"Anyway." Kianthe stroked his beak, giving him a bit of attention as Ponder explored the nearby vineyard. "I need you to do something. Can you fly back to Tawney and get Feo? We may have a situation here, and I'm going to need their help handling it."

Visk didn't love the idea. Eagle expressions weren't very identifiable, but Kianthe could tell in the way he lowered his head, how his talons dug into the dirt. She slid a note she'd hastily scribbled into a leather pouch strapped over the feathers near his neck, then scritched under his chin.

"I know, bud. But it shouldn't take long. You always know how to find me, so just point out that note and get Feo here. You can visit your other kiddos in the meantime."

The griffon reluctantly spread his wings. Even Visk couldn't deny the attraction of visiting his mate again. He and Kianthe would have an entire lifetime together, but his mate had no interest in leaving the imposing mountains that flanked Tawney—which meant he visited *her,* not the other way around.

Ponder had found the grapes and plucked one into her beak. It sliced open, spilling juice, and she squawked and dropped it like it burned her.

Her father sighed with his whole body, then turned a questioning gaze to Kianthe.

"Take her with you. I bet she's missing her siblings." The mage grimaced, thinking of how Reyna had slammed against the floor, the blood that smeared the back of her hand. "That ship isn't exactly safe right now."

Visk chirped, regaining Ponder's attention. They conversed in their griffon language for a few breaths, and then Ponder spread her tiny wings and launched into Kianthe's arms. She nuzzled Kianthe's chest, nipped at her ears.

Kianthe laughed, feeling better already. "Mamakie will see you soon, Pondie, okay? Be good."

The baby griffon promised to do no such thing, if the snide look on her face was any indication. She nibbled Kianthe's hair fondly, then fluttered into the skies. Visk bumped his head against Kianthe's chest and took off after her.

Retrieving Feo was a start, at least. With a heavy sigh, Kianthe trudged back toward Koll.

14

Reyna

As promised, Judd delivered.

And he did more than that. He *delivered.* They spent a day selling the vases and fetched a sum that would keep Serina afloat—another pun . . . Gods, what did Kianthe *do* to her?—at least through the fall season. (That day at the market involved a period of them dodging Bobbie and Kianthe through crowded stalls, which was both exhilarating and hilarious.) The next day, they returned to Judd's bar, and spirits were high as he presented a fantastic company of people.

There were two women; two men; a girl just exiting her youth; and her sibling, a teenager with a pin inscribed with "they/them" pronouns. Reyna looked at that for a bit longer than usual; she'd seen various pins that indicated it was polite to ask, usually bronze but not always, but one with pronouns explicitly written was new.

Judd gestured at the crowd, swelling in pride while Serina shook everyone's hand. "You asked for a crew, and you won't find any better. Allow me to introduce Pil, Rankor, Farley, Squirrel, Darlene, and Joe."

"Squirrel?" Reyna repeated, just in case she'd misheard.

The middle woman, who was shorter than Matild and had a similarly cheery smile, waggled a few fingers. "It's on account of the stealing. Squirreling things away." A pause. "I thought it was clever."

Serina grinned. "I like you already."

Judd walked down the line, pointing at each in turn. "Pil's your boatswain. He's been sailing longer than you two have been alive. Darlene and Joe are his kids."

"They won't hold you back," Pil said, crossing bulky arms. "They've *also* been sailing longer than you."

That was impressive, since Darlene seemed barely older than a teenager, and Joe was still in their gangly phase. Reyna's brow pinched together as she leaned close to whisper in Serina's ear: "Are we really okay taking a child with us?"

"Hmm. Joe. You know what to do if we're attacked?"

"Get belowdecks and hide," they intoned, sounding bored.

Serina shrugged. "Sounds good to me."

Pil pulled his shoulders back, clearly pleased. "No strangers to pirate work here. I got my sailing start on Dreggs's flagship."

"*Dreggs's* flagship?" Serina exclaimed, then clamped a hand over her mouth. Everyone watched in amusement as she laughed nervously. "Sorry. I'm a fan. Are they wonderful in real life? Or did the legends blow them out of proportion?"

Pil smirked. "Let's just say they got that reputation for a reason. If you're half the pirate they are, we'll get along fine."

Darlene tilted her head, gesturing at Reyna's sword. "I want to learn to fight for real. Pa said we're good, but I'm not sure I'd hold up." Her brows knitted together. "You know how to use that sword?"

"'Course she does." Joe elbowed their sister. "You heard her accent."

Reyna couldn't even tell them that the Queendom wasn't filled with vicious swordsmen, because she was indeed a professional in that regard. She heaved a sigh. "I can teach you. Always good to know self-defense."

"Then you're the ship's security?" Squirrel asked.

Reyna tilted her head. The motion smarted—she was still a bit sore after that slap of alchemy. "Something like that."

Judd smoothly inserted himself, gesturing at the remaining three. "Squirrel is your cook; I know you didn't ask for one, but trust me, you'll be glad to have her. Last but not least, we have Rankor and Farley. Rankor's the navigator, and Farley's a carpenter. They're married and work together as contractors." Judd smirked. "Farley's the flame, but Rank's the kindling."

"Please don't light my new ship on fire," Serina said good-naturedly.

"Don't give me a reason to," Farley replied, crossing her arms. She was a burly woman with muscles Reyna envied and a no-nonsense expression she could respect.

Her husband shrugged. "I just go where I'm told. Usually take the whole ship with me." He paused. "That was a navigator joke."

"Pray you never meet my fiancée," Reyna said.

Judd stepped back, clapping his hands together. "All right. My part's done. You make sure my cousin gets another shipment, and I'll be much obliged. In the meantime, I'll keep talk of you positive around here. Word is starting to spread that you're helping towns all along the Nacean."

Serina smiled. "Well, I wouldn't want to disappoint. It's a pleasure to meet you all. Let's go steal some food."

"My favorite." Squirrel rubbed her hands together.

Things moved fast after that. The crew settled into the ship and moved more efficiently than Reyna thought possible. Pil and his kids crawled around the lines like monkeys, unfurling sails, testing Serina's sewing job, shouting to Rankor as he settled into the helm.

Squirrel disappeared belowdecks, locating a galley Reyna hadn't seen during their original tour—it was down a second, narrow staircase hidden behind several crates. The diarn's ship must have been well stocked, because she made a mouth-watering lunch without any supply runs. Meanwhile, Farley strolled around the ship inspecting the handiwork, already tugging out tools to adjust things.

Serina stood at the center of it all, swelling with pride.

In fact, she seemed to be crying.

Reyna stopped short on her way to finish painting the ship's new name, her brush perched on the bucket of paint. "Everything okay?"

"More than okay." Serina drew a shaking breath, turning her gaze skyward. "I just—I've been at this alone for so long. Even back when I was a farmer. I tried to hire some help to till the fields, but . . . well. My family isn't good at farming, and word got around." She scrubbed her eyes with her palm. "This is all I've ever wanted."

It made Reyna think of Tawney, of the community that supported their shop, their lives, their passions and dreams. Truly, that was all anyone could ever hope for—friends who'd follow them through life.

"I'm glad you found it, Captain Serina," Reyna said, and meant it from the depths of her soul.

Serina pulled her into an awkward hug, then found a reason to get busy on the other side of the ship.

Smiling, Reyna strolled to the rope swing she'd secured over the hull of the vessel. With a flourish of bold black lettering, she wiped clean Diarn Arlon's old name and penned the new one Serina had chosen.

KNOT FOR SAIL

It was ridiculous. Kianthe would love it. Reyna chuckled, hauled herself off the rope seat, then stowed the small bucket of paint belowdecks. Shortly after, she helped Pil and his kids weigh the anchor—it was remarkably heavy, and the big reason why, once Serina docked here, they hadn't been able to leave. But now they had a real crew.

Darlene unfurled the final sail, Rankor took control of the helm, and they were off. Reyna expected they'd keep sailing downriver, but they didn't. Instead, on Serina's command, they angled north, heading back up toward Neolow.

Reyna approached the captain as the vineyards faded away behind them. The river air was cold and clean, and the sun kept everyone warm. Reyna was silent for a few moments before saying, "You're really going to flaunt Arlon's ship right in front of his estate?"

"We have to head north; I promised shipments to Oslop and Lathe," Serina replied. "There's plenty of divisions on the river, especially near where he lives. If he hears I'm sailing by, he might send constables out to chase us." She rolled her eyes at the thought. "This ship is fast, but I'd rather not get my new crew arrested."

"We'd all prefer that," Rankor said amicably from his perch at the helm.

Reyna snorted. "Okay, next question. What are we delivering? Because I distinctly remember Kianthe telling me your entire shipment went over that waterfall."

Their captain waved a hand. "A minor setback. We're reaching the end of harvest season, but there should still be some spring wheat on this river." She grinned, plucking a tricorne hat off a wooden peg near the staircase to the lower deck. Where she found that, Reyna had no idea, but she was clearly leaning into the whole "pirate captain" thing. Serina fit it over her long, wavy hair and pointed north. "Pirates pillage, after all. Let's show these folks what the fearsome crew of the *Knot for Sail* can do!"

A cheer erupted from the lower decks and their merry pirate crew was off.

It didn't take long to wind their way upriver. A few of the larger glacier lakes near Neolow were visible off the ship's left side, and they found their prey perched at the base of a hiking trail to the largest lake: a ship seemingly abandoned, its deck stacked with crates.

"That's it. Rankor, keep sailing north. Pil, hold on the black sail for now—we don't want to earn attention just yet." Serina scurried up the rope ladder to the crow's nest, borrowed the spyglass from Joe, and squinted through it as they cruised past.

Reyna climbed up beside her, relishing the thrill of seeing the deck grow small beneath them and the sudden strength of the wind that whipped her hair. There was nothing quite so freeing as watching the world from this height. It wasn't as amazing as traveling by griffon, but it had her blood pumping all the same. She took the spyglass Serina offered, peering through it.

"It looks empty." The ship had Diarn Arlon's insignia flying high on the mast and was a bit bigger than the *Knot for Sail*. Despite that size, the deck was laden with wooden crates and bales of hay, and Reyna only counted three constables milling on its deck.

"That ship came from Jallin, I think. See the hay? It's too cold for a final cutting this far north, so it must have been harvested in the south." Serina pointed, and Reyna scanned the winding dirt path that led up the forested mountain. "The biggest lake in Shepara is up that path. It's a huge tourist attraction. I bet they're southerners who stopped for a gander."

Reyna collapsed the spyglass, feeling very much like a swashbuckling pirate—perched in a crow's nest, anticipating their next theft. Maybe she did scheme after all. Excitement tinged her voice: "Which means most of the crew is gone."

"Ghost ship." Serina winked. "My favorite target."

She called a quick meeting, but they didn't have time to waste here. There was no telling how long the ship's crew would be gone, which meant their attack would need to be swift. Everyone huddled near the helm so Rankor could keep them nearby without being suspicious.

"It's best if we loop around and pull up alongside them. Pil will drop the black sail while Reyna and I board. We'll take care of the constables, and once the deck is clear, Squirrel and Darlene will drop the plank and everyone will help us steal the crates." Now Serina held up a hand, holding each of their gazes. "We take thirty percent of what's onboard. Nothing more. As much as I hate Arlon's business practice, we're not here to clear his entire back stock. He feeds a lot of people east of here, and we can't disrupt that."

Everyone nodded, and they separated quickly. Pil was a master of the sails, and with his sharp instruction, his family was able to catch a fierce wind and haul their ship fast—ridiculously fast—over to their target. Rankor positioned the ship so they'd pull alongside facing the opposite direction. Better for a quick getaway.

By now, they'd gained the constables' attention. "You ready?" Serina removed her tricorne hat, offering a wry smile.

"Always." Reyna perched at the upper deck and waved at the constables, holding up a big vellum map like they were lost.

The constables gripped their weapons, on guard, but once they were close, Serina shouted, "Hello, fine folk! Could you direct us to the town called Oslop? Our navigator thought it was here, but clearly we missed something . . ."

One of the constables shouted, "Don't come closer. We'll come to you."

"Now, Pil!" Serina called, and their black sail unfurled. The constables' eyes widened, but it was too late to respond—their ship was close enough, and Reyna traded the vellum piece for a sturdy line and took a running leap.

For a breathless moment, she was suspended over the water, and then her boots found purchase on the enemy's deck. A *thud* behind her proved Serina had followed suit.

Reyna unsheathed her sword, sprinting toward the first constable before he could react. A quick slash across the chest stunned him—the wound wouldn't kill, but pain had a way of shocking an enemy into stillness—and her foot connected with his kneecap. He crashed hard to the deck, and a swift kick to the head ensured he wasn't getting back up.

Reyna spun to the second constable, who lashed at her with the same thick, curved sword Bobbie used. It was slower than hers, but dangerous, like facing a machete in the Leonolan jungle. She parried, twisted out of the way, and used his clumsy weight to her advantage. When he stepped forward, taking the offense, she ducked under his arm and smashed the pommel of her sword against his skull.

He dropped like a rock, nearly on top of her other opponent.

Across the ship, Serina yelped.

Reyna spun just in time to see the third constable crashing down the narrow wooden staircase. He groaned, slumped against the rough wood, and didn't get back up.

Perched on the upper deck, Serina gripped her left arm and spat at him. "Good riddance," she snapped, and checked her wound. It was bleeding freely, deep red slowly staining her white tunic, but she didn't seem perturbed.

"Clear," she told her crew, and a second later, the wooden plank thumped between the ships. She observed it, one eyebrow raised. "This is a lot easier on a nice, tall ship. Should have seen me wrestling with crates on my old one."

Reyna sheathed her sword and knelt beside Serina's foe, swiftly tying his hands with rope and tugging a gag across his mouth. If the rest of his crew got wind of this takeover, they'd be in for a much bigger fight. They needed to load the crates quickly and be gone before anyone realized what had happened.

"I can help," Serina said, appearing at Reyna's elbow.

"I've got it. You should bind that." Reyna tied off the second and third constable just as fast, then turned to Serina. Blood was *tip-tip*ping off her fingers now, and she looked a bit woozy. A flash of concern, masked as irritation, wound through Reyna's chest. Been a while since she'd battled alongside a rookie. "I thought you knew how to fight?"

It was the wrong thing to say. Serina stiffened. "I'm plenty capable."

Reyna raised her hands. "I'm not doubting your ability. But combat isn't like pirating. This isn't a 'fake it 'til you make it' type deal." She nudged the sword dropped by Serina's target. "These are *real* weapons, and they cause real damage. I'm not here to help you get killed, Captain."

The title seemed to snap Serina out of her anger. She glanced back at their crew, noting the way Joe's jaw dropped when they saw her crimson shirt, the way Squirrel's brow knitted together. Already, Farley was tugging a roll of cloth bandages out of the captain's quarters, even as the rest of their crew continued to tow the crates over the wooden plank.

"I . . . always snuck around before," Serina admitted quietly. Her face was paling quickly, and Reyna stepped up to apply firm pressure to the wound. She hissed in pain, recoiled, but Reyna just pressed harder. It took Serina a moment to finish her thought: "My ship was small. I attacked at night, knocked people out or pushed them overboard, then grabbed what I could."

"Well, this brigantine is too big to sneak." Reyna's voice wasn't forceful or condescending. She was merely stating a fact, and it was vital their new captain understood. "If you can't handle this kind of approach, we'll need to downgrade the ship and dismiss your crew."

Serina clenched her eyes shut, wobbling a bit. "I—I can't give up now. We finally have the manpower to make a real statement here. My father's ship is gone. That loss needs to *mean* something."

Reyna nodded, guiding her back over the plank. "Then get patched up, and prepare for more of this. We'll start combat lessons tomorrow."

The pirate nodded glumly and took a seat beside an unimpressed Farley.

"You're lucky I have a bit of medical experience," their carpenter drawled. "Try not to get stabbed next time."

"I didn't get stabbed—" Serina said indignantly.

Reyna left them to it, wiped Serina's blood off her hands, and got to work helping with the crates. One of the constables woke up while they were moving the last of their haul, and he started screaming against the gag. She paused briefly to approach him, looking every bit the vengeful Queensguard she used to be.

"If you don't stay quiet, this theft will be the least of your worries," Reyna said darkly.

The theatrics worked. His eyes widened and he stopped thrashing, fear painting his face. It was oddly satisfying, knowing she hadn't lost that ability of her old profession. Reyna allowed a private smile as she turned away.

And then the task was done and they were gone, flaring the sails to catch a gust of wind, vanishing upriver while the anchored ship sat robbed and silent. The pirate crew was quiet until they'd gained enough distance, heading north toward Neolow, and then Darlene whooped.

"We did it!"

Squirrel pried open one of the crates, grinning at its contents.

"Quality wheat, here. Maybe the last of the season." She glanced at Serina. "What's your plan when the harvest is over? Is that when we start stealing gold?"

Serina's injured arm was tightly bound, and she pushed herself upright, standing tall. Her skin was still several shades paler than normal, but she spoke with confidence. "On this ship, we don't steal gold. We steal *food*. And once we've dropped this shipment off at Lathe, we'll shift our sights from grains to leafy greens." She paused, holding their gazes. "I recognize that's not glamorous, and I know that today got a bit more dangerous than we intended. If any of you want to disembark or return to Koll, now's the time to let me know."

Reyna quirked an eyebrow.

The rest of the crew stayed silent.

Serina clapped her hands together. "Then we sail north, drop off this haul, and find the next. Savvy?"

"Aye!" they shouted back, and got to work.

15

Kianthe

Bobbie must consider herself the unluckiest person alive, Kianthe thought, to keep missing Serina as she did. It was true misfortune.

Misfortune, and most certainly *not* Kianthe's meddling influence.

The constable spent two days canvassing the docks, locating private piers, smashing into bars and disrupting parties while hunting for information on Serina's stolen ship. Every single avenue turned into a dead end. No one had seen the ship—*Because it never docked here,* Kianthe thought in exasperation—and no one knew the pirate's true identity. Eventually, Bobbie started using her real name, asking for anyone named Serina, and even that didn't help.

The one lead that might have turned into something happened by complete accident, while Bobbie was interrogating a server out on a winery's terrace. It overlooked the harbor and had a very lovely view, one the constable was convinced would have highlighted Serina's stolen ship.

And so, Bobbie was currently trying to bribe the server with a set of poorly crocheted gloves to reveal information the woman *clearly* didn't have.

Kianthe, meanwhile, was more distracted exploring the wines. Bottle upon bottle of it, in all flavors. Reyna would be in heaven.

"I'll get two of these," she said, taking a wild guess. As someone who abstained from alcohol for the good of everyone involved, Kianthe had no idea which wine was best. "Wait, they're not too sweet, are they? She has a very narrow tolerance for sweet."

"Nah, this is my bestseller," the bartender remarked lightly. "Even the Queendom folk love it. One of them was just here last night, and she bought six bottles." He laughed robustly, smoothing his embroidered apron.

Kianthe grinned, checking to see that Bobbie was still outside. The server she was questioning looked confused, turning the purple gloves over in her hands. As if it might help, Bobbie produced a matching scarf to go with them, which made the woman's eyes brighten.

Confident she wouldn't be overheard, Kianthe drawled, "A Queendom woman, you say. Blond hair, light brown eyes? As gorgeous as the rising sun over the Nacean River?"

The bartender leaned across the table, lips quirking upward. "Lemme guess. You're the fiancée. She had plenty to say about you. Even tried to convince me you're the Mage of Ages."

"Well. I don't like to brag." Kianthe tossed her shoulder-length hair.

"She said you love to brag. Also said you could fix my squeaky floorboards just by persuading the wood to be quiet." Now the bartender raised an eyebrow in challenge.

Kianthe slumped over the bar. "Leave it to Reyna to give me chores even when she's not around." With a magical touch, she found the floorboards in question—wood that used to sing every time the wind whistled through its branches, and now was very annoyed that it didn't have the privilege anymore—and reasoned with it until it agreed that it could squeak all it wanted when customers weren't present.

All of this happened without the bartender realizing it, but she stepped over to demonstrate the magic, and he whistled. "I'll be damned. Glad I comped her a few extra drinks last night." Now he looked at the terrace. "That your constable friend? Serrie's lover?"

"Lover?" Kianthe tapped her chin. "Don't tell Bobbie that—she thinks they hate each other. Do you know if Serina already left? I'm supposed to keep us close, but not *that* close, and it's moderately exhausting."

The bartender was silent for a long moment, then sighed. "Between you and me, I helped her get a crew together. They left pretty quick. I bet they're halfway up the Nacean by now."

"Great," Kianthe muttered, and pushed away from the table. "Hey, do you have a supply line to Tawney, out east?"

He shrugged. "Can't say I do. You need one?"

"My fiancée would love nothing more than regular shipments of your wine."

Now the bartender grinned. "Shipping wine to the Arcandor. I'll get something established, but only if I can slap that on my storefront."

"'I'm Arcandor Kianthe, and this is my favorite winery on the Nacean,'" Kianthe drawled sarcastically. "You know mages don't drink, right?"

"I do. Some don't." The bartender winked.

Kianthe snorted and left, tugging a defeated Bobbie away from the very pleased server. "Hate to tell you this, Constable, but they've already sailed north. Bartender just told me he heard that she'd gathered a crew. I doubt Serina would stick around now that she has the bodies to sail that ship."

"What?" Bobbie spun toward the river. It was, of course, empty. She groaned, digging her hands into her corkscrew coils. "I can't believe this. A crew? What kind of person chooses to sail with a pirate?"

"Hey. My fiancée resembles that remark."

The constable leveled an exasperated stare her way. "Right. Thanks for that." She swept past Kianthe, trudging out of the tavern. Kianthe waved at the bartender and followed, catching up with her down the street. "I have to get my horse—"

"Oh, for the Stone of Seeing's almighty sake." Kianthe grabbed her arm, spinning her back around. "You are running that poor horse to death, and you will *never* catch up to her. Come on, Bobbie, how long have you been following her trail? She's one step ahead of you, and without similar transportation, you're going to keep missing her."

Bobbie looked close to tears. She'd slept for a decent amount of time, but she was still up far earlier than Kianthe would have been, and the nights at the inn clearly hadn't been relaxing—if her new supply of crocheted projects were any indication.

This entire search was wringing Bobbie raw, and it showed.

"Then . . . we need a boat. You're a mage. You can guide it upriver."

Kianthe's expression hardened. "I'm not sailing after Serina until we talk. Reyna is keeping Serina out of your grasp because you're insistent on destroying the life of your oldest friend."

"She's a *criminal*."

"That's negotiable. And she's also your friend," Kianthe snapped. "If you hand her to Arlon, you are guaranteeing her a lifetime trapped in a cell—and that's if she's fortunate. Is turning her in really the only way to solve this problem? Why not help her disappear instead? Reyna told me you wanted to make positive change from inside Arlon's organization; this is a damn good place to start."

Bobbie withdrew at the reminder. Her voice was thick. "She won't disappear. She has something to prove now."

"Right. And you can't relate to that at all."

The constable dug her hands in her hair, spun on her heel, then spun back.

"I can't—risk this job. When I wear this uniform, it's a reminder that *I* get to choose how to deliver bad news. No little girls will be crying because of me." Bobbie clenched her eyes shut. "You saw the constables flanking Diarn Arlon at his ball. They're his closest advisors. If I got that position, I could make real, positive change."

Kianthe crossed her arms. "Bobbie, I've heard enough policy talk to know that rulers will always act in their own best interests. You're fooling yourself if you think otherwise. If that's your goal, Serina's approach isn't the worst; Arlon will respond if she strong-arms him into a deal."

"I don't agree with that method." Bobbie hung her head. "But . . . you might be right about her punishment. Diarn Arlon would have settled for a fine at the beginning of the season, but now—"

"Now, he's out for blood. You're riding up and down this river trying to keep her safe, but your presence is causing her to get reckless. Worse, if you can track her, Arlon can track you. Did you think of that?"

Maybe it was all the time spent with Reyna, all that time fearing the queen's spies, but Kianthe was under no illusions that Arlon wouldn't assign constables to watch Bobbie. Now the idea seemed to sit like a hot coal in the constable's stomach, because she physically hunched over.

"He's not following me." But she didn't sound so certain.

"Bobbie, you're working yourself to the bone without understanding why." Kianthe pinched the bridge of her nose. "Sometimes you have to step back from your job and ask yourself what's right. The person paying your coin isn't always the good guy."

It felt like a repeat conversation, something she'd discussed with Reyna over and over, something she thought might break them up until *That Night*—the fateful moment Reyna fled everything to pursue the life she wanted, not what was determined for her. It had led to so many glorious things.

Kianthe suddenly understood why Reyna insisted she follow the constable. How the Arcandor's very presence and life experience could make people in this situation question everything.

But Bobbie wasn't convinced. "I . . . I don't know about that. But I'm a constable. I can't leave Diarn Arlon's service."

"Why not? There are plenty of people who would employ you." Serina, for one. She'd be gleeful to steal one of Arlon's guards. "Tell me what happens if you don't find Serina for him."

"Then I've failed—"

"Failed at what? Your job?"

"Failed at *life,* okay?" Bobbie snapped. Tears shone in her eyes, and she spun away when she realized it. "You think it was easy, being raised by the beloved sheriff of Lathe? My mother earned that job when she was younger than me. I wanted to do something equally impressive, so I tried to follow in her footsteps—and I still wasn't good enough. Then I trained to be one of Arlon's constables, and our neighbors threw a party to celebrate, and *finally* I was someone important."

Kianthe scoffed. "Your job doesn't make you important."

Bobbie jerked like she'd been burned. She opened her mouth to protest, but now the air crackled with heat, and Kianthe raised a hand to silence her.

"No, hang on. You're worth more than your work ethic. The only person who can decide if you're failing is *you,* Bobbie." Kianthe rolled her eyes. "Do you think anyone thought I was impressive before the Stone blessed me with its magic? I was just another kid training to be a mage. I could boil water at best."

"I'm sure you could do more than that," Bobbie muttered.

Kianthe laughed, and laughed again at the assumption. "I was *last* in every class. They tried to push me toward alchemy. 'A supplement for natural talent,' they told me, as if that didn't drive a stake in my soul. I left my family to make them proud, and I failed every time I tried."

Bobbie stayed silent.

Kianthe drew a breath, and the air around them cooled. "*I* had to decide my worth. And the minute I got the chance, I left the Magicary behind. Fuck those guys." She sighed, massaging her forehead. "Your opinion of yourself is the only one that matters. Your mom will love you either way. Your job doesn't denote how successful you are, and you won't suddenly become worthless if you quit."

"I'm not even sure what else I'd do." Bobbie looked lost.

"That's half the adventure, isn't it?"

For a long moment, the only sound was the footsteps of passersby, the occasional shout from the docks. In the distance, someone struck up a smooth violin, likely to accompany one of the fancier taverns.

Kianthe smiled.

And after a moment, Bobbie sighed. "Let's say I'm considering this. What's our next step?"

"You were right; we need a boat. Because I'm not hurting Reyna's precious horse thundering up the riverbank again." Kianthe held Bobbie's gaze. "We'll leave them stabled here for a bit, and catch up with Serina. We'll *talk*. No arresting anyone. No fighting. And at the end of it, you can decide what you'd like to do. Fair?"

Long moments slipped past.

Bobbie massaged the back of her neck. "Fine."

Well, it wasn't a *no*. And at this point, Kianthe would take anything.

"Okay, follow me." Kianthe led her out of the street, down several flights of stairs to the lantern-lit docks. They chatted about lighthearted things, leaving the heaviness of that conversation behind.

But Bobbie was thinking hard about it, Kianthe could tell. Which was probably good, because they'd only barely approached two constables at the dock when things went sideways.

Again.

"You said you're Bobbie?" the shorter constable huffed. "We got a notice about you this morning."

Bobbie stiffened.

"What kind of notice?" Kianthe crossed her arms, challenging them.

They barely paid her mind. The taller one plucked a thick sheet of parchment out of her pocket, unfurling it with a flourish. She read, monotone: "'By order of Diarn Arlon, in punishment for allowing the capture and use of the diarn's private ship, the *Prestige*, Barylea of Lathe's position as constable of the Nacean River has been revoked. This termination is effective immediately. Employment and privileges will cease. Bobbie of Lathe's badge and sword must be returned. If any struggle ensues, constables enforcing this order may use deadly force.'"

"By the Stone of Seeing and every Star in the sky," Kianthe snapped. "*Deadly* force? Is that necessary?"

The constable curled the paper back into a strict roll and tucked it away. "Well, that depends on her, doesn't it?"

The shorter constable held out his hand. "Nothing personal,

Bobbie. My grandmother still loves the scarf you made her, but . . . well. It's business."

Bobbie stood still, jaw clenched tight. Her entire body was trembling—with anguish or pent-up rage, it was hard to say—but she unclipped the silver badge from her chest, mutely handing it over.

"Bobbie," Kianthe said, feeling helpless. "You can't—"

"You're the one who told me I could do anything," Bobbie said, sounding lifeless. If a corpse could talk, that would be its tone. She moved stoically, untying her sword's leather strap with stiff fingers. "Apparently, I'm getting my chance earlier than expected."

"I didn't mean *now*. Stone damn it all." Kianthe stepped in between them before Bobbie could offer her sword. "No. Don't you dare. You can't have her sword."

The taller constable scowled. "We have to collect—"

"You don't have to do shit," the mage growled, and bright flame ignited from her hands. The constables looked shocked, stepping back, which pleased Kianthe immensely. Her expression was scathing. "This woman served alongside you. She crocheted your grandma a scarf. Doesn't that mean something?"

"Enough," Bobbie said, her voice trembling. She carefully stepped around Kianthe's flaming hands, offering her sword to the constables. "I accept my termination. Please tell Diarn Arlon that I'm—"

"Don't say it," Kianthe interrupted.

"I'm sorry." Bobbie glanced at her, then looked away as quickly. Without a word, she turned and walked toward the edge of the deck.

The constable holding Bobbie's things swallowed. "Mind putting those out?"

"Don't test me." Kianthe shook the flames off her hands, then stepped threateningly into the constables' space. "Since you're so good at following orders, let me issue one. I am the Arcandor, the Mage of Ages. By Magicary agreement with the Sheparan council, of which Diarn Arlon is a member, mages are allowed to temporarily claim Sheparan property for official Magicary business. Consider this my notice: we're taking your Stone-damned boat."

The craft bobbed behind the two of them, clearly intended as a river patrol for a pair of constables. It had a single mast and sail, but it would do for their purposes.

The taller constable opened her mouth to protest, but the shorter one elbowed her. He looked sheepish. "I am familiar with that law, Arcandor. We apologize for the . . . ah, unpleasantness." He stepped aside, allowing access to the boat.

"Yeah, well. She didn't have to enjoy it so much," Kianthe said scornfully. "Bobbie. Come on." And she stomped past the two of them.

There was a moment where Kianthe really didn't think she'd follow. A moment where the former constable just stood, expressionless, and then glanced over her shoulder at the town. As if she might just spend the night drinking her sorrow away.

Kianthe couldn't even blame her.

But duty won out again—an unspoken debt to Kianthe for defending her, or maybe the never-ending desire to find Serina—and Bobbie glumly followed the mage onto the boat and took a seat. Good. Kianthe waited to see if the other constables would say anything else, but they kept their mouths shut.

With little else to do, Kianthe magicked the water to push their boat out of the docks.

16

Reyna

The rest of the night, the crew of the *Knot for Sail* were riding high. Rankor was a skilled navigator who knew *exactly* how to use a sea anchor to catch an upriver current—a talent that surely would have netted him more than the paltry income Serina could afford, if he'd advertised it anywhere else. The fog had settled over the river again, thick enough that Farley kept watch over the railing and shouted instructions to her husband.

But it was Serina who directed them into a much smaller portion of the river, something thin enough to be reminiscent of the rivers near Wellia and in the Queendom, instead of the grand Nacean.

"This section is nearly impossible to find unless you're looking," Serina said as they cruised underneath towering pine trees. Only a couple sails were unfurled now, to take advantage of the mild wind, but they were slowly towed by the anchor's underwater current. "It meets back up just a little ways upstream, but it should be a safe place to anchor for the night."

The moon was starting to wane, which meant their shining silver light was dimming with every passing day. In turn, the Stars the Sheparans revered were glowing brighter and brighter. Serina lit a few lanterns on deck, and they dragged the wooden table out from the captain's quarters for their first meal as a crew.

Squirrel slipped between them like—well, a squirrel. She'd softened some dried meats in boiling water and spiced them to perfection, then cooked up carrots as a side dish. Reyna produced three bottles of her precious Koll wine, and the adults helped themselves.

Soon, they were laughing and chatting like they'd known each other all their lives. Darlene was fascinated with Reyna, leaning over herself to hear stories of her escapades.

"The queen? Queen *Tilaine*? I'm shocked you weren't killed."

Reyna was so tired of being ashamed of her past, and here was someone who was impressed, awed, not scornful or afraid. With the wine tickling her brain, loosening her tongue, Reyna leaned over the table dramatically. "We almost were. It's treason to leave the queen's employ. I'm the first palace guard to escape."

"No way." Darlene gaped. "Did you kill anyone?"

Reyna took a demure sip of her wine, aware that Joe was listening too. "That's a story for another time."

Darlene slumped back in her seat, and the conversation progressed. After a while, Reyna wound up talking with Farley and Rankor. Their navigator swelled with the attention. "I'm from Leonol. Born and raised. Farley came to study our use of carpentry—nowhere better to learn than cities built in the trees, after all."

"Too humid for me." Farley poured another glass of wine. She seemed to prefer the reds more than the sweeter whites, and her smile grew wider the more she drank. "But there is something to their meritocracy. The smartest, most proven folk lead. Their university has some of the best courses I've ever seen—and the strangest."

"My favorite was archeology," Rankor said. "Digging up bones of ancient magical beasts and old civilizations. We even found dragon remains in our jungle."

Reyna's eyes widened. "Incredible."

Later, Squirrel whisked away her plate and tapped her shoulder. "Reyna, will you follow me with the dishes? Once we clear off the table, we can start the music."

"Music?"

Serina, at the head of the table, laughed boisterously. Now that she was able to relax, she drank with the best of them, and had produced a bottle of amber liquid from Diarn Arlon's old room. "'Course there's music! Pil told me the Dastardly Pirate Dreggs has dancing parties every Stars-damned night. Can't let them show me up. I'd be a shit pirate captain."

"I play the fiddle," Joe said solemnly.

Darlene rolled her eyes.

Squirrel grinned, then led Reyna belowdecks, arms laden with food. The staircase to the galley was narrower than Reyna expected, and she had a newfound respect for how Squirrel had carted up all these dishes. The galley itself was just a small space underneath the cargo hold, with enough room for a tiny countertop and barrels of what appeared to be flour, salt, and sugar. Long wooden shelves along the back wall had been built with a metal bar to hold the cans in place when the waters grew turbulent.

Reyna set the dirty dishes in a large washing tin, and realized Squirrel was staring at her.

Scowling, actually.

She frowned back. "Is something wrong?" Her sword was on deck, but Reyna was hardly worried about an attack by this older woman. Nothing up to this point had pinned her as any kind of threat.

"These are good folk," Squirrel said.

"I agree," Reyna replied, suspicious now.

"Don't give me that tone. I'm from Mercon. Born there, fled west over the bay to Jallin while I was young enough to adopt the Sheparan accent." Squirrel's eyes were hard, untrusting. "I know all about the Queensguard. I know what you've done."

Reyna had spent many nights in the dark, shivering at the memories of the people she'd killed. Wondering about their families, their hobbies, their favorite kind of tea. She remembered every single face—and yet, she never had the luxury of ignoring her orders.

Either they died . . . or she did.

She crossed her arms, voice neutral. "I wasn't lying when I said I fled Her Excellency's service. If I weren't engaged to the Arcandor, she would have killed me for treason last summer. The very fact that I'm standing here should prove that story's truth."

"I believe the story. I doubt the intention." Squirrel began washing dishes, cleaning the metal plates with a quick pass of a wet rag. "The Queensguard is unforgiving. I saw how you fought today. What happens when you decide to turn on this crew?"

That hurt more than Reyna cared to admit. She closed herself off, smoothed her face so Squirrel couldn't see her pain. "I swore to protect this crew, and I will."

"Hmm. For our sake, I hope that's true."

Reyna swallowed a retort. "If that's all, Squirrel, I'll be returning to the festivities." She waited, but their cook didn't seem to have an opinion on that. Reyna began to climb the narrow steps, but paused to say, "Just remember, not everyone was lucky enough to sail west. Some of us didn't have a choice."

And she left the old woman alone.

Things passed in a blur after that. Reyna drank more wine, but never enough to dull her senses to the point of allowing Squirrel an opening. The cook came and went, danced for a short while, but wouldn't look Reyna in the eyes after that. Eventually, the kids went to bed, Farley and Rankor retired, and it was just Serina, Reyna, and Pil left on deck. The night had deepened and the chilly air was alive with the sound of crickets and the gentle glow of lanternflies.

"You said you're a tea maker?" Serina asked.

Reyna swallowed a yawn. "Amongst other things."

"You know, the diarn orders a special blend from the Roiling Islands. There's a flower that only grows on their tallest mountain, and it's supposed to taste like lavender and honey. They mix it with some kind of black tea that wakes you up."

"A yerba maté," Reyna said, perking up. "Do you have some?"

Serina grinned in response and vanished into the captain's quarters. A few minutes later, she returned with a teakettle and a small burlap bag of gorgeous-smelling tea. Reyna set the water to boil over one of their lanterns and partitioned out tiny cloth bags to steep.

Vividly, she missed New Leaf Tomes and Tea, missed the copper kettle she'd always used to heat her water, missed Gossley wiping tables while Kianthe showed Matild and Tarly the newest romance novel.

"I love wine," Reyna said, "but there's something about a nice cup of tea."

"I love tea, but there's something about *stolen* tea from Arlon's personal stash." Serina cackled wickedly.

Reyna set the tea bags into each of their mugs, letting them steep. She almost suggested retrieving honey or sugar from the galley, but she didn't want to see Squirrel anymore tonight. Once everyone had a steaming cup, Reyna settled back into her chair, inhaling deeply. It really did smell divine, and a quick taste proved why Diarn Arlon special-ordered it.

Delicious.

Quiet moments slipped past. All three of them seemed content to admire the stars, appreciate the cold weather, and hunch under their cloaks with stolen tea.

Finally, Serina glanced at Pil. "What led you to Dreggs's ship?"

He shrugged. "Bit of work here and there. Dreggs offers the crew of any ship they attack the chance to join their side instead. Half the ships in their fleet are just sailors agreeing to fly under a different flag. My chance came, and I figured, why the hells not?"

Serina chuckled.

Now Pil took a deep swig of his tea. "And what are you doing out here, Captain? Not every day we hear of pirates on the Nacean."

"I just . . ." Serina sighed. "I want things to be different. My family moved from Lathe when I was a kid, and I was so angry about it. I spent a decade convincing myself that moving *back* to Lathe, farming the family land—that was my path." She laughed, but the sound was dark, bitter. "I finally got my chance. Not the family land; that was gone. But he offered me a barren patch of soil so far inland that shipping to the riverfront ate nearly all my profits."

"How kind," Reyna drawled.

The pirate shrugged. "Yeah, well. Turns out, I'm as bad at farming as everything else in life. No surprise Arlon ordered my land reclaimed."

"But a pirate? Doesn't make much sense, career-wise." Pil quirked an eyebrow.

Serina finished her tea in another large gulp. "Hey. I already had a ship. It was either working for Arlon—or stealing from him. Seemed like an obvious choice."

They laughed at that. Once all the tea was gone, the three of them hauled the long table back into the captain's quarters, stowed his tea in a wardrobe behind it, and bid each other goodnight. As Reyna was climbing into her hammock near the small staircase, Pil clapped her shoulder.

"I saw Squirrel pull you aside. Just want you to know, me and my family? We judge by actions, not history . . . and so far, you seem okay to me." He offered a kind smile and climbed into the hammock above Joe, who was fast asleep.

Reyna blew out the lantern, getting comfortable in her own bed.

Maybe one day, she'd believe that.

"Where are we delivering this food?" Joe asked, peeking into the crates the next morning. The fog had shifted into gloomy rain, which chilled the air and pricked their skin. They'd begun sailing north again, moving at a snail's pace against the current.

Any slower, and Rankor joked they'd have to start rowing. Of course, Arlon's ship wasn't equipped for that—he probably assumed he'd always have a mage on board.

Reyna was alert, accustomed to running on a few hours of sleep, but Serina apparently forgot overnight that she captained a *crew* now. She took a sip of the bitter maté tea Reyna had provided and grimaced. "Ah, that. I have a mental list of places that need it."

"Anyone higher up on that list?" Pil, hanging from the lines, asked. He was busy tugging a knot into position, but spared a glance at them below.

Serina's brow had furrowed, and she appeared deep in thought.

"Typically, I try to focus on the folk outside of town, since they're usually worse off. The lack of a community around their homes means they're usually overlooked."

"Fewer people to complain if they're going hungry," Reyna said. "Arlon probably doesn't give them much mind."

Serina nodded, stepping lightly to the helm. She peered over the backside of the ship. "Exactly. There's a tiny cluster of homes on one of the islands nearby. It's the only place the hallerberry grows, but they can't survive on berries. I bet they'd appreciate a stop." Now Serina took another sip of tea, spinning back toward her crew. She seemed to have perked up considerably with the thrill of pirating. "You lot ready to see the back end of my work?"

"For a pirate, you don't do much actual pirating," Joe muttered.

Pil snapped his fingers at them, rolling his eyes. "Kid. You're hardly the definition of a pirate yourself."

Joe clamped their mouth shut, grudgingly resecuring the lid on the crates.

Serina chuckled, but Reyna didn't miss the nervous edge to her voice. "You'll like this. Promise." She raised her tone. "Rankor! You know where Qualla Island is?"

"About half a day's sail from here, judging by the sea anchor's current." Rankor rolled his shoulders, adjusting the helm to angle them directly north. "Pil, the sails. We'll need all the wind we can get."

"Isn't your partner the Arcandor?" Joe asked Reyna, crossing their arms. "She'd be handy here."

"She would indeed," Reyna replied drily.

Sailing a ship was a multi-person job, but Reyna wasn't needed. With Rankor handling navigation, Serina supervising, and Pil and his kids scurrying across the lines adjusting to the wind, Reyna was left with little to do. She spent her time along the ship's railing, watching the distant shoreline appear and fade in the fog. Eventually, the smattering of rain stopped, although the clouds were heavy overhead.

Farley joined her, munching on a buttered biscuit. She wore a light cloak in this weather, seemingly at ease despite the colder temperature, and she gestured at the water below them. "The river's beautiful, isn't it?"

Up here, the river was shockingly clear. It got murkier farther south, but this water showed everything on the surface, and faded into a black tinge at its deepest parts. Reyna smiled slightly. "It's lovely. We don't have anything like this in the Queendom."

"No one has anything like this. This river is a beast all its own." Farley let the silence stretch, then asked, "Anyone tell you the folklore of it? How the Nacean was created?"

Reyna turned slightly to face Farley, offering her undivided attention.

Farley smiled. "They say this land was barren—a desert, empty of anything. Any magic that settled over it was sucked into the ground and consumed. Early Sheparans viewed it as a death sentence."

"Sounds familiar," Reyna drawled. The Queendom lands were considered equally barren . . . equally devoid of magic.

Farley waved a hand to dismiss her. "More than your homeland. One story says that a mage walked fifteen steps into the desert, and withered into a husk. *That* kind of emptiness."

"A void."

"Exactly."

Reyna frowned, glancing at the generous foliage. Even from this distance, with the shoreline barely visible, the towering mass of trees couldn't be missed. The colors had dulled with the afternoon gloom, but they hinted at mystery. Adventure. "How'd Shepara go from that, to this?"

"The Stone of Seeing itself."

Reyna perked up. Anything to do with the Stone's history interested her; she hadn't seen it in person, but it always seemed odd that Kianthe worshiped a literal rock. "What happened?" Her words were a bit breathless.

"They say a blessed Star fell from the sky, angling to heal the land. It crashed into the mountains north of Lathe, an event that shook the very world. When the mages flew north to check, they found the Stone of Seeing perched in the center of a gushing river—water pulled from the very ground. All that water had nowhere to go but south, and it carved a path so intense that the entire region was flooded."

"*That's* how they found the Stone of Seeing?" Reyna asked. Kianthe had never mentioned anything like this before.

Granted, Kianthe didn't pay much attention to the Stone—unless it wanted something. History in general, she didn't really bother with. *Better to live in the now,* she said, shrugging. *All that was so long ago that we can only rely on biased retellings anyway.*

But if there was a grain of truth to this, Reyna was interested.

"The Magicary won't publish an official origin to the Stone, but that's the rumor." Farley smirked, leaning heavily against the ship's railing. She stared at the water flowing past their ship. A few fish were visible, leaping out of the waves. Birds soared past, eyes on their prey, and one gull dove sharply into the water.

It didn't catch anything, but Reyna admired the effort.

"Kianthe said this is the Realm's most powerful ley line," Reyna mused. "Perhaps that's why."

"Maybe." Farley pushed away from the railing. "All I know is that it's nothing to trifle with. This river will be respected, one way or another. But there's something enigmatic about that . . . I couldn't leave the Nacean if I tried. All my time traveling, and I've never found anywhere better."

Reyna laughed. "Good thing Rankor feels the same way."

"Oh yeah." Farley grinned and strolled up to the helm, leaving Reyna to her thoughts.

After another hour, they pulled up to a small dock on one of the islands. Unlike the other islands, which were mountainous and intimidating, Qualla Island was flatter, with a friendly cove carved out of the northern edge. The village nestled there was small, just a few shops with houses deeper in the trees, and fishing boats nearby. Several locals milled around the pier watching Pil and his kids fold the sails, squinting into the gloom as Farley and Reyna dropped the anchor.

"We'd better not stay long," Reyna murmured to Serina. "This is the perfect place for an ambush—if Arlon's constables block the cove's exit, we're trapped."

"If that happens, Arlon's really pissed." Serina grinned at the thought, then helped Pil and Farley lower the gangplank. It landed on the dock with an echoing *thud*, and Serina wasted no time strolling down it.

"Garinson," she called. "How've you been?"

"Oh, dandy." A full-bodied man stepped up to the pirate, clapping her in a hug so firm she wheezed. When he heard her gasp, he pulled back. "You hurt yourself again, kid?"

Serina's fingers feathered along the bandage on her arm. "Only a little, but it was worth it. Trust me."

Garinson squinted at her, but must have been satisfied with her overall state. He chuckled. "Well, you're certainly making waves. The constable that came last week couldn't stop ranting about you."

"Ranting, huh?" Serina folded her arms, puffing out her chest. "Serves him right."

"Serves them *all* right," Garinson replied with a booming laugh.

Reyna and the others eased down the gangplank, clustering on the small dock behind Serina. Reyna delicately cleared her throat, and the pair glanced at them. A look of pride overtook Serina's face, and she lifted her chin, gesturing grandly at them. "Garinson, allow me to introduce my crew." She went through names, and everyone waved in turn.

Reyna was included, which sent a rush of happiness through her soul. She didn't miss the suspicion that flashed on Squirrel's face at her name, but she couldn't dwell on it. Serina valued her, and that was what mattered here.

"You've upgraded. Pirating pays well, then, hmm?" Garinson drawled.

"I already told you. I'm an *entrepreneur,* not a pirate." Serina winked.

"Ahh. My mistake." Garinson swallowed a laugh, stuffing his hands in his cloak's pockets. "Well, Serina the Entrepreneur—I'm assuming you've either brought something, or you want something."

Serina clapped his arm. "We brought something. I remember you telling me stores were getting low, and it's shaping up to be a cold winter. Could you use a few crates of wheat?"

Garinson stared, and for a moment his eyes took on an incredulous shine. He blinked a few times, cleared his throat, and replied, "Ah—we'd—well, of course, we'd take what you have. How much?"

"Free, for your discretion." Serina smiled warmly.

"We can be *so* discreet," a teenager behind Garinson chirped, eyes alight.

Behind Reyna, Darlene snorted.

Garinson floundered, seemingly at war with himself. "We can't accept wheat for *free,* Serina."

Now Serina lowered her voice, and the raw emotion of her words made Reyna look away. "Gar, without you folk, I'd have starved last season. I told you I wouldn't forget it. Just needed a crew to improve my operations first."

At that, her crew shifted. Something between them solidified. Reyna watched it happen; it was subtle, just a few smiles, some shared looks. But in that magical moment, the *Knot for Sail* became less of a joke, more of a cause.

Reyna's arms prickled, and she swallowed past the sudden lump in her throat. *Ah.* This was the camaraderie she missed from the Queensguard. She really didn't think she'd find it again.

Even Squirrel avoided her gaze, shifting awkwardly as she said, "We're happy to help."

Serina held Garinson's gaze. "Folk like you are why I'm doing this. Accept the wheat. And feel free to share some of your hallerberries." The last part was said as a joke, and it elicited a laugh from Garinson and the other villagers.

"Of course, of course. Anything you need." He cleared his throat. "How about you folk stay for dinner? We'll have plenty to share, thanks to you."

Serina glanced at the crew, assessing their approval. Reyna almost told Serina they needed to keep moving, but it was starting to rain again, and the sun was beginning to set. In a short while, it'd be too dark to identify Arlon's ship by the dock anyway.

They could set sail first thing in the morning.

Serina seemed to arrive at the same conclusion, because she swept her arms wide. "We'd love to. Let's enjoy the night, shall we?"

And as Garinson instructed some of his folk to help haul the crates off the ship, and several other people ushered Serina's crew toward the few buildings along the shoreline, Reyna couldn't argue with the warmth inside her chest.

Maybe pirating wasn't the villainy it seemed.

17

Bobbie

Everything was gone.

Bobbie couldn't stop the mantra from repeating in a sickening spiral inside her mind. *Everything is gone,* her brain whispered. Her job, something she'd spent years perfecting, something she'd accepted to *prove* herself—and all it proved was that she wasn't good enough. Her family would be next; what kind of sheriff wanted a failed constable as a daughter? And then Serina . . . the antagonist to her story, not misunderstood but blatantly opposing everything Bobbie was.

It was dizzying, and for the first time in her life, Bobbie felt a little seasick. She clutched the tiny boat's railing, staring at the water below, her skin hot and cold all at once.

From the front of the boat, Kianthe craned her neck to see Bobbie. "You're not going to puke, are you? The river won't like that."

Helpful as always.

A surge of fury swept through her. The only reason she didn't snap was because this was the *Arcandor,* and she didn't want to add "screaming at the Mage of Ages" to her list of failures.

"Can we—not talk?" The request came out vaguely miserable.

Kianthe contemplated it, then shook her head. "Considering we've been sailing half the night and you've spent it moping, I'm not feeling particularly benevolent. I think we *should* talk. In fact, I think you should yell. Scream. Fight."

Easy for her to say. "There's nothing to fight for. Everything is gone."

Kianthe flicked a hand, and something smacked Bobbie from behind. Sensation flashed down her back, more shock than actual pain, but it made her jerk to her feet and spin toward an invisible opponent. Except Kianthe hadn't moved from her position at the front of the boat, and they were obviously alone in the center of a massive river.

The deck was wet. Bobbie narrowed her eyes. "Did you just slap me with water?"

"Maybe." Kianthe crossed her arms. "Talk to me. That was *shitty.* Aren't you angry?"

Yes. She was so, so angry, it simmered in her chest and lit her soul on fire. She wanted to scream and cry and throw things—but it was too late. All those outbursts would accomplish nothing. She set her jaw, drawing a slow breath. "I'm fine."

"Like hells." At the words, huge whips of water rose from the river, circling the boat. It seemed like the Nacean itself was enjoying Kianthe's spite.

This was ridiculous. All she wanted was a bit of peace to compartmentalize her thoughts. It didn't feel like too much to ask, but the Arcandor was scowling like she'd demanded the fucking world.

"What do you want me to say?" Bobbie snapped, then clamped her mouth shut. Her next sentence came out quieter. "My job is gone. I failed. Serina's never going to stop breaking the law, and the constables who finally catch her—" Bobbie cut off, clenching her eyes shut. "You told me yourself. It's nothing good."

Around them, the boat bobbed along the currents. Water splashed in the distance, and Bobbie caught a fast glimpse of a dolphin's fin as it dove again. Her words seemed to settle around them like a heavy fog.

Kianthe leaned against the boat's railing. "So. What are you going to do about it?"

So simple.

Bobbie swallowed a groan, sinking to the boat's wooden deck. She put her head in her hands and muttered, "I don't know."

Another slap of water smacked her head, and this one didn't pull back. Icy tendrils of river water slid down her shirt, causing her to flinch and yelp. When she pushed to her feet, she came face-to-face with the Arcandor.

The mage narrowed her eyes. "Get mad."

"I don't—"

"Damn it, Bobbie, you've been overly stressed since this began. You've been jerked up and down the river. Your best friend hates you. You were just *fired*." Kianthe stepped closer, decidedly in Bobbie's space now. "Get. Mad."

"I'm *already* mad," Bobbie snarled, and the suddenness of it had a wry smile tilting Kianthe's lips. It was encouraging, and for the first time in a while, Bobbie let fury consume her. The fire that prickled her skin burned hot, and they were alone on this Stars-damned river, and everything had gone to the five hells already, so *why not*? "I never even wanted this. You know that? Being a fucking constable for fucking Arlon!"

Satisfied, Kianthe stepped back, leaning casually against the helm's wooden post. The water writhing around them calmed as Bobbie paced before her, fists clenched, shouting at the sky.

"My mother was already the sheriff, and working for her sounded terrible. But I wanted to do her proud, so I didn't even let myself *consider* other options. I think I'd have loved to be a seamstress, or a carpenter, and instead I'm here, patrolling Arlon's land." Bobbie dug her fingers into her tight spirals, and tugging her hair felt good—a bit of release to the tension in her brain. Her volume was climbing. "Before Serina lost her mind, I thought I was *helping*. That's how I reasoned it away. I was committed to the greater good. You fucking believe that?"

"'Good' is relative," Kianthe inserted drily.

"No shit," Bobbie hissed. "Fuck those guys. The other constables. Arlon. All of them. Hells, if I have nothing else to do, maybe I *will* be a pirate. I wonder if Serina's hiring." And she laughed again, hysterically.

Eventually, it died down. Eventually, silence took over, filling the space with the warmth of hot cocoa on a cold day. Her skin cooled, and she suddenly didn't want to cry or scream anymore. Actually, Bobbie felt . . . good.

Kianthe smirked. "Sometimes, we all need a release."

"I haven't yelled like that in years." Bobbie massaged her face with two hands. "Screaming into a pillow is usually enough."

"Well, we're out of pillows, but an empty river is a good substitute." Kianthe strode forward, clapping her shoulder. "Every time a door closes in my life, it's for a reason. Something better always, *always* shows up. But feeling that anger in the meantime is justified."

Bobbie laughed, a weak chuckle now. "Maybe it's time to be a seamstress. I could just crochet for a living."

Kianthe shrugged. "Maybe. But I think you're destined for more."

Satisfaction spread through Bobbie's soul. It was nice to hear someone believed in her, especially after all this.

Exhaustion tugged at her chest now, and her eyes were burning. She swallowed a yawn. "I think . . . I'd like a nap. Can we do shifts?"

"We don't need to. The wind will keep us on course." The second sentence held a warning tone, and a gust of wind swirled around them as if to concur. A chill swept up Bobbie's arms at the magical display, but she forced a smile as Kianthe rifled through the supplies on one end of the boat. "They left us sleeping pads. Let's both get some shut-eye while we can, huh?"

"Okay." Bobbie took one from her and laid it out on deck. Kianthe settled adjacent to her, facing the sky with a satisfied sigh.

Overhead, the stars gleamed, paint on an inky canvas. Bobbie leaned back herself, bracing her hands under her head. Another splash farther down the river—possibly another dolphin, but maybe just a fish—but otherwise the river was calm. The gentle lapping of water against the side of their boat was almost soothing now. On the distant shoreline, crickets chirped, and the silhouette of an owl cut across the sky.

"Kianthe?" Bobbie ventured.

"Mmm?" The mage sounded half-asleep already.

Bobbie hesitated, keeping her eyes trained on the stars. "Thanks. I know you and Reyna didn't want to spend your season like this, but . . . I'm glad you're here."

"I always find myself exactly where I need to be, even if my expectations were different." Kianthe sounded amused. "All that to say, I am too. You're surprisingly good company when you aren't stressed about things you can't control."

Bobbie snorted—and for once, she didn't let herself pick that apart. "I'll keep that in mind."

Maybe Kianthe was right. Maybe now, finally, she could stop with the pretenses. Leave behind the professional constable, the perfect daughter, the lackluster friend.

She could just be . . . herself.

It sounded nice.

With a smile on her lips and the boat rocking gently, Bobbie drifted to sleep.

18

Serina

Qualla Island had one specific spot that Serina adored.

It required a hike out of the village, picking through a barely worn path, climbing a gentle incline, and finally emerging through the pine trees to a rocky outcropping at the edge of the bay. But what unfolded before her was worth it: a stunning view of the river, dotted with distant islands, one shoreline curling around them like a cat's tail. The morning fog was lighter today, more of a mist that added a cozy golden haze to everything.

The rocks at her feet were hexagon-shaped, oddly geometrical, and Serina perched on the edge of one, running her fingers along the soft moss that grew between the stones. Her crew would be sleeping for a while, but this was a nice way to wake up.

A nice place to calm her anxiety.

Everything would be fine. It had to be fine. But Serina's arm hadn't stopped throbbing all night, and even redoing the bandaging this morning was a task. The wound was a visceral reminder of what Reyna had discussed earlier.

Steps would have to be taken.

Decisions made.

How far *was* she willing to go to disrupt Arlon's rule?

Lost in her thoughts, Serina didn't realize someone had approached until they cleared their throat behind her. She yelped, pivoting so violently she nearly tipped over the edge of the outcropping. Reyna raised the two steaming mugs in her hands, clearly amused.

"Should I have made more noise when I approached?" she asked.

Serina coughed to cover up her laugh. "Yes. Always." Her eyes lingered on the mugs. She hadn't realized how badly she'd wanted a wake-up beverage until Reyna arrived with them. "Is that tea?"

"After last night, it certainly isn't liquor."

Serina snorted, taking one of the mugs as Reyna sat beside her. This morning, the tea maker had chosen a dark blend that smelled of mint and cacao. She'd clearly mixed in a bit of honey, and the result had Serina's mouth watering. It had cooled on the hike, especially considering the morning chill, so she sipped it quickly to savor the taste.

"Is everything okay?" Reyna asked after a moment.

Serina glanced sideways at her. "Why wouldn't everything be okay? Things are great. *Better* than great—I finally have a ship and a crew, and we can make a real difference."

It sounded hollow, even to her own ears.

"That is what you wanted." Reyna traced the rim of her mug, staring at the islands in the distance. Serina bristled for a fight, for some inspirational talk about the difference between *wants* and *needs*. Instead, Reyna pivoted. "Do sea serpents really swim in this river?"

The question took Serina by such surprise that she laughed. "What brought that on?"

"I saw a gift shop in Neolow that had carved sea serpents. They looked like dragons, so I got curious." Reyna tilted her head. "Are they real, or another part of folklore?"

Serina had forgotten that some people didn't grow up here. She couldn't keep the amusement from her voice. "They're definitely real. My parents used to sit along the riverbank and skip stones to call them from the deep. They like fish, and *love* elk." Serina frowned. "You really haven't seen one?"

"No." Reyna's eyes widened. "Gods, no. How big are they?"

Serina studied the river, gauging size. "At least as big as our ship.

Sometimes twice that size. But they're pretty mild. Dangerous to fish and dolphins and the like, but they don't really care about humans. They live at the bottom of the river."

"How deep?" Reyna craned her head over the edge of the outcropping.

"Deeper than you can imagine." Serina chuckled. "If the river wasn't deep, we'd have trouble sailing on it."

Reyna hummed affirmation, squinting at the mist settling over the river's surface. "Amazing. I hope I get to see one before we leave."

"I'll see if we can find one." One lived near Lathe, but Serina didn't really want to go back there. She couldn't look Viviana in the eyes right now—especially not with how she'd left things with Bobbie.

Silence fell over them again as they sipped their tea, basking in the morning chill and watching the rising sun color the mist a brilliant gold. After a moment, Reyna tilted her head. "How did you arrive on Qualla the first time? You seemed to be good friends with the people here."

Ah. Serina's cheeks burned, and she cleared her throat. "Ah, that. It's kind of ridiculous. Turns out, pirating is . . . not that easy. I had a couple rough escapes before I realized I needed to plan my attacks better—move at night, watch for ships left unattended, that kind of thing."

"Smart tactics."

"It'd have been smarter to try them sooner." Serina set her mug down on another flat-ish rock, then tugged up the sleeve of her uninjured arm. Her fingers trailed along the nasty scar that marred her skin. "One of the constables got a lucky hit. I was bleeding pretty badly, and realized I wouldn't make it to Neolow. So, I diverted course."

Reyna analyzed the scar, her brow furrowed. "Garinson helped you."

"They all did. They gave me food, water, and medical help . . . and no one asked questions." Serina swallowed, letting her sleeve drop again. "Four constables arrived while I was recovering and took half their food supply. *Half.* Garinson still insisted I stay until I'd fully recovered."

Reyna's lips tilted. "They're good folk."

"The best. Most of the people on this river are. Community is an easy thing to forget in a big city like Wellia or Jallin, but the Nacean breeds something different. I couldn't stay away."

"I'm sure." Reyna finished her tea, then set her empty mug nearby. She leaned back on her palms, the picture of relaxation. "You're doing something great. You're aware of that, correct?"

"I'm aware that I'm breaking every rule." Serina paused, lowering her voice. "And now if I mess up, others will be hurt too."

Reyna smiled slightly. She didn't have her sword this morning, but she somehow still seemed professional, cunning, ruthless. Serina hadn't met a Queensguard before her, but Reyna was everything she expected. "Any true leader takes on that responsibility. But you *are* doing something important, and it's natural people will follow you. That's a good thing."

Serina set her jaw, kicking her legs aimlessly. "I wasn't really thinking that far ahead."

"Now's the time to start. But I have a feeling you'll be just fine." Reyna pushed to her feet, stretching in the newfound sunlight. Today there were scattered clouds, which meant less cover sailing the river—but a prettier day overall. "We should probably head back before the crew awakes. What's our next stop, Captain? Continue sailing north?"

"Might as well," Serina replied. "A lot of shipments go through Oslop. I bet we can hit a couple vessels there and restock grain. There's a few other locations that might need—"

Reyna was smiling.

Serina cut off, feeling self-conscious. "What?"

"Nothing. Just, when you talk like that, it sounds like you were born to be a pirate." Reyna winked, retrieving her mug, offering to take Serina's.

Warmth spread through Serina's veins. If someone like Reyna approved of her work, maybe she wasn't so far off after all. Serina pushed to her feet, dusting herself off. It was a nice sunrise, but they had work to do.

"You're right." Serina smiled, pleased. "Thanks for the reminder."

"Anytime." Reyna grinned, and together they headed back to the village.

19

Reyna

As Qualla Island faded into the distance, an eerie feeling settled in Reyna's gut. Maybe it was the fact that the river was clear—which meant they were creeping along at a slow pace, in full view of the shoreline between islands. Maybe it was the fact that spirits were high and the crew was loud. Maybe it was just a premonition, honed from years of combat.

Either way, Reyna was unsettled.

"So, how do you avoid slicing your foot off?" Darlene asked.

They'd claimed the stern of the ship as a practice area, simply because Darlene had asked for sword-fighting lessons. With little else to do while the *Knot for Sail* crept north, Reyna cleared an area and was letting the teenager test her sword's weight. Darlene held it like one might an axe, squinting as sunlight reflected off the oiled blade.

Reyna glanced at the shoreline, which had just come back into view. The islands were behind them, and the river was narrowing again. They must be near Arlon's estate, even though they were hugging the western bank to avoid it.

No sign of an enemy . . . but that didn't mean much when Reyna felt this way.

"Ah—proper footwork, and treating the sword like the deadly weapon it is." Reyna pulled her attention back to Darlene, forcing a smile. "Keep the blade pointed up. Unless you're moving into an attack or sheathing it, the blade should be parallel with the ground or higher." She stepped behind Darlene, adjusting her grip, nudging her feet into a more stable stance. "How does that feel?"

Darlene grinned fiercely. "Like I need my own sword."

"Not a chance," Pil called from the crow's nest. He sounded distracted.

"You're no fun," Darlene called up to him. "This could be my future. Maybe I'm destined to be a—"

"Hang on, kid." Pil's tone instantly silenced his daughter, and he whistled softly to Rankor at the helm. "You see that?"

Rankor's tone was grim. "Yep."

A chill swept up Reyna's chest. She knew it. Without thinking, she left Darlene with the sword, taking the steps to the upper deck two at a time. Serina and Rankor were pressed against the railing, squinting through the trees.

"What is it?" Reyna asked.

"Maybe nothing." Rankor hesitated, leaning over the rail to squint at the river—as if his basic eyesight might be enough to see the sea anchor hauling them north. "But it looks like several ships anchored around this bend."

At their side, Serina whipped out her spyglass, squinting through the trees.

Reyna, meanwhile, didn't need a spyglass to identify the problem. Because Rankor was right—she could see two distinct shapes lurking in the shadows behind the trees, and two more drifting closer to the river's center. A mix of ship sizes, but all looked intimidating, and she was fairly sure one had cannons.

Reyna frowned. "You think they're here for us?"

"It wouldn't surprise me, considering we stole from Arlon two days ago."

Serina scowled, snapping her spyglass shut. "A blockade. I can't believe Bobbie set up a fucking blockade to catch me."

"This isn't Bobbie," Reyna replied quietly.

Her tone made the pirate flinch. Serina began to pace, running her hand through her long, unruly hair. Her arm was still bandaged, and it seemed painful to lift—which didn't bode well.

"Okay, so . . . a blockade. Which means Arlon will ask for surrender. He won't want to see his precious ship at the bottom of the Nacean, right?"

"Depends on how angry he is." Reyna rolled her arms, loosening up for a fight. But against four ships, she couldn't do much without Kianthe. Fear coiled in her gut, the sick knowledge that she might not be able to keep her promise—either to keep the crew safe, or to keep *herself* safe. "We know he has plenty of coin to buy a new ship. He might decide to make a statement."

Serina glanced at Rankor, then at Darlene on the lower deck, swinging Reyna's sword in a mock practice drill. Sweat gleamed on the captain's brow as she turned back to the blockade. "Then we turn around. There are plenty of places we can go—we don't have to visit Oslop anytime soon."

It was a fair point, and a far safer plan. Eventually Diarn Arlon would catch up, but for today it seemed like the smart idea. It gave Reyna time to find Kianthe, too—Diarn Arlon would think twice about attacking a ship with the Arcandor on board.

"I think that's—"

A flash of light from one of the ships.

There was just enough time to scream, *"Get down,"* before a sharp keening sound sliced through the air. Wood shattered above their heads, a deafening explosion, hailing splinters in every direction as the earsplitting crack of cannon fire finally caught up. A chunk of one of their booms spun into the water.

As the high-pitched whine in her ears receded, Reyna registered someone screaming. Darlene. She dropped the sword, covering her head.

"We're under attack," Serina shouted, taking command with impressive speed. "Darlene, Joe, get belowdecks! Pil, Rankor, turn us around. Now!"

Farley burst out from belowdecks, tying her dark hair into a bun. "Who's attacking?"

"There." Reyna plucked the spyglass out of Serina's hands,

locating a ship emerging from a small inlet she hadn't seen before. They'd been so concerned with the forward ships that she'd completely forgotten to check their flank.

Rookie mistake.

Reyna cursed. "It has two cannons, which means a second shot is inbound. We have to get out of here."

"The hull is too thick for a cannon to pierce at this distance. They can't sink us," Farley said, vaulting onto the upper deck beside her husband.

Overhead, Pil barked a hollow laugh. He was bleeding from several cuts—undoubtedly from the spray of splinters—but none of it looked serious. He moved in swift tandem with Rankor when their navigator turned the ship, even as his kids vanished belowdecks. "I'm less concerned about sinking in a river, and more concerned about the debris taking out our eyes."

Another *boom*. Sharp snapping sounds echoed as lines sliced clean through, whipping under the sudden loss of tension. Pil clutched one of the masts, bracing himself, but at least no wood shattered this time.

"If they get our mast, we're dead in the water," Serina said. "We need to get out of here."

"Trying—" Rankor grunted, wrestling with the helm. Under them, the ship lurched sideways, turning a slow circle away from the blockade. But it was too late—the four ships hidden around the bend had left their spots, and were advancing fast in the downriver current.

Reyna counted thirty constables, maybe more, marring their decks.

She retrieved her sword from where Darlene had abandoned it, but even its familiar grip didn't offer comfort. Fear thrummed in her veins, warring with cold determination as she held Serina's gaze.

"Prepare to be boarded, Captain."

Serina tugged out her own sword, her face pale. "Aye."

20

Kianthe

Kianthe lost track of how long they were on the tiny boat. With her magic, they made excellent time—and the Nacean was a powerful ley line, so sliding a ship up its width was as easy as breathing. Occasionally, they stopped on the shoreline for food, and once at midday, they visited a farmstead that boasted dried elk jerky.

"We set up a stand here every day, and ships always stop," the daughter proclaimed, wrapping their jerky in a checkered cloth. "Papa says we can buy a horse if we sell enough." Her chubby cheeks were bright with excitement. "Do you have a horse?" she asked Kianthe.

Lilac was left at the stables in Koll, almost certainly loving life. Kianthe shook her head. "I have a griffon."

"A *griffon*?" the girl gasped. "Papa, can we get a griffon?"

But the father was staring in horror at Bobbie's uniform—even crumpled from days of use, missing the identifying badge, there was no mistaking it was a constable's garb. He took the jerky from his daughter and shoved it at Kianthe. "We aren't doing well enough for a horse." The gruff statement came with an unspoken threat: *Nothing to see here.*

At her side, Bobbie swallowed hard and muttered, "I'll just . . . wait on the boat."

Kianthe handed them coin, knelt to the little girl, and whispered,

"Keep your eyes on the sky, and you might see my griffon." She ruffled the little girl's hair, nodded at the stoic father, and boarded their boat. A quick twist of magic had them back on the water, but neither spoke until the jerky stand was out of view.

"You okay?" Kianthe asked.

"I . . . want to get out of this uniform," Bobbie replied numbly.

Fair.

They sailed well into the morning, admiring the golden glow of mist on the river as they passed huge islands. At some point, Kianthe drifted to sleep, lulled into relaxation by the soft swell of the waves.

And a burning sensation at her chest wrenched her back into awareness.

"Ow, *ow,*" she hissed, yanking her moonstone from her skin. It was hot, and it only got hot with one signal from Reyna: *Emergency.*

And on cue, a *boom* echoed through the air.

"Shit!" Kianthe lurched to her feet, calling the wind to her. It was all too happy to oblige, a flurry of magic that carried its complaints at being slashed to hells by a careening metal ball. She tapped the moonstone, desperately awaiting a response, but Reyna must be too busy.

Or injured.

Fuck.

"Cannon fire." Bobbie leapt to the front of the boat, leaning over the railing as she scanned the riverbank for its source. But the river curved like a titanic snake, and their view was obscured. "You don't think Arlon attacked, do you?"

"Based on recent events, nothing would surprise me anymore." Kianthe leaned over the railing on the boat's side, her fingers drifting in the water. Magic spread along the river's ley line; farther upstream, the water circled around a ship desperately trying to turn away from four—no, five—attackers.

Horror spiked through Kianthe's chest. "I left her alone for *two days.*" And with a sharp tug of magic, their boat snapped forward, wind whistling against the sails as the elements themselves shoved her toward Reyna.

They weren't far. Another cannon echoed and Bobbie flinched as screams pierced the air. More shouts accompanied it—an army of them, it sounded like—and they curved the river bend into what looked like an all-out war.

Or rather, bullying. One ship with no defenses and . . . Kianthe counted five adults on board, maybe six? Meanwhile, five of the diarn's best ships seemed intent on sailing it down. Two were armed with cannons, and one was already in position, taking aim at the pirate ship's two masts.

"He's going to kill her," Bobbie exclaimed, horror seeping into her voice.

"That's what I've been trying to tell you." Kianthe didn't wait for Bobbie to comprehend the situation. Every moment those cannons were aimed at Serina's ship was another moment Reyna could be killed. "Hold on!"

And she wrenched the river *up*, encouraging it to drench, to consume. For once, the water could pretend it was fire, eating through its enemy. It soaked the ship, washed its constables overboard, and the vessel itself tipped onto its side.

The river sucked its sails down, and the entire thing tilted under, cannons directed at the sun itself now. The Nacean greedily devoured it, a bit too excited for Kianthe's preference. She sent a wave of soothing magic after it, and the ley line pulsed with her command.

The river pouted, but calmed.

It still left one ship with cannons, but that wasn't a big concern—not when a dozen constables were swinging onto the pirate ship. It seemed remarkably risky with Serina's vessel turning the way it was. A few constables overshot, landing hard in the river and sweeping downstream before they could fight it.

But several did reach the deck. And there was Reyna, sword glinting in the sunlight, facing off as the first line of defense.

Of fucking course.

"For the Stone's sake, Rain," Kianthe grumbled, and yanked their little boat alongside it. She pulled the wood out in strategic divots, creating a ladder straight up the side of Serina's ship. The new name caught her attention—the *Knot for Sail*—but Kianthe didn't have time to laugh.

She lunged up the makeshift ladder, dimly aware that Bobbie was following, and thumped on deck to find a sword's tip near her nose.

"Stand down and you won't be killed," the constable snarled.

"Cute." Kianthe grabbed the air in his lungs, but before she could yank, a sword clanged against his and a boot connected with his knee. He buckled, and Reyna moved swiftly in front of Kianthe, slamming her sword's pommel onto his skull.

The constable dropped like a stone.

"Don't threaten my fiancée," she told his dazed form.

Kianthe raised an eyebrow. "That was sexy as hells."

"Thank you, dear." Reyna spun toward another approaching constable, slashing his leg. The wound certainly wasn't shallow, and he swallowed a strangled cry as he crashed to the deck. Her boot connected with his nose, shattering it in a spray of blood. It was vicious and somehow beautiful, how she moved with such deadly grace. "We have to get—"

"Serina!" Bobbie exclaimed.

"Right," Reyna replied.

On the upper deck, the pirate had been thrown to the ground by another constable. He pressed a sword into her back, his boot applying pressure to a bandage on her arm. Serina yelped, thrashing under his hold, but he just dug the sword in farther and snarled something to her.

More constables had cornered three of Serina's crew and a couple extras were venturing belowdecks with swords and nasty expressions.

Bobbie only had eyes for Serina. She leapt past Kianthe, scaling the staircase to the upper deck and tackling the constable threatening the pirate. He raised his sword just in time, slicing down so the blade bit deep into Bobbie's shoulder. She yelped as he withdrew, but instead of retreating, she grabbed his hand and dug her nails in until he released his hold on the bloodied weapon. Newly armed, she slashed and jabbed to force him back—too far back, so far he accidentally toppled over the railing. Bobbie barely acknowledged the splash as he hit the cold water.

Reyna, meanwhile, was fighting her own battle. She moved swiftly across the deck, cutting through constables and leaving stains of crimson in her wake.

"Key," she shouted, "the cannons."

How she'd noticed that, Kianthe would never know, but she was right: the second armed ship was aiming their cannons at the masts. They were a lot closer—if they fired now, this fight would end badly.

Thoroughly done with their drama, Kianthe wrenched another wave over the enemy ship. It didn't manage to capsize this one, but the water assured her it would soak anything combustible.

That took care of that problem, but none of it addressed the constant stream of constables leaping onto their ship. Kianthe ignited her palms and shooed the fire onto the very flammable cloth of the enemy sails. It didn't take much prodding. Fire was the most gluttonous element, and it had just been gifted a feast and full permission to eat.

Shouts of anger turned to cries of panic as ropes were chewed to ash. Constables mid-swing crashed into the water around them, and two of the ships veered toward shore before the unnatural flames could devour their hulls.

It left one enemy ship circling, its sails alight—although they seemed to decide the constables on the *Knot for Sail* were more important to retrieve than fleeing for shore. Satisfied, Kianthe turned back to the fight, only to realize that Bobbie wasn't faring well.

Her fighting was decent, actually. She didn't move with Reyna's grace—the smooth motions of a lifetime wielding a sword—but the ex-constable had clearly practiced footwork, and she was fueled by something far more dangerous than a typical work ethic.

Despite that, blood soaked the front of her shirt, the wound on her shoulder clearly much deeper than Kianthe thought. And although Bobbie had sent her first opponent flying into the water, another constable thundered up the steps—one that resembled an angry seagull, one Kianthe had met before.

Tyal.

And he looked *furious.*

Bobbie staggered in front of Serina, readying her sword.

Serina didn't seem pleased by that. She said something (scathing, if her expression was anything to go by) and tried to pull Bobbie back—but Tyal seized the opportunity and lunged. Bobbie wrenched Serina away and met his blade, but wasn't prepared when he slashed sideways. The blade bit into her ribs, and her cry echoed.

"I have to help Bobbie," Kianthe called to Reyna.

Her fiancée was already moving over several fallen constables. In a true miracle—or a testament to Reyna's incredible skill—none of them seemed to be dead. Most were unconscious, and a few were curled around painful injuries. Kianthe counted seven . . . no, eight. Stone and Stars, Reyna was a force, and it was both terrifying and incredible.

"I'm going belowdecks; there are children down there. Stop that fight!" Reyna tossed a sword to one of the newly freed pirate crew, then strode toward the staircase leading belowdecks.

"One constable coming right up." Kianthe rolled up her sleeves, which proved difficult with the large cloak she wore. Meanwhile, Reyna vanished into the darkness, her bloodied sword gleaming in the firelight below. Stone help anyone who got in her way.

At the helm, Tyal was showing no mercy. He slashed and hacked, moving with vicious grace until he pinned Bobbie against the deck's railing. "Traitor," he growled. "I knew you were helping the pirate."

"I wasn't," Bobbie snarled, gasping for breath. Her skin, normally the shade of charred bark, was dangerously pale. Sweat gleamed along her brow, and her black uniform was obviously slick with blood, shining in the sunlight. A sharp *clang* rang through the air as she blocked his sword, grunting against his strength.

Kianthe called the wind—but before she could forcibly separate them, Serina did something very, very stupid.

She lunged at Tyal, and they both went crashing to the deck.

They grappled for a brief moment before Tyal produced a short knife—why did *everyone* have hidden knives?—and drove it into the meat of Serina's leg. It happened so fast, Kianthe barely had a chance to breathe.

Serina howled in pain.

"Serrie!" Bobbie lurched forward.

Without wasting more time, Kianthe wrenched the wood of the deck up, pinning Tyal's torso in a tomb of his own making. Serina rolled away. Bobbie pointed her sword at his neck, as if daring him to make another move.

He couldn't.

The fight was over.

For a long moment, everyone just gasped for breath. Bobbie's sounded a bit more rasping than the others', but she was still standing—even though she left bloody footprints in her wake. Her sword's tip trembled against Tyal's neck. "Was this blockade your idea?"

Tyal scoffed, fumbling for his sword.

Bobbie kicked the blade out of the way. "Tyal! Good people might have died today. *Did you order the blockade?*" Her tone was vicious.

"I don't give orders to a diarn." Tyal spat blood on the deck, wrenching against the planks pinning him. "And I'm not the traitor here. Once I told him you were working with the pirate, Diarn Arlon took action all on his own."

"She's *not* working with me," Serina hissed, grabbing Kianthe's shoulder to steady herself. "And she didn't 'let me escape.'" Now the pirate captain reached for the knife embedded in her leg, but she couldn't seem to convince herself to pull it out.

Probably for the best.

Kianthe propped Serina on the railing, then approached Tyal with the dangerous grace of a mage scorned. The air around her crackled. "I'm going to give you and your constables *one* chance to get off this ship. If you follow us, you'll find out what it's like to sail through a tidal wave. Is that clear?"

Tyal glowered at her. "The Mage of Ages, working with pirates now. The council is going to be furious."

"Oh, trust me. They've earned a visit. In fact, tell Arlon to expect me." Kianthe released his wooden bindings, then knocked him over the ship's railing in one smooth move. But he didn't hit the water—instead a burst of air swept between the ships, tossing him unceremoniously onto the neighboring brigantine. With another wave, she quelled the fire eating their sails.

"What about the others?" Serina gestured at the lower deck, where a few constables were staggering back to their feet.

There were probably ten left behind. Kianthe grumbled, "I can bundle them up in a tornado, but it might damage our own sails."

"We're pirates, right? Let's make them walk the plank." Serina gestured at a long wooden plank they could prop between the ships. "Just hold the ships close, Arcandor; they're going to drift otherwise."

It was a long process, hauling the constables up, quelling any lingering fighters, and then shoving them across a precarious wooden board between two massive ships. Bobbie stayed at the helm, tending her wounds while Serina's crew handled the minutiae. Reyna resurfaced with another pair of constables, shoving them unceremoniously onto the bloodstained deck.

"Your kids are safe, Pil," she said.

The man she addressed, a silver-bearded sailor, chuckled. "My kids aren't stupid. 'Course they're safe."

And finally, *finally*, all the constables were gone. Two of the diarn's ships had been capsized, carried downstream—two had constables desperately trying to extinguish flames as they anchored at shore—and Tyal's ship drifted like a rejected lover in the currents, its sails burned to ash.

Tyal himself was left glowering on his own deck, but when he shouted something, his words were magically lost to the winds. As they sailed north, Kianthe flipped him off, at which Reyna heaved a sigh.

"Darling, you are the picture of professionalism."

"No, love, that's you," Kianthe replied, pulling her into a fierce hug. Her nerves were buzzing after the fight, even though they'd had it well enough in hand. "Thanks for not killing anyone," she whispered against Reyna's sweat-slicked skin.

Her fiancée smiled, but the expression was pained. "Contrary to popular belief, I do not thrive on taking someone's life."

Shit. Kianthe scrambled to backtrack. "I didn't mean—"

"Uh—" A panicked tone caught their attention.

Both Kianthe and Reyna glanced back at the upper deck and the helm, where the tall, lanky sailor had taken control of the massive wooden wheel. The burly woman—his wife, Reyna had helpfully informed Kianthe—was tending to Serina's knife wound.

But Serina was the one who'd spoken, and her eyes were glued on Bobbie.

Bobbie, the ex-constable, who seemed to be attempting as much physical distance as possible from Serina and her crew.

Bobbie, who'd been hacked to bits and soaked with blood over the course of that fight.

Bobbie, who Kianthe had *completely forgotten* was acting faint *before* they sent Tyal's constables packing.

It was like watching a shipwreck from the shoreline. They saw the exact moment Bobbie's eyes fluttered. The exact moment her knees buckled. The exact moment the ship hit a wave, and instead of pitching toward the deck, she pitched backward—right over the polished rail.

And Kianthe couldn't even react before she hit the water.

21

Reyna

"Key," Reyna gasped, throwing herself against the rail as fear slid down her spine. That water was absolutely freezing—and Bobbie was unconscious. Bad combination. *Very* bad.

Luckily, Kianthe didn't hesitate when it came to the elements.

"Stay here," she said, and the urgency in her voice stilled Reyna. Then Kianthe threw herself overboard, and the river literally rose to meet her, swallowing her like a drop of water.

On the upper deck, Farley was holding Serina back; the pirate captain wailed in anguish as she staggered upright, surging to the railing where Bobbie had vanished. "She's going to drown," Serina cried. "Fuck—I should have—"

"Too late for that," Reyna said firmly, spinning away from the railing. "We have to be ready to fish them out of the water." Maybe Kianthe could persuade the river to lift them onto the deck, but for all Reyna knew, it would take too much magic—or be impossible with Bobbie in tow. Best to be prepared.

Serina set her jaw, taking control immediately. "Pil, get up high and tell me if you see them. Rankor, hold it steady. We don't want to crush them by accident. Farley, Reyna, get the rope ladder and be ready to toss it over."

Squirrel appeared from belowdecks at the commotion. Darlene

and Joe trailed in her wake—Joe looked vaguely ill at the crimson splatters on deck, but Darlene gripped a sword she'd stolen off one of the constables and seemed flushed with excitement.

"Another fight?" she asked, far too eagerly.

"Soul overboard," her dad grunted, heaving himself into the rigging.

That sobered her. She followed like a monkey, leaping into the crow's nest a breath behind him.

Reyna was helping Farley haul the rope ladder to the center of the deck, where they could toss it over either side depending on where Kianthe resurfaced. Her eyes locked with Squirrel, who'd hidden for the majority of the battle.

The older woman averted her gaze.

Good. If that fight didn't prove Reyna's worth, nothing would.

"I'll get some blankets, and hot water boiling," Squirrel told Serina. "Warm 'em up."

She vanished again, although her eyes caught Reyna's once more, brows knitted in apology before she went. Reyna barely noticed; enough time had passed that now she was worrying about *Kianthe*—although it was ridiculous to think an element would kill the Arcandor.

Still, as Reyna scanned the river's surface, waiting for a telltale break, her heart began to pound. This felt more tense than a fight. In a battle, Reyna knew how to seize control, how to save herself and her loved ones, where to step and stab and shift so the outcome was as expected.

She didn't know what to do with *this*.

Even if the elements would never hurt Kianthe, the river could consume Bobbie with one flick of a current. Kianthe had already been aghast to lose Serina's old ship. How would she feel if the constable was killed on her watch?

Chewing her lower lip, Reyna scanned the water, attempting to logic her way through the fear.

It worked, but only barely.

The rope ladder was rough under her hands, but she gripped it too hard, everything still as they waited for word. Silence settled over the ship like a tomb. After several moments, Serina's breath hitched in despair.

"This is my fault," she sobbed, her words nearly lost to the winds.

Reyna opened her mouth to protest—Serina wasn't the one who stabbed Bobbie—but a geyser-like blast erupted behind them. Everyone spun to see Kianthe hauling Bobbie headfirst out of the water, giving her the blessed ability to breathe even as the river escorted them both back to the ship.

Kianthe grabbed the rope, holding Bobbie in one arm and the rough hemp in the other. It took four of them and several moments of struggling to haul them onto the deck. Reyna tugged Kianthe and Farley towed Bobbie—and when the chaos settled, Kianthe was gasping on deck like a beached fish.

But Bobbie wasn't gasping at all.

"I'm glad you're okay," Reyna told her fiancée, even as she dropped to her knees beside the ex-constable.

Normally, Kianthe would joke about that statement. An Arcandor could be killed by the elements, but it took an extraordinary lack of focus on their part. Something like leaping off their griffon's back and forgetting to manipulate the winds to slow their fall. Not drowning in a river she was well aware she'd jumped into.

So Reyna did expect a bit of sarcasm at her comment.

Instead, Kianthe pressed a hand to Bobbie's chest, muttered, "You two have *got* to stop drowning," and made a yanking motion with her hand. Instantly, water spilled over Bobbie's lips, and Reyna barely had time to prop the woman onto her side.

She still didn't cough or gasp. She just lay there. Limp. Blood oozed from her wounds; her skin felt waxen, its color pallid.

"No," Serina breathed. Tears dripped down her face, and she fell heavily onto the deck, grimacing in pain from her own wound. She cupped Bobbie's cheek. "Come on, you stupid lug. Wake up. *Wake up!* Stars, not this way. Not like this." She shook Bobbie's shoulders violently, desperately, but her friend still didn't move.

Kianthe's expression hardened. "Get back. All of you." She accompanied the word with a gust of wind that pushed everyone away, clearing a circle around Bobbie. Then, with a growl and a crackle of magic, she pressed two fingers against Bobbie's heart and *shoved.*

A whipping sound echoed across the river, accompanied by a blinding flash of light and a thud as Bobbie's body wrenched off the deck.

And then—Bobbie gasped.

"What did you do?" Reyna asked, eyes widening. All her time with Kianthe, and she'd never seen anything like that before.

Kianthe glowed a bit, clearly pulling magic from the Nacean's ley line to replenish her supply. She mopped the sweat off her brow and pressed a hand to Bobbie's forehead, then her chest. "Lightning. It was just a hunch. I can feel similar energy in a human body, and I thought—maybe it'd work."

"You didn't *know*?" Serina tugged Bobbie into her lap and brushed sodden curls out of the ex-constable's face. Bobbie was breathing—unsteadily, but breathing. Meanwhile, Serina looked furious. "You just gambled with her life?"

It was unfair, driven by passion, but Reyna would have none of that. Not after what Kianthe just did, not when her fiancée was beginning to shiver in the icy wind.

"Her life was gone." The words cut through the air, hanging between them.

Serina blanched, looking like she might be sick.

Reyna, meanwhile, draped her cloak over her fiancée's shoulders, pressed a comforting kiss to her short hair. Kianthe offered her a grateful smile, which Reyna returned before pushing to her feet. "We need to treat Bobbie's wounds and get her out of those clothes, or this will have been in vain. Unless you'd prefer to continue yelling at the Arcandor?"

Serina had the decency to look ashamed. She ducked her head, muttered, "Thanks," and gestured at Pil and Rankor. "Let's get her into my quarters. I have some clothes she can wear." She pushed laboriously to her feet, grimacing, as the bandages on her thigh bloomed with fresh crimson.

Gods, what a mess. Reyna pinched her brow and said, "Captain, permission to take command of the ship."

Serina couldn't tear her eyes off Bobbie. Rankor scooped the ex-constable into his arms and Pil cleared a path to the captain's quarters. Even after they ducked inside, it took several seconds for Serina to process Reyna's words—and several more to accept she wouldn't be any help here.

"Aye. Permission granted."

She ghosted after Bobbie, staggering on her injured leg.

Farley pursed her lips. "I have some medical experience. Might be more useful than carpentry, considering we have an elemental mage on board now."

Kianthe stood as well, clutching Reyna's cloak around her shoulders. The wind that filled the sails somehow stilled around them, the elements once again trying to make her comfortable . . . but Reyna recognized the fresh anxiety painting Kianthe's face. Knowing Bobbie was breathing wouldn't be enough—at least not until the adrenaline of the fight settled.

Reyna drew a centering breath.

"Thank you, Farley. Address Bobbie's wounds first, and keep Serina off that leg if you can." Reyna turned, captured the attention of their boatswain's kids. "Joe. Go find Squirrel and help with the blankets and tea. We'll also need cloth for bandages, alcohol to sanitize, and heated water to warm Bobbie up."

They saluted, vanishing belowdecks.

Pil returned from the captain's quarters, pulling his shoulders back. "Are we still sailing north? I can navigate if Darlene handles the sails." He gestured to his daughter, still perched in the crow's nest awaiting instruction. She looked pale, but set her jaw and offered a reassuring nod when her eyes caught theirs.

Bless a versatile crew. Reyna nodded. "The helm's all yours, at least until Rankor is done helping the captain. Kianthe's magic will keep us moving north." It was safer than turning around at this point—safer than running back into those constables.

Pil nodded, climbing the staircase to the bloodstained upper deck.

Reyna surveyed the ship, ensuring everyone had a job. When it was clear no one was watching them, her hand found the small of Kianthe's back, guiding her toward the cargo hold. "Come on, Key. Let's get you into something dry."

"I can magic the water—"

Reyna put a hand on her cheek, silencing her. "Let me help you."

Kianthe nodded numbly.

They descended into the warm depths of the ship and immediately had to flatten against the bulkhead as Squirrel and Joe bustled past. The pair's arms were laden with blankets, strips of cloth, and steaming kettles. Good.

As she passed, Squirrel stopped, hesitated—but Reyna clapped her arm. "I know. It's okay."

The older woman nodded and followed Joe up the stairs.

Finally, they were alone in the quiet dark. Reyna led Kianthe to the hammocks, relieved for the modicum of privacy, and rummaged for a set of dry clothes in her bag. "That was brilliant, Key." Her words were firm, reassuring.

"It might not have worked," Kianthe mumbled, looking dazed now. She'd used an awful lot of magic to save them, and a bit more trying that lightning trick on Bobbie. The Nacean was a powerful ley line, but the glimmer of her magic drain was still evident. The mage mutely lifted her arms, allowing Reyna to undress her.

The trust they shared always hit in moments like this. Reyna pressed a kiss to Kianthe's bare shoulder before pulling a nice, comfy shirt over it. "It did work. Besides, if those two didn't have a death wish, you wouldn't have had to test it at all." A pause, a smirk. "And I thought *we* were reckless."

Kianthe laughed, forcing a smile. "We're reckless, but at least we're competent." She caught Reyna's hand, squeezing tight. "I missed you, Rain. I'm sorry I didn't get here sooner."

"Please. You arrived right on time." Now Reyna's smile dropped. "We should summon Visk and Ponder. Diarn Arlon is owed a visit after that stunt. I would expect a display like that from Her Excellency, but seeing it in Shepara is shocking."

"If I've learned one thing chatting with world leaders—it's that no one is above drastic measures. Even though everyone thinks they are." Kianthe hauled herself off the hammock, stripping her trousers. "I sent the griffons to Tawney. We need Feo if we're going up against the council."

"Feo?" Reyna handed her clean, dry pants. "They didn't exactly secure their title legally."

"Feo knows every law and loophole in Shepara. They're a tried-and-true diarn now, regardless of how they started. Plus, the council won't risk upsetting the balance of Tawney. Not when we live there, not with Tilaine watching that town like an eagle sighting prey."

Reyna sighed. "After what he just pulled, leaving Diarn Arlon unsupervised feels like playing with fire."

Kianthe snapped her fingers, pulling an ever-flame out of thin air. It drifted into the rafters, offering a cozy glow. "Please, Rain. Playing with fire is my specialty." She grinned, finally looking back to her normal self.

Of course. Puns always revived her.

"Been waiting to use that?" Reyna drawled.

"Elemental jokes? You *wood* not believe how many I have."

Reyna snorted and led her toward the galley. "Come on. Let's get you a cup of tea. Then we'll go check on Bobbie."

Clutching steaming mugs to their chests, chatting amicably, they resurfaced a short while later. Joe was on their hands and knees, swabbing blood off the deck. Darlene was making slight adjustments to the sails, calling out positions to her father as he tilted the helm. Squirrel exited the captain's quarters empty-handed, offered a slight smile, and disappeared belowdecks.

Inside Serina's room, things had settled. Bobbie's wounds were tightly bound, barely visible beneath thick blankets. She was still unconscious, but breathing well on her own. Propped on a pop-up cot, Serina was poking her leg, which was also bound in fresh linens.

Farley offered an exasperated sigh when Reyna approached. "Come to relieve us? Thank the Stars. They're terrible patients."

"Well, Bobbie's not bad," Rankor said.

"Bobbie's unconscious." Farley shoved her husband's shoulder.

Serina crossed her arms, almost petulant. She was braced against the bulkhead wall, but her eyes kept skirting to Bobbie. "Excuse you. I've been cooperative."

"You want to be cooperative? Try avoiding getting stabbed in the first place. Look, it's quite easy; I've gone my entire life without being stabbed." Farley held out her muscular arms to emphasize that point. "The key is not engaging with swordsmen."

"Or getting engaged *to* a swordsman," Kianthe piped up.

Reyna was startled into a laugh. "Darling, you've never been stabbed."

"Near thing in that bandit fight near the Capital, though."

Serina didn't seem in the mood for humor. Her eyes skirted again to Bobbie, and she asked, "Sorry to interrupt, but can we get some privacy?"

Farley shrugged, and Rankor held the door open for her. "Fine by me. I could use some lunch."

"Dinner, now," Rankor said.

Farley sighed. "Great."

And they were gone.

In the resulting silence, Reyna stepped to Bobbie, checking the pulse on the inside of her wrist. It wasn't as strong as she'd like, but it was steady, thrumming under the pad of her finger. Bobbie's breath was rasping, but present, and she'd started shivering at some point—which was better than the waxen stillness she'd displayed before.

"She'll be okay, right?" Serina couldn't seem to take her eyes off Bobbie's face.

"Do you care?" Kianthe's tone was neutral. She perched on the edge of Serina's cot, sipping her tea.

Serina puffed up indignantly. "She's my oldest friend. Of course I care about her recovery."

"Her recovery? Is that it?" Now Kianthe held her gaze, almost like a challenge. "Because this woman tracked you up and down the Nacean, kept the other constables off your back, and then leapt into battle to save you. I can tell you from firsthand experience that a person doesn't take risks like that if there isn't someone worthwhile waiting for them."

At that, Kianthe lifted her mug to Reyna, a pointed statement. Warmth spread over Reyna's cheeks.

Serina was silent for a long moment, fingers playing with the bandage around her leg.

When she did speak, her words were contemplative: "When Bobbie evicted me from my farm last season, I was so mad. Mad at her, mad at Arlon, but mostly furious at myself for leaving *everything* I knew. But I just—I thought if I could be successful like her, it'd even the playing field. She'd done so much while I was gone. I've fallen behind."

"I don't think comparing your life to hers means you fell behind," Reyna said, leaning against the wall of windows. Behind her, the river slipped past, golden in the setting sun. "You two were on different paths. One isn't better than the other."

"She was traveling the Nacean. She trained near Wellia. She's the definition of glamorous. My paths were working on my father's merchant ships . . . or trying to farm." Serina clawed her hair in frustration. "Did you know that I only came back to Lathe because of her? When Arlon seized my family's land, she and I swore we'd start our own farm one day, something he couldn't touch. We'd be terrible at it, but at least we'd be together."

Reyna understood that—it was a similar deal she'd made with Kianthe last spring. They knew exactly nothing about opening a bookstore and tea shop. And yet, together, anything seemed possible. Her eyes met Kianthe's, and they shared a private smile.

Serina sighed, her tone heavy with resignation. "When I got to Lathe, Bobbie was already gone. So, I figured I'd build the farm up . . . and maybe she'd come back. As if she could be happy with a simple life on the farm after being a constable."

"From what I can tell, being a constable just means she's collecting fabricated taxes," Kianthe drawled.

Reyna put a hand on her fiancée's shoulder, then addressed Serina. "I think you're missing the point, Serina. It isn't about the job you do. It's about the life you build together."

"She doesn't want a life with me. She made that clear," Serina muttered.

Time to try a different approach. "I told Kianthe for years I wouldn't leave with her—and I changed my mind. It only took one night to realize that we would be happier together than apart." Reyna beamed at Kianthe, brilliantly, gratefully. "She could ask me to become a slug harvester, and I'd do it. I don't care if we're having tea by a hearth, fighting on a pirate ship, or digging in the dirt. As long as we're together, it's a good life."

"Plus, digging in the dirt is fun." Kianthe sniffed.

Reyna rolled her eyes. "My point, Captain, is that people change. And Bobbie wants more than you're giving her."

Serina's face shifted, her tenuous expression giving way to a glimmer of hope. "Is that true?"

"Stone bless, you two are exhausting to watch. Serina, that girl is so head over heels for you that you could literally walk off a cliff, and she'd follow." Kianthe rolled her eyes, pushing to her feet. "With that settled, I want to make sure we pass Oslop without problems. Think about what we said and let us know when Bobbie wakes up."

Kianthe tossed an arm over Reyna's shoulders. Reyna pressed against her, warmth spreading in her own chest, and they strolled out of the captain's quarters.

22

Kianthe

They went to Lathe.

Naturally, they went to Lathe—it was the only town north of Oslop, and the only place they could sail without running into heaps of the diarn's constables. The journey took two days, mostly because the river was already icy this far north and avoiding it took both their navigator's skill and a touch of magic.

As the crisp air shifted into outright snow, Kianthe began to realize that normal life on a pirate ship was . . . pretty relaxing, actually. She got to know the crew, who—despite the chaos of the blockade battle—was already loyal and excited for adventure.

The older woman called Squirrel approached Reyna late that night and they murmured to each other for a while. By the end, Squirrel and Reyna were exchanging pastry recipes and discussing the best length of time to brew the diarn's private stash of tea. Squirrel even summoned up a true Queendom accent and gave Reyna tips for hiding her own when needed.

Kianthe watched it all from behind piles of parchment. After all, she'd promised to write Reyna a book and, Stone be damned, she'd deliver.

Especially after Reyna slyly drawled, "Did you give up on your dreams of authorship so soon?"

"I'm getting around to it," Kianthe had replied, crossing her arms.

"Hmm. I was under the impression that you needed to put pen to parchment to accomplish that goal. Then again, you're the expert on tomes—perhaps I'm mistaken." And she offered a winning smile before descending into the galley with Squirrel.

And so Kianthe buried herself in parchment, slowly realizing that writing a book was harder than *talking* about writing one. She spent two days struggling to pen her ideas while Reyna commanded the ship and Serina kept an eye on Bobbie—until finally the ex-constable awoke.

Instead of waiting in bed like a normal injured person, Bobbie staggered onto the deck and caught everyone's attention. Tough to miss her, considering her skin held an ashen hue and blood was already dotting her newly changed bandages.

"Ah, Captain?" Kianthe called, jerking a thumb at the doorway to the captain's quarters, where Bobbie had paused to grab the doorframe. It was very possible she'd topple over if she let go. "Your charge is up. Against carpenter recommendation, I might add."

Serina had created a makeshift cane to use while her leg healed, but she was doing better now, chatting with Rankor as he guided the *Knot for Sail* through mounds of ice. At Kianthe's words, though, she craned her neck over the railing, then groaned audibly. "Bobbie! What in the hells are you doing?"

"Just—making sure it wasn't a dream," Bobbie muttered, staring hard at the ship, the crew, Kianthe, and finally Serina. Her corkscrew curls were flattened on one side from where she'd been sleeping, and her expression was pinched.

Definitely shouldn't be up.

Kianthe stacked the sheets of parchment and set them under her inkwell, dispensing strict instructions that the wind not disrupt the pages while she was gone. She'd been writing on the deck, lying on her stomach like a kid drawing with charcoal, and it took a few moments to climb to her feet.

Reyna, who'd been in the crow's nest with Joe, dropped onto the deck. She stretched, pulling her arms above her head. "Done writing for the day?"

There was judgment in her tone. It was mild, amused, but definitely there.

"I'm sourcing content." Kianthe jerked a thumb at Serina, who'd just staggered down the staircase to cuff Bobbie on the head. "You know it's prime stuff when these two get together."

Reyna's lips quirked.

"I'll get back to it!"

"I know you will, love. Because I expect three pages by tonight or you're sleeping on the floor." Kianthe gasped indignantly, but Reyna was already stepping to help Bobbie back into bed. She slipped under the ex-constable's arm, taking most of her weight. "And you. Back to bed."

Bobbie didn't complain as they hobbled back into the captain's quarters. She dropped heavily on the mattress, her fingers feathering over the tight bandages on her shoulder. "What happened?"

"You were stabbed," Kianthe offered helpfully. She'd been drinking tea while she wrote, and cradled the cooling mug against her chest. Behind her, Rankor and Joe were squinting curiously at Bobbie, so she closed the door.

Nosy crew.

Serina loomed over her, glowering as she leaned on her cane. "*Stabbed,* Bobbie. Which means when I tell you the options are bed rest or bed rest, you'll obey your captain's orders." She puffed indignantly.

Bobbie flinched. "You're not my captain. I'm not supposed to *be* here. I have to . . ." She trailed off, clenching her eyes shut. "Stars, I don't—I really did lose my job, didn't I?" Now she looked at Kianthe desperately, as if the mage might wave it all away.

Kianthe cleared her throat. "Ah, yes. Yes, you did. But if it makes you feel better, Arlon is proving himself to be absolutely insane, so he's probably not long for *his* job, either." That was supposition at best, but if Kianthe trusted anyone to find a loophole and expel a diarn from his lands, it was Feo. And by her calculation, Visk would be bringing Tawney's diarn soon.

Bobbie's confusion melted Serina's icy irritation. The pirate captain sighed, dropping onto her cot. A flash of pain crossed her features, but it smoothed quickly as the weight was taken off her leg. "You're better off not working for him anyway."

That didn't seem to help.

"But what am I going to do, Serrie?" The words were wrenched from Bobbie's soul.

Reyna and Kianthe exchanged sympathetic glances. Their bookshop had been threatened last summer, and Kianthe knew the anxiety she faced trying to keep it—and Reyna—safe. And in the end, it was out of her hands anyway.

Serina, meanwhile, had softened further at the nickname. She swallowed hard, reaching for Bobbie's hand. "We'll be in Lathe soon. We couldn't go south, and I figured—well, at least you've got family there. You can take some time to heal, and figure out next steps." A smile, almost warm now. "It'll be okay."

"Family." Bobbie's voice was faint, and her free hand once again ghosted up to the bandage on her shoulder. The wound was deep enough to leave a wicked scar once it healed. She grimaced. "Y-Yeah. Because you're a pirate now, and I'm—" She cut off with a choking sound, and hunched into herself. "I'll go home."

Yikes.

Reyna pinched her brow, and Kianthe kept silent only by taking another sip of tea. This blend was one from Reyna's personal stash: rose and lavender. Soothing. Much nicer than the shipwreck happening across the room.

Serina hesitated. "You were hurt really badly, Bobbie."

"I'm—"

"Don't say you're fine. You weren't *breathing*." Serina pulled away, pushed to her feet, then winced in pain and slumped back onto the cot. She stared at the wooden ceiling. "You weren't breathing. You saved my life, and you almost died right in front of me and it's all because of my choices."

Her voice broke on the last word, and her eyes dropped to the bandages wrapping Bobbie's shoulder. "I think it's better if you stay in Lathe."

Maybe it was Kianthe reading into things, but Serina didn't sound very convinced.

On the bed, Bobbie looked dazed, either from fever or this conversation. Regardless, her filter was gone, because she replied: "Better for me, or better for you?"

Serina stiffened at the accusation in her tone. "You. Arlon crossed a line, and he won't stop at that fight. This is only going to get more dangerous. Are you planning to throw yourself in front of every sword that comes my way?"

"Maybe," Bobbie said stubbornly. Her eyes narrowed, but she was swaying a bit now. She probably should lie back down—a woman so perpetually sleep-deprived, now facing the lingering effects of drowning, blood loss, and a lightning strike. Kianthe almost stepped forward to intervene, but Reyna caught her arm.

A wry smile had settled on Reyna's face. She was enjoying this.

Kianthe almost buried her face in her hands in exasperation.

"Maybe," Serina repeated, deadpan. "And the next time it happens, when the Arcandor isn't around to *literally* send a bolt of lightning into your heart—what then? I get to watch you die?"

"Better than me watching you die," Bobbie retorted. "Better than some other constable towing you back to Diarn Arlon, watching you earn a life sentence because you didn't understand what you were doing."

That went south.

Reyna winced. "Perhaps we should let Bobbie rest—"

Kianthe did roll her eyes, now. "Too late for that, Rain."

"I don't *understand* what I'm doing?" Serina laughed, and then laughed again. The derision in her voice was as palpable as a hammer to the face. "Do you think I'm an idiot? You really think I'm just messing around? Playing pirate, like when we were kids?"

Bobbie set her jaw, but didn't respond.

"Arlon is hurting people. I'm taking a stand. Maybe it's not the best method, but everyone here joined my crew because his oppression is wrong. If you can't understand that, maybe you *do* belong in Lathe." Serina scoffed, pushed off the cot, and hobbled out of the room.

Silence lingered when she left. Bobbie stared after her, then slumped against the plush pillows of the bed.

"Fuck," she muttered.

Kianthe exchanged a quick glance with Reyna, then mouthed, *I'll handle this.* Reyna nodded silently, took Kianthe's empty mug of tea, and stepped after Serina. Alone again, Kianthe perched in the space the pirate captain had vacated, gently taking Bobbie's wrist to check her pulse. Just like Matild had taught her, she counted beats, but Bobbie physically was doing much better than expected.

Mentally, well . . . that was another story.

"I messed up," the ex-constable mumbled. "Didn't I?"

Kianthe dropped her wrist, leaned back with a sigh. "I won't lie to you; that wasn't ideal."

"I didn't think—" Bobbie cut herself off with a self-deprecating laugh. "I didn't think."

"Listen. When Reyna and I first started dating, we had these issues too. Conversations that seemed to veer into dangerous territory, hurt feelings after saying something we didn't mean, misunderstandings about our jobs and responsibilities. There was a huge culture difference, and overcoming that was tricky."

Bobbie stared glumly at her hands. "You don't seem to have those problems now."

"I mean, we worked on it. We both wanted to see what we could become together, so we created conversational cues to avoid those pitfalls. It's not that we don't have hard discussions anymore; those don't go away." Kianthe tilted her head, a ghost of a smile on her lips. "But if you start a conversation with the honest desire to understand . . . well, things go differently."

"I have a hard time understanding this." Bobbie gestured at the ship. "Arlon isn't perfect—maybe he's even the villain here—but there are other ways to take a stand. Legal ways."

"I mean, you're living proof that most legal options are slow, if they work at all. Serina did what she felt was best, it seems."

Bobbie bristled, pushing off the bed again. She wobbled as she stood, but kept her balance against the gentle sway of the ship. "Ah, yes. Because her only options were to start a farm . . . or be a pirate. Naturally."

Kianthe shrugged. "I'm not in the business of telling people how to live their lives. But if you approach her implying that she's wrong, you won't get very far."

Silence.

The ex-constable winced in pain and pressed a hand against her chest. "Did you really shoot lightning into my chest?"

"Just a bit, yeah. You should probably sit back down."

Instead, Bobbie staggered to the wooden table near the door, to the teakettle perched on it. "Is there water in this? I'd love a cup of tea before a few more hours of sleep."

"Ah, growth." Kianthe lit her index finger on fire, holding it under the kettle's metal framing to heat the water inside. As they waited, Bobbie dropped heavily into the wooden chair by the table. Kianthe bolstered her courage, then asked: "Do you think pirating makes Serina a bad person?"

"I think Serina is one of the kindest, most encouraging people I've ever met." The answer was immediate and honest. Bobbie buried her head in her hands. "This was a lot easier when we were kids."

"Kids rarely have to get involved in world politics." Kianthe shrugged, pouring the boiling water into a ceramic mug. Reyna had stacked a couple bags of Arlon's precious tea on the desk, and Kianthe wrinkled her nose as his alchemical seal pulsed at her proximity.

One day soon, she'd have to tackle it. For now, she just hoped Serina wouldn't get curious.

Risky—but the pirate was preoccupied right now, at least.

Kianthe dropped the tea bag in her mug and pushed it toward the ex-constable, then leaned against the table. "Regardless, you have a choice. It's easy to stay on the proud path, the 'righteous' one—but you'll lose a lot of friends that way. Time to identify what's important, then find a way to keep it."

Bobbie stared glumly at her tea. "You lost your hat again."

"That happens when you're diving into the river to haul out a corpse."

"Oh. I'll make you another one."

Kianthe chuckled. "I'm fairly sure Reyna has me covered on that front. We'll just pick our favorite people in Tawney, and they'll get the remaining souvenirs. Your yarn is with your horse anyway, isn't it?"

"Yeah. Wish I had some now." Bobbie glanced at her things piled on the table, the waterlogged belt, the custom crochet needles in their drying leather sheath.

"You could try reading. That's my stress relief." Kianthe pushed off the table, clapped the ex-constable's good shoulder. "Get some rest. We'll be arriving in Lathe later tonight." And she strolled into the sunshine, leaving Bobbie to contemplate her future.

23

Reyna

Night settled and Reyna assumed that meant a small town like Lathe would be empty, quiet. But they arrived to a welcome brigade: four constables flanking a stern-looking woman in a sheriff's uniform. They'd barely docked—it was a lot smoother with Pil managing the sails and Rankor at the helm—when the sheriff strolled up the narrow plank like she owned the ship.

Everyone stiffened as the constables followed, but based on their silence and nonaggressive stances, they were clearly deferring to the sheriff. Even though they must work for Diarn Arlon, it was obvious who they obeyed here.

"Serina," the sheriff said, her tone a cross between fond and exasperated. "How did I know you'd be stashing this monstrosity in my harbor?"

The constables spread out behind her. Eyeing them, Reyna rested a hand on her sword. One of them noticed and offered an amused grin. A peace offering.

Huh. Reyna's hand fell away from her pommel, and she surveyed the sheriff instead.

The older woman was tall, imposing, with tight cornrows and umber skin brushed with bronzing powder. Her eyes were deep green, a shade much darker than Bobbie's, but the family resemblance was obvious. Her uniform, like her daughter's, was impeccable, tailored to perfection with a shiny golden badge on her chest. When she moved, it was with the powerful grace of an eagle in the skies.

Reyna liked her immediately.

Serina forced a laugh, her voice cracking. "W-What are you talking about, Viviana? This is my new ship. Straight from my father in Jallin."

"Don't pull that shit with me, kid. We *all* got a notice about the theft." Sheriff Viviana jerked a thumb at the constables behind her. "Derik delivered it personally, then stuck around because we have such good booze . . . and even better company."

The one named Derik chuckled, and beside him a second constable flushed red. He purposefully separated from Derik, as if distance would hide the implication.

Kianthe snorted.

Reyna perked up. "You have wine?"

Sheriff Viviana quirked an eyebrow. "Oh, you're Queendom."

"Depends on the day," Reyna replied neutrally. She'd been lulled into a false sense of security now that she and Squirrel had made amends, but apparently her heritage was still the most interesting quality about her. A deep part of her soul yearned for Tawney, for people so used to blending cultures that no one cared anymore.

Viviana smirked, resting a hand on her own sword. The leather bindings were worn with use, but the blade was sharpened and polished to a shine. "Nothing nefarious intended. Just wondering if you're any good with that blade. Bandits love camping in the wilderness north of here; I'll happily put you to work."

"Please don't tempt her." Kianthe tossed an arm over Reyna's shoulders.

She *was* tempted, actually. Reyna had been handing out fake "assignments" to the bandits who visited Tawney for three seasons. She'd hidden behind a fictional boss, a leader so ruthless no one dared challenge the very idea of him.

Still, if the bandits of the Realm did answer to a leader, he'd be here in the untamed wilderness of northern Shepara.

A part of her was dying to check.

Of course, Sheriff Viviana's eyes slid to Kianthe, and her smile grew. "You must be the Arcandor. I heard rumors that you were drifting along our shore. Pray tell, what brings someone of your stature to the humble Nacean?"

"Humble." Kianthe snorted. "Don't let the river hear you say that."

"Not to interrupt, but we run a risk docking here." Serina braced herself against her makeshift cane, glowering at the constables behind the sheriff. It was obvious what she was implying.

Derik's shoulders drooped.

Viviana laughed. "Arlon may have fooled himself into thinking that coin is what it takes to buy loyalty, but these kids know better. We're a family here. No one's spilling your location on my watch, Serina."

"Good. Because your daughter is sleeping in my room, and she's going to want to see you."

At that news, Viviana's eyes widened. "Barylea is here? After all those years she swore to 'leave, and never come back.' Who'd have thought?" Sarcasm tipped her tongue, and she strode past Serina toward the cabin.

Serina ducked in behind her, and they closed the door for a little reunion. It left the constables staring down the pirate crew, a tense standoff. Reyna and Kianthe stood in the center of it, and Kianthe rolled her shoulders.

"So . . . you said there was wine. My fiancée would love a glass or six."

"Key!"

"I missed drunk Reyna the first time. I'm not missing it again," Kianthe replied, a wicked gleam in her eyes.

Reyna snorted.

The constables started laughing, and Derik's partner stepped forward. "The sheriff already arranged for rooms at the local inn. Got a bar there, too, if you'd like to come along."

Serina's crew hesitated. Farley crossed her burly arms, stepping in front of her husband almost protectively. "How do we know you won't shank us in the back or poison our drink? Constables haven't exactly been kind to us lately."

"Viviana's treated us better than Arlon ever has." Derik shrugged. "And frankly, Lathe has bigger issues than a pirate crew plaguing its docks. If we're filing a report, it'll be about the bandit activity, not you lot."

"Join us if you'd like," another constable said amicably. Chatting amongst themselves, the constables filed down the plank, heading confidently toward a little building lit with the cozy glow of lanterns.

Reyna shrugged, said, "Well, that's good enough for me," and followed.

Soon, everyone was relaxed. The bar was brimming with townsfolk who were excited to see Serina again, which meant their alcohol flowed freely. They also seemed to have a ridiculous amount of food—far more than Reyna had seen in other towns or villages.

In fact, Lathe didn't seem to be suffering from Arlon's taxation at all.

When Reyna brought this up, Kianthe shrugged. "I mean, Bobbie's a force. It wouldn't surprise me if her mother was equally impressive. I think there's more to Viviana's operation than we thought."

"Hmm," Reyna said, taking a sip of chilled wine. Across the tavern, a few townsfolk had tugged out instruments, and a lively jig had the crowd cheering. Reyna gestured at the festivities. "Should we dance?"

But she was still savoring her wine, a crisp reminder of her time in Koll. They were tucked in the back corner, pressed against the wall and each other, cozy as could be. Kianthe glanced at the wineglass, assessed her half-hearted tone, and smirked. "Maybe we just spectate."

"Killjoy."

"Do you *want* to dance?"

"Well, you're hardly graceful enough for it. But that's half the fun."

Kianthe gasped, mock-offended. "I'm not graceful? Didn't you see me diving into that river? Haven't you seen me leaping off Visk and soaring on the wind?"

Now Reyna was having fun. A sly smile tilted her lips as she took another sip of her wine. "Sounds like the elements are graceful. All I've seen is your struggle to ride Lilac, messy footwork when you steal my sword, and—well, we've barely danced, but a crowded tavern wouldn't be as easy as swaying in our bookstore late at night."

A competitive gleam overtook Kianthe's eyes. She stood with a flourish, sweeping her cloak behind her, then bowed over her outstretched hand.

A challenge.

Gods, it was too easy.

Heart fluttering, Reyna drained her wine and took her fiancée's hand. They wove through the crowd to the space cleared for dancing. Rankor and Farley were locked shoulder to shoulder doing some sort of odd jig, which Reyna vaguely recognized as a Leonolan step dance. Everyone was clapping along—no one noticed the bookseller and tea maker taking position in the back.

The music was fast, and Kianthe threaded her arms around Reyna's waist. "You ready?"

"Ready to have my toes stepped on, perhaps." Reyna draped her arms over the mage's shoulders.

Kianthe gasped in offense, and they were off.

It wasn't pretty, but just by virtue of leaping and twirling, excitement bubbled in Reyna's chest. The music swelled across the room and once people realized they'd joined in, the crowd pushed back to give them space. And to her credit, Kianthe wasn't bad—she led Reyna through a simple set that had the bystanders cheering in delight.

"Pretty impressive, huh?" Kianthe gasped after the song ended.

Reyna smirked, shifted her stance so she was leading. She took Kianthe's hands, stepped back a bit, and when the next song struck on the fiddle, Reyna didn't move.

Kianthe paused, panting for breath, eyes widening as the song slipped past and time seemed to still. On the eighth beat, Reyna raised her hand, pulling Kianthe's in a matching pose, and then twisted around her, fingers trailing along her shoulders, twirling her effortlessly. The music threaded through her veins, ignited her brain—after all, dancing was just like sword fighting at its base level.

And just like on the battlefield, Reyna had no trouble leading her partner.

Kianthe wanted to write, but *this* was storytelling. In Reyna's mind, the world faded to the two of them, and it became a representation of their life to this point. It started out dangerous, jerky movements and never-ending speed. Life in the Grand Palace, life on the move. Then she pulled Kianthe close, so their noses were almost touching, so their breaths intermingled—the moment of truth.

I like books. You like tea.

Care to open a shop and forget the world exists?

Reyna paused, pressing a gentle kiss to Kianthe's lips, smiling against her startled expression. When she pulled back, dipped Kianthe to the ground, it was a measured motion. Slower. Contemplative. The tavern had quieted, the fiddler slowing the melody in response.

Their journey to Tawney. Perusing the barn, gaining ownership, refurbishing it into their dream shop. The entire last year settled in her mind, and she wove Kianthe through the tavern like it was the cozy barn of New Leaf Tomes and Tea.

Because that's what Kianthe had forgotten. Dancing wasn't just swaying to music, and fighting wasn't just waving a sword.

They were tributes to everything that ever was, ever could be, and would never be again.

When the song ended, Reyna twirled Kianthe one last time, then pulled her close. "Still think you're graceful, dearest?" The words were lost in thunderous applause.

The mage looked dazed, blinking as reality set back in. "Shit, Rain. We should dance more often. You can lead."

Victory. Reyna laughed in delight and kissed her again. The dance floor was filling with drunken patrons, so they carefully slipped to the edges. Across the tavern, Viviana and Serina had joined the party—Serina was nursing a huge tankard of beer, chatting with Darlene and Joe.

Sheriff Viviana was staring right at them.

Reyna tapped Kianthe's shoulder, gesturing at the older woman. "I have a feeling we're being summoned."

Kianthe groaned. "I hate being summoned."

Viviana held open the door, and they ducked through it. Outside, it was frigid cold and snowing gently. Kianthe immediately ignited an ever-flame to clutch against her chest; she hadn't had a chance to raid their crochet gifts, which meant she didn't have a scarf, mittens, or her precious hat.

Reyna was not upset she'd lost that orange monstrosity.

When Viviana quirked an eyebrow, the mage huffed. "Look, just because we live in cold weather doesn't mean I like it."

The town was barren, and the snow muted all noise. While Tawney boasted more heavy stone accents—a nod to the quarries that littered the Queendom—as well as the type of wooden structures favored in Shepara, Lathe seemed more focused on utilizing the heavy pine lumber that surrounded it. Buildings had dramatically sloped roofs, most likely for easy snow removal, and rounded doors. To their left in the harbor, the *Knot for Sail* lurked like a dark shadow, and glowing lamps illuminated the street.

Conversation continued inside the tavern, but it felt like a world away.

"I spoke with Serina. Considering my daughter's condition and the fight that the crew endured, I convinced her to stay for a week and rest." Viviana's voice was low and authoritative, and she put a hand on her hip, holding Kianthe's gaze. "I heard what you did for Barylea. Fishing her out of the river, restarting her heart." Her tone quieted. "Thank you, Arcandor."

Kianthe shifted uncomfortably. "I mean, it'd have been more helpful if I kept her from falling overboard in the first place." A self-deprecating laugh accompanied the words.

Reyna drew a measured breath. "Key. For the last time, you saved her. That's the only detail that matters."

Viviana nodded assertively.

The mage sighed, but didn't argue.

"It's a good idea for Bobbie to rest for now." Reyna crossed her arms, hugging herself against the bitter wind—although it did seem like the breeze was purposely avoiding them. Elemental mages. Handy to have around. "But I'm wondering if it's safe to stay put for an entire week. The only way we've avoided Diarn Arlon lately is through constant movement."

His constables—the ones not loyal to Viviana, anyway—would be patrolling the river, she had no doubt.

Viviana smirked. "Luckily, you're in my town now. There's an outcropping farther upriver where we can stash the brigantine. Arcandor, with your magic, it shouldn't take much effort to hide." She waited for Kianthe to give an affirming nod before continuing. "We have plenty of room here for the crew, and the best doctor on the Nacean, thanks to the bandits here. Barylea will be back on her feet in no time."

Well, that certainly sounded safer than traipsing up and down the river, especially with Diarn Arlon out for blood.

Kianthe frowned. "Bobbie didn't seem excited to be here. Are you two on bad terms?"

It was bold, but Viviana clearly owed Kianthe. She glanced around the town square, but no one was nearby to overhear. "No. Well . . . I'd hope not. My daughter takes things at face value. She saw that Lathe was doing well, and assumed it applied to the rest of Arlon's land. What she didn't see was everything *I've* done to keep my town safe. Bribes. Negotiations. And sometimes staging attacks to physically force out the constables who can't be bought." Viviana set her jaw. "Arlon thinks we're a tiny town, and we give him grain accordingly. He doesn't know we have fields west of here, well hidden from his sight."

"Clever," Kianthe said, crossing her arms. "Trust me, Arlon won't be a problem for much longer."

Viviana snorted. "I'll believe that when I see it." She heaved a sigh, running a hand over her cornrows. "Bobbie has pure intentions, and she was *so* convinced becoming a constable would be good for Lathe. Good for me. I didn't . . . have the courage to tell her the truth."

Regret filtered into her tone.

"She's been trying hard to make you proud," Kianthe said.

"I know. And she has. But the best news I've heard all week is that she was fired." Viviana wasn't joking.

Reyna sighed. This brought up another concern, one far removed from a mother's relationship with her daughter. She nudged Kianthe. "If the crew is staying here, perhaps we should go speak with Diarn Arlon." Reyna glanced at Kianthe.

The mage's expression soured. "Oh, I have words for him. But it'd be difficult to get to his estate without Visk or your horse. Plus, I'd rather wait until Feo arrives; they're going to be our winning card here."

"Does Feo know that?" Reyna drawled.

"I left a note."

"A descriptive note?"

Kianthe pursed her lips. "It told them to come quick, and that it was important."

Reyna rolled her eyes. "So, they're just going to be pestered by a mythical creature until they agree to be carried halfway across the Realm to solve a political battle worthy of history books?"

Kianthe rubbed the back of her neck. "Yes . . . ? I mean, Visk won't force them onto his back, but . . . I doubt Feo will refuse."

Reyna tilted her head skyward, wondering if the Gods could give her comfort. "Glad we're on the same page."

Muffled through the tavern door, the fiddler switched to a new song, and the patrons began clapping in time with the music. Viviana was watching this entire back-and-forth with an amused smile, and now she smoothly interjected: "Well, if you're staying in town, I wasn't joking about the bandit intervention. I'm certain we can keep you two busy."

"We're technically on our own quest—" Kianthe said.

Reyna silenced her with a hand. "I meant to ask about that, Viviana. You've been sheriff for a while, right? Decades, even?"

"Longer than you two have been alive, that's for damn sure." Viviana offered a wry smile. "Why? Here to remind me how old I am?"

Reyna chuckled, then plowed ahead: "Here to ask about a shipment. It was delivered somewhere along the Nacean River in the

741st year of the Realm. We believe it was labeled as a candle shipment, but what was inside was . . . not candles. There might have been alchemical seals on the crate."

It was vague, an absolute longshot, but Reyna had a hunch.

And it paid off.

Viviana stiffened, hazel eyes widening. But just as quickly, she smoothed her expression, forcing a casual smile. "That was a long time ago. I'd have to explore my shipping statements; I wasn't as diligent about records when I started this job."

Reyna kept her expression clean, mind racing. "I see. There's no rush; we'll be here all week. In fact, we should probably check on Bobbie before we wind down for the night. Most of the crew is enjoying themselves, but I worry about her alone on that ship."

Viviana let them pass. "I'll search my records and see what I can find. Hopefully we can solve this mystery."

"Indeed."

Kianthe followed Reyna toward the ship, but neither spoke until they were a fair distance from the sheriff and tavern. As they stepped onto the dock, Kianthe rolled her shoulders, clutching the ever-flame against her chest. Her face was cast in harsh shadows.

"Well, that was suspicious as hells."

"We know bandits stole the dragon eggs. We know they headed west on orders from a mysterious benefactor." Reyna paused at the ramp leading up to the ship, tossing her hair over her shoulder. "We know the shipment ended somewhere near Arlon's estate, and we know Lathe has had a long-standing issue with bandits up north."

"Viviana knows about those eggs."

"That's my theory. But to verify it, I think we're going to need Bobbie's help."

And Reyna walked up the plank onto the deck.

24

Kianthe

Getting Bobbie awake and alert enough for a conversation took the better part of the following morning. The crew relocated to rooms at Lathe's inn, sleeping off their hangovers—except Darlene and Joe, of course, who spent their time adjusting sails for the short trip to Viviana's hidden cove and complaining that they were too young to drink.

"It's just ridiculous," Darlene muttered at one point. "Like I've never snuck a sip of Dad's wine."

"Not going to work, Darlene." Serina, as the ship's captain, had strolled on deck bright and early—but it was obvious even she'd enjoyed the evening a bit too much. She spoke quietly, hid her eyes under the tricorne hat, and seemed grateful that it was a perpetually gloomy day.

The young girl heaved a sigh. From the rigging, Joe rolled their eyes. "I don't know why you'd want to drink. Just makes you stupid."

"It looks fun!"

Serina offered an exasperated glance to Reyna, who was helping tie off the lines. Reyna ducked her head to hide a laugh, yanking a knot tight.

Kianthe, meanwhile, slipped into the captain's quarters. Bobbie was lying in bed, awake. She glanced up when Kianthe closed the door behind her, then breathed a sigh—of relief, or disappointment? Tough to say.

"Serina's still not talking to me, huh?" Her neutral tone felt forced.

Stone bless that Kianthe and Reyna were past this "does she, doesn't she" point in their relationship. Kianthe flopped onto the bed's edge, rolling her eyes. "You two are exhausting to watch. You know that, right?"

"What's that supposed to mean?" Bobbie sounded more alert than on previous days, but even sitting upright was clearly still painful. It was probably good they were in Lathe now, near an actual, trained doctor. He'd already paid a visit, Kianthe knew.

The mage waved a hand. "If you want to talk to Serina, she's literally right outside."

"It's . . . um. It's hard to stand."

"Sure, that's the reason." Kianthe snorted. "Unfortunately, we're relocating the *Knot for Sail* and staying in Lathe for a short while, so you'll see her anyway. Someone has to help you hobble to the inn."

Bobbie hesitated, playing with a loose string on the blankets.

Kianthe frowned. "I figured you'd be happy she isn't dropping you off and sailing away. Are you that afraid to talk to her?"

The ex-constable pinched her brow. "No. But—" A pause, a frustrated sigh. "I'm not sure what to say. It seems obvious that she doesn't want me to tag along. And I'm . . . not going to be great company on a pirate ship."

"I think you're looking at this the wrong way." Kianthe pushed to her feet, gesturing at the door. "You're still viewing Serina as a criminal—and she might be, by Arlon's standards. But to everyone else on this river, she's the only one who cared enough to ensure they're fed all winter."

Bobbie winced. "I mean, the diarn does distribute food—"

"People who aren't facing starvation wouldn't accept stolen food, Bobbie. Not considering the consequences if they got caught."

The woman fell silent.

It made sense, in a twisted kind of way. If Bobbie acknowledged what was staring her in the face, she'd be admitting her entire career was a waste of time. A fool's errand. She'd be admitting that she *could* have run away with Serina and lived happily, if only she'd been brave enough to make a different choice when she approached Serina's farm that day.

Instead, she followed procedure, and it shattered Serina's life again. And now Bobbie was here trying to pick up the pieces . . . even as they sliced her hands to shit.

See? That was poetic. Kianthe needed to start writing again.

The mage massaged her neck. "If you want to salvage this relationship, you need to reframe what you're seeing. Serina isn't the villain here. Serina didn't fire you, and she didn't order the blockade battle. From everything I'm seeing, these pirates are victims of a powerful enemy, and it's pretty damn brave that she's standing up to him."

"That's true," Bobbie admitted.

"Or, you can be stubborn and lose the person you nearly died for." Kianthe's tone was deadpan. "Your choice."

Bobbie grimaced. "Okay, okay. I get it. Did you come here to scold me, or did you need something?"

Kianthe strolled to the windows, squinting at the town. "Oh, we definitely need something."

"Great."

It didn't sound great.

Kianthe chuckled, stretching her arms above her head. "I have no faith in Arlon following through on our deal of pirate for paperwork. Luckily, we're fairly certain your mom knows something about the shipment we're looking for."

"She knows everything about anything that passes through Lathe," Bobbie admitted. Then her brow furrowed. "Why won't she tell you?"

Kianthe snapped her fingers. "That's for you to find out. Be a dear and ask, won't you? And think about what I said." With a broad smile, she strolled out of the room.

❦

They relocated the ship, then strolled through the snow back to town. It took the better part of the day; Serina spent most of it in silence. That wasn't surprising—before they left, she'd helped Bobbie into one of the inn's rooms and didn't resurface for a long while. Clearly, they'd had a discussion, although it was anyone's guess how that turned out.

On the walk back, Darlene and Joe started a snowball fight, and it took so long to kick their asses that darkness had fallen by the time they entered Lathe again.

"Never challenge an elemental mage to a snowball fight," Kianthe told them smugly.

"Pretty sure that's cheating," Darlene grumbled, rubbing a spot on her arm where Kianthe had landed a particularly good hit. Joe heaved a sigh and trudged into the inn. Their sister followed.

Serina shoved Kianthe's arm. "Stop beating up my crew."

Kianthe gasped. "They started it!"

"They're *kids*." The pirate captain rolled her eyes and followed them inside.

"Next time, no magic allowed," Reyna replied, lips tilting upward. It was ironic, since in the moment, she hadn't said anything of the sort—her competitive spirit was intense enough to take any advantage she could find. Especially three against two.

Kianthe opened her mouth to say that, but Viviana interrupted them. She ducked out of a building across the street, one adorned with a hanging wooden sign that read: SHERIFF. "You two. Care to chat?"

It sounded like a death march—the kind Kianthe had experienced walking to Master Polana's office for a "discussion" about her classroom performance. Considering she'd left the Magicary years ago, the mage wasn't enthused. She crossed her arms. "Why? Are we in trouble?"

Reyna rolled her eyes. "Darling, please." She strolled for the building.

So much for a hot meal after a long day.

The sheriff's office was surprisingly pleasant. Viviana had adorned the building with cozy armchairs, three desks for her staff, and a refreshment bar with a kettle and jars of tea leaves. A lively hearth kept the place warm, and a single cell occupied the corner, empty.

She was missing books, but to each their own.

Reyna eyed the tea. "May we? We're quite chilled." It was too late for permission, however; she was already perusing the selection with affirming hums. One glance at Kianthe had the mage flicking a tiny flame into the stove under the kettle.

Viviana waved a hand belatedly, then took a seat at the desk nearest the door. It was stacked with meticulously organized folders, one of which she plucked off the top. "Barylea had glowing things to say about you, Arcandor. Also, she apparently crochets now. I'm pleased she picked up a hobby."

"She's great at it," Kianthe said, almost defensively.

"She certainly has skill to crochet something like that." Viviana gestured at one of the shelves above her desk, where a tiny crocheted redspar perched. It had more detail than the bee or the whale, but it was still a bit misshapen. And yet, it was on full display, and Viviana's chest puffed with pride. "Redspars are my favorite. We also talked at length about Lathe's . . . ah, unique position in Arlon's lands." Now Viviana cleared her throat. "It helped, and I should have had that discussion much sooner. As a thank-you, your shipment, as requested."

She handed over the file.

Well, this was a lot better than Polana's office. Kianthe dropped into the chair opposite Viviana's desk, cautiously tugging the folder closer. Record reading was more of Reyna's domain, but her fiancée was pleasantly distracted steeping their tea and Kianthe knew better than to interrupt.

"If this investigation weren't a matter of life and death, trust me, Sheriff—we wouldn't be asking for it." Kianthe opened the folder, half expecting it to be empty, some kind of cruel joke. They'd been hunting for this shipment for two seasons now, and it felt odd to be so close to new information.

But inside was a list of all records of the 741st year, and she'd even kindly marked the shipment in question. It was delivered in the fall season, right on schedule based on previous information. And the deliverer . . .

"The Golden Eagles?"

"Bandits. Up here, they're organized enough to call themselves a 'guild,' which is ridiculous." Viviana pinched the bridge of her nose. "But they've been around as long as I have, and back then, they weren't so bitterly opposed to honest, paying work."

Pouring water from the steaming kettle, Reyna said, "They stole what was inside that shipment. You know that, right?"

The sheriff set her jaw, pushing away from her desk to lock the front door. The heavy *click* of iron echoed in the small space, rather ominous. Then Viviana leaned against the wooden door, expression deadly serious.

"After speaking with my daughter, I trust you both. We have good folk here in Lathe, loyal to this town and its well-being, much like you have in Tawney. But I didn't keep my title—or my life—by being stupid. So, when I say this doesn't leave my office . . . I mean it."

Dramatic.

Reyna paused while the tea steeped, her hand drifting to the pommel of her sword. "I'm surprised a shipment from so long ago would put you at such risk." Now she frowned. "Unless the person responsible for ordering that theft is still in power."

Viviana sighed. "Indeed. And considering what was inside that shipment, you understand my caution."

"You've seen the dragon eggs," Kianthe said, wonder tinging her voice. Her eyes dropped to the shipment paperwork in her hands, and a thrill raced up her spine. "They *were* here."

"They were here," the sheriff confirmed. "I shouldn't have peeked inside; it was above my pay grade. But a diarn doesn't contract bandits to steal for him unless it's something important . . . and possibly illegal."

Reyna quirked an eyebrow, carefully removing the linen tea bags from their mugs. "Then Arlon *was* responsible for ordering the eggs stolen."

Viviana raised her hands. "Arlon accepted the shipment. I couldn't tell you who ordered the job."

"The crate would have been sealed with alchemy; how did you get it open?" Kianthe accepted the mug from her fiancée and handed off the folder in response. Reyna put her own mug on the desk and began skimming the folder with sharp eyes.

Leaving the locked door, Viviana instead leaned against one of the armchairs. Behind her, the hearth flickered merrily. "The bandits had an alchemical mage working with them—or maybe he wasn't a mage, but he had alchemy training. Either way, he opened the crate to show me that the contents were all accounted for."

Kianthe's brow furrowed. The idea that any Magicary mage would wind up in bandit territory was concerning, let alone one practicing alchemy. Then again, that brand of magic was somewhat bloody, based on sacrifice for success. Maybe it wasn't so surprising.

"Inside were three eggs." Viviana winced. "The mage said they didn't have magic, that they'd never hatch, but—I can't quite explain it. I felt *something* coming from those poor things."

"Dragon magic is more powerful than anything we humans can harness," Kianthe said, wincing. Only the Arcandor could stand adjacent to it, and she'd been sick for a week when it was forced on her. Sometimes, even the memory of it turned her stomach.

Reyna patted her leg sympathetically, but never took her eyes off the shipping records.

Viviana set her jaw. "Well, those things weren't dormant. I don't know what Arlon planned for them, but—Arcandor, I just couldn't hand them over like that."

"What did you do?" Kianthe asked, eyes widening.

"I took one." The sheriff of Lathe spoke confidently, but a challenge lingered in her words. "Arlon expected multiple eggs, so I couldn't take more. I tricked the bandits into leaving without their mage resealing the crate . . . and I took the egg that had the most energy back to dragon country."

Kianthe's jaw dropped. "What, *all* the way back?"

"There's a piece of the Northern Bay where Shepara nearly touches dragon country. The round trip took a while, but I rode there and left it on the shoreline. Close enough that a dragon could have flown over and retrieved it."

"Did they?" Reyna finally lifted her gaze to the sheriff. Kianthe hadn't realized she was paying such close attention to the conversation.

Viviana sighed. "I haven't had the time to go back and check, and to be frank, it dropped farther down my priority list when I had children."

Kianthe pushed to her feet, pacing with her mug of tea. It was a rose blend flavored with chamomile and honey, but right now she couldn't quite enjoy it. "Okay, let me get this straight. Bandits stole the eggs. In Tawney, their mage somehow stripped the dragon magic and left it beneath that church—but they clearly didn't do a great job. Regardless, they carted the eggs west and handed them to you. You stole one and left it near dragon country, and it may still be there. And Arlon has the other two."

"I couldn't say if he still does or not." Viviana frowned. "All I know is my role in this. I'm sorry, Arcandor; I should have brought the egg to the Magicary. But considering that an alchemical mage was working with the bandits, it didn't feel particularly safe."

"You did what you could, and it came with the best intentions." Reyna closed the folder in her lap, tucking it under her arm. She leaned forward, her tea forgotten. "I'm more concerned about why Arlon wanted three dragon eggs, personally."

Kianthe heaved a frustrated sigh. "I'm not. I'll deal with him soon; right now, I want to know what happened to that third egg. If I can't return all three, the bindment is at risk." The agreement she'd made with the dragons: find the eggs, and they wouldn't attack Tawney in the meantime. Dragons operated on a different timeframe than humans, but that didn't mean she could ignore this task for long.

Reyna frowned. "You don't happen to have a map of where you left that egg, do you, sheriff?"

As it turned out, Viviana did. Which meant they were headed back into the cold.

Again.

25

Reyna

It was a two-day ride north to where Viviana left the dragon egg. After the snow, it should have taken three, but traveling with Kianthe meant the only thing that slowed them down was their borrowed horses. Considering Lilac's personality, these two were absolute delights, but Kianthe was clearly itching to reunite with Visk.

"Stone be damned, we could have done this in an afternoon if we were flying," she muttered.

"You're the one who sent our griffons to kidnap Feo, darling," Reyna reminded her. Not that Ponder would have been much help here, but still. A deep ache settled in her chest; the reprieve from Ponder's antics was nice, but Reyna missed her feathery child.

Kianthe glowered, hunching further under her heavy winter cloak. "They aren't being *kidnapped*. They'll get on Visk willingly."

"Because they'll think we're in danger, and a griffon can't communicate how far they'll be flying." Reyna snorted. She was rather enjoying this little excursion; after so many days on a ship with their new friends, it was nice to be back traveling alone with Kianthe again.

It was no surprise why her fiancée was pouting. It was frigid here, rivaling Tawney's temperatures without any of the warm company and cozy bookstore aesthetic. The wind wasn't strong, considering the mountains that flanked them, but the ice along the river didn't help warm anyone.

The Nacean River itself tapered away this far north, separating into multiple smaller streams gathering from the mountains. They followed the largest one, keeping a steady pace as Kianthe glumly sifted snow out of their path.

"We could be sitting at a vineyard in Koll right now."

"Hmm. But where's the adventure in that?" Reyna teased.

They rode on.

When the sun began to set, they made camp—which was essentially Kianthe carving a hole in the mountainside. She started a fire while Reyna tethered the horses. Firelight caught her gaze farther downhill, along the western slope.

"I suppose we found the bandits. I was wondering how far north they camped."

It looked like a huge gathering of them, like a second town. Distant music had struck up, nearly swallowed by the gentle snowfall, but the fire from their torches blazed in the darkness of night. Kianthe paused beside her, squinting at the camp.

"Please tell me you aren't planning on disrupting their party." She produced Reyna's chosen hat, the deep blue one, and gently undid Reyna's bun. With her long, ice-blond hair falling over her shoulders, Kianthe tugged the hat onto her head.

Reyna sighed. "Why does everyone think I live my days dreaming of murder?"

Kianthe gestured at her, a fond smile tilting her lips. "It's a whole vibe. Don't pretend like you don't carefully foster it, either. I notice that sword hasn't left your side since we left Tawney."

"I keep my sword nearby because the Realm isn't as safe as Tawney, and I'm not one for chances. But no, I don't particularly care to attack a camp of people living their lives in the wild north." Reyna strolled back toward their own camp, sitting close to the fire. Kianthe paused to magically dust the ice off a luscious patch of grass, and then joined her, tucking herself under Reyna's arm.

"I think it's sexy," Kianthe said after a moment.

Reyna laughed. "You think everything is sexy."

The mage rested her head on Reyna's shoulder. "Guilty. Remember when I got you that moonstone?"

Except for the last few days, Reyna had barely needed to use hers lately, but she wore it regardless: a physical reminder of Kianthe's devotion. Now she tapped it, knowing the touch transferred to Kianthe's matching necklace. "Are you referring to the day I fainted in front of you while on duty, or the first time you told me you loved me?"

"The day you fainted. You stood *all day* with that wound because you wanted to prove you were good at your job. Right?"

It wasn't Reyna's proudest moment. She sighed. "That's true."

"That's what I think is sexy. Not the stupidity of working while bleeding out, mind you, but the dedication you showed. You're good at the things you're good at, and I love that about you."

Reyna's cheeks warmed. "Thank you."

Kianthe smiled. Her fingers began tracing a light circular pattern on Reyna's leg, the touch so feather-light it sent a shiver along her skin. "I appreciate that you're here, Rain. The dragons aren't your problem—not really—but you never once asked to stay home."

"I'm with you through anything . . . and I told you before: I don't think I'm built to live in Tawney all the time." Reyna couldn't keep the frustration out of her tone at that. "I want to. It's perfect there. But fighting, traveling, meeting new people . . . that's what I love. It's not surprising, considering I was raised for it."

Kianthe was quiet for a moment, watching the fire flickering before them, tracing that circular pattern absently. "Do you think that's something you need to fix?"

"I think, just by virtue of marrying you, it *is* fixed." Now Reyna gestured with her free hand at the cave, the horses, the stars glimmering through the dispersing clouds. "This is an adventure. And you're here too, which makes it better than anything Queen Tilaine could offer."

"Okay, well. Promise you'll tell me if you change your mind. Because our life doesn't have to be Tawney forever—I'll take you to the Roiling Islands if that's where you'd rather be."

"The Roiling—" Reyna cut herself off with a laugh. "What's there?"

"Arlon's favorite tea, for one."

They both dissolved into laughter.

After a moment, Kianthe untangled herself and plucked their dinner out of one of their packs, setting the strips of meat in a cast-iron pan over the flame. Reyna swallowed a yawn, watching her cook, appreciating the warmth of the cave contrasting with the frigid scenery outside.

High overhead, a glimmer of blue and green glowed past the clouds.

An aurora. She'd heard of them but hadn't seen one in person—even in Tawney, they were rare. "Key," she gasped, stepping to the cave's edge.

Kianthe joined her, and her fingers threaded with Reyna's. The mage waved her free hand to magically disperse the clouds, offering them an unhindered view of the brilliant stretch of green, blue, and purple. Amazement filled Reyna to her toes; no wonder the Sheparans worshiped the Stars, if this was their view.

"No matter where the adventure is, I'm happy if you're in it," Kianthe said quietly.

Warmth—unlike anything a fire could create—spread through Reyna. Instead of responding, she leaned against Kianthe's shoulder, smiling at the cold night sky.

The next day, they reached the spot Viviana marked on the map. It was a clearing nestled between several towering cliffs and even taller mountains. The Northern Bay glimmered before them, big enough that it looked like another ocean. The other side of the bay wasn't even visible except at the northern tip, where dragon country reached for Shepara like a prying hand.

Reyna squinted at the opposite landmass. "I don't see any dragons flying over there."

"That's why I'm worried. Dragons tend to stick closer to the southern border, along the Vardian mountain range. I'm not sure one would have seen an egg over here, unless they felt the magic from this distance." Kianthe bit her lip. "I doubt that egg made it back."

Reyna picked along the shoreline, her boots kicking snow away from the cold ground. "I feel like if it *had,* the dragons would have communicated it. Feo said their eggs are rare. If one showed up after three went missing, the dragons might have diverted attention from Tawney to Lathe."

That fact settled between them, cold as the day.

Kianthe heaved a sigh. "Well, we're already out here. Let's spread out. Look for clues."

"Your enthusiasm is catching, love," Reyna drawled.

"Look. After all the pirate action, this feels like a side quest."

"Saving Tawney from dragon fire is a side quest?" Now Reyna faced her fiancée properly, unable to control her exasperated tone. "This is literally why we're on the Nacean at all. It wasn't for the pirates."

Kianthe crossed her arms and muttered stubbornly, "You're the one who got me on pirates. Now you're mad I'm enjoying it. I can't win with you."

Reyna laughed, rolling her eyes. "Just clear the snow, dear. We're looking for *any* clue the dragon egg was here." And she busied herself with canvassing the area.

They searched all day—and found absolutely nothing. The day eased into night, and as a heavy darkness settled over the bay, they set a campfire and unpacked for the evening. The ground was so cold here that Kianthe raised a rock-bed for them, then covered it in a carpet of moss. That, plus the furs they'd brought to sleep on, made for a very cozy evening.

As they sat shoulder to shoulder under heavy furs, sipping tea and staring at the bay, Kianthe passed the time by explaining her book's plot. She was only a few pages into writing it, but already characters had started to form: two women madly in love, but one was a pirate captain and the other her captive prisoner.

"Hmm. Do you think the prisoner would fall for her kidnapper?" Reyna's brow furrowed. "That seems problematic."

"Worked for me, with you." Kianthe grinned.

Reyna raised an eyebrow. "Dearest, I was never your prisoner."

"Really? Because I remember capturing your heart." A burst of bright laughter echoed off the moonlit bay, and Kianthe slapped her knee, her legs dangling off the edge of the makeshift bed. Reyna swallowed a heavy sigh, barely refraining from smacking the mage's arm.

Apparently, this was the height of humor on this trip . . . and if that was the case, the next two days back to Lathe would be terrible.

At Reyna's behest, they reworked the plot: the prisoner was now a captive princess, stolen for ransom. But she spent her time killing ogres—"That's pretty mean," Kianthe said. "Ogres are lovely creatures." Reyna sighed and suggested unicorns, and vicious glee sparked in Kianthe's eyes—so the princess spent her time killing unicorns, right up until the day she followed a herd too close to the ocean. The pirate captain, who sounded suspiciously like the Dastardly Pirate Dreggs, scooped her up, and thus began an adventure where the brave princess taught the cunning pirate how to love.

As the night settled and their eyelids began to droop, Reyna leaned against Kianthe's shoulder and murmured, "It sounds a bit like our lives. You once told me that only inexperienced authors use self-inserts."

"Every author puts a bit of themselves in the character," Kianthe said, with such self-assurance that Reyna began to wonder when she'd become an authority on these matters. Especially when she added, "Besides, the Realm will love to see us in print. We're a delight."

Reyna chuckled, the sound fading into the quiet night. "If you say so. Do you have a working title for the tome?"

"Oh, *so* many." Kianthe literally rolled up her sleeves, a shocking choice in this icy weather. Reyna grimaced before she even got started. "How about *Seas Her Fortune*? Or *The Pirate's Bountiful Booty*. Maybe *Seas Likes It Rough*. Get it?"

Reyna began to regret that Kianthe knew where she lived.

The mage was still going. "Something . . . something about firing cannons through your porthole. Oh! How about *This Treasured Chest,* but the chest refers to—"

"Darling, I beg of you, please forget I asked."

Kianthe wrinkled her nose, tugging her sleeves back down with a shiver. "I thought these were gold. Pirate's gold! Get it?"

"I get it."

"You sound like you're dying."

"Only on the inside."

Kianthe smirked, winding her arm over Reyna's shoulders and pulling her closer. "I'd apologize, but you know what you're marrying. I will be courteous enough to accept any and all title suggestions, so I can veto them in favor of *This Treasured Chest.*"

Reyna massaged her temples. Kianthe's warmth was a pleasant comfort—she'd missed her over the days they spent apart, trailing after Serina and Bobbie. Still, it wasn't hard to infuse exasperation in her tone. "Splendid. How will you face your family at our wedding, knowing that book sits on our shelves? How will we face our friends?"

"Well, our friends include Matild, and you know the stuff she likes." Kianthe waggled her eyebrows. "And my family won't be there, so—at least there's that."

They'd started this conversation in Oslop, and now it screeched into existence again: the glaring point that Kianthe didn't seem to care about her parents . . . or their role in her life. Reyna frowned, contemplating a tactful way to approach it.

Luckily, her furrowed brow was a cue, because Kianthe heaved a sigh. "Go ahead, Rain. Tell me how you're feeling."

Hmm. Well, that made things easier.

"I'm feeling a bit perplexed, if I'm being honest." And they always were when that statement was spoken. Reyna admired the bay's shimmering water, listened to an owl hooting in the distance and the fire flickering before them. She sighed. "I'd give anything to spend another day with my mother. I just can't fathom what your family did that would result in excommunication."

"It's not *excommunication.*" Kianthe set her jaw, hunching into herself. "I still write them . . . sometimes. I just . . . I don't know. I moved to the Magicary when I was a kid and barely talked to them after that. But even before the Stone blessed me with its magic, before I became the Arcandor, they kept writing about how proud they were of me. I was failing every class, and they still kept implying that I was smart, or capable. One of their letters even said I'd be 'the greatest mage alive.'"

"You *are* the greatest mage alive." The words weren't minced; it was a truth neither would deny.

"I was *seven* when they sent that."

Reyna frowned. She'd been raised by a mother who expected success. It would sound crass to admit outside her thoughts, but—that kind of pressure only pushed her to grow. She succeeded because there was no alternative, and when that success paved the way to a prestigious career, it felt like nothing Reyna didn't deserve.

The only thing she felt like she hadn't earned in life was Kianthe. It took years longer to accept her presence.

"I suppose that could be a lot of pressure on a child."

Her words were neutral, because she didn't really understand. She wanted to, but this was . . . odd.

Kianthe shifted, pulling away from her. "You're laughing at me." Under her tone was a deep-rooted fear that she'd be right.

Reyna scrambled to backtrack. "No, darling. Not at all. I'm sorry; I forget sometimes that we're two different people, and similar experiences affect us differently. My mother had an unwavering belief in my talents, but I never once doubted I'd meet them. I worked hard and was rewarded, which is how we're raised in the Queendom." She paused, puzzling through this now. "But if your performance isn't exceeding the standards set by the Magicary, well. I can imagine how encouraging letters might feel like a knife to the heart."

"It wasn't even that I was failing classes at the Magicary. I mean, I was, but—that doesn't really matter for a mage." Kianthe's voice took on a distant tinge. "It's hard to explain. Our classes aren't like . . . well, like the university in Leonol. There isn't a degree, even for alchemists. If you have magic and believe in the Stone of Seeing, you're a mage. It's that simple."

"And yet, that does make it more complex."

Kianthe snapped her fingers. "Exactly. How do you measure success when there's no standard? We can try to judge magical talents, but a person only ever has what the Stone allows. By placing a title on that, or claiming merit, it's akin to questioning the Stone's whim. All mages are equal in the Stone's mind. The Arcandor may be its favored mage, but everyone else is equal. And even the Arcandor would never forget what it was to have normal magic."

Reyna had never thought to inquire about this before. It was shocking to her that after so many years, she still knew so little about the Magicary's inner workings. Originally, that was intentional—she didn't want more information for Queen Tilaine to pry out of her. Later, their lives formed and it seemed less important.

This trip across Shepara was reminding her that she should never stop discovering things about Kianthe. Otherwise, their relationship would become very dull, very quickly.

"If being a mage is such a vague conclusion, how did you still fail your classes?" Reyna's voice was teasing, now.

Kianthe chuckled, but it was much more strained. "I'm not really one for classrooms. It's hard to stay focused, so I . . . didn't. Focus, I mean. Mostly I was in trouble for disrupting the teachers, but even when we did skill tests, I was the worst in the class." She sighed, tugging at a loose string on her cloak. "My parents thought I was an amazing mage, but before I became the Arcandor, that was so far from the truth."

"You became the Arcandor as a teenager." Reyna traced a soothing circle on Kianthe's thigh. "You can't possibly expect to be great at that age, even if you're a prodigy. Or the class clown."

Kianthe didn't reply.

Reyna sighed. "Did you ever consider that you've been great this entire time, and it wasn't your parents holding you to this imaginary standard?"

Several moments passed, and Kianthe opened her mouth and

closed it multiple times. A slow smile tilted Reyna's lips as she watched her fiancée splutter. She straightened, kissed Kianthe on the cheek.

"No matter what, I love you. And I'm convinced I'd have loved you even if we met as children. Even if it took you a long time to love yourself."

Kianthe's face flushed, and she waved the emotion off. The intimate conversation seemed to make her very uncomfortable, but she didn't divert attention; she just forced herself to sit in it. "I don't think I liked myself until I met you, anyway. But I guess that's not my parents' fault."

"So, perhaps we can invite them to the wedding? I doubt you'd feel inadequate facing their praise now, considering all you've done."

Kianthe grumbled. "Let me think about it."

Reyna scootched back on the stone bed, which was surprisingly cushy thanks to the thick layer of moss. She swallowed a yawn and bundled up, waiting for Kianthe to join her before tossing the furs over them both. Her feet were cold, and she pressed them against Kianthe's leg with vicious pleasure.

Different venue, same evening routine.

"That's all I ask, darling," she murmured, and let her eyes fall shut.

She barely heard Kianthe whisper fondly, "I know, and I love you for it."

The next day, they spent a bit longer searching, but found nothing. As Reyna tidied up the campsite, Kianthe draped over a pine tree's low-hanging branch. "What a waste of time. I bet Bobbie and Serina are having more fun than us, and they're recovering from battleground wounds."

"This morning wasn't fun?" Reyna asked slyly.

Waking up in the middle of nowhere, with no pressure and no one expecting them for days—well, it loosened their time considerably.

It started with a kiss, and quickly dissolved into much, much more. Reyna was still pleasantly warm.

Kianthe grinned deviously. "Okay, aside from that." She pushed off the tree, wheeling toward the bay. "I guess I expected a magical signature or *something.* Any indication it was here at one point."

Reyna paused in stocking her saddlebags, checking the map inside her pocket again. But she was excellent at following directions, and they were definitely in the spot Viviana denoted. She shared Kianthe's disappointment that it amounted to nothing after all.

Her eyes slid to the bay, and a thought crossed her mind. Absently, she left the horses to stroll to the shoreline, hunting for a nice rock. There were several suitable for skipping, and the bay's waves weren't so intense that she couldn't get a few jumps in. Reyna picked one, fitting it in the curve of her finger, and lowered herself to the waterline.

"Do we have any elk?" she asked absently.

"There's a bit left, yeah." Kianthe joined her at the shoreline, raising an eyebrow. "What are you doing?"

"Skipping rocks."

"In the waves."

Reyna let one fly, and it admittedly jumped once, then vanished in an oncoming swell. She hefted another rock to try again. "Serina said sea serpents live in the Nacean River. Water dragons. I just . . . with dragon country so close, I wondered if some lived here, too."

"And throwing rocks at their heads is the way to get their attention?" Kianthe sounded amused now.

Reyna pushed her partner jokingly. "Come on. Help me."

Kianthe was always ready for this kind of thing. With a satisfied smile, she hefted a boulder off the shoreline, something big enough no mortal could budge it. Reyna gasped, "Not *that* big—" but it was too late. With a shock of magic, Kianthe catapulted the boulder deep into the bay.

The loud *kersploOOSH* echoed across the water.

Kianthe cackled. "Okay. That *was* fun."

"You are terrible—" Reyna started to say, but at that moment something incredible happened.

The waves seemed to pull out from shore, reversing direction toward the center of the bay. Everything got eerily quiet. And just as Kianthe grabbed Reyna's arm and began to haul her from the shoreline, a huge jet of water slammed toward them. Kianthe barely had time to react, twisting it to their left, but the mist drenched them both.

Deep in the bay, half its body raised from the water, an iridescent serpent with a dragon's head, massive frills, and glimmering purple scales perched in the water. Its deep black eyes stared directly at them, and after a moment's assessment, it grumbled—which sounded suspiciously like laughter. With a flick of its tail, the serpent sent another spray of water at them. Kianthe was too busy gaping, and it caught them in a salty downpour that left them both shivering.

Then the creature twisted, vanishing deep into the bay again.

Silence filled the space, and the waves resumed their gentle trek to shore.

"Well," Reyna said, wiping her eyes. "You deserved that."

"Yeah. Probably." Kianthe shivered, pulling water from their clothes with a magical tug. She balled it up and let it drop into the rocks, where it began draining back into the bay. "A sea serpent. That's a first."

"We could have had a better experience if you'd fed it instead of hurtling a rock at its home." With a shake of her head, Reyna trudged back to the campsite, where the horses were both staring wide-eyed at the bay. "Come along, love. Let's return to Lathe and wait for Feo. I'm dying to see what's inside Arlon's desk drawer."

At the reminder, Kianthe perked up. "Fine. But I'm opening it this time, okay?"

"Your wish is my command." With a smirk, Reyna packed up the last of their campsite for the long trek back.

26

Serina

Kianthe and Reyna had been gone for two days, and Serina was bored.

And not just bored. Frustrated-bored. "Antsy," Farley had said knowingly when Serina breezed into the tavern. She and Rankor were deep in a game of chess, passing the time in the most benign way possible. "Go ask the sheriff what you can do. I'm sure she has a list."

"Or go make up with your constable friend. Not every day someone leaps in front of a sword for you." Rankor grinned, hunching into himself when Serina glared. He raised his hands. "Or not."

"*Not* is right," Serina muttered, and stomped away. She didn't want to think about Bobbie, recovering in one of the inn's spare rooms. She didn't want to think of the way Bobbie had been groaning in pain last night, or how she awoke in the early hours with fever-glazed eyes and begged Serina to "come to her senses."

"He'll kill you," Bobbie had whispered, tears in her eyes. "What am I going to do if he catches you?"

Serina had stroked her hair, traced a gentle line on her forehead until Bobbie fell into another fitful sleep—but she couldn't be near that anymore. Not with the way anxiety was roiling in Serina's chest. She kept picturing Reyna gripping her sword, facing off against constables. Darlene and Joe fleeing belowdecks while the adults faced deadly enemies.

That fight wasn't even theirs.

Was she losing her mind? Maybe the *Knot for Sail* should stay where it was hidden . . . forever. Maybe Serina really should just get on a nice, neutral boat and sail for Jallin again. Her father ran a nice business as a merchant now. She could probably find some kind of job on his ship.

Glumly, Serina sat on the docks, legs kicking over the edge as she stared at the clear water. Far below the surface, seaweed swayed in the current, clinging to algae-coated rocks, coloring the water bright yellow.

Pretty. She and Bobbie used to sit here, shoulders pressed together, making guesses about which fish lived in that seaweed forest.

"Okay," a gruff voice said behind her. Viviana's heavy boots fell against the wooden dock, and she crossed her arms, looming over Serina's slumped form. "I've been told you need a job."

Behind her, Rankor smirked. He'd gathered the crew, even Darlene, who'd been gleefully absent practicing techniques with her newly claimed sword. It was strapped to her hip now, and she stood prouder because of it.

Pil didn't look happy, but he also didn't take it from her.

The fact that they'd all paused their days for this was . . . actually touching.

Viviana clapped Serina's shoulder. "Get up. Lucky for you, we have a family south of here that needs an extra shipment of grain."

A delivery. Serina perked up. "Do you have grain to spare?" For a moment, she imagined pirating on a smaller ship, just like the old days. Stealing quickly and fleeing fast. Her favorite method.

But Viviana just chuckled. "We always have grain to spare, Serina, or I'm doing my job wrong. It's loaded on that schooner, just waiting for a crew to sail it south. You remember Humalt's homestead, right?"

Of course she remembered Humalt, and his charming family,

and their bountiful crops. It felt like Serina's entire body drained of blood. "I—I can't go back there."

"They'd be excited to see you, Serina."

Her tone was almost scolding, like Serina was a child again, facing the disappointment of her mother and Viviana together. They'd been friends, but Viviana hadn't intervened when the constables took their land. Her mother didn't hold ill will. She said there was nothing Viviana could have done.

Serina felt differently.

She wanted to scream, *I am not a child anymore,* but that made her sound childish by definition.

Instead, she took a slow breath and replied, "Why do they need grain? I thought they were doing well." Far better than *she'd* done, farming the adjacent land last year. After all, Bobbie only evicted her, not Humalt and his family.

Viviana read between the lines. She crossed her bulky arms, her words neutral. "If you don't have the time, I'll send someone else. Your crew seemed willing, but—"

"We'll do it," Pil called. "My kids live on the water. Sooner we get back to it, the better."

Everyone looked at Serina. With nothing else to say, she sighed and trudged up the plank onto the little schooner.

Her crew fell in behind her, Farley humming merrily as she worked to tie down the crates of grain for the journey. Pil's kids slid into the sails, although Darlene had to leave her new sword at the mast first. Squirrel strolled on next, carrying two baskets of fresh bread and cheeses. "For the trip," she said, and merrily stepped belowdecks.

Finally, Pil and Rankor weighed anchor as Serina took the helm. She knew these waters better than she cared to admit, so it wasn't a problem to navigate for a while. As they eased out of the harbor and left Lathe behind, a dark irritation settled in Serina's chest.

Rankor approached the helm, clapping his hands together. "Ah, I thought this would keep your mind off Bobbie. Now I'm wondering if I messed up."

"N-No, you didn't mess up!" After everything they'd given her, Serina didn't want her problems to become his. "I'm sorry. I just . . . we used to be neighbors. Me and them."

"When you were a kid?" Rankor leaned against the ship's railing, the wind rustling his dark hair. They were making great time, catching all the right currents, and everyone moved with enthusiasm after several days off the river.

Schooners were known for speed. Maybe Serina could channel that once they reached the homestead.

She carefully guided the ship through patches of ice. "No, the second time. The land next to theirs was the closest I could get to Lathe, according to Arlon. But it had a tendency to flood, and it was so far from the shore that shipping costs were a nightmare." She winced. "Plus, it's a lot. Farming land all alone."

"Mmm. So, you couldn't make your quota, and Arlon replaced you with another farmer?"

"Bobbie came herself to do the deed." Serina rolled her eyes, even as her heart shriveled at the memory. "As if her presence would make her actions bruise less."

Rankor hummed. After a moment, he cleared his throat. "Can I be honest, Captain?"

The title took her off guard. She waved a hand.

Her navigator smirked. "Sounds like Bobbie did you a favor."

"Bobbie ruined everything I'd spent my adult life pursuing." Serina narrowed her eyes, a fire igniting in her soul. "*Bobbie* represents everything I hate."

"Well, right now, that constable is barely conscious because she was trying to protect you." Rankor shrugged. His tone was easygoing, even if his words cut like a knife. "Watching you the last couple days, I feel like you weren't meant to farm. And I think you know it, too. Sometimes, the worst event in our lives can turn into the greatest treasure."

Rankor smoothly inserted himself at the helm, pointedly dismissing her—even though *she* was the captain, and should be dismissing him. But that was fine. After his words, she didn't want to be near Rankor right now anyway. Silent, almost sulking, Serina trudged to the staircase. At least downstairs, she wouldn't have to pretend to stay busy.

Squirrel was down there, puttering away. There wasn't a proper galley on this schooner, but she'd made do with the space she had, establishing a lovely spread of food on a couple wooden crates. The rest of the space was living quarters, and a second set of stairs that led to a rowing station one deck lower. Hopefully they wouldn't need those today; Serina's muscles still hurt from the blockade battle.

"You like brie?" she asked cheerfully. "A good brie and apple sandwich will cheer you up."

"I don't need to be cheered up," Serina muttered. She was feeling decidedly less like a feared pirate captain today, but she couldn't fight the fact that this week's events had left her in a sour mood.

Squirrel appraised her and tutted. "Just a hunch." She swiftly prepared a mouth-watering sandwich of brie, apple, and fig jam. When she presented it on a napkin like it was a meal befitting a king, Serina swallowed a laugh.

"I'm really glad you guys are here," she admitted, taking the food.

Squirrel blinked, clearly taken aback. She cleared her throat, busying herself with cleaning the knife of excess jam. "I'm no good in a fight, Captain. During that battle, I hid down here with the kiddos. I'm . . . not sure what we'd have done if Reyna hadn't intervened when she did." Now Squirrel winced, then set her jaw. "But food? I can do that. It's not a large contribution, but it's an important one."

Serina sank her teeth into the sandwich, and the sweet jam played off the crisp crunch of apple slices and soft flavor of the cheese. A moan escaped her lips, and she chewed slowly, reverently. "It *is* an important one. Not everyone's a fighter, and that's okay."

"You are, though." Squirrel smiled. "I feel safe on your ship, Serina."

It brought sudden tears to Serina's eyes. She lowered her sandwich, chewing absently, blinking to clear her vision. "T-Thank you."

Squirrel patted her cheek. "Send the others down when you can, will you? I'm sure they're hungry too." And she began to whistle a familiar sea shanty, one Serina's father used to sing every time they hoisted the anchor.

Feeling lighter, Serina returned to the deck.

It didn't take much longer to reach the homestead—the long part would be the journey back to Lathe, considering the geography of the river. Serina guided Rankor to a small inlet, where she was shocked to see Humalt and his son standing on the shore, waiting for them.

"Viviana sent a carrier pigeon," Humalt called, waving enthusiastically. "Serina, it's so good to see you again!"

"Same," Serina called, falsely cheerful.

Rankor snorted somewhere behind her.

She ignored him, and they loaded the crates into a smaller boat to take to shore. Rankor, Squirrel, and Pil stayed on the schooner. Darlene and Joe were curious about Humalt's son, and soon the three teenagers had dissolved into excited chatter. That left Farley and Serina to greet Humalt.

He gave her a hearty handshake, his grin splitting his face. "I miss our cookouts. How've things been?"

The worst part was that it wasn't Humalt and his family at all—they were absolutely delightful. The very definition of fantastic neighbors. They'd even offered to host Serina after her land was reclaimed.

That was why Serina hated this. She'd loved living by them. Loved their cookouts, loved the hard work of a farm. And now he was here, a stark reminder of everything she'd lost. Her voice trembled. "Ah, good. Good. Got a new ship, and I'm . . . in the merchant business now. Like my father."

"Excellent." Humalt beamed proudly, like he was complimenting his own kid. "Always knew you'd turn that luck around. You're resourceful."

Farley chuckled. "She is that. Where do you want the grain?"

"Ah, we have a cart over there." He gestured at it. The horse was untied, grazing on icy grass, but the cart was clearly awaiting a shipment. His ruddy complexion reddened further, and he rubbed the back of his neck. "Flooding got bad this year again. I'm . . . not sure how much we'll be able to hold on before the constables come for us too." He laughed, self-deprecating, but the sound had true agony in its depths.

Serina paused, releasing the crate she'd been about to retrieve. "You—he can't reclaim your land too, Humalt. I was new, but your family has—"

"Been there since the beginning. Long enough to remember when we *owned* it proper." Humalt scrubbed his face, forcing a smile that barely twitched his mustache. "It'll be okay, Serina. Don't you worry about us. This grain will help through the winter, and after . . . Well. We'll just have to ensure we have a great harvest next season."

But no one could control that, and they both knew it.

Any ill will centered around her own insecurities faded. All that remained was a simmering reminder about *why* she'd turned to pirating in the first place. It wasn't about Serina's past, or her desire for a future. It was about Humalt, and his son, and Garinson and his neighbors, and everyone else who was just trying to make an honest living.

Serina would be dishonest for all of them.

"Don't worry, Humalt. I don't think Arlon will be a problem much longer," Serina said, narrowing her eyes. "We're going to do something about him."

And at her side, Farley grinned. "There she is. Welcome back, Captain."

27

Kianthe

Kianthe and Reyna had barely returned from their trip north when Feo intercepted them. And by the Stone and Stars above, they were *angry*.

"Kianthe!" they bellowed, leaping off Visk the moment the griffon touched down in the town's square. Nearby folk stopped in their evening errands to stare, jaws dropped as this smartly dressed Sheparan stomped up to the Arcandor like they might slap her.

Kianthe promptly ducked behind Reyna, who was just about to lead their horses to the stables for some rest. Even the horses couldn't hide the mage from their wrath. It was as futile as trying to avoid Ponder, who screeched in happiness and launched off Visk's back to tackle Reyna with full force.

She squealed in delight. Apparently, all her rigid training was abandoned after days apart. The horses forgotten, Reyna pulled the baby griffon close and smoothed the feathers on her head and kissed her senseless. And to Ponder's credit, she ate it up, nibbling Reyna's clothes and ears and chittering away.

Visk, meanwhile, shot Kianthe a look that clearly expressed distaste for his passenger. Without waiting, he spread his wings and took off into the night, leaving Ponder with the two of them.

Leaving *Feo* with the two of them.

The diarn's expression was stormy and a bit crazed.

Reyna glanced up long enough to see it, then hummed, "Someone's in trouble," and released Ponder to the sky. The baby griffon circled as Reyna took the reins of the horses. Her tone switched to something cheery, amicable. "Diarn Feo. What a pleasant surprise. Kianthe has been waiting to speak to you. Now, if you'll both excuse me, I have to stable the horses before Ponder upsets them."

Traitor.

"You're not excused. You have to help me," Kianthe hissed.

"I'm not the one who summoned them without warning, love," Reyna replied wryly, and led the horses away.

Feo was too close to avoid now. Their short hair was ruffled, windswept, and it looked like they hadn't slept in days. When they spoke, they literally spat the words. "I absolutely can't believe I'm in *Lathe* right now, and you're perfectly *fucking fine*."

"I am fine, aren't I?"

"Don't joke with me, Arcandor," Feo snarled. "You said you needed help. I thought you were in trouble. I thought you or Reyna or someone had *died*."

Kianthe frowned. "I—I said we needed help. Not that someone was on death's door." She would never openly welcome that kind of sentiment. She liked her friends and family healthy and happy, thank you.

"You could have clarified in the note," Feo ground out, although now they looked a bit sheepish.

Kianthe clasped her hands over her heart. "Aww. You were worried about me. You do care."

Feo rejected that wholeheartedly. "Not in the slightest. I care about my position in Tawney. A position *you* have put in jeopardy. I bet Wylan is already taking over in my absence." They tossed up their hands, pacing.

"That seems extreme." Kianthe was enjoying this now, just a bit.

Feo growled, lifting their hands like they might strangle her. "Do you realize the predicament this puts me in? A diarn, abandoning their lands without any kind of warning? Are you insane?"

They were attracting a crowd. Already, people heard the word "diarn" and began whispering. If rumors here spread half as fast as in Tawney, Diarn Arlon would know about Feo's presence far sooner than Kianthe liked.

She twisted the wind with a hand, ensconcing them in privacy. Anything said now would swing right back to them rather than carrying to the ears of others. Feo stiffened at the magic, raising both eyebrows.

"Are we in danger?" They stared at the townsfolk like any one of them might produce a knife and a murderous attitude.

"Well, based on your reaction, *I* might be," Kianthe said. "Are you going to kill me, or can we talk about this?"

Feo set their jaw, drawing slow breaths through their nose. For a long moment, there was silence. The townsfolk gave the two of them a good amount of distance, skirting into the tavern and other shops like they carried a plague. Finally, Feo spoke through gritted teeth. "I want a room, a bath, and a hot meal."

Without another word, the diarn spun on their heel and stomped toward the inn. The door slammed so hard in their wake that snow actually fell off the roof, landing perilously close to a bystander.

"Sorry," Kianthe called, swallowing her laughter. "They're a bit touchy."

The sun had set before Feo joined them at the tavern. Reyna had strategically secured a table in the back corner, one with enough privacy from the crowds that they could speak freely. It came with the bonus of hiding Ponder, who clearly didn't want to leave Reyna's side again. She curled up on Reyna's lap, almost too big for it now, her lion's tail curling possessively around Reyna's thigh.

Kianthe scowled at the griffon.

"Oh, for the Gods' sake, Key. You can share." Reyna ran a finger between Ponder's closed eyes, lightly petting the feathers above her beak.

"I *can* share. Doesn't mean I want to."

"This was your idea." Reyna gestured at the creature on her lap. "Remember? I didn't even want the egg."

Kianthe sighed. "And I'll forever lose this argument because of that." A pause, a sly smile. "At least soon she'll be too big to come inside."

Across the table, Feo drained a glass of amber rum in one gulp. They were a bit calmer now, but anger had hardened into bitterness, sharp as one of Reyna's knives. "Arcandor, why am I here?"

They waved for a refill, and Reyna took a slow sip of her wine, her ash-brown eyes calculating. "I thought mages didn't drink."

"I'm not a mage. The Magicary made that quite clear when they exiled me." Feo didn't sound at all bitter about it. They held out their glass, and the server delivered another robust pour. Their eyes held Kianthe's as they took a deep swig. "It's a ridiculous rule for alchemists, regardless. I have no natural magic; any magic I conduct requires carefully researched spells."

"Most alchemical mages refuse to drink out of solidarity to their elemental counterparts." Kianthe crossed her arms, sulking in her chair.

"Excuse me if my viewpoint on 'solidarity' is currently lacking." Feo's voice was dry as a bone.

Reyna tapped the table to regain their attention. On her lap, Ponder shifted with the movement, chittered quietly, and fell back asleep. A deep-throated purr slid from the griffon, fading in the noise of the tavern. "Let's focus. Feo, I'm deeply sorry Visk whisked you away without any real warning, but we do require your expertise. And advice."

At the mention of expertise, Feo straightened in their chair. If the diarn of Tawney loved one thing in particular, it was being an expert. A smug smile tilted their lips. "I knew it. Let me guess. You found the eggs, but they're hidden behind an alchemical barrier."

"Stone damn it all, I wish." Kianthe heaved a sigh, gesturing at another table across the tavern. It was one of the livelier ones, with Serina currently challenging Pil to a drinking contest—and winning. Rankor and Squirrel were pounding the table in glee, cheering them on. Farley rolled her eyes, smiling into her drink. Darlene and Joe sat in the corner murmuring to each other; they'd point at various patrons, confer for several moments, and burst out laughing.

Bobbie wasn't there, but that wasn't a huge surprise. She'd only just started getting out of bed reliably, and her time awake was spent avoiding Serina—at least according to the quick update Darlene offered when Reyna got her alone.

So, clearly Serina and Bobbie's most recent chat went well.

Feo followed Kianthe's gesture, squinting at the table. "Who are they?"

"Pirates."

"Pirates—?" Feo cut themself off, frowning. "There aren't pirates on the Nacean River. At least, none I've ever heard of."

"They're the first."

Feo chuckled, taking another swig of their drink. "Arlon must be shitting himself."

Reyna stroked the fur along Ponder's back, just between her wings. They fell open at her touch, stretching up over the table as Ponder waited for scratches. "Diarn Arlon attacked them seven days ago. He sent five ships to sink theirs. Cannons, constables . . . the works. We only barely made it out alive."

"It was a declaration of war, Feo." Kianthe didn't pull punches, and her tone was deadly serious now.

Feo's eyes widened.

And then a sly smile tilted their lips.

"War against his own citizens. You don't say."

Kianthe rested her chin in her palm, smirking alongside them. Much as Feo annoyed her, she always imagined this was what having a younger sibling would be like. Equal parts irritation and utter amusement at what they unleashed on the world.

And frankly, Arlon deserved what was coming next.

Already, Feo had tugged out a leather-bound journal from the pocket of their trousers. They flipped through it, tapped on a page of handwritten notes.

Kianthe raised an eyebrow. "Got a quill in there, too?"

The look they shot her could peel paint. But after a moment, they did, in fact, produce a quill and a tiny inkwell. It was like Reyna and her secret knives but far less interesting to watch.

"Take notes, Key," Reyna said mildly. "Maybe this will help you meet your daily word count."

Kianthe grumbled, "You are absolutely no fun. You know that?"

Feo was already scribbling, fast and furious. They muttered under their breath, wrote something, scratched it out, and started fresh. After a moment, they tapped the paper resoundingly. "That's it. This kind of thing happened over two centuries ago. A famine swept over Shepara, and a diarn began ordering their citizens to surrender shipments of grain. When the people fought back, the diarn responded with violence."

"Sounds familiar," Kianthe drawled.

Feo's smirk grew wider. "I think most people forgot this even happened, but the council instituted a law to prevent it in the future. If a diarn attacks his people outright, it's cause for an immediate trial in Wellia. If he's found guilty, Arlon will be stripped of his title."

"Promising," Reyna said.

"Hang on. We have to assume Arlon will fall back on a technicality. Before we present it to the council, this needs to be ironclad." Kianthe set her jaw. "That law might only apply if the diarn was physically present, but Arlon wasn't *there* for the blockade battle. His constables fought us, not him."

"Hmm." A pause. More scribbling. Feo drained their glass, but didn't raise a hand for another. "Is there a library here?"

"Stone damn it all, I wish."

Reyna's eyes shone with amusement. "You wish for a lot."

Kianthe shrugged. "Sometimes I get it, too." She glanced at Feo. "We could always break into Arlon's library. He said it was under construction, which seems suspicious to me."

"Darling, don't blame paranoia for the fact that you want access to the biggest library outside of Wellia." Reyna finished her wine with a final sip.

"Actually, Wellia's library would be the best option. Arlon is a councilmember. If he gets wind that his position—either position—is being threatened, he'll rally the council and shift public opinion. Aside from you, Arcandor, your witnesses aren't exactly reliable in a court of law."

Now Feo jerked a thumb at the table of pirates in the corner. Pil had lost the drinking contest, which left Serina drunkenly swaying her way to the empty space, dancing like the fiddler was back on duty. Darlene had started singing, with Joe adding a deep baritone. The pirate captain raised her glass and laughed loudly, and a few of the patrons began to clap in time with the impromptu music.

"The faster I can move to pitch our case, the better." Feo drained their own glass and set their jaw. "I'll work on this tonight. Let me borrow your griffon, and we'll overthrow Arlon by the winter solstice."

"You were ready to move on this awfully fast," Kianthe drawled, raising one eyebrow. "Almost like you've spent time planning this coup before today."

Feo's lips curled into a cunning smile. "I have a coup planned for everyone I dislike. You've only recently teetered into safe territory, Arcandor, and it's only because your fiancée serves an excellent cup of tea."

Reyna inclined her head graciously. "I appreciate that you are no longer plotting to murder my future wife."

"Please, Reyna. As if you don't have seven schemes to remove *me* from power if I were ever an inconvenience." Feo scoffed.

Reyna simply smiled. "I don't 'scheme.' I plan."

"Semantics."

This was getting off topic. Kianthe pinched the bridge of her nose. "Before you go rushing off to Wellia, Feo, you should know *why* Serina decided to become a pirate. The reality of life on the Nacean River is not as idyllic as it should be."

They spent the rest of the evening discussing politics, with Feo taking careful notes as they relayed all they'd learned. Eventually, discussion shifted onto the dragon eggs, and it coincided exactly with them finishing a robust dinner. The tavern was getting loud, and Kianthe wasted no time saying, "Are you up for an excursion before bed?"

"I'm in Lathe instead of Tawney tonight, so apparently so." Feo didn't sound as upset about it after a night of drinking and political upheaval.

"Bring your coat; it's a bit of a hike." Reyna lifted a sleepy Ponder to her shoulder, where the griffon balanced like a cat on a branch.

They waved to Serina on the way out. The pirate's crew was in various stages of "tired enough to vacate for the evening" and "just getting the party started." Serina stumbled after them, catching Kianthe as she slipped on her winter cloak.

"Where're you going?" she was slurring her words a bit, eyes glassy.

Definitely drunk.

Kianthe smirked. "Your ship. We won't be long."

"My ship?" It sounded like *mysship*. "I'll come too! We have to take Arlon down."

At that, Feo snorted.

Reyna, just about to step out the door, smoothly stepped in. "Captain, with all respect, we're just checking on it. It's a hike. But . . . you spoke with Bobbie, didn't you? How did that go?"

A distraction.

Serina blinked heavily, her expression souring. At the door, Feo scowled impatiently, but now Kianthe was too invested to interrupt the conversation. The pirate huffed. "She's so *confusing*. Why are the pretty ones always twisting my mind in circles?"

"Got me," Kianthe said.

Reyna rolled her eyes. "So, you two didn't make up? I thought Bobbie might like to accompany us when we sail again."

"She's staying here." Serina crossed her arms, her chin jutting out. "I thought we were fine, but this morning I told her to come with us. She told me to stop stealing. I'm a pirate. Who the fuck—" A pause, like she lost her train of thought. "Who's she to tell *me* what to do? To the five hells with her!"

"Kianthe, if we don't leave soon, I'm retiring for the night." Feo's cold voice carried over the tavern's din.

Serina craned around them, narrowing her eyes at Feo. "Who'ssat?"

"A friend," Reyna said with a sigh. "Drink some water before you go to bed, all right, Serina?"

The pirate captain waved a hand in dismissal and staggered back to her friends. But when Farley poured her a large glass of water, she did take a deep swig. Kianthe followed her fiancée and Feo outside, and in the sudden quiet, Kianthe drawled, "Well, that's it. I officially give up. Those two aren't meant for each other."

"I do agree we've reached the end of our meddling." Reyna tied her hair into a high tail with a piece of twine. "I suppose we'll have to return to matchmaking someone closer to home."

Now her eyes roamed Feo, who had a notorious crush on their Queendom counterpart, Lord Wylan. Feo seemed to realize what she was implying, and they set their jaw. "We're *friends*."

"Three seasons ago, you weren't even that. My plots span years, Diarn Feo."

Kianthe swallowed a laugh. "No wonder you two get along so well."

Feo grumbled something and plowed ahead.

They hiked the short distance back to the ship, which was still hidden in the cove north of town. Feo scanned its new name, clearly painted in Reyna's cursive handwriting, and glanced at them suspiciously.

"Diarn Arlon had one of these ships commissioned years ago."

"What a coincidence," Kianthe drawled, and pulled a sheet of ice up to the edge of the ship. The makeshift ladder she'd carved into the wooden side was still there, and they climbed in one by one. "You weren't wrong about the alchemical spell, though. Arlon really doesn't want us snooping in his private records . . . and we *really* don't care what he wants anymore."

Feo followed them into the captain's quarters, looking vaguely pleased. "I never cared what that pompous asshole wanted." They gravitated immediately toward the rolltop desk, pressing a hand on the drawer in question without any prompting.

Kianthe truly didn't understand alchemical magic the way she probably should; it just seemed unnatural, like reciting a script without any feel for the emotion behind it. But she wasn't going to argue as Feo settled into countering the seal.

At least Reyna wouldn't get hurt this time.

Luckily, Reyna was only half paying attention. Ponder was soaring around the ship, rifling through the lines, clawing up the masts with her tiny wings outspread for balance. She was every bit the menace Kianthe expected when they brought her here, and Reyna was not pleased.

"Ponder. *Ponder.* No! Form up."

It was comical how little that feathery creature cared about Reyna's orders.

After several moments, Reyna finally waved a strip of jerky where Ponder could see it. The griffon squawked, dropped like a brick to the deck, and folded her wings in the perfect image of a mini-mount.

Kianthe had to give her fiancée credit; that was pretty handy.

"I need a bit of blood to make this work. It can't be mine." Feo glanced at Kianthe, who was lingering in the doorway. "Probably shouldn't be yours, either. Not sure how your precious Stone will react to that."

"Probably the same way it reacts to being called upon with sarcasm," Kianthe drawled.

Feo rolled their eyes. "Get Reyna, if you please."

Kianthe hated this. She almost told them to fuck off, that her fiancée's blood wasn't a commodity to be traded for services, but Reyna had overheard and clearly felt this was more important than reining Ponder in.

"Here." She slipped past Kianthe and tugged a knife from . . . somewhere in the folds of her shirt. Under the armpit, maybe? Impossible to tell, for how fast she retrieved it. Even more concerning was how fast she sliced the meat of her forearm, near the elbow—and how little she flinched at the blood that welled from the wound.

"Rain." Kianthe inhaled sharply. "Wouldn't a small cut on the palm be enough?"

"Why *ever* would I injure my palm? I'm a swordsman." Reyna shook her head and stepped closer to Feo as blood beaded along the cut on her arm, dripping down her elbow.

Feo was unperturbed. "Excellent. Right here, please." They guided her bleeding arm to a sigil they'd etched along the top of the desk. The moment the blood made contact, it glowed a sickening red, so different from the gorgeous yellow of her magic, or even the deep, respectable blue of dragon magic.

Kianthe set her jaw, but Reyna was already retrieving one of the bandages Bobbie never needed, wrapping her arm resolutely. Meanwhile, Feo popped open the hidden drawer.

Inside was a single folder, leather embossed in gold, brimming with parchment.

Feo flashed it. "Success."

"Let's see what Diarn Arlon was so intent on hiding." Reyna smirked.

28

Reyna

Whatever it was, Diarn Arlon was clearly determined to protect it—because everything in the leather folder was written in code.

Kianthe wasn't pleased. As they trudged back to the inn, she grumbled about Arlon, his business practices, his general paranoia, and why couldn't he make any of this *easy* on them? Reyna and Feo followed behind, letting her rant while they exchanged ideas on cracking the ciphers. It turned out that Diarn Feo held a passion for this kind of thing.

"I'll postpone Wellia for a day. Shouldn't take me long to decode this." They smirked wryly. "Arlon isn't known for his intellectual acumen, after all."

"Well, *I'm* going to bed," Kianthe stated petulantly. "We woke up in a cave this morning, and I'm aching for a mattress."

Reyna and Feo were left in the inn's quiet sitting area after she stomped up the stairs. Ponder wasted no time soaring after her, nipping at her heels like it was a fun game. After they were gone, Reyna sighed. "I do apologize for how you were summoned, Feo. Had I known, I'd have written a better note explaining matters."

The diarn scrubbed their face. "Kianthe's always been this way. But to her credit, she doesn't usually waste my time with frivolous matters. And this . . ." They hefted the folder. "Well. I'm not disappointed."

"How *is* Lord Wylan doing?" Reyna kept her tone mild, neutral. "And the shop? Matild and Tarly? Gossley?"

Feo barked a laugh. "First, I see what you're doing, and it won't work. The shop's fine; the whole town takes turns managing it for the day. Everyone is good." A pause. They weren't an emotional person, so it clearly took a lot of mental energy to admit: "We miss you two. Tawney's not the same without you both at New Leaf."

Homesickness swept over Reyna like a wave. She forced a smile. "We'll be back soon. We just need to locate this shipment; I'm hoping that folder has answers." The small sitting area was warm and comforting, and Reyna noticed a desk by the window, near the hearth. "In fact, I'll be up for a while longer; shall we divide and conquer with this folder? I have some experience with ciphers."

Queen Tilaine's spymaster loved a good hidden message, after all.

Feo nodded, handed over half the contents. "You heading up?"

"Only to say goodnight to Kianthe. Light keeps her awake, so I'll come down here to work."

Feo shrugged, leading the way up the stairs. "Best of luck. We'll reconvene tomorrow; I truly doubt it'll take us long if we're working together."

Reyna wasn't sure when she became a diarn's intellectual equal, but she vastly appreciated the camaraderie. She bid Feo goodnight, then ducked into her room to see Kianthe already in bed. Normally, the mage fell asleep reading, but tonight her eyelids were already drifting shut. She probably hadn't even changed before falling under the covers.

Ponder was curled on a fluffy stack of blankets near Kianthe's feet, but she watched Reyna with rapt attention.

"You comin'?" Kianthe mumbled, patting the mattress. "Cold without you."

Reyna felt guilty hefting the parchment, but her mind was racing with the possibilities of what was inked on its pages. "I'll just be awake for a little while longer. Don't stay up, all right, love?"

"Ugh. Fine." Kianthe rolled over, then waved a hand as an afterthought. The candles in the room extinguished immediately.

A smile tilted Reyna's lips as she pressed a kiss to Kianthe's hair, then stepped back into the inn's hallway. Heavy snoring echoed from Serina's room; well, at least the pirate captain found her way to a bed. Hopefully the rest of her crew did as well.

Hopefully, Bobbie came to her senses before Serina left Lathe for good. But somehow, Reyna doubted it.

She took up residence at the desk in the lobby, poring over the cipher. It was written in Common, so she recognized the letters. They were gibberish, but it was a start. She began working through common ciphers used by Queen Tilaine, then more obscure ones she'd picked up after years of watching Her Excellency's spies—and the assassins who tried to outsmart them.

It was painstaking work, and she almost didn't hear a door opening, closing. The inn's front door remained tightly shut, and the innkeeper had long since gone to bed. Even the hearth was dying down by now.

But footsteps moved quietly through the back of the inn. Whoever had intruded clearly entered through the kitchen's back door. A service staircase led to the upper hallway's opposite side—Reyna had scouted it on their first night here. They were heading for the guest rooms, and they clearly had no intention of being discovered near the inn's main entrance.

How intriguing.

A wry smile crossed her lips, and she eased away from the desk. Arlon's papers were folded into a tidy stack, which she tucked into the deep pocket of her pants. Silent as a cat stalking prey, Reyna climbed the main staircase, sticking to the shadows.

If someone thought they were going to murder the Arcandor in her sleep, they had another think coming. Reyna slid two of her favorite knives out of their hidden sheaths, twirling them absently as she crouched in an alcove near the top of the staircase.

But the intruders—two of them, one bulky enough that Reyna wished she'd taken her sword, the other thin and willowy—clearly weren't after Kianthe. They moved with confidence not to the Mage of Ages's room . . . but to Serina's.

Well, that was a surprise.

Reyna watched, curiously, as they ducked into the pirate captain's room. Reyna lurked on the edges, waiting to see if they were going to hurt her—but all they did was press a cloth to Serina's face, then slide a burlap bag over her head and toss her over their shoulder.

She should probably intervene, but Serina wasn't in immediate danger and now Reyna's curiosity was piqued. They didn't move like Arlon's constables. They clearly weren't bandits, or Her Excellency's spies. Their practical clothing implied they were sailors, but this close to the Nacean, that could have been intentional.

So, who were they?

Well. There was one way to find out . . . and she just had to hope Kianthe didn't absolutely loathe her for it. Reyna turned on her heel, sheathed her knives, and snuck back down the staircase. By the time the kidnappers entered the kitchen, she was perusing the cabinets as if looking for a midnight snack.

"Oh—" she said, feigning shock. She made sure to look pointedly at the unconscious woman over the bulky one's shoulder, and then meet the willowy figure's gaze.

"Get her," the big one ordered, panic in his voice.

The willowy figure moved faster than Reyna expected. Not fast enough she couldn't have countered . . . but then again, that was hardly the point. Reyna opened her mouth as if to scream, sucked a quick breath, and when the person pressed a cloth to her nose and mouth, she exhaled.

Then, she did exactly as they expected—and dropped.

"Should we leave her?" the willowy figure asked. Their voice was deeper than she expected, considering their stature.

"Not after what she's seen. We take them both."

A burlap sack was crammed over her head, too, and her ankles and wrists were tied with rough rope. She stayed limp as they hauled her over the big one's shoulder, opposite Serina, and carried her outside. Reyna counted paces, tracked direction, and determined they were headed to the harbor well before they stepped foot on a boat.

Perhaps a disgruntled merchant and his crew?

If she'd been smart, Reyna would have prodded Serina for her list of enemies sooner. Far too late for that now. They carried her belowdecks, and a stern voice shouted, "Weigh anchor," and then they were off, sailing fast out of Lathe.

Kianthe was *not* going to be happy.

Reyna, however, was feeling quite satisfied with herself.

They eased her to the floor, laid Serina down beside her, and their footsteps receded. Silence filled in their wake, although on deck footsteps thudded and commands were shouted as they angled the ship south. Reyna waited several more moments, then plucked out the knife sewn into a secret pocket along her waistband. It didn't take long to slice the bindings at her wrists and ankles and remove the burlap hood.

The knots were the same kind Pil had taught her for the rigging. Interesting choice for a captive.

They were in a tiny cell. Serina was still unconscious, but Reyna patted her cheek anyway. "Captain, with respect, a development has occurred that demands your attention." Her whispered words were lost on the woman, though; she'd had enough alcohol, and whatever tincture they'd used to knock her out was doing its job.

"All right, then. Let's see who these folk are."

Reyna left Serina against the bulkhead wall, stepping lithely to the metal door. The ship was rocking now, firmly back on the river, and moving faster than Reyna expected considering the wind here. It was wholly possible they had a mage onboard.

She plucked two hairpins from her bun. One was angled with a sharp turn, and the other had a slightly curved edge. She swiftly picked the lock, then eased the cell door open. She closed it behind her; for anyone passing by, Serina would look like the only captive.

After all, she wasn't supposed to be here anyway. Odds were, no one would notice.

At least, not fast enough to intervene.

Reyna lifted a cloak off a hook near the staircase, and a hat off one of the hammocks near Serina's cell. At first glance she'd look like a sailor, and that was good enough for her.

The ship was smaller than the *Knot for Sail* and clearly moved faster downriver. Through the small windows in the lower deck, the dark trees seemed to blur past. Definitely a mage on board, which meant she'd have to be careful.

Reyna moved through the lower deck, sifting through crates, personal belongings, anything that might tell her the truth of their captors. Unfortunately, it was unproductive; whoever they were, they clearly didn't spend much time on this ship . . . or have any identifiers other than "sailor."

Hmm. Reyna returned to the cell, letting herself back in.

Mystery sailors, doubling as kidnappers. A boat they clearly didn't use for long. And no insignias—which implied a professional.

Her lips curled into a smile.

Well. If her hunch was correct, Reyna was about to secure incredible bragging rights.

The next day, someone slammed a wooden baton against the bars of the cell. Reyna had been awake from the moment she heard boots thudding toward them, but Serina jolted upright like she'd been burned.

"What—" She clenched her eyes shut against the midmorning sunlight, swallowing a groan. "Oh, Stars above, it's so bright. Are we . . . moving?" Her skin paled, and she groaned for a different reason. "On a boat. Right after a night like that. Why do pirates *drink* so much?"

"We don't. That's a rookie mistake," someone drawled.

The person before them was confident and poised. Their thumbs were hooked on a leather belt adorned with both a spyglass and a well-polished sword. They wore black breeches and a loose-fitting white shirt. Perched on their shoulders was a crimson cloak studded with black buttons and trim.

And on their head, a tricorne hat with a ridiculously large feather.

Good to see Reyna's instincts were on point, as always.

The Dastardly Pirate Dreggs quirked a wry, almost friendly

smile. They were older, with maybe two decades on Reyna and Kianthe, but it didn't stop their charming demeanor. Their skin was tanned from the sun. Short hair tousled playfully over blue eyes—eyes like steel, light enough to seem gray.

Gods above, it was no wonder they had such a reputation.

"Did you enjoy your midnight romp around my ship?" They addressed Reyna, lips tilting in amusement. Their accent was unplaceable—it might have once been Sheparan, but now was as unique as Dreggs themself.

Reyna found herself smiling in return, cocking her hip. "Whatever do you mean? I'm a humble captive here."

Dreggs laughed, the sound bright and airy. "In my experience, there are no coincidences. I sent my quartermaster and boatswain out with very specific instructions, and they returned with my intended captive . . . and an extra who just 'happened' to catch them in the act." Now Dreggs's smile grew into something cunning, dangerous. "Plus, my cloak wasn't where I left it."

"How odd," Reyna replied, tilting her head.

Dreggs laughed again and waved a hand at the bulky person beside them. "Ladies, I'd love to introduce you to my esteemed quartermaster, Mister Mom."

"Your name is Mom?" Serina said, looking baffled.

"On this ship, it's *Mister* Mom to you." The man growled the words, setting his jaw in irritation.

"He's a delight. Truly." Dreggs wasn't actually wearing their jacket—it was just draped over their shoulders like a cape. They shrugged out of it, hooking it over one shoulder. The picture of confident ease. "You're new to piracy, but in the Southern Seas, the captain is elected . . . and everyone else falls in line based on seniority. I'm the alluring one—" At this, they offered a flirtatious wink. "—but Mister Mom is the real authority."

"Don't get on my bad side," Mister Mom grunted.

Serina, meanwhile, looked like she'd just swallowed a lemon. "Holy shit. Shit, fuck, *shit*."

"Took her a moment, didn't it?" Dreggs asked Reyna.

"You're the Dastardly Pirate Dreggs!" Serina dug her hands into her long hair, tilting her face toward the wooden ceiling. "Stars be damned. I must be *good* at my job to pique your interest."

"Good enough to warrant a visit and a chat, certainly." Now when Dreggs smiled, it was like a shark scenting blood. Serina stiffened, but the infamous pirate was already gesturing at the locked cell door. "Why don't you two join me for a cup of tea? Mister Mom, if you please."

The quartermaster unlocked the cell door, motioning for Reyna and Serina to follow Dreggs upstairs.

Well. At least now they'd get some answers.

29

Kianthe

Kianthe awoke to an empty bed.

Well, "awoke" sounded far too calm. What really happened was Ponder sinking her tiny talons into Kianthe's chest *through the blankets*. The mage yelped, jackknifed upright, and Ponder deftly glided to the chair in the corner. She squawked irately, spread her wings, and screeched for good measure.

In the hallway, someone slammed a fist on their bedroom door.

Kianthe barely heard it—she was too busy staring at the empty space beside her. "Reyna never came to bed," she muttered, her chest tying into knots.

Ponder chittered, pacing along the thin back of the wooden chair. It wobbled under her weight, and she spread her wings farther to balance herself. Her lion tail thrashed.

There was no reason to think Reyna was in danger, but it didn't stop Kianthe's mind from going to dark places. She threw the covers off, already clothed from the night before, and stopped short when her eyes settled on the sword propped against the wall by the door.

Reyna never went anywhere without that sword.

Fuck.

"Kianthe," someone—Bobbie—shouted through the thick wood of the door. "Stars damn it all, please wake up!" More pounding, so intense it might break down the door soon.

Kianthe wrenched it open, sparks of magic flashing around her. Ponder landed on her shoulder, digging in to steady herself, and screeched in Bobbie's face. Bobbie yelped, scrambling backward.

The chaos ignited the mage's temper, which heated the hallway considerably. "Quiet!" Kianthe snapped.

Silence fell. Down the hallway, a few doors were easing open. Pil, his kids, Squirrel—they all stepped out of their rooms. Farley was coming up the staircase holding two mugs of tea. Kianthe compartmentalized it all, then lifted Ponder off her shoulder, setting her with a *thump* on the wooden floor. The mage stared past Bobbie at the open door behind her.

Serina's bedroom.

Where someone had clearly ripped her from her bed.

"I couldn't have chosen a *normal* fiancée," Kianthe muttered, scrubbing her hands across her tired face. She swept into Serina's room only briefly, acknowledged no one was there, then stepped past Bobbie to the staircase. Farley skirted along the banister, giving the mage space. As expected, the inn's sitting area was empty. Kianthe wanted to laugh—or cry. "Couldn't have picked someone who'd hide when kidnappers came. No, I had to pick a Stone-damned Queensguard, someone literally trained to run headfirst into danger."

Bobbie was on her heels, undeterred by the magic sparking around her. Ponder nipped at her clothes and Bobbie gently shooed her off, panic tinging her voice. "Serina wasn't kidnapped." The ex-constable swallowed a gasp as the movement pulled her stitches, expertly placed by Lathe's doctor days ago.

It didn't mean she was better. It just meant she wasn't bleeding outright anymore.

Even though anxiety pulled at Kianthe's mind, made her hands shaky, her breath scarce, she forced herself to calm down. It didn't work, not really, but she'd been spending time with Reyna discussing contingencies. The last time they were separated, Kianthe assumed she was safe, and then Arlon attacked with five ships.

Now, Kianthe took control, and tapped the moonstone on her chest three long, pointed times.

Emergency?

Long, agonizing moments passed—and then two long taps replied in their personalized code: *All okay.*

So, Reyna was both alive and well. It settled Kianthe's racing heart just a bit. Whatever had happened, whoever took her, Reyna clearly chose it. They had limited speaking capabilities through the moonstones—their communication was purely through taps and warmth, but she would be alerted if Reyna was injured, at least.

For now, Kianthe stayed focused. It was a work in progress, but at least she could do something here.

Serina's whole crew had shown up now. Rankor had clearly just rolled out of bed, and he accepted one of the steaming mugs from his wife. Squirrel muttered something about stress-baking and stepped toward the kitchen. Pil and the kids were watching solemnly.

Bobbie was still frantic. "Serina *can't* have been kidnapped. No one wants her that badly. Right?"

"Arlon might." Kianthe drew a short breath, tapping three short taps on her moonstone now. *I love you.*

And three came back instantly: *Love you too.*

It helped. It didn't fix her pounding heart, her jittery nerves, but it helped.

Feo appeared at the top of the staircase, their expression utterly disgruntled. "Arlon wouldn't have orchestrated a kidnapping; it's far too messy. A fast attack like the blockade battle can be cleaned up and denied, but a kidnapping means you're holding a hostage—often for long periods. Even he's not that stupid."

"She hasn't been kidnapped," Bobbie insisted. "She was drunk; she probably just stumbled into the snow. She . . ." The ex-constable trailed off when no one spoke in agreement. Bobbie scoured Kianthe's grim expression, then sank into the desk chair. "No. Stars, the last thing I said to her—she can't be gone."

"She's not gone," Kianthe said, exasperation lacing her words. After all, if something happened to Serina, Reyna would be fighting to save her. And *that* put Reyna in danger . . . so Kianthe had to pray neither of them were in that situation. "Bobbie, I'm telling you. She's okay."

A startled scream arose from the kitchen.

"For the Stone's blessed sake." Kianthe stomped past everyone, around the lower hallway into the kitchen. Squirrel was there, arms laden with a bag of flour, and she pointed at the floor.

A single dagger gleamed on the ground, its blade pointing toward the door.

"That's Reyna's." Kianthe knelt beside it. Her eyes followed the path out the door. Ponder prowled beside her, clawing at the dagger, chittering curiously. "Whoever took them left through here." Magic nudged her, circling around a lingering residue of blue locke in the air. When extracted properly, blue locke could put even the largest creature to sleep. Matild, Tawney's resident medical expert, had Kianthe procure it for sedating patients during nastier operations.

Now, the golden magic of the plant swirled around her, acting like a trail leading Kianthe straight out the door. She ran her thumb along the hilt of Reyna's dagger as she absently followed it, weaving through the streets until they reached the docks.

The procession followed *her,* something she didn't realize until she stopped at the water's edge.

"They got on a ship?" Bobbie asked.

"Mmm. Not Serina's ship, either." It was still docked in that cove north of here, and two people couldn't have gotten it out—not with all the ice present. Already, the cold whipped through Kianthe's clothes; she'd left her cloak at home, and she didn't bother stifling her shiver.

Overhead, Ponder circled, screeching sadly. A louder, deeper screech echoed, and Visk appeared on the horizon, summoned by her misery.

Kianthe flagged him down. He landed with a heavy thump on the dock, twisting his head to watch her. But before she could swing her legs over his back, a hand stopped her.

"Arcandor." Feo spoke firmly, clearly. "I know you're worried.

But Reyna is capable, and you've already confirmed they're alive."

Of course they'd seen her tapping her moonstone. Nosy bastard. She scowled, but Feo didn't release their hold on her arm. "We need to think about this. I've told you before and I'll tell you again: nothing good comes from rushing into a fight."

"What's there to think about?" Kianthe demanded. "They were taken on a ship. If we fly south, we'll find them."

"I'm coming too." Bobbie set her jaw. She was swaying a bit, but managed to stay upright, which was frankly impressive.

Feo ground their teeth, exasperated. "You can't track a ship on the river. They could be halfway to Oslop and you'd never realize it."

A slow smile tilted Kianthe's lips, and she hopped off Visk with a smug smile. "Oh, Feo. Sometimes I think you forget the capabilities of an elemental mage—especially one with my magic." And she casually dipped her hand into the water lapping the dock.

It was eager to please. The river traced a path in her mind, a yellow imprint of the small ship that had docked here late last night, then weighed anchor and sailed south, fast. Too fast. Magically fast. "Interesting," she drawled, pulling out the word just to feed Feo's confusion. "A small ship. Closer in size to her original vessel than the *Knot for Sail*. They have a mage on board, so they're likely past Oslop by now. Maybe even to Neolow."

"Or Arlon's estate," Bobbie mumbled.

Kianthe prodded the water, but it iced her hand petulantly. "The river didn't carry them to Arlon. It's frankly offended you'd suggest it."

"Wow," Pil breathed.

Feo set their jaw, but knew better than to argue again. They heaved a sigh, massaging their brow. "Regardless, I was hoping to borrow your griffon to get to Wellia. The sooner we rally the council, the better off we'll be against Arlon."

Visk ruffled his feathers, stretching his wings as he awaited Kianthe's orders.

She hesitated. Much as she hated to admit it, Feo did have a point; she'd summoned them for a reason, and it'd be incredibly rude to abandon them in Lathe while she flew off to rescue Reyna. Besides, she doubted Bobbie would let her leave alone—and the ex-constable certainly wouldn't be able to handle a day in the skies. Not in her condition.

The last thing Kianthe needed was to rescue the rescuer.

"I suppose it'd be more useful to follow on a boat, with backup." Her words were begrudging, tugged through a clenched jaw. "I can get the ship moving faster downstream than the crew can alone."

Bobbie tensed. "If Serina's in trouble, we can't waste time."

Kianthe heaved a sigh. She already hated this day. "Reyna's with her; they'll be fine. Until then, you should start thinking of who might want Serina in a precarious position. Because the last I heard, Arlon was her only real enemy, aside from a few disgruntled farmers."

"Dad," Darlene said quietly. At her side, Joe elbowed their father.

Pil grumbled something, rubbed the back of his neck, and raised his voice so it carried through the group: "It's Dreggs."

Everyone glanced at him with varying degrees of shock.

His kids shifted uncomfortably. Pil heaved a sigh that shook his entire body. "I wasn't entirely honest with Serina when we came on board. My kids were raised on Dreggs's ship; they're like family to both of 'em. Dreggs heard about Serina pirating on the Nacean and asked us to scope things out, so we got hired on. Wasn't hard."

"But Serina's really nice," Darlene mumbled. Her hand drifted to her ever-present sword. "And Reyna's teaching me to fight. Dreggs won't do that."

"Dreggs doesn't want you on deck during a fight, and neither do I," Pil said sternly.

Joe crossed their arms. "I like Serina's ship. It's quieter."

Kianthe started laughing and found she couldn't stop. It bubbled up from her chest, filled her lungs, and had her whole body shaking. "You—you infiltrated Serina's crew? Anyone else? Rankor, are you one of Queen Tilaine's spies?"

"Not that I'm aware." Rankor laughed.

"We weren't planning anything bad. We were just supposed to watch her. Figure things out." Darlene set her jaw, daring them to challenge her. "And we figured out that we liked her, so that's what we wrote when Dreggs sent a messenger pigeon for an update."

At Kianthe's side, Bobbie fingered the crochet needles at her hip. Then her hand drifted to the sword she'd obtained from . . . somewhere. Viviana, perhaps. "Serina *trusted* you three." The betrayal cut through her voice.

Pil crossed his arms, moving in front of his kids like Bobbie might attack them. "You're one to talk. You've been causing Serina stress long before we met her. Based on what I've seen, Dreggs won't hurt her—especially not the way you have."

The words took the fight out of Bobbie. She hunched, like she was two breaths from falling over.

Diarn Feo heaved a sigh, raising their hands. "Listen. All I need to know is whether I'm staying here or going to Wellia."

"Go to Wellia. But decipher the contents of that folder before you leave." Kianthe massaged her brow, edging away the headache that had settled between her eyes. "Visk, you're with Feo. Anything they need, got it? Ponder's staying with me; she'll be able to find Reyna faster than my magic. Pirates, we're going sailing. Anyone who has a problem with the people on board can stay here."

Bobbie frowned, but didn't volunteer to stay in Lathe.

Pil and his kids didn't either.

"Great," Kianthe said glumly. "This should be fun. Let's go find the Dastardly Pirate Dreggs."

30

Reyna

The Dastardly Pirate Dreggs was something of an enigma, and Reyna wasn't pleased about it. It was a rare moment when she wasn't in control, and she was forced to admit that the infamous pirate wasn't quite what she expected. Dashing and debonair, certainly, but there was something about this situation she couldn't quite place.

In Reyna's vast experience, her gut was rarely wrong.

And so she lingered in discontent, racking her brain for obscure facts about Dreggs. They were rumored to be Sheparan-born, which meant they probably worshiped the Stars. They'd started with a single ship and gathered a fiercely loyal crew through honesty, competence, and a bit of charm. They didn't kill unless they had to . . . but once someone was identified as a threat, they had no problem eliminating it.

None of that helped her in this immediate moment.

Dreggs casually led the procession toward the staircase to the deck, with Mister Mom lagging behind and Reyna and Serina sandwiched in the middle. It was a short walk spent in awkward silence.

Serina broke it by whispering to Reyna, "Are we about to be killed? Stars, I figured Arlon would do that, not Dreggs."

"If they wanted you dead, you already would be," Reyna replied.

Serina closed her eyes, drew a shaking breath. "Great. Tell me there's an escape plan."

Reyna's lips quirked into a smile she didn't really feel. "I always have an escape plan. But right now, I'm more intrigued with what they want."

"No one pirates unless it's under Dreggs's flag. Not for long, anyway. Maybe this is a job offer." She wasn't speaking quietly; Dreggs could certainly hear her. But as they climbed onto the deck, the pirate didn't acknowledge them.

Serina huffed, falling into agitated silence as they reached the deck.

And their location was surprising. Reyna knew they'd made good time heading downriver, but she didn't give Dreggs enough credit. In the span of an evening, their small ship had somehow traveled past Oslop, past Diarn Arlon's estate, past Neolow. The mountains had given way to rolling hills, the snow-coated pine trees shifting to the colorful deciduous blend. They hadn't reached the vineyards near Koll yet, but it was a near thing.

It got worse. As Reyna's eyes adjusted to the sunlight, she realized she was wrong about something else, too. She thought Dreggs had sailed this smaller ship north to remain sneaky, agile . . . but that was another misconception. Clearly, the Dastardly Pirate Dreggs didn't care about subtleties.

As Arlon's constables had expected, Dreggs's notorious flagship, the *Painted Death,* was anchored in plain sight along the coast: huge crimson sails secured, a black flag with the skull and crossbones flapping merrily in the breeze. It was several times the size of the *Knot for Sail,* with multiple levels, at least twenty cannons, and a working crew of a hundred.

Well, a hundred and four, if that steamy biography was to be believed.

No wonder no one stopped them before this point. Suddenly, Reyna wondered what had happened to that huge group of constables marching south from Neolow.

Concern must have flitted across her face, because Dreggs

paused, grinning triumphantly. "Ah. You *can* be surprised. For a moment, I was worried you knew more than me."

"Did you kill them? Arlon's constables?" Reyna demanded.

Dreggs tilted their head. "Please. I only kill those who attack me first. I lured that group onto a boat and deposited them onto one of the islands. They might be hungry until someone notices them, but they're not dead. Probably."

Reyna narrowed her eyes.

The pirate captain chuckled. "Believe me or not, it's the truth." With a charming salute, they raised their voice. "Lower the plank, if you please!"

A huge plank shot out from the massive vessel, unnaturally fast. So, not just one elemental mage under their employ. Multiple.

Reyna had to admit, this was an impressive operation.

As they crossed the wobbling wood, leaving the smaller ship behind to board the massive flagship, Serina grew more irritated. "I know you offer a job to any crew you capture, but maybe we can all save some time. I don't steal gold. I steal food."

Dreggs glanced at her. "What an interesting business model." They hopped onto the deck like a kid hopping into a pile of leaves, arms wide, sticking the landing.

Behind them, Mister Mom boomed monotonously: "Captain on deck."

"Aye," several sailors echoed from the rigging, the deck, over the side of the ship. There were so many that Reyna severely hoped they wouldn't need to fight their way out—because without Kianthe, that attempt would almost certainly fail.

Dreggs straightened, hooking their coat over their shoulder with a finger. With their free hand, they gestured extravagantly at the captain's quarters—which, once they stepped inside, was revealed to be more of a captain's suite. The parlor rivaled anything in Her Excellency's palace and every piece of furniture put Arlon's décor to shame.

"This is quite fancy for a bloodthirsty pirate," Reyna remarked.

"I told you, it's a rare mood when I'm feeling bloodthirsty.

Mostly, I operate through business deals and common courtesy. Please, take a seat." Dreggs pointed at a set of armchairs beside the wide bank of windows. "I love the open ocean, but there is something spectacular about the fall colors along the Nacean River."

Behind them, Mister Mom stomped to a long, ornate table, its wood polished to a shine, and lit a small fire beneath a gleaming silver kettle. They rustled through a small wooden cabinet laden with teas.

Serina balked, sinking into her chair like they'd just ordered her execution. "W-We're not going to the Southern Seas, are we? The ocean?"

Now Dreggs smiled, perching on the armchair across from her. "Serina of Lathe, failed farmer turned pirate. Your father told me you almost drowned in the ocean as a child, and now you're deathly afraid of large bodies of water . . . which makes your current career choice fascinating."

"You've met my father?"

"I heard you nearly drowned again recently; I'm surprised the experience didn't turn you off of the Nacean River, too."

Reyna's senses sharpened. "How did you know she almost drowned recently?"

But Dreggs just smiled, held up a hand. "Quiet, dear. The pirates are having a discussion, and if you get involved, I fear we'll be sailing down a different stream." They paused, met her gaze in an almost chilling fashion. "But don't worry, Reyna. I have you earmarked for later today."

This situation felt like it was careening out of control. None of the biographies of the Dastardly Pirate Dreggs mentioned they'd be quite like this. Reyna hated it—and simultaneously respected it. She sat back in her chair, crossing her legs, watching this unfold.

Serina set her jaw. She was too stubborn to realize the danger they were in. "I'm not going to join your crew. I won't sail on the ocean, and I don't steal gold. So, if that's all you wanted, you might as well let us go."

"But you just got here." Dreggs flashed a predatory smile.

"I'd like to leave." Serina met it squarely.

"Regrettably, we do have business to attend." Dreggs pushed to their feet, their bootsteps muffled by an expensive rug laid between the chairs. They smoothed an upturned corner before pausing by the windows. "What you're doing is admirable, and I appreciate anyone trying to disrupt Diarn Arlon's careful world. Believe it or not, I started pirating on the Nacean River decades ago—and he swiftly brought an end to that operation."

They swiveled around to wink at Reyna. "Your biography didn't tell you that, did it?"

Reyna certainly respected them. She leaned back in her chair, the picture of ease. "I'll be honest; my fiancée and I were more focused on the explicit scenes than your pirating history."

"Oh, Stars." Serina buried her face in her hands.

Meanwhile, Dreggs exploded into laughter. They slapped their knee and bellowed, "You hear that, Mom? The Arcandor, reading smut about little old me. Did you pass a copy to Queen Tilaine, too?"

It was actually concerning how much this pirate knew. It was getting harder to fake her smile, even as Mister Mom handed her a porcelain cup of . . . vanilla chai, it smelled like. "Her Excellency's reading tastes are a bit more refined than mine, admittedly. The Arcandor especially liked the knot-tying scene. It was educational."

"A sailor's knot is always useful." Dreggs grinned. They sobered, looking again at Serina. "I didn't call you here to hire you, and Reyna was right: if I wanted you dead, I wouldn't have bothered with the kidnapping."

"Then why am I here?" Serina scowled, refusing a matching cup from Mister Mom.

"You don't want tea?" Dreggs sounded upset.

Serina slammed her hands on the coffee table, shocking the room. "I want answers, damn it."

Silence lingered in her wake. Dreggs accepted a cup of tea from Mister Mom and took a delicate sip. "Touchy." They gracefully perched again on the edge of their seat, tracing the rim of their teacup. "I'll be blunt, since you asked so nicely. I want to break into Arlon's warehouse, and I need your help to do it."

Serina's brow knitted together. "What?"

"Oh, *now* you want the buildup. Do you see what I'm dealing with here? Start with the dramatics—enough of the dramatics—okay, wait, though, the dramatics." Dreggs heaved a sigh at Mister Mom, who'd taken a seat in the chair beside the pirate like they were all old friends. It should have been amusing, watching someone of the quartermaster's stature sipping tea from a cup so small.

Reyna wasn't amused, now.

Now, she was wishing Kianthe was here.

"Fine, I'll backtrack." Dreggs took another sip of tea, then offered their cup to Mister Mom. Stoic as anything, the lumbering man clinked their glasses together in quiet cheers. "Arlon has a warehouse where he keeps all the produce shipments before sending them east. He's stockpiling a huge haul for the winter months, and just announced he's boosting prices."

"He's *what*?" Serina looked ready to fight. "He can't boost prices. If he does, people won't survive—"

Dreggs held up a hand. "Trust me, I'm aware. I operate in the Southern Seas, but my parents live in Neolow and I'm rather fond of them." A vicious smile spread across their amicable features. "Arlon picked a fight with me three decades ago and assumed he won. He'll find out just how wrong he is."

"That warehouse is heavily guarded. My crew isn't trained in combat." She spoke the words begrudgingly, rubbing the bandaged wound on her thigh. It had healed nicely in a week, but she still walked with a bit of a limp.

"Luckily, my crew is. Even more fortunate is the fact that your partner was a constable. Once your crew finds you—and I'm sure they're already on their way, considering the Arcandor's magic—we'll be able to formulate a plan of attack."

Serina seemed dazed. It wasn't hard to remember that half a day ago, she'd been absolutely wasted. Now she pinched the bridge of her nose, mumbling to herself. Reyna sipped her tea; it was a shockingly good blend with a fifty-fifty chance of poison. But she'd built up a tolerance to most poisons guarding Queen Tilaine, so she wasn't that worried.

Serina set her jaw. "Say we do attack the warehouse and steal what we can. It's not going to fix the root of the problem."

"We're working on that." Reyna finally intervened. She waited to see if Dreggs would silence her again, but they seemed mildly amused that it had taken her this long. Reyna parsed through what felt safe to reveal here, and ended with: "Arlon attacked his citizens in broad daylight, with force that was shockingly disproportionate to the crime. We believe that might be cause to remove him from the council—and his lands."

"I knew I could count on you." Dreggs drained their mug, then handed it to Mister Mom. "You have some kind of reputation, you know. The retired Queensguard turned Arcandor's fiancée. The only thing you're missing is an information network outside of that town of yours."

"Perhaps you'll lend me access, since yours seems so robust." Reyna's tone was measured.

Dreggs smirked. "I can tell you're disgruntled, but I've shown you all my cards. Think back to your time on the Nacean River. Who could have possibly revealed the information I know?"

Reyna had been thinking—this entire conversation, she'd been thinking. And now, the answer came easily. "Judd. The bartender in Koll, the one with the great wine and that excellent apron." She heaved a sigh. "I suppose this is a lesson in liquor. If Judd was eavesdropping on my conversations, the queen's spies could do the same."

"That's a sobering thought."

Silence.

Dreggs burst into laughter again. "You two are no fun. Can't wait for the Arcandor to get here. Her jokes are legendary."

Well, it did make Reyna feel better about the pirate . . . and the knowledge they wielded. But Serina had paled, clenching her hands into fists. "*Judd?* Judd is working for you? He found my pirate crew! Stars, I knew he collected them too fast." She sounded agonized, like everything was crashing around her. "Did . . . did they even want to be on my ship? Or were they just following your orders?"

Dreggs's brow knitted together, and they leaned forward. Their tone was soft now, almost encouraging. "Serina, I feel it's important to stop and acknowledge what you've done this season. You became a pirate in an area where piracy has been eradicated. You don't kill, maim, or slaughter; you poke at a giant and somehow avoid his fist." A pause, a sigh. "Pil is one of mine. His kids are practically *my* kids. But even if they come back to my ship, I could find you seven pirates tomorrow who'd take their place."

Serina didn't know what to say to that, clearly. She hunched into herself, drumming her fingers on her leg, seemingly torn between swelling at the praise and processing that betrayal.

While she figured it out, Reyna smoothly redirected the conversation. "Since you know so much, I'd be remiss if I didn't at least show you this." She fished the folded papers from Arlon's rolltop desk out of her pocket, slid them across the low table. "We're attempting to crack this code."

"Oooh. My favorite." Dreggs picked it up, then took one look and huffed, tossing it back to Reyna. "Arlon's writing. Of course. It's a Leonolan cipher; swap the letters into Leonolan script, then translate the new words in Common. He's been using that one since I've been old enough to read."

Reyna stared, jaw unhinged.

Dreggs raised an eyebrow. "What? Listen, if you want a better cipher, I'd be happy to oblige. Mister Mom and I have been playing around with a code that uses numbers and multiplication—it's quite complex."

"And secret," Mister Mom said with a scowl.

"Yes, yes."

Reyna stowed the letters again. "Any chance you have a library aboard this vessel?"

Dreggs stared at her, deadpan. "This is a pirate ship, dear."

She quirked an eyebrow.

They sighed. "Who am I kidding? You remember *that* scene, don't you?"

"My fiancée and I re-created it in our own bookstore." She smiled soft and slow, chest warming at the memory. "It was a wonderful night. I don't need access to the entire thing; I'll just need a book on the Leonolan language. I haven't brushed up in years."

"Lucky for you, I have several bilingual crewmembers. I'll send someone to help." They paused, smiling. "See? I'm not so bad, am I? If you disagree, please refrain from killing me in my sleep; Mister Mom would be beside himself."

"Then I'd be captain," the quartermaster said, almost amused.

"Or the crew would vote and our new bilge cleaner would get an upgrade. He's fairly charismatic."

Serina pushed to her feet. "Are we still talking about a possible siege on Arlon's warehouse, or has that conversation fallen completely to the wayside?" She sounded a little desperate, a little hysterical. "Because I'm not quite done with that yet."

Dreggs drummed their chin. "To be fair, you'd tuned out. And to be more fair, it'd be less of a siege, more of a heist. I'm not starting a war on my parents' doorstep. Imagine the family holidays." They shuddered in mock horror.

A heist. Reyna quirked an eyebrow. "What did you have in mind?"

And a slow, devious smile spread across Dreggs's face.

31

Kianthe

It was an agonizing day of sailing.

Bobbie spent the majority of it at the bow of the ship, staring at the river as if it might produce Serina anytime. Unfortunately, Pil and his kids were *also* on deck handling the sails, which Kianthe kept so full of air that the ship was practically careening down the Nacean. Several times, she had to holler at Bobbie to get away from the railing, because Stone forbid they lose her overboard again.

Around midafternoon, they paused to eat. Rankor, who'd taken over as acting captain, insisted they sit together and bond—"since we are a crew," he said firmly. Everyone protested, but he held up a hand, silencing them.

"Listen. Serina is doing good work here and she needs a crew she can rely on. If we're all upset with each other, we won't last longer than her rescue . . . and I, for one, don't want to leave her like that."

That shut them up. Everyone filed in, glumly sat down, and dug into Squirrel's carefully prepared feast.

Farley gave Rankor a quick kiss, then took a seat beside him. "So. Who wants to apologize first?" She looked between Pil and Bobbie.

And to everyone's shock, Bobbie raised a hand. "I do."

Kianthe nearly spit out her carrots. High overhead, Ponder had found a perch in the crow's nest. She was watching the dinner with rapt attention, waiting to see if anyone dropped food, and she spread her wings when Kianthe started choking.

"Sorry." The mage coughed, swallowed, coughed again. Squirrel thumped her back with surprising strength as Joe pushed a glass of water her way. She chugged it, tears in her eyes. "Sorry, I'm okay. I just—thought I misheard."

Bobbie heaved a sigh. She was picking at her food, pushing it around her plate with her fork. "I think . . . if I admitted Serina was right, it was accepting all this was worthless. The training. My entire career. My dream of change. It was a hard thing to stomach, so I kept looking for reasons why you all were the enemy. But I don't think that's true anymore."

"Arlon's the enemy. That's why we leapt at the chance to join this crew." Rankor smiled warmly. "I'm personally very happy you're here, Bobbie. It was obvious how much you cared about Serina and this crew the moment you stepped on deck during the battle."

Murmurs of agreement.

Bobbie ducked her head, her cheeks flushing. Her green eyes were glued to the table. "T-Thanks. I got more yarn in Lathe. If anyone has any crochet requests . . . well, I think I'll be sticking around. Happy to make what's needed for the crew."

"I want a sweater," Joe said.

Bobbie grimaced. "Ah. A sweater. Something I definitely know how to make."

"Hang on, before we get distracted. I'm sorry too," Pil said, abashed. "We never meant any harm to Serina, or I wouldn't have accepted the job. Dreggs is a good soul."

"They're just curious about her. She's done *that* good a job out here." Darlene gestured at the ship. "I mean, stealing Arlon's private vessel? Even Dreggs wouldn't be that bold."

Pil chuckled, taking a bite of bread. "They tried, once. Did they tell you that?"

"No!" Darlene gasped.

Everyone dissolved into conversation and the meal picked up. As people broke off, chattering with their seatmates and reaching for more food, Kianthe flashed Bobbie a smile across the table. *Good job,* she mouthed.

Bobbie smiled, clearly pleased.

The night slid into casual conversation, which shifted into raw determination when they continued sailing after dinner . . . but at least now the whole crew was on the same page. Kianthe's wind shoved the sails forward, but even that didn't override the pleasant conversations happening on deck now.

And finally, they found the Dastardly Pirate Dreggs's flagship.

"Bit obvious, aren't they?" Bobbie peered into the darkness as they rounded the riverbend.

At her side, Pil sighed. "Subtlety is not their strong suit."

The vessel was huge, certainly—but the obvious part was the lively party happening on deck. It was late at night, the moon a bare sliver over the vessel, and unnaturally bright torches burned across its deck. Music thrummed through the cold evening air, what sounded like an entire orchestra.

Darlene and Joe lurched to the bowsprit, practically hanging off it as they squinted at the deck. "They're having so much fun! Without *us,* can you believe it?" Darlene gasped in offense, shoving her sibling. "Dreggs told us they wouldn't have fun while we were gone."

"They lied," Joe said solemnly.

"Or they're putting on a show for their guests—er, captives. Back to work, kids," Pil commented, tugging a set of ropes to ease the sails in the right direction. Under their guidance and Kianthe's gentle magic, the *Knot for Sail* soon eased alongside the long edge of Dreggs's ship.

"The *Painted Death.*" Kianthe read the name, rolling it around on her tongue. "Sounds dark. I like ours better."

"Of course you do. Ours is a pun." Bobbie chuckled, stopping beside her. She'd grabbed a bit of sleep after dinner, and while it hadn't magically healed her, she did look refreshed now. Her hand drifted to the sword at her hip as she squinted at the deck. "Think they'll attack us?"

Kianthe barked a laugh. "Did you *see* their cannons? They have at least three mages on that ship; they could have sunk us anytime."

"Mages?"

Kianthe gestured at the deck, at Ponder circling high overhead. "Griffons always know. And their magic felt mine as we passed Neolow. They knew we were coming."

"Plank coming down," someone with a deep voice hollered from the massive ship, and a large plank slammed onto their deck.

The moment it stabilized, Reyna careened across it. Normally, this would be a very graceful affair, but Ponder had just identified her and shifted into a dangerously fast dive. With a screech, the baby griffon plowed into her.

Reyna tipped off the plank as she scrambled to keep her balance. Ponder squirmed from her grasp, sweeping open her feathery wings to catch a drift between the ships. Reyna, as someone without wings, just started to fall.

"Rain—" Kianthe gasped and swept a vicious gust of wind to catch her. For a breathless moment, Reyna's feet left the plank . . . but the wind righted her almost instantly.

Reyna straightened, smoothing her windswept hair. "Gods, that was a bit of excitement, wasn't it?" She carefully stepped off the plank before slamming into Kianthe, pulling her into a hug much fiercer than she normally would.

Sure enough, when they separated her cheeks were pink, her smile a bit too wide.

"Drunk Reyna," Kianthe breathed.

"Hello, darling. I was accidentally kidnapped by the most delightful person. Come on; I'll introduce you." She pressed a kiss to Kianthe's lips, then towed her across the plank. Ponder followed behind, clearly sullen that Reyna wasn't prioritizing cuddles and pets over some party with humans.

The mages on the ship waved as Kianthe approached—the magic from each of them shone bright yellow, blending in with the magic in the trees on shore, the wind teasing the wrapped sails. Kianthe waved back cheerfully, beyond pleased to finally be reunited with Reyna and facing something new.

Reyna tapped someone on the shoulder. The person was wearing a crimson jacket and a tricorne hat over short, messy hair. They glanced at Reyna—and their eyes landed on Kianthe, and the mage gasped so loudly everyone nearby turned to stare.

"Holy Stone of Seeing and Stars in the sky, it's you. The Dastardly Pirate Dreggs!"

The pirate in question tugged off their hat and swept a low, charming bow. "And you must be the Arcandor, the esteemed Mage of Ages, our elemental expert and pun-maker extraordinaire." They paused, lips quirking. "I hear you're writing a book. Perhaps you'll let me star in it. My last one was a bestseller, you know."

"Oh, I know." Kianthe bounced on her toes. "Will you sign my copy? And maybe my arm? I can make the ink magically permanent . . . or is that weird?"

"Do it on your chest," Reyna said, giggling. A hulking man of a pirate daintily handed her a glass of wine, and she raised it with a gleeful laugh before taking a deep swig.

Kianthe pulled her shirt down a bit, lifting her cloak to reveal bare skin. "She's right—sign my chest."

"Ladies, ladies." Dreggs laughed, but they were clearly enjoying this. "You'll both get signed copies. And as much as I'd love my signature on your chest, I'm afraid gouging the Arcandor with a quill might be an international incident."

Kianthe released the neck of her shirt with a huff. "Or, maybe it'd just earn you *more* bragging rights."

"Tempting," Dreggs drawled.

Across the ship, Bobbie and the rest of the crew had crossed the plank and were staring at the festivities in admiration. Darlene and Joe had already rejoined two other kids near the captain's quarters, and Pil was chatting amicably with a few other sailors by the bow. Rankor and Farley cheerfully joined the dancing; Squirrel gravitated to the buffet table laden with incredible food. The cook cast a glance over her shoulder, then stuffed a few rolls into her pockets.

Bobbie, meanwhile, had locked eyes with Serina.

Kianthe elbowed Reyna, pointing at them. At Reyna's side, Dreggs put a hand on their hip. "Ah, their eyes meet across a crowded room. Take notes, Arcandor; this is how a romance is made."

"Our eyes met across a crowded room once, too." Reyna latched onto Kianthe's arm, pressing a kiss to her cheek. Her eyes never left Serina, though, who'd just noticed Bobbie stepping slowly toward her.

The three of them held their breaths, watching unabashed.

Bobbie moved—slowly at first, then picking up speed. Serina glanced sideways like she might attack her, like a weapon might be needed. But then Bobbie was upon her, and without warning, she pulled Serina close and kissed her hard.

"Yes!" Reyna shouted, so loud a few people nearby spilled their drinks. "I knew it. *I knew it.*" She hopped, tugging on Kianthe's arm. "Key. Look. I pinned it on the first day. Tell Dreggs that my matchmaking skills are superior."

"Considering *I'm* the one who talked Bobbie off a cliff over and over, I'd say I'm the one with matchmaking skills." Kianthe grinned.

Dreggs snorted at Reyna's mock-offense.

Across the ship, Bobbie had pulled away from Serina with a noticeable wince—although whether that was from her injuries or her brazen action was anyone's guess. Serina's fingers fluttered against Bobbie's cheek, and she smiled softly. Bobbie matched it, leaning forward so their foreheads touched.

Now it felt intimate. Kianthe glanced away.

Reyna didn't. She sipped her wine, a sly smirk tilting her lips.

"Didn't you have a code to crack?" Dreggs asked casually.

"I would like to bask in the glow of my success, thank you."

Kianthe swallowed a laugh, pointing at Ponder, who was currently fleeing two very invested children following her through the ship's spiderweb of lines. The griffon apparently saw it as a gleeful game and leapt between the ropes, waiting just long enough that the kids—maybe seven or eight years old—could grab at her before taking off. They laughed gleefully, loving the chase.

It didn't look very safe, but then again, this *was* a pirate ship.

"You may want to call your griffon before she hurts someone, Rain. And then tell me about the code; you actually deciphered it?"

Reyna followed her gaze, heaved a sigh, and whistled sharply. High overhead, Ponder screeched unhappily, but reluctantly drifted to the deck. Reyna tossed her a particularly big slice of jerky and the griffon forgot all about the kids and their game.

Dreggs watched in fascination. "Oh, no, she's *so cute*."

"Cute and fierce," Kianthe cooed, taking the jerky away for a brief moment. Ponder, who was used to this game, heaved a frustrated sigh, but sat quietly until Kianthe tossed it back to her. She was rewarded with both food and pets. "We're working on training."

"Let me try—" Dreggs bent down, and Ponder hissed at them. They wheeled back. "Ah, perhaps I'll let you two handle the mythical beasts."

"Probably best," Reyna replied. She was still watching Bobbie and Serina, who'd retreated to a private corner of the deck and were sitting on a bench, hunched in intense conversation. It seemed to be going well, though, because Bobbie trailed her fingers up and down Serina's thigh.

Adorable. Sickening. Kianthe wrinkled her nose and said, "Arlon's files, Rain?"

Her fiancée huffed and tugged a stack of annotated papers from the pocket of her trousers. In a breath, her focus was back, because she pointed to the second page and said, "It's shipping manifestos, absolutely. Hopefully Feo isn't spending too much time cracking their side, because the information we need was all here."

"All of it?" Kianthe's eyes widened.

Reyna took another sip of her wine, clearly pleased with herself. "All of it. It's probably the only shipping record he kept, and he figured it'd be safe since . . . well, no one would steal from his ship, on his river."

"Ha," Dreggs said drily, and raised a salute at Serina.

Across the ship, she was solidly ignoring them. She and Bobbie were too busy laughing at something. Her hand traced Bobbie's cheek, and Bobbie took ahold of it gently, then kissed the back of her hand.

Nope. Not adorable. Just sickening. "Get a room," Kianthe called across the ship, and then twisted the wind to make sure it delivered over the loud music.

Serina startled, noticed them, and flipped them off.

Bobbie, meanwhile, flashed a grin.

"All right, you win, Key." Reyna watched Ponder fly off again, then tugged Kianthe away from the festivities. "You remember Dreggs has a library on this ship, right?"

"Please. Everyone remembers chapter twenty-six."

Reyna waved at Dreggs, who'd struck up a conversation with the hulking pirate beside them. The infamous pirate captain waved back, and Reyna smugly led Kianthe belowdecks. Unlike the tiny space on the *Knot for Sail,* they descended into an entirely new realm: not a low-set cargo hold, but a cavernous hallway that led to a dozen rooms.

Reyna opened the door to one, cheerfully waving at two pirates exiting it. Both were clutching books and looked surprised to see her . . . but word of their capture had clearly spread, and no one stopped them.

"Arlon's code was based around the Leonolan language. Dreggs pinned it immediately; I guess they've seen it before—" Reyna was saying, but as she closed the door behind them, she realized Kianthe wasn't listening. "Never mind. I'll let you gawk for a moment."

Gawking was appropriate here. Considering they were on a literal ship, this was an expansive collection. Floor-to-ceiling bookshelves lined every wall, and each had a long metal bar nailed to the center of the shelf space—just enough to hold the books in place during turbulent waters. They were high enough above the waterline that the room should have windows, but instead they'd installed watertight portholes. The entire room glowed with water-repelling magic.

"I knew I liked Dreggs," she said, awed. "What a great use for those mages."

"I was undecided on liking Dreggs for most of the morning, but as expected, they won me over." Reyna gestured toward a table in the center of the room, where she'd clearly set up shop earlier today. Books on Leonolan language and culture were strewn about the table, beside a half-depleted inkwell.

She set the fruits of her labor out for Kianthe to see. "Thirty years ago, Diarn Arlon ordered multiple dragon eggs to be stolen from dragon country. As we know, three were shipped here. Viviana saved one, which left two in his hands."

Kianthe slid into the desk chair, skimming the shipping manifesto she was pointing to. "Delivered in winter under armed guard."

"Indeed. Viviana, and seven of Arlon's constables. He has their payroll information on a later page. They were all compensated handsomely; it wouldn't surprise me if those constables were quite rich now."

"Hmm." Kianthe glanced up, smirking. "Considering how much you drank, you're pretty coherent."

The look Reyna gave her was somewhat acerbic. "Please, Key. I know how to sober up in a pinch." A pause, a scowl. "And I was recently reminded of what I stand to lose by dismissing that ability."

Uh-oh. Kianthe opened her mouth to ask, but Reyna tapped the papers again.

"We're focusing here, darling. Now, Arlon received the eggs. Transported them on Serina's ship, in fact. But he didn't take them anywhere public. Instead, the only stop he made was to his own, private library."

Hope soared in Kianthe's chest. "The eggs are in the library?"

"You said you couldn't visit it because it was 'under construction.' I'm beginning to wonder how long that construction has been ongoing." Reyna smirked. "It's wholly possible he uses that guise to keep everyone but the highest dignitaries out."

"People have seen his library in the last three decades, though," Kianthe said, brow furrowing. "That's how we know it's so spectacular."

Reyna shrugged. "The finer details remain. I have no reason to believe Arlon moved the eggs after placing them in his library. Further in the paperwork, he has payment records for a basement he built below it, and I think that's our target."

"So, now we just need to figure out how to access his ultra-secret, very exclusive library." Kianthe massaged her forehead.

Reyna, however, was still smirking. "Indeed. And how convenient that the pirates of the Nacean are coordinating to steal from Arlon's warehouse soon. It'd be such a shame if Arlon's constables were diverted from one high-profile spot to another."

All right, then. Kianthe chuckled, pulling Reyna in for a triumphant kiss. "What a shame, indeed."

32

Bobbie

The party lasted so long, Bobbie began losing steam.

Problem was, Serina was having an absolute blast. After they talked, after they kissed, they lingered on deck. It was a lot of noise and stimulation for Bobbie, so many people filling so many crevices of the deck and lines that she thought she might never find quiet again. But watching Serina in her element made it worthwhile. Bobbie sagged against the ship's scuffed railing, her head pounding, as Serina chatted with pirates and drank and danced.

She was marvelous. Bobbie had never seen her so blindingly happy.

It's hope, she realized belatedly.

And after so many years of operating alone, Bobbie knew first-hand how nice it was to find that community. So, even if it wasn't in her best physical interests, Bobbie couldn't pull herself away from the festivities.

Unfortunately, Serina noticed.

Of course she did.

"Bobbie," she gasped, breathless from the last dance. She swept closer, eyes alight, face pink with the ship's energy. "You look terrible."

I feel terrible, she wanted to reply. Instead, she rolled her eyes.

"You always know the right thing to say." It was meant as a joke, but Serina's expression fell. Bobbie immediately scrambled backward, dissecting her words, her delivery. Shit. "That wasn't—I didn't mean—"

"No, you're right." Serina grimaced, and the alcohol seemed to wear off as she centered herself. She offered a hand and a kind smile. "Come on. I have a room belowdecks. It's not big, but it'll be a good place to rest, at least."

"What about the party?" Bobbie half-heartedly gestured at the festivities. Kianthe and Reyna were gone, and Serina's crew was spread across the deck, chatting with various pirates from Dreggs's crew. The infamous captain themself had retrieved an instrument and joined the musicians, much to the apparent exasperation of their quartermaster.

It all faded as Bobbie glanced back at Serina.

She shrugged, that easy smile never leaving her face. "You're more important than a party. I'm sorry I didn't notice you fading sooner." And with a strong grip, she eased Bobbie off the bench, supporting her weight, leaning into her side.

Warmth spread through Bobbie's chest, and she didn't argue as Serina led her to a grand staircase near the stern of the ship.

The ship was large, and Serina's tiny room was deep in the bow. Most of the pirates had hammocks in a big area near the cannons, but these quarters were nestled in the back, clearly set aside for visitors or families. Serina unlocked a wooden door with a heavy key and helped Bobbie inside. It was barely half the size of the inn's room back in Lathe, but the narrow bed looked *grand* after such a physically taxing day.

And best, the music upstairs didn't penetrate the walls. Here, it was quiet. Calming.

Bobbie's energy left in a *whoosh,* and she sank onto the cotton mattress. "*Thank* you."

"Don't thank me; we should have been here ages ago." Serina fluffed a pillow, helping her get situated. Her touches were coming more freely now, but every graze of her fingers against Bobbie's skin felt like fire. It was almost enough to temper the throbbing pain of her healing wound. Bobbie followed her cues, lying heavily against the pillow, half propped up.

Her body felt like it was crying in gratitude. A good night's sleep, and she'd be ready to get back to it—but for now, everything felt distant. Numb.

Serina brushed her forehead, then pulled back. "Sorry. I just . . . I think I missed you."

"I *know* I missed you," Bobbie mumbled. Maybe she was a little drunk too. Exhaustion had her words flowing freely. "I'm sorry I wasted so much time. I'm sorry I didn't visit your farm until there was bad news. I was afraid of what you'd think of me."

"I'm not innocent there either." Serina's tone was frustrated. Her eyes dropped to the wound on Bobbie's chest, and she felt the bandages through Bobbie's thin shirt. Yet again, her touch cut through the fog of Bobbie's mind. "Stars above, you tried your damnedest at every turn to keep me safe, and I just spit in your face. How can you forgive me for that?"

Bobbie laughed weakly. "What if we just . . . agree to forgive each other?"

"That feels like cheating," Serina teased. She settled in a chair beside the bed, but was leaning over enough that their faces were very, very close. Her eyes were that same blue-gray that had floored Bobbie as a teenager: the color of fog on the Nacean itself. Bobbie found herself lost in them.

Serina stopped chuckling when she noticed Bobbie staring. "Are you okay?"

"I'm trying to remember if you were always this beautiful, or if I just forgot." Saying it didn't even feel embarrassing. Bobbie was so far beyond pretenses at this point. She just wanted to speak her mind and be done with it.

Serina flushed from head to toe. Her wheat-colored skin literally shifted into an amusing red that splotched her cheeks and made her reel backward. "Stars. You can't just *say* things like that. We have issues. Old rivalries. Lots of unresolved problems. We can't move into the good stuff until we've come to terms with all of that!"

"Oh."

"Yeah." Serina set her jaw, stubbornly avoiding Bobbie's gaze.

Bobbie's eyelids were fluttering shut. "I'm not sure it matters right now."

Serina hesitated. "It should matter."

"It should. It just . . . doesn't. Not to me, not anymore." Bobbie drew a slow breath, sinking deeper into the cushions. "I think I've loved you for a long, long time, and the rest feels like noise." Like being on a party deckside, music thrumming, head pounding—but then they come downstairs and it's quiet and private and peaceful. Bobbie didn't have the energy to say all that, but she wanted to.

Instead, she found herself drifting. She wasn't even aware that Serina had moved until she was fitting herself against Bobbie on the bed. Serina was being careful of Bobbie's wounds, but her body was a warm comfort after a long day on a cold river.

Bobbie tried to shift to accommodate her, but Serina whispered, "Don't hurt yourself more. I'll find a spot." And she fitted herself around Bobbie like a well-worn hat, curling into the space left behind. Her cheek rested near Bobbie's shoulder—not enough to apply pressure or cause pain, but close enough that her breath tickled Bobbie's neck.

Tears pricked Bobbie's eyes, and she leaned her head against Serina's. "I'll make it up to you, Serrie. I'll do better."

"Me, too. I swear it." Conviction wound into Serina's tone, same as with the other avenues of her life. And in that moment, Bobbie realized she'd become someone Serina would fight for.

And if she knew one thing about the feared pirate, Captain Serina of the Nacean River would never lose once she set her mind on something.

Happiness spread through Bobbie's chest, even as her eyes drifted shut again. Serina relaxed, her breathing slowing to match Bobbie's. And as the rest of Dreggs's crew partied the night away, they shared an intimate moment of love and compassion.

Nothing else mattered.

33

Reyna

The next two days were spent scheming on the Dastardly Pirate Dreggs's ship.

Not planning, mind. *Scheming.*

Bobbie, Serina, and Dreggs spent most of their time hunched over a table with self-drawn blueprints of the river, the warehouse, and the constables' rotation among them. Dreggs offered suggestions on pirate warfare, which varied depending on the situation: sometimes a frontal assault, sometimes chasing an enemy into dangerous waters, and sometimes it was even sneakier.

"I once infiltrated Queen Tilaine's private ship on a diplomatic mission to Leonol." Dreggs winked.

Reyna, sipping their luxurious tea near the bank of windows, nearly spit out the drink. "You did not."

"No one noticed. Not even your mother." Dreggs leaned back, crossing their arms in utter satisfaction. Reyna balked, but the pirate was moving on. "The key is acting like we belong—and knowing just enough about the procedure that no one questions it. That's where you come in, Barylea."

"Bobbie. Please," the ex-constable said, wincing. Her wounds clearly didn't pain her more than her real name. Serina sat close, nearly shoulder to shoulder, and Reyna had it on good authority—her own—that they'd shared a room the last two nights.

Fortunately, Bobbie wasn't just interested in Serina. She now had a vested interest in taking down Arlon; loyalty to her old career was a thing of the past, apparently.

"The warehouse is right on the shoreline for easy transport access. On the east side of the river, because everything ships to Wellia and out from there. There are two guard towers with archers, dogs patrolling the perimeter, and several alchemical mages who've undoubtedly spelled the entrances."

"Luckily, I employ four alchemists as well." Dreggs smiled.

Kianthe, draped over one of the armchairs rereading their signed, sexy biography, quirked an eyebrow. "Does the Magicary know you're poaching people?"

"What can I say? Even mages are enamored with the pirate's life."

"Oooh. New title idea: *A Pirate's Wife for Me.*"

"Charming, dear," Reyna said, adding a tiny bit of honey to her porcelain cup. "The heist?"

Serina rapped the diagram of the river with her knuckle. "We send Bobbie in first, have her tell Arlon we're planning an attack on the warehouse. She regrets her part in my stealing his ship, but there's still time to stop us . . . if he moves fast."

"The constables are removed from the library, giving us free access." Reyna nodded at Kianthe.

"Right." Serina snapped her fingers, looking amused. "Then my crew heads in. We make a big show of the cannons we mounted on deck. While all eyes are on us, Dreggs takes over."

Dreggs bounced in their seat. "What an exciting time. My crew is heavily trained in combat, and we have mages on our side. We can handle the alchemical seals, and break into the warehouse from the back side while you're keeping them busy at the river."

"Don't kill anyone." Bobbie set her jaw. "I know these folk. A lot of them have families, just like us."

"Dear, and I mean this in the nicest way, death will happen in a battle of this scale."

Bobbie narrowed her eyes.

The pirate captain heaved a long-suffering sigh. "Young and

idealistic. Fine. My crew will *try* to avoid death. But if it comes down to the constables or my crew, I can guarantee who will be left standing. Fair?"

"Fair," Bobbie said begrudgingly.

"We'll take what we can and get out; I'll leave a little calling card to Arlon in the mix. Then we use my network to distribute the food. Arlon knows he's not top dog on the Nacean anymore, and my parents are happy." Dreggs paused. "I mean, I'm happy."

Kianthe snorted.

With the battle plan in place, they all separated to prepare. There wasn't much point in wasting time, after all. Dreggs waited until they left the *Painted Death,* traipsing down the plank onto the *Knot for Sail,* before sounding an alarm to rally their crew.

Kianthe and Reyna paused on deck, drawing in one last moment of peace before the storm. It gave them full view of Serina's crew dispersing, of Mister Mom boarding the third vessel—the one used to kidnap them from Lathe days ago.

Bobbie paused near the plank to it, hesitating. The immediate plan was that Mister Mom dropped her off close enough to borrow a ship from the constables in Neolow, where she could sail north to warn Diarn Arlon.

Now, Bobbie only had eyes for Serina. "Are you going to be okay? Arlon has the best archers in Shepara." She gnawed at her lower lip. "A lot could go wrong with this plan."

Serina flashed a confident smile and pulled her in for a kiss. "Don't worry. I'll be careful." Now her gaze sharpened. "You too, okay? Arlon may see through all of this. If he does, you know how to stop the attack."

Bobbie tugged out Kianthe's moonstone, begrudgingly handed over for long-distance emergency communication.

The mage huffed, crossing her arms.

Reyna elbowed her. "It's just for a few days, Key. We'll get it back. And I'll be with you the rest of the time."

"I know. I still feel naked without it."

Reyna's eyes roamed her fiancée. "Wouldn't that be something?"

Kianthe smirked, and her sour mood was forgotten.

Meanwhile, Bobbie heaved a sigh. "You two say *we're* ridiculous, but you're acting like you're already on a honeymoon." Bobbie paused, fidgeting. "I'm happy I met you two, though. Things would have been different without your help. Thank you."

"We expect an invitation to the wedding," Reyna said resolutely.

Serina paled. "Moving a little fast there, huh? Let's see if we survive the season first."

After a few more moments of discussion, Bobbie boarded the smaller vessel, waved as Mister Mom ordered the willowy pirate—who wound up being Dreggs's sailmaster—to get them to Neolow. Only once she was out of sight, vanishing around the river bend, did Serina heave a sigh.

"I think I might love her after all."

"Shocking," Reyna said delicately.

"A griffon would be very helpful right about now," Kianthe muttered.

They'd left Dreggs behind, and Serina dropped them off at the stables near Neolow's eastern shore. Regretfully, Lilac was still stabled in Koll, so they had to rent horses from the stables themselves. Normally, *renting* a horse was an absurd request, but considering the Arcandor herself asked, no one argued. Reyna tossed them a few coins as an afterthought, and they rode into the night.

Of course, that meant they were still trudging up the shoreline hours later. It had started to rain again—not quite snow, but the drops that pelted their faces were icy. Even after Kianthe placed a magical bubble around them, the air was still freezing.

Reyna swallowed a laugh. She wasn't much happier than Kianthe, considering the weather. "We have a griffon."

"Ponder is a *baby*. She's no help."

Kianthe squinted through the trees, didn't see the griffon in question, and whistled. Ponder chittered in response, skillfully weaving between the trunks. One day she'd be unstoppable in the skies—Reyna could already see her dedication, the drive she'd develop with age. She was smart. She was resourceful. Pride swelled when Reyna looked at her.

So, her voice was overly fond when she replied, "Oh, she'll be helpful someday. How long does it take to ride a griffon, again?"

"By summer, she'll be full size. By this time next year, you should be able to ride her safely." Kianthe waggled a hand. "Give or take."

"See? Just a year's time before we can fly. That's helpful." Reyna held out her arm, grinning when Ponder landed on it. She wasn't as heavy as one might expect, thanks to her hollow bones, and she nibbled Reyna's ear before taking off again.

Kianthe heaved a sigh. "Doesn't help us now. Are you still craving adventure?"

Reyna considered it. "Mmm. Not quite. After seeing Diarn Feo, I'm actually feeling a bit homesick. This would be a wonderful night to curl up by the fire together and read a book. I love the way you narrate."

"Stupid voices and all?"

"Indeed."

The mage seemed to swell with the praise. "Well, good. I'm glad Tawney will be a nice reprieve from this. I know the career change has been difficult for you, but we can take trips like this anytime, Rain. Seriously. Between the two of us, there'll be no lack of adventure."

Reyna inhaled the damp scent of petrichor, smiling. "I think I'm finally ready to believe that."

Kianthe returned the smile, and the night pulled forward.

They arrived at the library near sunrise but didn't get too close. They'd timed it well—Bobbie should just be entering Arlon's estate now, which meant the call to shift the constables farther north would be happening anytime. Reyna scouted the area while Kianthe watched Ponder, who was a bit too unpredictable to take on a stealth mission. Frankly, if they could have left her with Serina's crew, they would have—but Ponder only listened to Visk, Reyna, and sometimes Kianthe, so that was out of the question.

Alone, Reyna prowled along the edges of the clearing, squinting at the large building before her. Unlike Arlon's estate, this library was a display of wealth. It was circular, with multiple levels that reminded her of the luxurious towers in Wellia. Huge windows revealed books on every floor, so many her head spun. Forget Ponder—*Kianthe* would be the wild card here.

The grounds were heavily guarded. Reyna perched on a cliff overlooking the clearing, lying on her stomach in the rain while the sun painted the horizon a dull gray. In the incrementally brightening light, she counted no less than twenty-seven constables on rotation.

Gods, Arlon must have an entire town's worth of constables under his command. How did he even train an enforcement group this large?

Then again, it was wholly possible he'd relocated the people he had left to guard his most prized possessions: the eggs.

She had just finished mapping their rotations when a call sounded on the library's far end. The constables stormed toward the sound, leaving the opening Reyna expected. Moments later, her moonstone tapped twice against her chest. It was clumsy, nowhere near the professional taps Kianthe had mastered, but it would do.

Two taps meant the plan succeeded. Bobbie had warned Arlon and he was clearly responding.

Reyna watched for a while longer, but most of the constables didn't come back. Their window was open, and it wouldn't stay that way long. She crept back to Kianthe, wringing water out of her hair before tying it into a bun again.

Kianthe and Ponder were hunched under a bubble of empty air, the rain falling off it like blown glass. A tiny fire flickered merrily, one Kianthe extinguished when she saw Reyna. "Tell me we're ready to get out of this storm."

"Bobbie sent the signal. The constables are moving north."

Kianthe grinned, pushing to her feet. The bubble collapsed, and she tugged her hood over her head to get out of the rain. "Great. Let's go steal some dragon eggs."

"It's hardly stealing if he never owned them in the first place," Reyna replied primly, catching Ponder's attention with a slice of jerky. "Pondie, dearest, I'm going to need some focus from you, okay? Absolute silence inside the library. Can you do that for me?"

Ponder stared at the jerky, then assumed her "form up" position.

It was as much of an acknowledgment as they'd get. Reyna tossed it to her, showed the rest of the jerky, and pressed a finger to her lips. Ponder's chittering quieted, and she hunched on her haunches, looking more feline than eagle now. When Reyna led Kianthe toward the library, Ponder stalked behind them like a tiny jungle cat.

Five constables remained guarding the library.

"Plan?" Kianthe murmured, crouching in the bushes. "I can take them out."

"Hardly necessary. Dreggs added a new plant to my repertoire." With a wink, Reyna produced a cloth of the extract the pirate had used to keep Serina unconscious. "They call it blue locke."

"Are you seriously identifying a plant to an elemental mage?"

Reyna raised one eyebrow. "Do you want me to use this on *you,* next?"

Kianthe laughed and waved her on, one hand on Ponder's back to keep the griffon close. Reyna left them, doing what she did best: general sneaking, lurking in shadows, lunging at unsuspecting people, and incapacitating them before they could scream.

At least this time, she wasn't slicing throats. That was always a messy affair.

By the time the morning sun had settled behind the storm clouds, illuminating the forest with dull gray light, Reyna was picking the library's lock while Kianthe tugged the constables' unconscious bodies into a pile. As an afterthought, the mage waved a hand and vines snaked over their arms and legs.

The blue locke *should* keep them out half the day, but neither of them were leaving much to chance.

A soft *click* made Reyna pause in satisfaction as the final pin fell into place. She carefully opened the door. "All right. This is going to be difficult, but I'll remind you, darling, that we own a bookshop. We can order anything inside this library. Please stay focused."

She pulled the door open and held her breath.

"You act like I'm a toddler who's going to . . ." Kianthe stepped into the library and trailed off, tilting her head up, up, up. Her jaw dropped, and she scrambled to finish her sentence. ". . . to . . ." She clearly couldn't do it.

Reyna closed the door behind them, pinching her brow. "We have a goal here, Key."

"I know. I know." Kianthe didn't *sound* like she knew, not anymore. "Just a peek?"

"Kianthe."

The mage heaved a long-suffering sigh and grumbled under her breath, but she dutifully followed Reyna and Ponder farther inside. "Watch for alchemy traps. We know that's Arlon's favorite." The moment she finished speaking, her eyes landed on a set of glass cases in the center of the library. Old tomes lined the shelves, carefully preserved. It was obvious from their covers, their carefully sewn spines, that they were ancient.

"T-Those are one of a kind," Kianthe breathed. She moved as if possessed, reaching a hand toward the glass. "Surely he wouldn't miss these—"

Reyna stepped in front of her. "If you were a paranoid diarn who used alchemy to protect your things, where in this library would you have spells applied?"

Kianthe stared over her shoulder at the books, but admitted sadly, "The rare book section."

"The rare book section." Reyna guided her away, whistling for Ponder to follow. "Come on, love. I'd rather not see you unwittingly shocked today."

"It wouldn't be a shock; it'd be raw alchemical magic—"

Reyna offered a stern glance over her shoulder, and Kianthe clamped her mouth shut.

It'd have been smarter to split up, but Reyna didn't trust Kianthe not to sidle her way back to the ancient tomes. Instead, they scanned the perimeter together—after a few moments of searching, Reyna noticed a scrape on the floor near one of the bookshelves.

"How curious," she murmured, running her fingers along it.

Kianthe peeked over her shoulder, squinting. Then her gasp echoed through the massive space. "It's a secret door! A hidden bookshelf door—secret hinges—a secret *room*!" Her glee manifested in disjointed screaming, followed by an excited, "Hang on, I know this! I've read this book before," before she began tugging tomes off the shelf one by one.

Reyna watched her chaotic enthusiasm with amusement. While she was busy, Reyna traced the bookshelf with her eyes, noting a box near the top that was clearly designed to blend in with the wall. Gears to shift the bookshelf, almost certainly. And that meant a pull somewhere, larger than a book . . . something closer to a fake statue.

With confidence, she stepped toward the nearby statue of—how quaint—a dragon. It only took a few moments to notice the oil stains on its raised arm. She pressed it, and a scraping sound echoed as the bookshelf turned out.

"Damn it, how did you know that?" Kianthe said, disappointment evident in her features.

"I would never have thought to look if you hadn't realized it was a hidden room," Reyna lied, and strolled inside.

Behind her, Kianthe swelled. "I know you're lying, but the fact that you'd lie seems like true love. So, I'll take it."

"It is indeed true love," Reyna agreed, descending the staircase. The mechanism must have been timed, because the door shifted closed behind them, casting them in darkness. Ponder chittered in unease. Kianthe put a hand on Reyna's shoulder to stop her.

"Hang on. Let me lead." She ignited her palms effortlessly, then shooed the flame into a ball. She raised it up, illuminating the steep staircase, and shot Reyna a tentative smile. "This is kind of creepy, Rain."

"Don't worry. I'll protect you," Reyna teased. Despite the joke, she reached for one of the daggers strapped to her back.

Ponder landed on her shoulder, talons gently gripping her for balance. Ah. That would make a defense harder. Reyna thought about ordering the griffon off, but Ponder looked agitated—griffons didn't like being underground, after all.

"I know, Pondie. You're okay."

Kianthe glanced over her shoulder, brows knitted together, and they continued on in silence. Finally, they reached the bottom, where the staircase opened into a cramped room with a single door on the other end.

Kianthe was leading them, focused on illuminating the space and checking for constables in the corners of the room.

She didn't see the spellwork etched into the floor, so light it looked like part of the marble.

She didn't realize . . . but Reyna did.

Three things happened in rapid succession. First, Kianthe set one foot on the spellwork. Second, Reyna gasped her name, shoved her off the circle. Third, a flash of light and a shock of pain slammed into Reyna instead.

She didn't even have time to scream.

The world went black.

34

Kianthe

The alchemical ward exploded and the world ignited with it.

Time seemed to slow, passing in flashes of horrid images. Kianthe slammed to the ground, twisted in time to see light catching Reyna, swallowing her. She arched back in obvious pain; her scream silent, black against white. Then the spell slammed her off the circle—onto the staircase, crumpled in a heap.

She didn't move.

Kianthe was aware of a scream filling the room. It took several moments to realize it was *her* scream.

Ponder had taken flight right before Reyna's sacrifice, but she wasn't spared from the blast. Now, she screeched like a siren, blood trailing down her dark feathers, coloring one golden eye crimson. She curled into herself, trembling violently, offering the occasional pained clicking sound from the back of her throat.

She was hurt. Reyna was—

Kianthe didn't even know.

The mage acted on instinct. In a breath, she erected a wall of earth between them and the alchemical ward, physically blocking the staircase from the room beyond. A similar one slammed up behind Ponder on the staircase, closing them off with aggressive certainty.

Inside their tiny tomb, they had privacy. It wasn't enough. Kianthe's brain shut off, and she crashed to her knees beside her fiancée. "R-Rain." She choked on the nickname, sliding her hands under Reyna's crumpled form. She wasn't moving. Why wasn't she moving? "No. *No.*"

Ponder swiped at her eye, smearing the blood, and squeaked pathetically. It was the closest an eagle could come to crying, and it broke Kianthe's heart.

"I know, sweetie," she whispered, her voice breaking, tears blurring her vision. It was dark, but magic sparked around them, taking shape in thousands of pinpricks of firelight. Nothing that would burn, but enough that it cast Reyna's pale face in light.

It took far too long to determine she was breathing. Kianthe pressed a hand to her chest, but her own body was shaking so hard that she couldn't feel Reyna's heart. So, she ignored the conventional way, and instead magically reached for the air in Reyna's lungs.

It was circulating—and at her desperate command, breath flooded into Reyna's body.

Her fiancée gasped, jerking violently in Kianthe's hold.

Too much. Fuck. Kianthe recalled some of it, ordered the rest to keep going, and fought the panic swelling in her chest. It was impossible to know what kind of magic had attacked her—impossible to know what that alchemical spell was warded for. There were no surface wounds, nothing for Kianthe to fix.

Reyna's breaths were getting weaker. Kianthe could see it waning in her lungs.

Helplessness smothered her. "Rain, y-you have to help me. Tell me what's wrong." Kianthe bent over her, her fingers fluttering along Reyna's cheeks, her chest, her ribs. Hot tears fell like raindrops onto Reyna's face, and it seemed like a self-fulfilling prophecy.

If she didn't help, Reyna would slip away, and she would never get to help again.

But her last attempt didn't *fix* things.

"What do I do?" she cried, asking the magic now, the Stone of Seeing itself. It didn't concern itself with human affairs, but for its Arcandor, its magic would come to her aid. Sensing her anguish, it flooded her now, like a warm hug she didn't deserve.

She still had to direct it.

In her arms, Reyna was unresponsive.

And with the Stone's magic around her, things suddenly seemed very clear. Her brain was a gnarled mess, her body shaking so hard her teeth were rattling, her magic vibrating alongside it—and it just wasn't *useful.* The moment that thought passed through her, everything stilled.

Filled with instinct, Kianthe settled the magic over Reyna like a blanket, and it seeped into her body. Electrical impulses, once weakened, sparked to life. The water in her blood, her veins, began circulating strongly. Air poured into her lungs, helping now instead of hurting.

After all, the elements were life itself. Humans could be nothing else.

It was easy, and Kianthe gently extended the magic to Ponder, too. The griffon flinched away, then relaxed into Kianthe's touch. It didn't fix the bleeding wound on her head, but it seemed to calm her down.

Kianthe felt calmer, too. She pulled back, letting the Stone's blessed magic fade, watching Reyna with careful attention. Her chest tightened but she focused on her breathing, matching inhales and exhales with Reyna's.

And then . . . Reyna opened her eyes.

For a moment, neither spoke. Kianthe's grip tightened, but she gave her fiancée space to breathe. Reyna oriented herself, lifting her gaze to Kianthe's dark eyes, the firelight surrounding them. An apologetic smile tilted her lips. Her words were rasping, quiet. "You can scold me, but I'd do it again."

In response, Kianthe pulled her into a bone-crushing hug.

Reyna's breath hitched, but her arms wound around Kianthe's neck, her hand threading into the mage's short, messy hair. Kianthe didn't kiss her, not this time. They just embraced, close enough that it felt like their hearts were beating together.

"Are you okay?" Reyna finally whispered.

"Am I—" Kianthe choked on the sentence. "Don't ask me that. Not now."

Reyna laughed quietly. The motion must have hurt, because a grimace overtook her features. "Alchemy is not my favorite. I can't even tell where I was hit." She suddenly stiffened in Kianthe's arms, eyes widening. "Ponder—is she—"

"She's all right. Behind you."

Hearing her name, Ponder took a tentative step forward. She moved gingerly, but nothing seemed to be broken. The blood had been blinked from her eye, but her black feathers were still wet with it. Reyna shifted out of Kianthe's hold, held open her arms, and gathered the baby griffon into a comforting embrace.

"Dearest," she murmured against the griffon's feathers, stroking the velvety fur along her back. "I'm so sorry. But you're so brave. Someday soon, this will be a distant memory, and you'll be stronger for it."

Kianthe closed her eyes against the words. Her panic was still there, a deep thrum in the back of her brain—and once they had the luxury, she'd surely succumb to it. But to be fair, even Reyna still had nightmares about finding Kianthe in the snow, unconscious, surrounded by the shadows of dragons. That kind of horror never really went away.

Maybe that was love: knowing those negative emotions would linger . . . and choosing to focus on the positive ones instead.

"Why do I feel like you're having an existential crisis?" Reyna broke the silence, releasing Ponder with a forced smile.

A laugh bubbled, unbidden, from Kianthe's chest. "I'm always existential."

"That's what worries me." Reyna heaved a sigh, swallowed a hiss of pain, and pushed to her feet. The process was laborious, and she had to take Kianthe's arm to keep from falling over. "Gods, what a spell. Why does it feel like I almost died?" She laughed at that.

Kianthe didn't.

Reyna searched her face, paling. "Ah."

"We'll be having a conversation about your self-sacrificing tendencies later. Don't worry." Kianthe set her jaw.

Reyna snorted, then hissed in pain, her hand tightening on Kianthe's arm. "Oh, that's rich," she wheezed. "Considering you were the one who challenged an entire dragon brood on griffon-back, with a ley line that barely supports your magic on a *good* day."

"I'm the Arcandor—"

"Don't even get me started on that."

Kianthe gasped, sliding easily into mock-indignation. "In case you forgot, the dragons started that fight. I merely—" She paused when she realized that Reyna was laughing, her whole body trembling with it. "It's *true*. I hardly overextended myself!"

"I'll remember—" Reyna cut off, wheezing, laughing, which only made Kianthe grin too. "—I'll remember that the next time you're vomiting into a buck—into a bucket—" And she broke down, unable to finish.

"Hey, you said—"

"Key, please, stop. You'll kill me all over again." Reyna buried her face into Kianthe's shoulder.

Kianthe heaved an exasperated sigh, pulling her into a fierce hug. At their feet, Ponder lightly dug her talons into Reyna's pants. Despite their humor, the baby griffon wasn't having the best time—they were still underground, and their tomb must feel very suffocating to anyone who wasn't in control of the elements.

It reminded Kianthe that they had a goal here, and it wasn't banter after a traumatic incident. But the dragon eggs were hardly her priority now, not when Reyna looked like she was one strong breeze from falling over. "We should abandon the mission. Get you and Ponder somewhere safe."

"Darling, you know I never abandon a mission." Reyna's tone was factual. She picked up her sword from where it fell, tied it to her waist again. Her fingers fumbled with the leather straps, but she made it work.

Kianthe stayed close, panic lancing through her chest. Reyna was up and moving, and that was something, but her heart still pounded. "I'll come back alone. I won't get distracted by the books again. Promise."

Reyna leveled an amused stare her way, one eyebrow arching.

Kianthe wanted to shake her senseless. "Please, Reyna. They've been down here for decades; a few more nights won't make a difference." When she didn't budge, Kianthe whispered, "I need you safe."

"Then keep me safe, all right?" Reyna stepped closer, pressed a kiss to her lips. "Arlon could decide to move them after this attempt, and then we're back at the beginning—minus our paper trail. We simply cannot afford to abandon our goal." She gestured at the stone wall blocking them from the alchemical ward. "Whenever you're ready. Or sometime before that, since we aren't getting younger."

Kianthe hesitated.

Regretfully, she had a point. The dragons expected their eggs—and she couldn't risk losing them again.

After a long moment, Kianthe begrudgingly tugged down the wall, revealing the marble spell. Ponder landed on her shoulder, balancing there. Reyna still looked unsteady, breathing too hard for a casual stroll, so Kianthe hooked her arm around her fiancée's waist. It spoke volumes that Reyna leaned into her with a sigh of relief.

The sooner they finished this, the sooner she got Reyna to a bed and medical attention.

"Now, we need to find a way around this spell—"

With a huff, Kianthe yanked the marble floor deep underground, filling the small room with the scent of freshly upturned dirt instead. It was the same move she'd done with their bookshop in Tawney, back when they were first renovating, and it swallowed the spellwork whole.

Reyna grimaced, shooting Kianthe a knowing look. "Was that necessary?"

"Worked, didn't it?" Kianthe's grip tightened on Reyna's waist. She moved forward, Ponder still balancing on her shoulder, but Reyna dug in her heels. Kianthe glanced at her, brow knitting together. "What? Did I hurt you?"

"If you aren't okay with this, I can wait here." Reyna's voice was gentle. "You've walled off the staircase; I won't be taken by surprise. Ponder can keep me company."

A peace offering. The fact she felt it was necessary made Kianthe deeply ashamed of her own attitude. She clenched her eyes shut and drew a breath. "No. I'll be okay. Let's finish this."

This time, Reyna moved with her, and they crossed the tiny room without incident.

Kianthe inspected the wooden door alone, reaching out with her magic—which was less than helpful against alchemy—and then visually checking for signs. But Arlon must have assumed any intruder would be finished off by the spell in the center of the room, because the door opened easily. It wasn't even locked.

They stepped into a magnificent room laden with expensive artifacts. It truly looked like the museum in Wellia, or the records hall in the Magicary. The ceilings were high, considering they were underground. Long tapestries covered every wall, some pressed between glass to preserve the fraying edges, some vibrant and fresh. Suits of armor from every known period and country lined the four walls. More books were framed in display cases or on wooden podiums.

And in the center of the room were two dragon eggs, perched on a velvet pillow.

They were each the size of a sack of flour—small enough to carry, big enough that Kianthe worried about how she'd carry them *alone,* with Reyna in this state. Their leathery shells gleamed lavender, like a flowery sprig on a spring day. And they did pulse with magic. It was so obvious that she winced, because if this was a dragon egg after a spell designed to strip them of power, what did a normal dragon egg feel like?

No wonder Viviana took pity on them. The eggs were basically screaming at Kianthe to help.

She stopped in the doorway and helped Reyna against the wall. "Let me check things out."

It was telling that Reyna merely nodded, then wasted no time easing to the ground. She winced, closing her eyes for a brief moment. Ponder floated off Kianthe's shoulder, nudging Reyna's arm, and she smiled at the griffon before saying, "Be careful, dear. I doubt I'll be able to save you twice in one day."

"Ha, ha." Kianthe's voice was dry as a bone.

It was a slow process getting to the eggs, and it made Kianthe wish she'd borrowed one of Dreggs's alchemists—or at least kept Feo around. She could feel alchemical magic, but it was an echo, a possibility. Dormant until triggered, then unleashed in violent, crimson fury. It took extensive concentration to switch magic types, and even then the elements nudged the back of her mind, asking why she was ignoring them.

But if she'd ignored them earlier, Reyna wouldn't be hurt—so Kianthe focused, even though it was draining.

It was all for naught. There weren't any more traps, although she walked the length several times to confirm. While she tested the room, Reyna's eyes had slid shut, which made Kianthe want to scoop her up and take her somewhere safe—*somewhere* to be determined, but "not here" was good enough. Luckily, Ponder was taking her job of guarding Reyna very seriously. She perched beside the tea maker like a statue, keeping an eye on anything that moved . . . which, here, was just Kianthe.

Still, considering how the baby griffon was injured too, her dedication was impressive.

At least someday, Kianthe wouldn't be the only one protecting Reyna.

Get the eggs. Get out.

Kianthe didn't reach for them. She didn't trust Arlon at all anymore, and the last thing she needed was to be trapped in an alchemical cage. Instead, she stood a fair distance back and swept up a windstorm, a literal tornado that lifted one egg off the perch, then the other.

As expected, the tile floor around the pedestal began to crack and decay—literally sinking anyone standing nearby into the mud and trapping them there.

Kianthe wasn't nearby, and she rolled her eyes at the theatrics.

Another careful twist of magic, and the eggs touched the ground at her feet.

Applause from the doorway. A panicked screech, muffled by a

thump of heavy fabric. Kianthe spun on her heels, realizing too late that someone new had joined them—and that someone had just yanked Reyna to her feet and pressed a knife to her throat.

Arlon.

35

Serina

"We should have mounted cannons on deck ages ago," Serina called over the wind. They'd taken two of Dreggs's four mages, and with Pil and his kids at the sails, the *Knot for Sail* was cruising up the river at a frightening speed. Gone were the days of creeping through fog—now the mages just manipulated it out of the way. Overhead, heavy clouds hung in the sky, threatening rain, which honestly might help the fight.

Joe snorted from somewhere above her, entangled in the lines as always. "They're loaners. Don't get excited."

"Too late," Serina quipped, grinning wide. "Nothing says 'pirate ship' like a couple cannons."

Joe rolled their eyes, but Darlene flashed her a thumbs-up. The girl had gotten permission to stay on deck for the fight—at least as long as the constables aimed at them from the shoreline. If they boarded somehow, it was right back to the galley with Squirrel.

"We're coming up on the warehouse," Rankor called. He and Farley had taken this turn of events in amicable stride. They just liked adventure, Serina was learning.

Good. She'd happily provide it.

"Manipulate the fog to hide us. I want a dramatic entrance," Serina called, just because she could. The mages at the bow of the ship shared an amused glance, but they obediently twisted the fog in a display worthy of Kianthe herself. As Pil and his kids bundled the sails and the ship slowed its pace, everything took on an ominous tilt.

Creepy fog. Light rain. A pirate ship appearing out of nowhere.

Oh, yeah.

"Do we have a musician on board?" Serina asked Farley.

The carpenter, who'd so far done everything but carpentry on this vessel, had taken position by one of the cannons. She caressed the iron frame, deep in thought. "I'm fairly sure Rankor can hold a tune on the flute."

"Rankor," Serina whispered. "Get your flute."

The navigator shrugged, relinquishing the helm to a gleeful Serina before strolling belowdecks. A few moments later, he resurfaced. He could indeed play a tune, and he chose a somber, almost eerie melody that drifted through the fog like a death sentence.

The two mages began snickering. They were twins, a few years younger than Kianthe, and they were clearly delighted by this.

"Shhh," Serina whispered. "Now's our time. Places, everyone."

Anticipation had everyone holding their breaths. Joe scurried belowdecks, but Darlene took position beside her father, gripping her sword. Farley held the matches close, ready to light the fuse for the cannons. Serina took her position between the two cannons, even as the mages slowed the ship to a drifting stop.

On the shoreline, a row of constables awaited. They stared in shock at the pirate ship, shifting the swords in their hands. Among the lineup was the constable Serina had fought at the blockade battle—the constable who'd nearly killed Bobbie.

Tyal.

No matter what, *that* constable was going to be tied in her brig soon. She swore it.

Serina raised a hand. At her cue, Rankor twiddled a few final notes and let the flute fall silent. A hush carried, and Serina's heart thudded with anticipation. Archers took position at the two watchtowers that framed the huge warehouse, a wooden monstrosity that could feed most towns on the Nacean all fucking winter.

But, no. Arlon was squandering the food away for the highest bidder instead.

No more.

She set her jaw, cupping her mouth to carry her voice. "Arlon, diarn of the Nacean River. Consider this a challenge. We declare you unfit to rule—unfit to control our food supply, our coin, our land. Time and again, you have acted without grace or integrity. No more. Step down now, open the doors to your warehouse, and ensure your people are fed."

It was a good speech. Properly dramatic.

Serina scanned each constable's face, hunting for Bobbie . . . but of course, she wasn't there. She'd only arrived at Arlon's estate a little while ago, and she'd still been fired. Even if the diarn believed her—and it looked like he did, based on the dozens of constables lining the shore—Bobbie would be kept far from this fight.

Serina just had to hope Bobbie wasn't facing a fight of her own.

A constable with silver epaulets stepped forward. "As pirates, you are in contempt of Diarn Arlon's proclamation. You threaten the peace and prosperity of this fine land. Stand down immediately, or you will be dealt with."

Welp. She tried.

Serina snapped her fingers. "Light them."

"With pleasure." Farley was grinning as she struck the match, igniting both cannons. They both stepped back, covering their ears—and on the shore, realizing what was happening, the constables broke their pretty formation, scrambling for cover. Shouts of panic filled the air, competing with the fizzling of the fuse.

For dramatic effect, Rankor began playing his flute again, a faster tune that heightened Serina's anticipation.

BOOM. BOOOOM.

The cannons shook the ship, recoiling several feet from the blast. One cannonball buried itself in the rocky shore where the constables had been standing, and another crashed into one of the watchtowers. The archers perched atop it yelled, screamed, scrambling for purchase as it slowly crumbled. A couple leapt for the rooftop of the warehouse, barely making it, and one latched onto a nearby tree branch.

"Attack!" the lead constable called, his voice bellowing over the river.

Pil and Farley moved swiftly, hiking up two more cannonballs and stuffing ignitable powder into the back with a long tool. They shoved their cannonballs in, and Rankor and Serina pushed the cannons back to the railing of the ship, grunting with the weight.

"Incoming," Darlene shouted, panic in her voice.

Serina pivoted to see a volley of arrows angling at them. The archers in the remaining guard tower had clearly recovered from their shock. "Wind," Serina called forcefully, and the twin mages dutifully twisted the air, diverting the arrows.

No time to celebrate. Two dozen constables had seized the distraction to wade into the water. Serina was about to laugh until she realized they all had grappling hooks. Fear shot into her chest. Farley and Pil were distracted aiming the cannons at the second tower, and the constables knew it.

"Phase two," Serina shouted, seizing the sword at her hip.

Her crew moved like a well-oiled machine. There were only nine souls on the *Knot for Sail,* after all—they couldn't possibly defend against a full frontal attack. But before Serina had cannons . . . she had the element of surprise.

By the time two dozen constables boarded the ship, scrambling onto the deck with their swords extended, the ship was empty. Not a soul remained on deck—not a single sign anyone had been there at all.

Serina perched with the twin mages in the captain's quarters, watching it all through the glass windows that looked onto the deck. "You sure this won't damage the ship? I really like this thing."

"It'll damage it," the taller mage said. She grinned at her brother, her expression devious. "But don't worry. We'll push it back together. Ready?"

Serina slipped to the opposite side of the room, squinting through the bank of windows to see her crew resurfacing by an outcropping of low-hanging pines. Pil waved from the shoreline—the signal. Everyone was with him, safely on land.

"Ready," Serina replied, holding her breath.

The two mages nodded at each other, then pressed their hands against the wooden deck. They glowed yellow, the magic of the Nacean infusing them. Kianthe had seemed to bend the elements to her whim with a mere thought, but it took more concentration for this pair: they chanted under their breath, whispering a spell over and over until the words lost meaning, twisting into sheer power.

Constables were swarming the ship. A couple began pounding on the quartermaster's door, hunting for them.

And under their feet, the deck began to ripple. The wood bucked and bowed at the magical command, sprouting new branches that wound around the constables' feet, boards snapping in half to suck their bodies into an impossible hold. Controlled shouts shifted into harried screams as they fought the elements themselves.

But no one could escape the elements.

Serina chuckled as two mages finally straightened. They were sweating, still glowing, but already they looked refreshed. Kianthe said the Nacean River was a ley line, that mages could play around with its power for years and never be drained.

She hoped that was true. They weren't done yet.

"Come on," she said, and tossed open the door, striding into the fray with her sword extended.

Everyone who'd dared to board had been captured. It cut the number of constables fighting her in half, easily, and had claimed everyone's attention. More constables tossed new grappling hooks over the railing, but Serina wove between the trapped constables, stepping over bound arms and legs as she sliced the ropes from the new grappling hooks.

"Next time you decide to fight the Dreaded Captain Serina," she told the one with the silver epaulets, "don't."

"Dreaded Captain Serina?" the male mage drawled. "Sounds familiar."

"Everyone knows my inspiration," Serina replied, and grabbed the rope to twist off the ship. "Now, if you'll excuse me. Said inspiration will be here anytime, and I can't let your crew have *all* the fun."

As if on cue, a horn echoed across the battlefield. The constables had been scattered by Serina's attacks, and now they twisted in panic as pirates leapt out of the trees. Swords clanged and people shouted and yelled as chaos descended on the beach. But now that Serina had trapped half of their force on her ship, they were badly outnumbered.

Behind the *Knot for Sail*, the *Painted Death* slid into view—and they elevated her ominous look entirely. Their crimson sails were a clear warning, their cannons poised to fire.

In that moment, it was no surprise that Dreggs ruled the Southern Seas with that ship.

Serina grabbed one of the ropes hanging over the side of the *Knot for Sail*. "Keep them contained," she called to the mages. "I'll be right back." And with a gleeful laugh, she catapulted off the railing of her ship.

For a breathless moment, she was airborne, *flying*.

Then she landed hard on the ground, the impact thudding through her body. Her leg had healed nicely over a week, but after that it throbbed in protest. Serina barely noticed, her entire body buzzing with anticipation.

Especially considering Tyal had noticed her crew lurking in the pine trees north of the shoreline, and was striding to them with a wicked sword in hand. None of her crew could fight. *Serina* couldn't fight, not really, but an unreasonable anger surged in her chest that made her think she could. She started after him, hobbling a little as she shouted, "Hey!"

He paused, turned, and in the chaos of the battlefield, it was like two lovers watching each other across a ballroom. He paused, and the world seemed to still. Serina stiffened. Recognition flashed in Tyal's eyes, and a dark smile cut across his face. "Ah. The pirate of the Nacean. Let's finish what we started."

Serina unsheathed her sword. "Let's." She slid into the stance Reyna had taught. There was no fear—only anticipation.

Behind Tyal, Farley watched in horror. Rankor was standing in front of Squirrel and Joe—but Pil clenched his fists. Serina watched two things at once: Tyal advancing in the foreground, and Darlene mutely handing her new sword to her father with a triumphant smirk.

Huh.

Too late to think on it. Tyal had reached her, prowling around Serina like a jungle cat. She matched his pace, keeping her sword angled at his. The constable narrowed his eyes. "You have caused a *lot* of problems for us lately."

"And yet, you seem to be taking it personally," Serina replied.

"I was *one job* away from a promotion." Tyal's face twisted in anger. "You were one fucking pirate, but you somehow got the *Arcandor* on your side. The Dastardly Pirate Dreggs, for the Stars' sake. You're making me look like a fool. Of course this is personal."

He lunged, and instinct took over. Her form wasn't perfect, but she was able to parry his thrust. She danced away, distracted him with talking. "It's personal for me, too. Does Arlon know you attacked your own cohort? You almost *killed* Bobbie."

"I didn't—" He scowled. "I was fighting *you*. It wasn't my fault that she inserted herself."

"Bullshit," Serina hissed, and this time *she* lunged. For Bobbie, for Humalt and his family, for Garinson and his folk. For everyone on the Nacean, Serina fought. She lashed with such ferocity that even with her poor form, she was able to keep him on defense, driving him back toward the pine trees.

For a moment, it looked like she was winning.

And then Tyal twisted, his blade sliding against hers as he stepped into her space. Serina strained against his weight, sweat trailing down her face, her breath coming in short gasps. Their noses were very close, and he whispered, "I'll forever be known as the constable who captured you."

And with a vicious grin, he—

—froze.

"I don't think you'll be doing much of that," Pil grumbled at his back.

The pressure on Serina's blade lessened, and she seized the chance to escape Tyal's proximity. Gaining distance, the situation unfolded. Pil had Darlene's new sword poised at Tyal's back—right behind his heart—and was pressing hard enough to draw a tiny spot of blood. The statement was clear: move and be skewered.

"Your constable friends are laying down their arms. I'll give you one breath to do the same." Pil's voice was suddenly dangerous, ruthless. The perfect pirate. Behind him, Joe and Darlene had moseyed out of the brush, wearing matching expressions of satisfaction.

"Dad's a badass. Forgot to mention it," Darlene said.

Serina laughed.

Tyal's eyes scanned the shore, but Pil was right. All the constables had realized they were defeated. Some were on the ground, bleeding, curled around wounds, but the rest had laid down their weapons.

A successful siege.

With a frustrated scowl, Tyal gently followed suit.

Serina swiped his blade. Pil stepped back, and Serina twirled her own blade, sheathing it resolutely.

"Yo ho ho, you bastard."

36

Reyna

Reyna heard new footsteps—but after the hit of alchemy, everything sounded kind of murky, like she'd fallen overboard and was clawing toward the surface of the Nacean. Her instincts screamed, *Move,* but her brain lagged behind and whispered, *Why, again?*

She was in Arlon's hold before she could fully comprehend what had happened. Once she did, Reyna began to think that maybe, just maybe, she should have taken Kianthe's advice and left the dragon eggs alone.

This was just embarrassing.

The blade against her neck was dull, the bite of it against her skin paling in comparison to the agony of leftover alchemy. Everything in her body thrummed—it felt like she was a violin string vibrating out of tune. Pain had been washing over her in dull waves since she'd woken up, but reassuring Key had been her priority then.

Now, she just had to *not die.*

It seemed glaringly simple, but considering her body wasn't responding to her commands, there were complications.

One was Kianthe, and the utter horror draining her face of color. She surged forward, but Arlon said, "Ah, ah. One more step, one spell of magic, and she'll be dead before I am." His voice was beside Reyna's ear, low and gravelly, and she shuddered as his breath hit her skin.

At her feet, Ponder screeched, clawing at the confines of a heavy blanket, twisting herself deeper inside it with every panicked thrash.

Reyna had to do something. An elbow to the ribs, a hit to the wrist, and *she'd* be the one pressing a knife to Arlon's neck. In her mind's eye, it played out so beautifully. Over in two breaths, and then she and Kianthe could go home.

But the world was spinning. She felt vaguely nauseated, and tried hard to focus on one stationary point.

She chose Kianthe, who was a sight to behold. When faced with a challenge, her fiancée was as fierce as she was beautiful. Fury had painted her face with murderous tones, and she didn't even seem to notice the wind picking up. Her dark eyes blazed, her voice booming.

"Let her go, Arlon."

He tightened his grip. She was his insurance, after all.

It made Reyna chuckle, which pressed the knife harder against her throat. She stilled, clenching her eyes shut against the dizzying twist of the world. "You must be truly desperate to pick a fight with the Mage of Ages."

When she pried open her eyes again, Kianthe was several steps closer, calling his bluff.

Reyna didn't even need to twist to be free. She just needed to reach the knife along her thigh. Keeping as still as possible, she fumbled for it, but another rumble of pain trampled over her. Agony. This alchemy lingered like nothing she'd ever experienced—when she sat perfectly still, it had faded to a manageable thrum, but now that she was standing, breathing, moving, it roared back to life.

It made it very hard to concentrate on her surroundings.

Hard to do anything but shudder in pain, actually. The banter she'd shared with Kianthe after she woke up was a distant memory now.

"You aren't leaving with those eggs." Arlon spat the words.

Ah. Then he didn't have a plan. That sharpened Reyna's senses: this entire time, she'd assumed Diarn Arlon came down here with a scheme in mind, something he could use against Kianthe to keep himself alive. Apparently that something was, quite literally, *Reyna*.

It was a shortsighted thought, and it made him even more dangerous.

Animals backed in a corner lashed out, after all.

"I don't give two shits about the eggs." Kianthe's voice rang loud, reinforced with unnatural power. "But if you don't release my fiancée, *I will kill you*."

"Step closer and I'll—"

He didn't get to finish the sentence.

This entire time, Reyna had been planning how to rescue herself. Her fingers were already curling around the knife, even though she could barely stand, even with immaculate pain stunning her. She had a dozen and one ways to stay alive.

She'd forgotten about the dozen and second: the Realm's most powerful mage.

A mage who only became unhinged when Reyna's safety was threatened.

Kianthe twisted a hand, and suddenly Arlon was choking, clawing at his throat. The knife he'd used against Reyna clattered to the ground. He wheeled back, slamming into the wall, writhing as he gasped like a fish for air that didn't come.

Reyna tried to keep her footing, but her balance was gone. Immediately, Kianthe's arms wound around her shoulders, catching her before she toppled.

"Are you okay?" Her voice was low.

Reyna was beginning to admit that, in this moment—no, she was not okay. But she forced herself to focus, because Diarn Arlon was turning purple. He turned pleading, watery eyes on them before crashing to the tile floor, suffocating under the deadened stare of the Arcandor herself.

Kianthe would let him die for hurting her.

Reyna couldn't let that happen. She gripped Kianthe's arm. "Not like this, love. Please. Feo's working on justice, but—not like this."

For a long moment, Reyna thought it might be too late, that

the goddess of a mage had already decided this human's fate. But just as Arlon's eyes fluttered shut, Kianthe twisted her hand again. He seized a ragged breath, then another, pushing himself onto his hands and knees as he hacked and coughed.

Nearby, Ponder had clawed the blanket to shreds. She emerged, screeched, and landed on Arlon's back, tearing at his flesh without mercy.

"P-Pondie," Reyna gasped, surging forward. "No!"

Her words seemed to register, dimly. The griffon pecked at Arlon's head for good measure, then took off on shaky wings toward Reyna. If she felt this bad, she could only imagine how Ponder was doing.

Of course, with her blood-soaked talons, she clearly got her revenge.

Kianthe eased Reyna to the ground, leaning her against one of the wooden podiums. She pressed a gentle kiss to Reyna's forehead and murmured, "I won't kill him, all right? I'm just going to talk."

"Thank you," Reyna replied, resting her head against the podium in exhaustion. She had no concern for Arlon's life—but she cared deeply about how Kianthe would feel about these actions later. There was already a lot to unpack.

Ponder perched beside Reyna, guarding her yet again.

Meanwhile, Kianthe strode toward Arlon, looming over him.

This time, he cowered under her ire. "S-Stay back," he gasped. "You can't kill me."

"Considering you were planning to kill us both to hide these eggs, I don't think you realize what I'm capable of." Kianthe knelt beside him, her fury heating the air. It rippled above them, made sweat bead along Diarn Arlon's brow. She lifted his chin, so their eyes met. "You might walk out of here if you answer one question: Who asked you to steal the eggs?"

"No one," he ground out.

"You're lying. Think carefully, Arlon."

A flash of panic overrode his features—Reyna watched it with dispassionate interest. Arlon clenched his eyes shut, and gritted out: "You're not the most dangerous person in the Realm."

"Rude."

"There are people with more power—"

She waved a hand, pinning him in a tomb of rock. A vine slid over his mouth, gagging him—Reyna noticed belatedly it was lined with vicious thorns. Blood trickled down his neck, and he went very still, eyes widening.

"Turns out, I don't care." Kianthe pushed to her feet, stretching her arms over her head. Despite the casual gesture, her gaze was icy now, a direct contrast to how warm the room had gotten. An impossible breeze still tousled her hair, but it had died down significantly now that the danger had passed.

"I truly don't know what possessed you to lose your Stone-damned mind this season, Arlon. One pirate shouldn't have shattered your sense, but . . . well. When we see you next, it will be petitioning the council for your immediate removal as diarn. And if this powerful person comes knocking about the missing eggs—" She paused, flashing a cold smile. "Well. Tell them I'm in Tawney, and I'd love a chat."

With a sweep of her cloak, she strolled back to Reyna.

"You ready?" Kianthe knelt beside her. Gone was the fearsome Mage of Ages—in her place was a chivalrous knight carefully helping her stand.

"I might be falling in love with you all over again," Reyna told her. Since sitting again, the pain had quieted, but she wasn't looking forward to walking out of here. She grimaced, staggering on unsteady feet. "Or just falling over you. I truly hope this isn't permanent."

Kianthe frowned, smoothing Reyna's hair off her face, squinting into her eyes. "You don't look good. I kept your body functioning, but that spell was designed to attack intruders. I doubt it'd stop just because I told it to." Kianthe shot a nasty look at Arlon, who was watching them with venom in his eyes. "Come on. Let's get you to an alchemist and see if they can help."

"Agreed."

Ponder wound between her legs as Reyna braced herself against the podium while Kianthe retrieved the dragon eggs. Holding both was awkward, one in each arm, and she grunted under the weight. "Can you hold on to me? I might be able to carry you on my back—I don't really trust you carrying one of these." A pause, a humorless chuckle. "No offense."

"None taken," Reyna said. "I can walk."

Kianthe frowned. "I . . . highly doubt that's true."

Reyna set her jaw, pulling the last dregs of her energy. This was the reserve she relied on—the determination that pulled her through days of exhausting travel, through bloody battles and back to Queen Tilaine's side. It narrowed the world to point-by-point directives: walk past Arlon. Tread up the stairs, one step at a time. Fight the encroaching darkness. Get out of the library.

Kianthe followed close, almost too close. She grunted under the weight of the eggs, but kept a steady one-sided conversation.

"So, he didn't get past my earth wall. He must have another entrance here somewhere; maybe a tunnel from his estate." She nodded at the wall she'd erected to block the staircase and it collapsed under her glance, crumbling into dust.

Reyna murmured a prayer of gratitude to the Gods that she didn't have to stop her forward motion—she truly wasn't sure she'd start again. She tried to reply, but her breath was gone.

Kianthe seemed to notice. She hovered close, still talking. "Dreggs has alchemists; once we get up top, I can hide you and Ponder and go find them. You'll be okay, Rain. And then we'll load up the eggs, stop in Wellia for the council, and we're home before winter really begins. I could use a nice cup of tea right about now."

One step.

Another.

"I can drop the eggs off upstairs and come get you, Rain—" Kianthe said.

"No," she wheezed, pausing to gasp for air. Sweat trailed down her face, and the pain was rippling through her chest again, but she forced a smile. "There might be constables waiting upstairs. G-Gods forbid, Arlon's alchemist. It's best to go together."

Kianthe's fingers clenched on the eggs, like she wanted to toss them aside and scoop up Reyna instead. "Just—take it slow, okay? For me?"

"I doubt I can go faster." Reyna laughed, which sent a spike of pain through her chest. She began moving again, barely noting Ponder flying on ahead, angling toward the top of the staircase. They were close, so close.

Of course, when Kianthe elbowed the lever and the bookshelf swung open, people were lounging on the other side.

Kianthe stiffened, stepping in front of Reyna, hands igniting—but almost instantly, they recognized Dreggs and Bobbie.

The pirate captain quirked an eyebrow, lowering a wicked-looking sword. "And here I thought you'd be Arlon. Found your booty, I see."

"Thank the Stone of Seeing itself." Kianthe didn't even laugh at the word. She just handed the eggs off—one to Dreggs, one to Bobbie—and immediately took some of Reyna's weight. It was a huge relief, and Reyna sagged against her.

"A pleasure to see you both," she said, her eyelids fluttering. "Please don't be concerned if I pass out."

Bobbie looked alarmed. "What happened? Is Arlon down there?"

There were several bodies littering the library floor—constables who'd apparently swarmed the place as backup to Arlon, but couldn't make it downstairs to help. That wall probably saved her life . . . or at the very least, kept things downstairs from escalating beyond their control.

Relatively speaking, Reyna acquiesced silently.

"Arlon is secured. We'll have to transport him east for a trial. Attacking the Arcandor with intent to kill is a grievous offense." Kianthe didn't sound upset about that. Her jaw was hard, and she looked like she wanted to go downstairs and finish the job properly. "How'd things go on your end?"

"Well, Arlon was originally engaged . . . and then the bastard slipped away when he realized where you two were." Dreggs didn't sound pleased about it.

"The alchemical ward must have alerted him when it triggered," Kianthe muttered.

Dreggs held their egg in one hand, sheathed their sword with the other. "Well, however he knew, it cut into my triumphant vengeance. I had a whole monologue planned."

"Your half of this mission relied on stealth," Bobbie said, exasperated. "*Serina* was the one taking focus on the shore. Why did *you* prepare a speech?"

"Lesson number one, dear: always have a monologue ready. You never know when the opportunity might arise." Dreggs winked. "Actually, you had Arlon trapped in a study. That was a missed opportunity right there."

Bobbie groaned. "I'm not going to monologue to my old boss. He sprinted out the door once I told him Serina was attacking, anyway."

Reyna listened half-heartedly, trying and failing to focus amidst the sudden roaring in her ears. Ah. Then she wasn't going to make it farther than this. Pity. She sagged more against Kianthe, drawing everyone's attention.

"We need an alchemist—" Kianthe sounded like she was underwater.

Dreggs's reply was inaudible.

The darkness washed over her, and everything went black for the second time that day.

37

Kianthe

Reyna blinked awake, and Kianthe told her, "Next time you crave adventure, I'm going to slap you upside the head."

Her fiancée's lips curled into a wry smile, and she pushed herself into a sitting position. They were on Serina's ship. Kianthe had claimed the captain's quarters after they'd pried the trapped constables off the ship and she restored the deck to its pre-attack state. Serina's crew was safe—Dreggs's folk had a few injuries, but nothing major. Once Arlon fled the warehouse mid-fight, his constables surrendered to the pirates rather quickly.

Even Tyal, which was pleasing. He'd been tied on the shore, bandaged and gagged, awaiting judgment.

Apparently Keets, Tyal's friend, had been the first to surrender.

Reyna surveyed her surroundings, Kianthe's relieved expression, and landed on the dragon eggs perched in the corner of the room. She pushed upright with ease, stretching. "Then I gather we were successful?"

"Well, we kept the eggs. That's something."

It was late evening now, so far into the night they'd nearly reached sunrise again. The room had a cozy glow, warm with Kianthe's ever-flame, and was blessedly empty. That gave Reyna all the time she needed to orient herself.

Kianthe watched her carefully, but Reyna didn't seem to be

struggling. Relief spread in Kianthe's chest. "Looks like the alchemists helped. We had two of them working in here for half the day, eliminating any trace of that spell. Apparently, the alchemy wouldn't have lingered if I hadn't intervened, but—well, then you *actually* would have died, so I stand by my actions."

Reyna chuckled, flexing her hand into a fist, testing her dexterity. "I also stand by your actions." She paused, offering a charming smile. "I must say, it's nicer for the unconscious person. I wake up and everything is fixed. Saves me quite a lot of stress."

Kianthe might kill her all over again.

"Don't get any ideas, Rain. We're avoiding mortal peril in the future, remember?"

"Mmm. I'll take that under advisement." Reyna swung her legs off the bed, pushed to her feet. She moved with her usual easy grace, although Kianthe still surged closer to help steady her. Their hands touched, their eyes met, and Reyna's gaze softened. "Thank you for saving me."

Kianthe's cheeks burned under the attention. "Well, if he'd tried taking you captive any other day, he'd have earned a knife to the stomach. I'm not even sure this counts as saving you."

"I wasn't in any physical state to intervene, much as I hoped I could." She paused, her cheeks coloring. "It's nice, knowing I don't always have to save myself."

"If anyone else presses a knife to your throat, I reserve the right to kill them slowly." Kianthe wasn't joking, and her magic responded to the promise, swirling in sparkles around them. "Turns out Queendom citizens aren't the only ones with a penchant for murder."

Reyna's fingers ghosted over Kianthe's arm. "Anyone can kill under the right circumstances. I'm just glad I found more with you. Now, please tell me we're finally ready to go home."

"We're ready to go home." Kianthe paused, wincing. "Almost. Feo came back while you were under."

"Already?" Reyna blinked in surprise, starting for the door. It was such a relief to see her moving like usual—this time, when she tied her sword to her hip, it was with deft fingers and practiced motions.

Kianthe followed, as always. "Well, Visk isn't a slow flier. And you know Feo. Their case couldn't be argued, not by the time they presented the evidence."

The two of them emerged onto the deck to a party.

Reyna paused, arching one eyebrow. "Pirates waste no time when it comes to celebrating, do they?" Her tone was wry.

The deck of the *Knot for Sail* had been transformed—long buffet tables lined the railing, to which Squirrel was bustling past, stacking more food. In the distance, similar revelry was happening on the *Painted Death*'s deck. The massive ship loomed, crimson sails yet again tied tight, anchored behind trees flickering gold and red in the firelight. Several pirates were on the shore, too, milling among the captured constables.

Any constable not glowering in fury had been released to enjoy the party. Kianthe wasn't sure who'd overseen *that* decision, but as the night wore on, no one could argue they were having a good time. Without Arlon making terrible decisions, the constables were simply normal people doing a job.

Tyal notwithstanding. He looked murderous, but no one was undoing his ties anytime soon.

In the distance, Ponder was taking her father on a tour of the *Painted Death*. Visk was too big to fly between the lines like she did, so he perched on the crow's nest, his wings spread for balance as she flitted among the masts.

Serina stepped up to them, pulling Reyna into a big hug. The pirate was still limping a little bit, but it didn't seem to slow her down. "You're awake! Ah, you look so much better. I'm glad the alchemists could help."

"Me too," Reyna replied, gripping her forearms when they separated. "I suppose this means Arlon's reign is over. Now that you've toppled the king of Shepara, what's your plan?" Her eyes roamed Dreggs and Mister Mom, currently having a drinking contest across the deck. Mister Mom was winning, and Dreggs seemed increasingly annoyed about it. "I'm certain Dreggs would let you keep sailing, if you choose."

"Dreggs couldn't stop me if they tried." She raised her voice when she said that, waving to catch the infamous pirate captain's attention.

Dreggs paused mid-drink and flipped her off.

She cackled. "They're fun. I'm not sure what my plan is yet . . . it'd be awkward to pirate the same river my girlfriend supervises."

Kianthe rubbed the back of her neck, embarrassed she didn't mention it before. Of course, the look of shock on Reyna's face was priceless, so she didn't feel *that* bad. "Ah, that's the other thing. The council asked Feo for recommendations on who should replace Arlon. Someone local, with extensive knowledge of the towns here. They put forth Bobbie's name, with the Arcandor's 'full endorsement.'" Kianthe grumbled, "Not that I gave them explicit permission for that, but—"

Reyna cut her off with a squeal. "Bobbie is the Nacean River's new diarn?"

"One of them." Bobbie had stepped up beside Serina, winding her arm around the pirate's waist. Although her wounds were healing, it was a slow process; she still moved gingerly. Despite that, her eyes were bright, her tone pleased. "The council agreed that a diarn's power should be limited. A few towns, not entire regions. Feo advised them to truncate Arlon's land, so there will be three new diarns. I'm responsible for Lathe, Oslop, and his old estate."

Serina snorted. "Viviana's going to love that oversight."

"You didn't get the vineyards," Reyna said sadly.

Bobbie stared at her, exasperation slathering her tone. "*That's* your takeaway?"

"Is Koll up for grabs? Because I feel like we could make a good . . . case . . . for it." Kianthe paused. "Get it? A case of wine? Wine is transported in cases, right?"

"Crates, dear."

"Ah. Well, this is embarrassing."

Bobbie pinched her brow, then reached into her pocket. The crocheted toy she pulled out this time was brown and black, a perfect representation of a tiny griffon. She'd spent a painstakingly long time getting every stitch right, and it showed.

"It's Ponder. She modeled for me."

That was a stretch; the baby griffon had formed up for about three breaths, and then got distracted. But she did stay close while Bobbie crocheted on deck for half the day. The woman tried to teach Kianthe—stress relief while the alchemists worked on Reyna, she'd said—but the Arcandor *also* had trouble focusing. Eventually Bobbie gave up.

Still, when she handed it over, Reyna was the one squealing in delight. She clutched the toy to her chest, adoration in her gaze. Kianthe couldn't tear her eyes away, her own heart swelling at Reyna's happiness.

"It looks just like her!"

Bobbie shifted, clearly embarrassed. "Thanks. I thought you'd like it."

Reyna lovingly tucked it into her pocket, a bright smile on her face, and turned to Serina. "Then what's your plan, if not pirating?"

Serina beamed. "I might switch into the family business. Not farming—Stars know I'm terrible at that—but my father already has the books set for merchant work. Transporting food up and down the river sounds relaxing."

"You mispronounced *boring,*" Dreggs called. How they even heard this conversation over the din was shocking.

Serina flipped *them* off this time.

"Her crew's staying on regardless," Kianthe told Reyna. "It was a whole thing. Lots of tears."

Serina bounced on her toes. "Even Pil and his kids! Although Dreggs made me promise to let them visit from time to time." Behind them, music began, a bouncy jig that competed with the music echoing off the *Painted Death*. Serina gasped and, without warning, towed Bobbie toward the area cleared out for dancing.

Bobbie let herself be dragged away, but called to Kianthe, "I'll get the problematic constables to Wellia for trial, and put the rest to work distributing the food Arlon's been stockpiling. Don't worry about us. You guys should go home and relax."

"You really want us gone, don't you?" Kianthe drawled, crossing her arms.

Bobbie simply laughed. "I would never imply that." But the glint in her eye told a different story.

"Don't leave without saying goodbye," Serina called, and then they were dancing. Well, Bobbie was more swaying to the music, considering her injuries, but Serina made up for both of them.

It was cute to watch.

Kianthe was already bored.

"Come on. Feo's prowling around Arlon's estate, poaching what they can. If we move fast, I bet we can snag those rare books."

"You really want to test the spellwork in that library again?" Reyna followed Kianthe down the plank someone had set up along the dock.

The mage shuddered. "Never mind."

"Hang on. Am I worth more than a set of rare tomes? How kind." Now Reyna smirked. "Speaking of, how's your book coming, dear? You had some time to write while I was unconscious."

"I was *distraught.*" Kianthe huffed, digging her hands into the fur-lined pockets of her cloak. "I can't create under those conditions. Bobbie learned that firsthand."

"Mmm. How convenient."

Kianthe started to protest, but just then Feo stepped out of the warehouse and Reyna jogged off to greet them. Tawney's diarn had deep bags under their eyes, a heavy coat over their shoulders, and a stack of books under one arm.

Rare books.

One-of-a-kind books.

"Hang on. Those are mine!" Kianthe exclaimed.

Feo shot her a smug look. "Technically, they belong to the estate—and as a thank-you for aiding in her instatement, Bobbie agreed to let me claim them. A professional courtesy between diarns. Surely you understand."

Kianthe lit her palm on fire. "Feo, I will burn you."

"And ignite the books? I can hardly trust these priceless artifacts around your temper."

Reyna stepped between them, holding up her hands to stop Kianthe from doing something stupid—like pulling the ground over

Feo's ankles, grabbing the books, and fleeing. The tea maker addressed Feo. "We have the dragon eggs, but I need to retrieve my horse from Koll."

Shit. Kianthe had totally forgotten about Lilac. The horse was certainly basking in the stables' luxurious care.

She also caught the gleam in Reyna's eyes; she wouldn't go home before having one final glass of wine at Judd's place. Kianthe supposed they could make a stop. Serina would certainly sail them south if they asked.

"I'd feel safest with the eggs in our possession. Are you all right to take Visk and Ponder home, or is that asking too much?" Reyna smiled. "Kianthe and I can follow behind at a more leisurely pace."

"The sooner I'm back in Tawney, the better." Feo paused. "Although the council is debating on a replacement for Arlon's seat. If you cared to stop by Wellia, the Arcandor's endorsement would hold a hefty weight in that discussion."

"You want to be a councilmember?" Kianthe spluttered.

Diarn Feo sniffed. "Well, if there's an opening . . . We all know I'm capable."

Kianthe's eyes dropped to the books in their arm, and a devious smirk tilted her lips. "Then you should know that my recommendation doesn't come cheap."

A standoff. They locked eyes, battling in silence. The war behind Feo's eyes was absolutely priceless—and triumph spread when Feo reluctantly offered the stack of books. "I suppose I'll still be able to appreciate them in New Leaf Tomes and Tea." They didn't sound happy about it.

Kianthe snatched the books, grunting under their weight. "Glad we could reach an agreement."

"To be clear, she'd have given the endorsement regardless," Reyna said curtly, shooting Kianthe a stern look. "Don't manipulate people, dear."

The tomes were heavy in her arms, and she clutched them against her chest like a child might with a precious toy. "But—but there were *books* at stake." At Reyna's obvious disapproval, Kianthe muttered something inaudible and offered the stack to Feo again. "Oh, fine. Fine!"

Reyna heaved a sigh.

Feo stole the books back, expression smug. "A pleasure doing business with you both. Next time, send a better note if your griffon abducts me." And they strolled for the ship, whistling to gain Visk's attention. It spoke volumes that the griffon abandoned the *Painted Death* to glide over, then let Feo mount him without any fanfare.

"Traitor," Kianthe grumbled, although she wasn't sure if that was directed at Reyna or Visk.

Reyna took her hand. "Let's get Lilac and say goodbye to Judd. I'm ready to go home."

38

Reyna

If they thought the Nacean River was cold, it had absolutely nothing on Tawney in the winter.

A literal snowstorm raged. Unlike on the Nacean, one of the Realm's most powerful ley lines, here Kianthe's power was minimal. There was no magical shielding from the ice pelting their faces. Lilac looked miserable, trudging through the snow only because Reyna was tugging her reins. The cart she hauled kept getting stuck in the snow, and Kianthe seemed to be struggling to keep the path in front of it clear.

"Perhaps we should summon the dragons, rather than hiking all the way to dragon country," Reyna called over the wind.

Kianthe wrenched another pile of snow out of their path. "We might have to. This is ridiculous."

Reyna squinted against the storm, but even at midday, it was dark and gloomy. They weren't far from Tawney, but it had taken the better part of the morning just to make it this far. Reyna was thoroughly chilled, and already anticipating the little get-together they were hosting at New Leaf tonight.

Lilac, meanwhile, was clearly anticipating the quiet, warm stables of Tawney's inn. She tossed her head, resisting the steady pressure Reyna was putting on her reins.

"I know, girl," Reyna said, patting her neck. "Just a bit more, okay?"

The eggs had been packaged inside carefully padded crates for the journey home, which had taken the remainder of the fall season. The winter solstice came and went as they reached Wellia, and now they were well into the darkest season of the year. It was a miserable time to hand off the dragon eggs, but Reyna wasn't keen to wait until spring.

Not when they were so close to true freedom.

Ahead, Kianthe groaned. "Ugh. Between Tawney's ridiculous ley line and those things pulsing with dragon magic—" She jerked a thumb at the crate with the eggs, secured in the small cart. "—I am so done."

She looked pale, slightly nauseated. They'd spent so much time on the Nacean River that Reyna had almost forgotten magic drain was a real problem here. She stopped, running a hand over her snow-soaked hair. "Then let's summon the dragons and be done with this. Can you call them?"

"If they can see me. Maybe." Kianthe set her jaw, stepping through the snow to put some distance between them. She pulled her hands together and went quiet for several moments—clearly tugging on magic that wasn't hers to command.

Reyna hoped it didn't poison her again; she sincerely didn't want to cancel their evening plans.

Whatever she did must have worked, because an earth-shattering roar echoed over the icy plains. Kianthe dropped her arm, drawing an exhausted breath. "Well, I think it's safe to say they're coming."

"Just in time," Reyna said, offering an arm to steady the mage.

They stood together near Lilac, who was looking increasingly nervous. Reyna held on to her reins tightly, whispering reassurances as the horse's eyes widened, ears flicking toward the approaching wingbeats.

One dragon landed with a thump beside them, seemingly unbothered by the snow.

Two more followed suit, literally shaking the ground as they folded their wings.

Reyna would recognize the leader anywhere: it was the same dragon who'd given Kianthe its magic last spring. The same one who'd offered the bindment in the first place—the eggs for Tawney's safety.

Now, Kianthe separated from Reyna's support, addressing them. "We found the eggs. Two of them, anyway." She went quiet for a moment. She'd told Reyna once that she communicated with the dragons through flashes of magic, images that slid between an invisible link. Reyna wondered if she was showing the dragons the location of the third egg, the one lost to time.

The dragon lowered its head. Its skull was massive, bigger than Lilac, bigger than the cart. Its intelligent eyes shifted from Kianthe to Reyna, and she swore she saw recognition spark in its gaze. The beast inclined its head, straightened, and carved a circle into the snow with one intimidating talon.

"Thank the Stone," Kianthe muttered under her breath, and stepped into the circle.

Reyna gripped the worn leather straps of the reins, watching in interest as the circle glowed blue, then flashed yellow. When the wind died down, Kianthe looked exactly the same, but she heaved a sigh like a huge weight had been lifted.

"The bindment is complete," she said. "I wasn't sure they'd allow that, considering the missing egg. But they're just happy to get two back."

"Will they hatch?" Reyna asked, handing off the reins to pry open the crate, revealing the eggs for the dragons' inspection. They'd brought them to the storage room beneath the burnt church the moment they'd arrived in Tawney, and Feo undid the spell binding the dragon magic. It infused the eggs now, powerful enough that even Reyna could tell the difference.

Now, when she pressed a hand on the eggs' leathery shells, she felt life pulsing from them.

Kianthe kept ahold of Lilac's reins, since the horse was wide-eyed now that the dragons were closing in. "They'll hatch. Not sure when, but I'm sure the dragons will be happy. Arlon could have done a lot worse than storing them in a basement for decades."

Reyna hauled one egg out, carried it to the lead dragon, then repeated the process with the other one. The main dragon studied each of them, a satisfied grumble echoing in the back of its throat, before scooping them both up with surprising tenderness. Cradling the eggs in its talons, it spread massive wings, nodded again at Kianthe, and took to the skies.

Its backup followed suit, and the dragons left.

"I expected that to be more complicated," Reyna remarked, closing the empty crate.

Kianthe looked ready for a nap. She swallowed a yawn, but seemed much less sickly now that the dragons were gone. "What about dragon magic melding with elemental magic to bridge communication between two nations isn't complicated?"

Reyna snorted. "When you put it like that, I suppose it's a miracle that only took a few moments." She took the reins from Kianthe, guiding Lilac back to Tawney. "Come on. We're hosting tonight."

It seemed like the entire town of Tawney showed up for their homecoming.

New Leaf Tomes and Tea was absolutely packed. Every table was filled, every shelf being perused, every armchair taken. Lively conversation filled the bright space, even as the snowstorm raged outside.

Reyna flitted from customer to customer, offering ceramic mugs of hot tea and plates of scones. She smiled at Sasua and her son, their next-door neighbors, and ruffled Gossley's hair as she passed. The teenage boy flinched against her touch, shooing her away.

"Miss Reyna, please." He cast a surreptitious glance at his new girlfriend, the carpenter's daughter. "I'm hardly a kid anymore. I managed the shop more days than anyone. I'm basically a business owner." He puffed up his chest, and it looked as silly as the day he stepped into their store asking for a bandit assignment.

She had to swallow her laughter, but her shoulders shook anyway. "Of course, Gossley. Thank you for your help while we were gone."

He grinned, satisfied, and she moved on.

She paused at Diarn Feo's table. They were lounging across from Lord Wylan. The lord looked absolutely flabbergasted, pushing thick hair out of his eyes. "A *councilmember*? How in the five hells did you snag that job?"

"I told you, Wylan," Feo said, examining their nails with casual indifference. "You don't explore opportunities outside of Tawney. When the Arcandor's griffon appeared at my doorstep, I knew Kianthe had discovered something. I was happy to give her some time, and I was greatly rewarded for it."

Reyna snorted.

The lord and the diarn glanced her way. Feo's eyes flashed.

She busied herself cleaning the table beside them, smiling at the town informants, Sigmund and Nurt, as they helped her stack the plates. Clever that they'd sat so close to the town leaders, considering their line of work.

"I'm sorry," she told Lord Wylan. "I didn't mean to eavesdrop."

Wylan hooked an arm over the back of his wooden chair. "Feo is lying, aren't they?"

"The council is still deciding on their candidacy," she said neutrally. "And I heard their first act of business is to donate several very rare books to New Leaf Tomes and Tea. Help Tawney become even more of a destination."

Now she shot a wry look at Feo. She wanted Kianthe to be above this kind of thing, but it was right down Reyna's alley. She hadn't spent her life circling Queen Tilaine's court for nothing, after all.

The diarn set their jaw. "I thought Kianthe didn't want those?" The words were pulled through gritted teeth.

Reyna smiled prettily. "She might not, but I'd view it as incredible generosity. Especially considering how valuable we've been to you of late. Councilmember." She winked and strolled away, but not before she caught Wylan's sly smirk.

"How generous, Feo. Good for you."

The diarn grumbled something inaudible.

Reyna carried the dirtied plates past the counter, smiling at Kianthe as she ducked into the storage room. When she emerged, wiping her hands on her apron, she realized Matild and Tarly had arrived. The midwife strolled to the counter with all the confidence of someone who owned the place, and she slammed two bronze coins on the wood. "Cuppa tea, and *all the details*. I heard you found pirates."

"I heard you overthrew a diarn," Tarly drawled, draping over the counter.

"You didn't hear the best part." Kianthe bent forward, beckoning them closer. "We met the Dastardly Pirate Dreggs."

Matild's face was one of absolute glee. "You did not!"

"They kidnapped Reyna."

"It was a strange accident," Reyna drawled, kissing Kianthe's cheek before pouring a pitcher of water into her trusty copper kettle.

Matild clapped her hands together, elbowing her husband. "That's it. Next time they leave town, they're taking me with them." Tarly arched an eyebrow, and she quickly backtracked: "Ah, I mean, *us*. Come on, Tarls. We could use a vacation, right? It's about time."

Tarly heaved a sigh. "A vacation to reconnect, just the two of us? Or a vacation to pitch your case for a one-night stand with a notoriously promiscuous pirate?"

"Who *wouldn't* want a threesome with Dreggs?"

Solemnly, Tarly raised his hand.

His wife shooed him off. "Oh, stop it. You don't even know what you want."

He shot Kianthe and Reyna an exasperated—albeit amused—stare. "Tell me you got their biography signed, at least. Otherwise, she'll be stealing your copy when she comes over next, and I really don't want either of you infiltrating our shops to get it back."

Reyna reached under the counter and handed Matild a book wrapped in heavy paper, tied with a cloth bow.

Matild squealed and tore at the wrapping, gathering the attention of several townsfolk. Whoever wasn't looking before certainly glanced her way when she squealed, "It's the sexy version, Tarly! And they signed it with a little heart!" and then swooned.

"Her most prized possession, as of two breaths ago," Tarly drawled.

"It's sleeping in bed with me tonight. You can have the couch." Matild only half sounded like she was joking. As an afterthought, she added, "Welcome home, you two. We missed you." Without another word, she fled to the corner of the cozy bookshop, where she folded into a velvet armchair and opened the biography.

Tarly took his cup of tea and asked, "Are you two sticking around now that the dragon business is settled? I hear Tawney was listed as Shepara's 'up-and-coming town' in the *Wellia Times*. Come spring, we'll get a lot of tourists—especially since the risk of, you know, being burned alive is gone."

Reyna grimaced, finally pouring herself a cup of tea as well. They'd taken several boxes of Diarn Arlon's imported tea, and its scent filled the air as she opened one of the boxes. "We're so happy to help keep folk from dying by dragon attack."

"And after the pirates and alchemical magic and lovesick drama, I'm happy to stick around for a bit." Kianthe heaved a satisfied sigh, watching the bustling folk filling every corner of their shop. "It's good to be home."

As the hearth blazed and warm laughter filled their bookshop and a snowstorm raged outside, Reyna smiled, pouring steaming water into her mug. Satisfaction filled her soul. "It really is."

Perhaps adventure was much closer to home.

Epilogue

The bees were distressed.

Tessalyn squinted at the honeycomb, mentally tallying the eggs, watching how the bees moved over the brood cells. Many were already capped, and many more had larvae visible to the naked eye: tiny white squigglies—*The technical term,* Tessalyn thought—that were still developing inside their cells.

But there weren't as many larvae as Tessa expected. Which could mean the queen was taking a break from breeding for a time . . . or it could mean something more ominous.

It could mean the hive's queen had died.

"Notice anything?" her professor, a man with an easy temperament, sharp brown eyes, and bronze skin, asked. He was wearing a thin shirt as his protective gear, which was a bold choice by her standards—although to her recollection, he'd never once been stung.

Around them, Natilau—the capital city of Leonol—was bustling. The city was built near the ocean, close enough to see glimpses of it through the dense rainforest, buildings constructed right into the ridiculously thick tree trunks. The rainforest flooded, after all, so raising the homes off the ground just made sense. Homes littered the space between branches, connected with swinging rope walkways and open-air balconies. It was humid, as it always was in the summer, and even the ocean breeze didn't temper the stickiness.

Tessalyn was sweating in her protective gear, but she didn't dare take it off. Not with the bees this agitated. Not when they didn't recognize her like they recognized Professor Leen. Inside the mesh hat, she tried to blow a stray strand of blond hair out of her face, but it was a futile attempt.

"Either a brood break, or . . . they're queenless." She frowned, squinting again at the honeycomb. She'd only recently taken up beekeeping, but it was a fascinating subject. After archeology, sociology, hydrology, and a deep voyage into ethics, it was nice to explore a trade instead of theory.

For now, anyway.

Professor Leen inclined his head. "Indeed. Look here." He guided her around the hive, lifting another frame out of its protective wooden box. The bees buzzed around them, but as always, none viewed him as a threat. He pointed at the dark brown spots of a new honeycomb. "Uncapped queen cells. I noticed this issue several days ago, but I believe there's a virgin queen within the hive. Until I know for sure, I can't pair a new queen with this hive."

"So, they'll just panic until she starts laying eggs again?"

"A hive without a queen is a dead hive. The workers are doing everything they can to prevent that." Leen replaced the honeycomb, closed up the hive by lowering the lid at the top. "It's a delicate process . . . but we *can* intervene if necessary. It's just very, very tricky to decide when the time is right."

Tessa opened her mouth to respond, but someone cleared his throat behind her. She stiffened, grimacing. Professor Leen, meanwhile, smiled wide. "Ah, James. I've been wondering when I'd see you back in class."

"Regretfully, I'm only here for Tessa today."

"Of course you are," Tessa muttered.

James was well-built and moved with powerful grace, so when he crossed his arms, the intention was clear. *Not right now, Tess.*

She stuck her tongue out at him. She was far too old for that kind of thing, but it felt good in the moment. When his lips twitched, she ignored the surge of irritation and glanced at Professor Leen again. "I appreciate the insight. I'll be back tomorrow."

"We'll continue from there, then." The professor hummed,

waved, and strolled around the wooden balcony to another set of students.

Tessa peeled off protective layers, following James to the spiral staircase built around every tree trunk. The beekeeping tree was one of several educational pillars in this part of the city, and students of all ages bustled around the others. She'd toured nearly all of them by this point.

James had toured . . . exactly one. The swordsmanship tree. Because he was a stick-in-the-mud who saw no value beyond the one skill he already knew.

In Leonolan society, he wouldn't amount to much. Not that he cared about that, considering his roots.

Their roots.

They emerged on ground level, and he led her silently toward the cabin they shared outside the city. Once upon a time, she'd shared it with his mother and his aunt, but they were long gone—one perished in a flood, and one . . . well. One fought to the death.

James held open the door to the small home. It was dangerous to build on ground level, but they'd chosen a hill that rarely flooded, and the privacy couldn't be beat. He didn't speak until the wooden door closed behind him, until they were truly alone.

"A letter came for you. From a Lord Wylan." He fished it out of his jacket, tossed the envelope at her. It was sealed with crimson wax hued in gold, a private gift to all lords from Queen Tilaine herself.

She bounced on her toes. "By the Stars, he wrote back?" She moved to snatch the letter from James, but he danced out of her reach. His expression shifted into something stormy, so she cut him off at the pass. "Oh, come on, James. You know the Arcandor is the only one who can help us."

"The Arcandor is dating a former Queensguard." The words were pulled through gritted teeth.

"She's *marrying* that Queensguard soon. Don't be disrespectful."

James looked ready to strangle her, which was very amusing. "Tess, we are trying to stay hidden. They already know we're somewhere in Leonol. With my aunt—" He choked on the word, clenching his eyes shut.

"She took care of that problem, didn't she? They're all dead." Tessa fingered the hem of her shirt now, nervously. It was a lighter hemp material, breathable in the sticky heat of the rainforest.

It didn't stop the sweat that dripped down her neck.

James inhaled slowly. "Yeah, and what's a bigger red flag than four spies missing at once?"

"Why do you think I wrote Lord Wylan?" Tessa set her jaw now, finally snatching the letter from his grasp. She danced away—dance, yet another thing she studied before academic learning took over—and unfolded it. Her eyes skimmed the meticulous script, and she smiled slightly. "He can house us. Hide us."

"We'll be safer in Shepara—"

"I thought we were safe *here*." Tessa sank into a chair by the window, wishing she could open it to let some air in . . . but they had a rule against that too. Just once, she'd love to just *live*. It shouldn't seem too tall an order.

She'd heard a rumor that the Arcandor's Queensguard fled the palace. Fled Tilaine. That she'd opened a bookstore, a tea shop, and settled near dragon country—a spot even Tilaine would hesitate to attack.

She had to know if the rumor was true. If Tawney really was a safe spot for refugees from the Queendom.

Silence stretched between them. James paced, digging his fingers into his short hair, which was shaved nearly to the scalp. His eyes flicked to the sword propped by the door—a Queensguard sword, tucked away in a leather sheath.

"If anyone there finds out who you truly are—" he whispered.

"They won't." She spoke so quickly she nearly tripped over the words.

More silence.

Finally, James glanced out the window, at the two gravestones propped between the curving roots of a towering pentandra tree. In the late afternoon, they were almost entirely cast in shadow. Tessa followed his gaze, swallowed hard.

They hadn't been related to her, but they were family nonetheless.

"We travel *my* way—"

Tessa flicked the parchment. "Actually, Lord Wylan called in a favor. Well, Diarn Feo did. *Well*, the Arcandor did. A ship will dock on the spring equinox to transport us north. Apparently, they were already headed this way for the wedding."

James balked. "*Who*'s already heading this way?"

Now Tessa smirked. "The Dastardly Pirate Dreggs, of course."

THE GAME

A Tomes & Tea One-shot

Note: This is a spicy one-shot, not suitable for underage readers. It has no bearing on future books or their plot. It's just a fun time.

"Let's play a game," Reyna said smoothly, lips pressed to the ceramic edge of Kianthe's favorite mug. Her fingers traced the deep purple glaze, flecked white like the Stars themselves, and Kianthe found herself watching how they caressed the glaze.

Whenever Reyna had a game in mind, Kianthe paid for it.

The mage's chosen tea blend, a yerba maté with notes of cacao, held enough caffeine to be a morning staple—and her simple sentence was *still* more effective at alighting Kianthe's nerves. Reyna knew it, too. Her eyes roamed Kianthe's body language, compartmentalizing, identifying advantages.

Kianthe barely refrained from swallowing. If Reyna sensed weakness, she'd pounce—and this "game" might already be afoot. "Ah. What did you have in mind, dear?" A subtle reminder that they were *supposed* to be on the same page.

A fated pair, and all that.

It didn't seem to matter much now.

Reyna's lips tilted upward, and she drew another delicate sip of her tisane. Unlike Kianthe, she didn't need the caffeine in the morning. She always woke up with something gentle, a chamomile or lavender blend, and then slid into more robust teas as the sun climbed higher. Today, she lounged in the armchair with her legs tucked underneath her.

Soon, they'd have to open New Leaf Tomes and Tea for the day. It was frigid cold outside, deep in the throes of a Tawnean winter, and their neighbors relied on reading material and hot tea between snowstorms. But for now, it was just the two of them, a quiet hush of contentment before the hustle started.

The silence stretched. Kianthe grew tenser with every passing moment, struggling not to fidget. Her fingers tightened around her own mug, which was ironically Reyna's favorite: a large mug with a thick handle, glazed in red and blue that curled like flames.

"Our anniversary is in one week." Reyna's voice was like butter over warm bread. "Did you forget?"

Kianthe absolutely *had* forgotten. Mostly because "weeks" were a Queendom thing, a desperate attempt by Tilaine's mother to keep better track of the days by grouping them arbitrarily. She had loved control, Queen Eren. The rest of the Realm, meanwhile, operated by phases of the moon—which were steady, yet somewhat vague.

All that to say that Kianthe *would* have remembered, if time-keeping were easier—

Reyna's lips quirked.

Fuck.

Kianthe fumbled with her mug, drawing a swig so large a few drops escaped the corners of her mouth and slid down her chin. She hastily wiped them away. How was she *already losing* when she didn't even know what they were playing yet?

"If you're looking for an anniversary gift, you should know yours is en route." Luckily, Kianthe had gifts arriving for Reyna every season, just because she kept finding things her partner would love. She squinted at Reyna, gauging her reaction, hoping that was the point of all this.

Reyna pushed to her feet, moving as gracefully as a dancer before royalty. "This isn't about gifts." Now she stepped closer . . . intoxicatingly close. She was a tad shorter than Kianthe, but her standing position gave her every advantage as she circled the mage. Her fingers trailed along the armchair's velvet backing, close enough that Kianthe could hear their path.

Gooseflesh pebbled along the mage's arms, and she held her breath. "No?"

"No." Reyna paused behind her, leaning close to Kianthe's ear. Her lips were close enough that her whisper felt like a scream. "It's about rewards."

Fire was eating Kianthe from the inside out. Her mouth was dry, the mug forgotten in her hands. She shifted, clenching her thighs to find a modicum of relief. "I'm going to need some blatant clarification here, Rain. Talk to me like you didn't just scramble my brain with a few words."

Reyna's lips brushed against Kianthe's ear, there and gone in a heartbeat. She stepped back, her voice nonchalant. "Success tastes sweeter after tribulation. All the best things"—now she waved a hand at their barn, their hard-built home—"come from patience."

Patience was not Kianthe's strong suit. She tugged at her scarf, which had been a comforting warmth when she woke up and now felt *far* too tight around her neck. "Okay. What does that have to do with our anniversary?"

"Oh, simple." Reyna finished her tea in another sip, offered a wink that made Kianthe's stomach flip. "I propose one week of hands-off contact. No hugging. No kissing. And certainly nothing else. And then, on our anniversary . . . we'll reap our rewards."

A whole *week*?

Kianthe had spent a lifetime alone, held at arms' length by Magicary mages, world officials, and everyone in between. Reyna had been the first person to treat her like a *human* rather than a goddess. Someone to be loved rather than idolized.

Those casual touches, the kisses they shared so freely—those were moments of proof. Reminders that Kianthe wouldn't, in fact, die alone. She'd spent so many nights curled against Visk, hidden in the darkest corners of the Realm, craving a loving embrace. Now that she had it, she didn't want to go back.

She couldn't mask her disappointment.

"Oh."

Reyna paused, hearing it in her tone. Her brow knitted, her sultry attitude gone. "It's okay, Key. It was just a thought I had last night." Now she held out a hand, offering to take Kianthe's cooling mug. When Kianthe handed it over, Reyna brushed her fingers, a pointed reminder that the game was discarded as easily as it was proposed. Her brilliant smile held no strings. "We don't have to do it."

Stone and Stars, Kianthe loved her.

She pushed out of the chair, trailing after Reyna like a puppy as her fiancée set both mugs into a basin of soapy water, fresh for the day. Kianthe draped over the polished wooden countertop, watching Reyna for any sign of disappointment. "I feel like you brought it up for a reason."

Reyna quirked an eyebrow, lips tilted in amusement. "Dear, this isn't a trick. If the game doesn't excite you, we won't do it." And to punctuate that, she leaned over the counter and kissed Kianthe on the lips.

Warmth blossomed in Kianthe's chest.

But more than that.

Curiosity.

"You were thinking about this last night?"

Reyna smirked, dunking the mugs again, using a nearby rag to wipe them clean. "We've found something wonderful, but . . . sometimes I miss the anticipation after you'd been traveling, when we met under the cover of darkness. Swallowing sounds because my cohorts might hear. Knowing what would happen if we were caught." Reyna's eyes drifted upward, like she was drenched in a memory. "There's something thrilling about the chase. That's all."

Kianthe's brow furrowed, because Reyna was right. Their sex life was hardly unadventurous, but . . . well, it lacked the urgency, the desperation, of their courting years. Everything in the Grand Palace felt like a stolen pleasure. Kisses were more passionate. Touches could ignite. Even a fast glance held enough weight to make Kianthe squirm.

Hmm. Amazing that Kianthe hadn't noticed it before. Now

that Reyna pointed it out, everything lately felt a little boring. Like things were too easy.

But damn it, they were the Arcandor, the Mage of Ages, and the *only* Queensguard to ever flee her post and survive. "Boring" didn't fit their lives—or their relationship—at all. Competition flared.

She and Reyna were a lot of things, but *boring* was not one of them.

"How long is a week, again?"

"Six days, love." Reyna sounded amused. She laid the mugs on a custom rack to dry, then wiped her hands on a clean towel. Her apron was hung by the storage room, and she plucked it off the wooden dowel. "If you're actually considering it, we can lay ground rules to make you feel better."

Now Kianthe was embarrassed that she'd ever doubted the longevity of their relationship. Of course a week without kissing wouldn't kill her. Hells, when she traveled for her magical duties, she was gone for huge chunks of any given season. They survived without each other then, too, and it never weighed on her.

"I don't need ground rules," Kianthe said, stubbornly.

Reyna tied the apron behind her back. "You balked at the suggestion half a conversation ago."

Kianthe straightened, pulling back her shoulders. "I didn't understand what you were asking. It's not an excuse to avoid me for a week. It's—well, the opposite." Like spinning a top; anticipation would build every time it wobbled, wondering if that was the moment it might fall.

Actually, the very idea made Kianthe a little breathless.

"An accurate revelation." As Reyna strolled past, her hand slipped seamlessly under Kianthe's shirt. The calloused pads of her fingers trailed Kianthe's bare skin, causing her breath to hitch—but Reyna was gone before Kianthe could enjoy it, stepping lightly to unlock the front doors.

Shit.

Kianthe unwound her scarf; the barn was always chilly in the mornings, but after the tea and . . . well, *this* conversation, she hardly needed the added warmth. "Okay. If this is something you want to try, let's do it. A week without contact should be easy."

Reyna stepped outside, barely flinching in the bitter wind as she flipped the "closed" sign to "open." Then she closed the doors to block the cold, pausing by Kianthe again. Despite her casual words, her expression was sly. "Easy, hmm?"

Reyna's lips crashed against hers. Her hands wrapped around Kianthe's neck, tangling in her shoulder-length hair, her body pressing against Kianthe's form. She tasted sweet, like the honey she used in her chamomile tea, but her lips were ravenous, hungry, mind-numbingly *good*—and gone, far too fast.

When she pulled back, Kianthe actually staggered after her. Then her mind made sense of the world, and she caught herself at the last second.

Unfairly, Reyna didn't seem at *all* phased. She strolled back to the counter, humming as if she hadn't just ruined Kianthe's day. "Then we'll start now. No cheating, Key. First person to touch the other in any real capacity loses."

"What do we lose?"

Reyna considered for a moment. "Bragging rights. For eternity."

Oh. *Oh*.

Kianthe balled her fists. "Gonna be like that, then, huh?"

"Dearest, it's *always* like that." Reyna winked. "Game on."

It sounded so easy.

It *should* have been easy, damn it.

But Kianthe was already seriously regretting agreeing to this. They were only one night in—*one night*—and Reyna was making her wild. It started when they retired to bed, and Reyna wedged two thick pillows in the space between them.

"Try not to think of me," she'd said, in a voice that made Kianthe think of nothing else.

She pushed upright, staring at Reyna over the linen pillow cases. "Well, that's nearly impossible."

Reyna had chosen Kianthe's favorite nightshirt—because of *course* she had—and it dipped tantalizingly low over her ivory skin, showcasing a subtle swell of her breast while leaving *everything* to the imagination. She'd let her hair down, too, and it fanned over her pillow like a halo.

It'd be so easy to roll over the barrier and kiss her senseless. Kianthe wanted it so, so badly. It'd start with cuddling . . . and then her fingers would roam, circling Reyna's nipples. Reyna's lips would part, soft inhales that shifted to quiet moans. Kianthe would bury her nose in the crook of Reyna's neck, kissing just under her ear, along her collarbone. Her fingers would venture farther down, down, pressing *right there,* just to hear Reyna gasp.

"Dearest," Reyna said, shattering her thoughts.

"What?" Kianthe grumbled.

"Your fingers."

They were draped over the pillow wall, nearly brushing Reyna's bare skin. Her fiancée didn't move, as if waiting to see what Kianthe would do next. Her hazel eyes held Kianthe's, and her lips parted ever so slightly. The energy that sparked between them was a physical heat.

Heat pulsed elsewhere, too, spreading between Kianthe's thighs.

"Well, love?" Reyna breathed, statue-still.

Kianthe hated losing, and she absolutely couldn't give Reyna the satisfaction. With a groan, she pulled away—which might have been the hardest thing she'd done all night. "You know that telling me *not* to think of you only does the opposite, don't you?"

"I'm aware." Reyna traced the blankets above her body, watching Kianthe with lidded eyes. For a moment, Kianthe was certain she'd delve below the covers, take pleasure into her own hands—which would be *hot*—but then she blew a kiss and chimed, "Good night, love. Sweet dreams."

Kianthe's dreams would be *anything* but sweet. She audibly groaned in frustration, to which Reyna blinked innocently.

"Problem?"

Kianthe's body throbbed. She gritted her teeth. "No. No problem."

"Excellent. Don't forget to extinguish the ever-flames." And Reyna let her eyes drift shut.

Kianthe flopped onto her back, waving a hand and casting their room into darkness. The rest of the night was spent utterly aware of Reyna's body near hers, close enough to feel her shifting in her sleep, but never touching.

This was fine.

It was most assuredly *not* fine.

Reyna's tactics grew even more unrelenting. It was almost like she took *pleasure* in making Kianthe squirm—which, knowing her fiancée, was probably true. She wore all of Kianthe's favorite outfits: tight corsets and well-fitted trousers and belts that left little to the imagination. She smiled to their neighbors, chatted to their customers, and every chance she got, she'd get so close Kianthe could *feel* her body heat. And then she'd stroll away, acting as if she wasn't doing it on purpose.

By the third day, Kianthe was ready to rip her own hair out.

Reyna slid behind the counter, twirling a quill over deft fingers. "What do you think, Key?" Her voice was contemplative, and she fanned out a sheet of parchment. "Two containers, or three? We've been going through the cinnamon spice blend pretty fast."

The parchment was noting their most recent shipping order, which was important. Bethette would be here any day to collect it, and she didn't like to wait. Kianthe forced herself to focus on the numbers, *not* on the way Reyna's blouse showed off her shoulders, or how the neckline framed her collarbone.

"Three? It's not like we won't use it."

There. That sounded appropriately coherent.

Reyna hummed, licking the quill's nib. Wetting the tip made it easier to write, Kianthe knew, *she knew,* but it lingered a breath too long. Reyna's eyes flashed to hers, and a sly smile flickered—gone the minute Kianthe registered it.

"Three is expensive, but you're right. It's the season for spiced teas." Reyna wrote a few notes on the shipping order.

She did that on purpose. Kianthe leaned over the counter, her fists clenching as heat spread between her legs. "You're not playing fair."

"Fair?" Reyna blew on the ink, so gently that Kianthe could imagine she was blowing on her bare skin instead. She glanced at her fiancée through heavy lashes. "Love, I never said I'd play fair. In fact, we only set one rule."

They were so close Kianthe could nearly taste her. Her breath caught. The urge to kiss her fiancée was overpowering, and Kianthe absolutely would have lost their bet right there—but then someone said, "Oh, shit! Reyna, can I get a towel?"

Reyna straightened immediately, all business. Only the slight flush to her cheeks belied their conversation, something Kianthe noted with smug satisfaction.

"One day, Brennia, I'm going to start putting a lid on your mugs."

Brennia, the town exterminator, laughed. "It's not *my* fault. The tables are too small. Can't properly spread out." She took the rag Reyna offered, and the pair of them began wiping down the table and floor.

Kianthe definitely didn't stare at Reyna's ass.

Okay, she did, but once she realized it, she forced herself to look busy behind the counter. There were dirty mugs near the wash bin, so she started cleaning what she could. Might as well be useful, even when she felt pretty damn useless.

After a little while, Reyna said, "Rose mint, right? I'll steep you another."

"That'd be divine."

Reyna whistled cheerfully as she strolled toward the back storage room. On the way, she produced that quill—and brushed the feather ever so gently against Kianthe's bare wrist. It felt like a passing kiss.

Okay. Fine. She wanted to play it that way?

Kianthe set the mugs on the drying cloth and followed her fiancée into the storage room. Reyna was sifting through their back stock, and when she saw Kianthe, she said, "Key, good. Make a note that we'll need more rose mint—"

"You're doing this on purpose." Kianthe stepped too close, almost taking Reyna by the waist. But then she'd lose, and the game would be over—and that heat on Reyna's cheeks was everything Kianthe ever wanted. Reyna was standing beside the dormant oven, which hadn't been used in hours. The brick would be pleasantly warm now, a straight backing that sloped gently near Reyna's head.

Kianthe glanced at it, an idea already forming.

Reyna, meanwhile, pointedly avoided her gaze, setting a box of tea leaves on the counter beside the stove. Her tone was innocent. "On purpose? I don't know what you mean."

She'd barely finished when Kianthe swept a gust of wind, pushing her back with magic instead of touch. It was so sudden that Reyna gasped, the sound cut off as her back thumped against the oven's brick wall. Shock overtook her beautiful features.

Kianthe stepped in close, her hand slamming beside Reyna's ear. Trapping her here, in this moment. Reyna was a trained Queensguard. She could kill someone with a hairpin and three moves, tops—but now her breath caught, and her eyes flicked to Kianthe's lips. A dark flush crept over her cheeks, her ears. "A-Ah. Hello, love."

"Hello, dearest," Kianthe whispered, leaning even closer. Their lips were almost touching, *almost,* and she swore magic fizzled between them. The world narrowed to her fiancée, the woman she loved. She'd *asked* for this. And in this moment, Kianthe could see why. "You've had days to tease me, but you seem to forget that there are two players in this game. I hope you've enjoyed keeping me up at night, all those fleeting looks, because it's *my* turn now."

She punctuated the moment with a twist of magic. The stone under Reyna's feet surged up in a rolling wave, forcing Reyna to arch against the curved brick near the top of the oven. Reyna gasped, but it cut into a breathy sigh as a caress of heat slid between her thighs, touched her skin like a wicked promise.

And then, it was gone. Kianthe stepped back, offered a wink, and said, "Don't forget about the rose mint tea."

She left Reyna alone, bracing herself against the dormant oven, breathing heavily.

Maybe this *was* fun.

After that, it became a game of scoring points.

Kianthe took her to dinner at the tavern, chose a table in the back corner—and sent a strand of ivy creeping up her leg, caressing Reyna's inner thighs as she tried to maintain a conversation. Kianthe didn't drink, but hearing Reyna stumble over normally articulate speech was nothing short of intoxicating.

Reyna got back at her by ignoring her nightshirt after a hot bath. She stepped out of their washroom with pink skin and lidded eyes, fanning herself, everything on full display. "It's just so hot in there," she said. And she sat on the other edge of their bed, *always* on the opposite side of the pillow wall, giving Kianthe enough of a view that she was squirming in discomfort.

Kianthe was working on her pirate novel one evening, lying on the floor while Reyna read in a nearby armchair. "For research," she said as she started pitching positions for the sexy scene, where the woman was ravaged by a crass pirate captain. Reyna joined in, offering suggestions that got raunchier by the moment. Kianthe kept going until Reyna's eyes glazed, until her breath came a bit too fast—and then the mage gathered up the pages and said, "Well, time for bed."

It culminated one night before their anniversary.

The tension between them was tangible now, and it seemed like everything set Kianthe on fire—a smile, an innuendo, a heavy look. Reyna didn't seem to be faring much better. Her gaze lingered on Kianthe, eyes roaming her form. She found more and more reasons to get close—which was both nice, and absolutely tantalizing.

They were finishing up a cup of tea before bed when Reyna said, "You know, we never said we couldn't . . . touch ourselves." Her tone was one of casual disinterest, but her eyes cut to Kianthe's. Illuminated by a roaring hearth, they seemed to be fire themselves.

Everything in Kianthe ignited, too. It was well after closing at New Leaf, so the shop was clean and empty. A quick glance proved the front curtains were drawn. They were well and truly alone.

Which was dangerous as shit.

Kianthe cleared her throat, crossing her legs. "Ah, n-no. I suppose we didn't."

"Hmm." Reyna went silent again, her eyes skimming the pages of her book. There was no way she could be retaining *anything* on those pages, but she flipped through a few more anyway. Sweat slipped down Kianthe's brow. Her heart was beating too fast.

After a week of *this,* it really wasn't taking much at all, was it?

Just the idea of Reyna touching herself, giving Kianthe a show, was—almost too much. Definitely too much. Kianthe had to stop her own hand from drifting downward, had to clench her jaw to keep quiet. Tomorrow. The day of reckoning was *tomorrow.*

"Won't that ruin it?" she finally ventured to ask. It was like pulling teeth to say the words.

Ruin it! her mind screamed.

"Oh, I don't think so." Reyna snapped her book closed, and the *thump* sound had Kianthe going ramrod straight. Reyna's hazel eyes roamed Kianthe's rigid form, and she smiled.

Shit.

"In fact," Reyna said, pushing to her feet. She didn't approach Kianthe. Instead, she spread out on the rug before the hearth, patting the space beside her. "I think it might give us something to look forward to. Something to . . . imagine. One more barrier, right before they all come down."

"You are a menace," Kianthe murmured, but she slid to the floor beside Reyna.

"I'm not the one who's used magic all week." Reyna's words were a bit breathless. Holding eye contact, she lifted her shirt over her head, revealing smooth skin and stunning breasts. Kianthe's heart thumped.

"Don't think I didn't appreciate the change of pace, love. Thinking of you cornering me in the storage room. Touching me in the tavern." Reyna shuddered, letting her eyes slip closed as she traced the swell of one breast, followed the curve of her stomach to the divot of her belly button.

"I—" Kianthe's voice caught, and she swallowed and tried again. "I didn't touch you in the tavern."

Reyna smirked, opening one eye. Already, her pupils were blown out with lust. *Fuck.*

"Semantics."

Reyna's fingertips delved deeper, disappearing into her trousers. It was obvious the moment she settled in, because her entire body tensed, and a slow moan escaped her lips. "Gods, that's almost everything."

Kianthe's own fingers drifted toward her—and stopped just in time. "I can't—I really can't touch you?"

Reyna lay back on the rug with a contented sigh. One hand stayed in her trousers, but the other was roaming, feeling her stomach, her breasts, her neck. "Are you prepared to lose the game?" Her voice dissolved into a whimper, and it made every muscle in Kianthe quiver.

No. She couldn't lose the game. Not after an entire week of this. But it got *so* much harder to remember why when Reyna's breath caught and a shiver wracked through her. Reyna laughed softly. "Wow. This won't take long."

Kianthe released a moan of her own, lying parallel to Reyna. Fuck it. In the absence of touching her fiancée, she let her own fingers flutter along herself, slipping under her shirt, delving below her waistband. Kianthe's clit throbbed, she was already *wet,* and two fingers pressing hard was enough to leave her writhing. "Stars and Stone," she groaned.

"Tell me," Reyna gasped, breaths growing ragged. Her eyes locked on Kianthe, watching her pleasure herself. "Tell me how it feels."

The phrase they always used, twisted into something so incredibly sexy, sent another shot of desire through Kianthe. Reyna was visual, but Kianthe was stimulated by the *noises* her partner made—the sharp inhales, the breathy moans, the hoarse whines as she arched against the rug. Kianthe clenched her eyes shut, feeding off those noises, and it took a moment to remember to speak.

"It feels like—like *everything*, Rain. Like I can almost imagine it's your fingers here instead of mine." Kianthe shuddered, her clit pulsing under the attention. "And—and—*Stone*, it feels so good. Knowing you're that close, it's all I n-need." She swallowed past another tremor, cracked open an eye, watching her lover.

"All—all I need, too." Reyna aggressively palmed her breast, and *fuck* if that didn't send another shock through Kianthe's body. Her hand curled on the rug, close enough that Reyna could reach for it. They hadn't done anything like this since they'd first started dating, quiet kisses punctuated with moments of vulnerability as they discovered how to feel good together. But back then, it was quieter. Now, nothing was stopping the pleasure washing over her—or the cries they made in response.

"K-Key," Reyna said, her voice strangled. "I-I'm not going to last long."

Kianthe rubbed faster, the tight circles making her shudder and twist. "Come for me, love." She groaned, wishing they weren't so far away. "You're the most beautiful thing in the Realm."

"*Gods—*" Reyna gasped, and her body froze in an arch, shudders rippling through her.

The sight of it, the sound of her staccato breaths, the way her eyelids fluttered, it was enough to tip Kianthe over too. She shouted—light *exploded*—Stars—everything igniting as the world fell away and all that was left were torrents of ecstasy coursing through her veins, her body, her soul.

She was vaguely aware of Reyna whispering—"Stunning, my love. *Magnificent.*"—before the keening faded and awareness seeped back and she felt the rug under her boneless body, heard the crackling fire above her head.

It took several more breaths—mostly gasps, shuddering inhales—to remember how to speak.

"S-Stone be damned," Kianthe whispered, her voice hoarse. She withdrew her hand, turned on her side to face Reyna. Even that felt like a monumental effort. Her body was leaden, weighted with satisfaction—and yet, something new thrummed beneath the undercurrent of satisfaction.

Desire.

Yearning.

Reyna looked tantalizing, cheeks pink and chest heaving, and in the afterglow, Kianthe wanted nothing more than to touch her. To make her scream, but not on visuals alone. She wanted to make her fiancée writhe, beg, *come* with Kianthe's head between her legs. She reached for Reyna's hand.

"Dear," Reyna breathed, although she didn't pull away.

Kianthe stopped herself just in time, and her groan was pulled from her very soul. "Rain, come on. We're close enough." The frustration in her voice was evident.

It was exactly where Reyna wanted her. She offered a serene smile, and dread crept along Kianthe's spine. Her next words weren't surprising. "Close enough, indeed. My darling, all the greatest things come from waiting. From *anticipation*."

Kianthe felt like she was physically on fire. She actually checked to see that her hands hadn't accidentally ignited. A shiver wracked through her, and she clenched her jaw. "I'm anticipating enough."

"Let the memory of this sit for a day. Then, tomorrow night . . ." Reyna murmured, leaning close so her breath brushed Kianthe's lips. "We'll see if it was worth the wait."

"You're the worst." But Kianthe's brain was already swimming, aware of nothing else but Reyna's face so close to hers, of her body near and so, so far.

"Perhaps." And then it was gone. Reyna pushed upright, gripped the mantle to steady herself, and laughed a little. "Lightheaded. See you in bed, dearest." And she waved a few fingers, strolling for the washroom.

Kianthe flopped back to the rug. "Yeah, yeah."

The next morning dawned dark and dreary, and Kianthe awoke from a restless slumber to a frantic knock farther into the barn.

She cracked open an eye, saw Reyna already twisting out of bed. Her fiancée's hair was bedraggled, and she clawed it into a bun, moving swiftly for the hallway.

"Whassaproblem?" Kianthe mumbled.

"I'm not sure," Reyna replied. "But people don't bang on our front door for no reason."

That woke Kianthe up. She pushed out of bed, shuddered in the cold, and grabbed a robe. As she followed Reyna, a distant part of her brain whispered, *But it's our anniversaryyy.* Even in the lingering throes of sleep, she hadn't forgotten their gifts to each other.

"This better be good," she said darkly. "I was going to keep the shop closed and enjoy you all fucking day."

Reyna raised one delicate eyebrow, tying her own fleece robe around her waist.

"Pun intended," Kianthe added.

"Is that a pun, love?"

"I don't know. I'm half-asleep."

Another knock on the door, louder this time. A booming voice followed: "Kianthe, we need that fancy magic of yours!" It was Tarly, which only made Reyna yank the door open faster. A gust of icy wind swept into New Leaf, and both of them shivered. Outside, it was snowing heavily.

"What's the problem?" Reyna's voice was sharp.

Above his short beard, Tarly's cheeks were splotchy from the cold, and he rubbed his hands together. Even his heavy cloak didn't seem to protect from the freezing weather. "Sorry to bother you two so early, but there was an avalanche on the rim. We think the Klancons are trapped inside their house."

"Shit," Kianthe said. "Just let me change." And she stepped past Tarly, pressed two fingers into her mouth for a sharp whistle. It wouldn't travel far in the snow, but griffons had excellent hearing. Visk—and probably Ponder—wouldn't waste time.

Sure enough, by the time Visk landed outside New Leaf, Kianthe was tying her scarf and Reyna was securing a thick winter cloak around her neck. Tarly was standing in the entranceway, dripping as the snow on his cloak melted, shifting his weight. Reyna tossed him a towel and asked, "Anyone else caught?"

"Just the Klancons. Lord Wylan's house was affected too, but he's higher up. Just got a dusting of snow in the courtyard—nothing that would impact the house." Tarly jogged back outside. "Matild is prepping the clinic, just in case. I'll meet you guys there with some shovels. The whole town is mobilizing."

"Shovels?" Kianthe said drily, her hands flickering with flame. "Really?"

"We don't know what we're up against, love. Lives are at stake." Reyna stepped outside after Tarly, waiting for Kianthe to follow before closing the front doors tightly. Ponder landed hard on her shoulders, which almost knocked her over—in just half a season, she'd doubled in size, and now was akin to a large dog.

A large, *flying* dog. With talons and an impulsive attitude.

"Pondie, dearest, not now," Reyna said, which offended the griffon greatly. She began chittering, her talons digging into Reyna's cloak—at least until Visk screeched. It was enough to still Ponder, enough to make her slink to the ground and hunch under her father's ire.

Kianthe leapt on his back, offering a hand to Reyna. She took it, and lightning flashed between them. The first contact in days—and Kianthe couldn't even enjoy it. But an emergency took priority, and they both knew it. She hauled Reyna on behind her, waited for a breath as she settled into her usual spot on Visk's back.

"See you there, Tarls," she said, and they were off. Ponder stubbornly stayed behind, clearly petulant. Kianthe patted her griffon's neck. "You'll be paying for that later."

Visk huffed.

The whole town *had* emerged—which was good, because the snowstorm was getting worse. Visibility was so bad that Visk had to fly lower to town, skimming rooftops just to stay on course. When they came upon the avalanche, peppered with their neighbors attempting to dig into the snow, Reyna swallowed a gasp.

"Gods." Her grip tightened around Kianthe's waist, and the mage tried to ignore how it sent a rush of heat between her legs.

Not the time, damn it.

"I've seen worse," Kianthe said. That was true, but it had been deep in the mountains before. She'd never seen an avalanche so viciously consume public property. Most of the houses here were of the *burnt* variety, the portion of town targeted by the dragons, so that explained why only the Klancons were involved. Still, the avalanche had clearly thundered down the curved edge of the rim, swiftly swallowing entire streets in its way.

Reyna's voice was stern. "*Why* did they move here? You told them it was too dangerous with Tawnean winters."

"They wanted land, and this house was already built." Kianthe guided Visk to the ground. "If this drains me too much for tonight, I'm going to be pissed."

As they landed near the edge of the avalanche, Reyna pressed a kiss to Kianthe's cheek. It felt like she'd ignited every nerve in Kianthe's body, but when the mage turned to kiss her properly, Reyna pulled back. "Key, the reward for saving lives will *absolutely* be worth your while." Her sultry tone implied far more than social rewards. "Impress me."

Kianthe's mouth went dry, and her shudder wasn't from the cold. "S-Sure. Anything for you, love."

Reyna winked and slid off Visk, striding with confidence toward Lord Wylan and Diarn Feo. Kianthe didn't wait to see how she'd help from the ground. She just urged Visk back into the air, magicked the snow from her eyes, and squinted at the avalanche.

Okay. Showtime.

"To the Arcandor," Rylo Klacon shouted, hoisting a beer in Kianthe's direction. "And to everyone who helped dig us out."

"Our pleasure. Now, time to move," Tarly bellowed, which elicited a cheer of amusement from the rest of the crowd.

The inn's tavern was swarmed with people, folks who'd spent hours in the icy cold and now wanted a fireplace to warm the skin and a drink to warm the veins. Through the windows, the blizzard was still raging, and snow reflected off the flickering lights of the inn. At the table of honor near the hearth, Kianthe and Reyna lifted their own drinks in kind.

"Moving isn't necessary; I should have reworked the physical structure of that rim seasons ago." Kianthe chugged her water, then heaved a sigh and massaged her head. "Just—give me some time to regain my magic. Avalanches are a bitch."

That raised another hearty laugh from the crowd, and conversation separated like strands from an unraveling rope. In the resulting din, Reyna bent her head toward Kianthe, turning her face so her words were private.

"Are you tired?"

There was an obvious connotation, emphasized by the way her fingers trailed along Kianthe's thigh under the table.

She *was* tired, but the Stone of Seeing had felt her misery and was replenishing her magic supply faster than expected. Already, her headache was fading, replaced with a more insistent throbbing much farther south. Kianthe shifted, casting a glance at the crowds. "I feel like some folks will notice if we leave."

"Let them. It's our anniversary, and I've waited too long." The heat in Reyna's voice, murmured low for Kianthe's ears alone, made her swallow a groan. She followed obediently as Reyna pushed to her feet, drained her wine, and strolled for the door. Her voice was casual. "If you'll all excuse us."

She offered no more explanations. Matild quirked an eyebrow, and across the tavern, Feo wrinkled their nose. But otherwise, they slipped out unnoticed.

They walked arm-in-arm, huddled close for warmth. It took Reyna a few steps to realize that Kianthe had magicked a bubble to keep the snow off their faces. "Are you sure you're up to this?" she asked, her voice mild. Despite the casual tone, an undercurrent of worry lingered.

Neither of them would forget what a true magic drain felt like, or how it could put Kianthe out for days.

But today wasn't that. "Trust me, Rain. I'm all in for tonight." Her body pulsed with want, and she tightened her grip on her fiancée's arm. "You looked so sexy in the tavern. All I wanted to do was kiss you."

"Soon," Reyna replied, promise heavy in the word.

Kianthe swallowed and picked up her pace. Reyna kept up easily, and soon they were back at home. Anticipation buzzed through her veins as she checked the curtains were still drawn, as Reyna locked the front door resolutely. The snow muffled all noise, and the barn was silent, save for some light creaking in the wind.

"Should I steep some t—" Kianthe's words were cut off as Reyna pulled her into a passionate embrace. *Apparently,* she'd been putting on a calm façade all evening, because now passion emanated from her desperate grip on Kianthe's arms, the feverish press of her lips as she left Kianthe's behind to kiss her cheek, her jaw, her neck.

"Stone b-bless." Kianthe was suddenly breathless. She hadn't been ravaged like this in a while, and it was making her lightheaded. "Right here?"

Reyna pulled off her cloak, then tugged her own shirt over her head. She wasn't wearing any undergarments today, and her bare breasts made Kianthe stop and stare. Reyna wasn't having that. She pushed Kianthe against one of the bookshelves, pressing her body against her partner's. Her words were heavy with lust.

"Clothes. Off."

Anything. *Everything.* Kianthe stripped so fast she barely remembered doing it, but soon her clothes were on the floor. Reyna kept her pants on, too enamored with stroking Kianthe's waist, palming her breasts, ravishing her collarbones. Kianthe shuddered when Reyna closed her lips over one nipple, then swallowed a strangled groan as her tongue flicked the peak. Hot desire coursed through Kianthe, and she writhed against the shelves.

"E-Enjoying yourself?" she managed to gasp.

Reyna pulled back, and the sudden rush of cold air on her tit made Kianthe moan. The sound only seemed to incite Reyna more. Her voice was a sultry purr. "Oh, I'm enjoying this *immensely.*"

With little pretense, Reyna wrenched her thigh between Kianthe's bare legs. The sudden pressure *right there* almost made Kianthe see stars, and her hands fell back to the books, knocking a few over as she struggled for purchase.

Reyna chuckled, which only sent heat pooling against the friction. Kianthe's hips moved on their own accord, pumping against Reyna's thigh. Her trousers had pockets and buttons and they'd never done *this* before, not with one clothed and one completely bare, but somehow the fabric barrier and all its *interesting* assets pressed against Kianthe's folds just right, and her head fell back as she ground against Reyna's fantastically strong thigh.

"*Rain,*" she barely managed to breathe, but pleasure was pulsing through her in waves now, and she'd never come this fast, not until last night, and certainly not without earlier stimulation, but *somehow* she was right on the precipice of something divine. Reyna seemed to realize it, too, because she pushed to her tiptoes, which only gave her a better vantage point for *more* pressure, and by the Stone and Stars themselves, it was too much—and it hit her exactly right, and oh fuck fuck, *fuck*—

"What was that?" Reyna nipped her skin, scraping teeth along one sensitive breast. Kianthe was shuddering in waves of bliss, and that made her cry out, stiffen against the shelves, but Reyna didn't stop. Instead, her voice was louder, somewhere by Kianthe's ear now. "Talk to me, Key. Tell me how you're feeling."

That *phrase*. Kianthe could never deny her partner an answer to *that* phrase. Her brain was scattered, lost in a cacophony of *oh Stars and Stone, oh my fuck, Reyna, Rain, keep going, please never stop* and she finally began babbling those words, because it was all she could manage. "Rain, f—uck, keep going, yes, right there, *yes, YES*—"

"Gods, you are the sexiest thing when you're like this," Reyna breathed, wrenching her thigh up yet again. Kianthe did scream this time, her hands gripping Reyna's bare waist now, squeezing muscle and soft skin and digging her nails in because *nothing had ever felt this good*—

"I'm—I'm gonna—"

And Reyna pulled away.

The loss was like a physical pain that ratcheted through her.

Kianthe actually cried out in frustration, sagging against the bookshelves, shuddering with desire, arching against the books as her throbbing, dripping center convulsed in the emptiness. It felt like a wash of heat that swelled too much, but she was alone, no stimulation, no touch, and for several ragged breaths it seemed like it wouldn't matter, like Kianthe might explode anyway, just off the memory—but eventually awareness seeped back in and she was left absolutely drained.

And pissed.

"Y-You're an asshole," she wheezed.

"Am I?" Reyna asked innocently.

Reyna hadn't moved far, clearly staying close in case Kianthe actually buckled at the knees—which felt like a near thing, honestly. Her partner wore a smug smile and didn't bother hiding how her lidded eyes roamed Kianthe's naked body. The look brought back all kinds of recent memories, and Kianthe trembled, resting her head against the books in a fit of frustration now.

"Yes," she finally said, when she'd caught her breath and felt like she wouldn't topple over.

Reyna stepped closer again, her fingers feathering along Kianthe's bare chest. Every touch was *fire,* and one pinch of her nipple had Kianthe groaning.

"I told you this week would be worth it. I don't want to give you multiple orgasms. I want to give you the *best fucking orgasm* you've ever had." Reyna pressed a kiss to Kianthe's lips, smirking against them as Kianthe's hands desperately wound around her body, feeling Reyna's breasts, stroking her back. "Do you want that, love?"

"*Yes*. More than anything." Kianthe kissed her hungrily, and the feeling of their breasts pressing together was more arousing than she expected. She mimicked Reyna's earlier motion, trailing kisses to that soft spot under her ear—the one that sent gooseflesh up Reyna's arms.

"Ah, ah," Reyna breathed, and stepped back again. "This is about you, dear."

For the first time tonight, a spark of competition flared in Kianthe's chest. Reyna was going to be insufferable tonight if she didn't *do* something, and luckily, Kianthe knew exactly how to regain control.

Really, Reyna should have just let her come. Then Kianthe would be more pliable. But now, she was heightened with desire and that *smug smile* on her partner's face made her instantly aware of the fact that this had always been Reyna's game, even if Kianthe won a few rounds.

Well. Tonight, she'd take the true victory.

"About me, huh?" Kianthe advanced, getting into Reyna's space again. Her voice was dark, heady with lust. Reyna's eyes were just as dark, and it was *hot*. "You want to give me the greatest orgasm I've ever had? You want to fuck me senseless all night? Dearest, I'm going to need something to think about first."

Reyna saw what she was doing, and one slender eyebrow rose. She held her ground, nodding at the disheveled bookshelves. "*That* wasn't enough?"

"After the week we've had? Nothing close will be enough." And she scooped Reyna into her arms. Her lover yelped, barely a squeak of surprise, and Kianthe marched her to their bedroom. As much as she loved ravaging Reyna all over their shop, she didn't want to leave her partner with an aching back.

Not this time, anyway.

She dropped Reyna on the bed, then bent over her, kissing her senseless. Reyna was more turned on by Kianthe's pleasure than she let on, because she barely remembered to kiss back—half of them were just gasps as Kianthe's hands roamed. She traced Reyna's breasts, feathered along the ticklish part of her stomach. Normally, that'd make Reyna giggle, but tonight it just seemed to heighten everything else. The moan that left Reyna's lips was an elixir.

"I'm setting a new rule," she breathed in between kisses. "If I haven't come, *you* don't come."

"C-Changing the rules so—" Reyna cut off, arching against the mattress. "*Gods*—so late in the game?"

Kianthe smirked. "The only rule we set already expired. Remember?" To punctuate that, her fingers slipped under Reyna's trousers, finding her clit with practiced ease. She was rewarded by Reyna's breath cutting off entirely, her eyelids fluttering as she sank into pleasure. Beautiful. Nothing would ever be more stunning than Reyna in this state.

"I'm going to need these off." Kianthe withdrew her hand, then began unbuttoning the trousers.

Reyna helped, kicking them to her ankles and shivering in the cold air. In response, Kianthe cast a few ever-flames, letting them drift toward the ceiling. It warmed the air slightly, but she didn't want things too hot. Reyna was already sweating, her body slick, her cheeks flushed.

Perfection.

"You are incredibly beautiful," Kianthe murmured, peppering kisses along her stomach, drifting lower. She felt Reyna's muscles tense under her ministrations, and she smiled against her skin. "I barely slept this week—I haven't been that aware of your body since we met." Another kiss, this time on her inner thigh. Close, so close. Reyna seized a gasp, her body trembling with want. Kianthe chuckled. "And last night. We haven't enjoyed ourselves like that in so long, but I don't remember it being that fun."

"It—I couldn't help it," Reyna whispered, clenching her eyes shut as Kianthe's fingers stroked her folds.

She went silent, and Kianthe tsked. "Couldn't help what, love?"

"C-Couldn't help t-touching myself," came her breathless reply.

It sparked another fire inside Kianthe, and she twisted, giving her own clit a couple hard rubs. "Really?"

"You were on my mind all week." Reyna moaned, her hands tangling in Kianthe's hair. She was rambling now, as Kianthe kissed closer and closer to where she needed. "Every time you looked at me, I thought I might die. It was so hard to s-serve our customers. And that—*fuck, Key*—that oven trick? You—you cleared my mind."

That took some doing. "Tell me more." Kianthe rewarded her by pressing her lips to Reyna's hot center, her tongue delving between the folds. She was soaking wet, which only incited Kianthe more. They'd been together long enough. She knew exactly how to make Reyna writhe, and she wasted no time.

"*Kianthe—*" Reyna cried, grinding against her mouth. "*Gods.*"

"Tell. Me. More." Every word was muffled, punctuated by her tongue darting to the nub of Reyna's clit. She could imagine the waves of ecstasy washing over her partner, could feel her body tensing and trembling as Kianthe worshiped her.

It took a few breaths before Reyna started talking again. "I imag—*fuck*—imagined *this.* I knew you'd—" She cut off with a keening groan, her thighs clenching, her body twisting to find the best angle. Her fingers tightened on Kianthe's scalp, and the way she tugged on Kianthe's hair was intoxicatingly incredible.

Pleasure mounted in Kianthe, too, and she touched herself with little regard. *It took some doing,* she thought distantly, *to keep Reyna* and *herself satisfied.* It didn't take long to get herself back to the heightened state she'd experienced against the bookshelves. Her breath came hot against Reyna's center, even as she sucked and twisted her tongue.

Reyna had fallen silent, consistent trembles arching through her body. Even her moans had quieted, but she managed to gasp, "I'm n-not going to last long, Key—"

"You don't come until *I* come," Kianthe growled against her. But she didn't slow her pace, didn't have the willpower to leave. In fact, she paused in her own pleasure, fingering Reyna's opening, testing a finger inside, then two. Reyna arched, shuddering, swallowing a scream. "*Key, YES,* Gods, that! Please—I can't—"

"Don't come," Kianthe snapped, mostly because it was damn fun to watch Reyna *trying her hardest not to.* A vicious pride overtook her chest, and she slid back between her partner's legs, sucking relentlessly, her tongue circling Reyna's clit, her fingers pumping hard until her partner shouted loud enough to echo off the rafters and her body dissolved into violent shuddering.

Kianthe wanted to see how far she could take this. She kept up her sucking, her pumping, but paused just long enough to whisper, "I told you *not* to come."

It seemed to incite another round of pleasure for Reyna, and she whimpered, eyes clenched as she writhed against the bed. "Gods, *Gods,* Key, I've never felt this good—*Gods—*"

Damn. This was as close to cosmic bliss as Kianthe would ever reach.

Her climax finished in stages—where Reyna eased herself back to the mattress, slowly unwound her muscles, blearily opened glazed eyes. Kianthe coaxed her through it, kissing instead of sucking, stroking instead of pumping, and eventually, she withdrew entirely to lie beside her lover.

Reyna glanced sideways at her, a weary smile on her lips. "You're terrible."

"I'm not the one disobeying orders." Kianthe lightly traced Reyna's bare stomach.

The touch sent another wave of shivers through Reyna, and she breathed a satisfied sigh. "I can confidently say that was the best orgasm I've ever had."

"Even better than our first trip to Wellia?"

Reyna paused, thinking back. "Well, shit. It's tied."

"Hard to compete with toys." Kianthe smirked. "You look tired, Rain. Had enough already? What happened to fucking me all night long?"

"You went off-script." Reyna swatted her shoulder.

"I always go off-script. I'm the Arcandor."

A bit of fire lit in Reyna's light brown eyes, and she rolled over, draping her cooling body over Kianthe's. Her bun was coming out now, soft strands framing her face. The ever-flame above her cast her form in shadow, but Kianthe could see the wicked curve of her lips. "Did you know I kept one of those toys? From Wellia?"

"Did you now?"

"Mmm." She kissed Kianthe hard, then rolled over. From the depths of their wardrobe, Reyna produced a silk bag. She pulled out a smooth stone cock, meticulously shaped from granite—undoubtedly by an elemental mage's hand. Kianthe twitched just looking at it, eyes widening. "That must have cost a fortune."

"Worth it, for nights like this." Reyna eased back on the bed, trailing the tip along Kianthe's stomach. The contrast of cold stone against hot skin had her swallowing a groan, and Reyna smiled, her fingers taking position for some slow, steady circles.

Kianthe hissed, pressing her head back against the bed. "Rain, I'm so turned on that you might not get to *use* that." Heat had flooded her center, and she let her eyes drift shut. But that allowed too much focus on the stimulation, which was *good, so fucking good, shit,* so she forced them back open.

Reyna's lips were tilted in a perpetual smirk. "I need to make sure you're ready for it. Besides, there's nothing wrong with a prelude."

A prelude.

Stone and Stars, Kianthe might not survive this night after all. Already, her body was coiling, something tremendous building in her center. Her clit pulsed with want, and Reyna didn't let up, and her breaths were already coming heavy again. She wasn't sure how long Reyna pleasured her like this, but the climax snuck up on her, slamming into her like—

Well, an avalanche.

She cried out, shivering, gripping Reyna's forearms as she came. Pleasure cascaded through her, but on the heels of it, immediate want for more. She'd had such a week, been teased *so* much, that this wasn't enough—not by a long shot. As the post-climax haze settled over her brain, her body ached for more.

And Reyna delivered. "You say I'm beautiful, but I don't think there's more stunning than you." Her fingers continued to massage *right there,* but now a third finger dipped toward Kianthe's opening. Everything was raw with pleasure, bright with anticipation, and Kianthe felt breathless as Reyna slipped a finger inside.

It felt good.

It wasn't enough.

"More, Rain," she breathed, nearly begging. "Please, *more.*"

"You mean that first orgasm wasn't the best yet?" Reyna hummed disappointment, but it was all a ploy. She traced the stone cock over Kianthe's chest again, trailing it smoothly down, down. When it brushed against her sensitive clit, Kianthe whined a bit, but it kept diving deeper, burying in her folds, playing with her entrance.

"*Yes,*" she said. "Please, Reyna—"

Reyna lifted herself off Kianthe's body, pressing a kiss to her left breast. "Tell me if something hurts, Key. I'm serious."

"I—I know." Kianthe was always, always safe with Reyna.

Her lover hummed against her nipple, nipped it lovingly, and when Kianthe arched backward—she slid the stone cock inside.

Everything *exploded,* and for a moment, there was only the blissful senselessness of unbridled satisfaction. She was vaguely aware she was chanting again, but Reyna covered her mouth with fierce kisses, and the world fell silent. All Kianthe could do was groan against her lips, lifting her hips to meet Reyna's rolling movements of the toy.

"How's that feel, dear?"

Reyna pulled back to rub her clit, and the added stimulation made Kianthe seize another ragged breath. "Good. *Stone,* Reyna, that's so, so g-good."

"Stone indeed," Reyna replied smugly, and picked up her pace. Her gentle rotations with the toy shifted into light thrusts, which steadily grew in intensity and fervor until she was pounding the toy into Kianthe. Ecstasy rolled off Kianthe in waves as she ground against Reyna's fingers, rolled her hips against the toy.

The best orgasm, *indeed.* Kianthe wasn't even sure where she *was* right now. All that existed was Reyna, and a feeling of being so, so full that she almost couldn't stand it. And all the while, her partner spoke to her, a running dialogue that caressed her brain while her body was pounded into the bed.

"I can't stand how gorgeous you look right now, Key. The way your lips are parted, the flush of your cheeks. Your eyes are my absolute favorite—but the fact that you can't keep them open for long—it's so, so sexy." Reyna kissed Kianthe's stomach, like she couldn't bear to wait any longer. "You are everything I've ever wanted. All I've ever hoped for in a partner. I can't wait to marry you, to live our lives together forever, to see you like this any. Time. I. Fucking. Want." She punctuated that with thrusts of the toy—and it was Kianthe's undoing.

"Oh, *Reyna—*"

Her words cut off into a staccato scream, punctuated by, "*Oh, oh, oooh,*" as her entire body clenched around the toy. Reyna was relentless, and she was still sensitive from her first orgasm—which meant this one was a *fucking beast.* Stars burst behind Kianthe's eyes, she ground her head into the mattress, her fingers clenched the sheets, her body shuddered and writhed, and wave upon wave of pleasure left her absolutely mindless.

Everything.

Was.

Perfect.

When she came to, there was an actual *ringing* in her ears. Reyna had removed the stone cock, tossed it to the side, but she still rubbed Kianthe's folds softly, easing her back to awareness. Her entire body throbbed in the best way, and her clit pulsed with aftershocks. She shuddered once, then again for good measure, cracking open her eyes.

"W-What the fuck," she said.

She was pretty sure she was slurring.

Reyna kissed her cheek, her neck, the swell of her breast. "You are incredible."

"I—" Kianthe lost her train of thought, struggled to locate something articulate. "I don't think I'm the incredible one, Reyna."

Her partner chuckled. "Agree to disagree. So, what would you say? Better than Wellia?"

"Better than a *thousand* Wellias."

"Well, damn. I am good." Reyna dropped beside her on the bed, heaving a sigh. For a long moment, they just lay beside each other, content in their haze. Kianthe was pretty sure she was falling asleep until Reyna nudged her shoulder. "I'd like to clean up, swap blankets, and cuddle you until high noon tomorrow."

Nothing sounded better. Kianthe swallowed a yawn. Her headache was definitely gone now, but she'd be aching tomorrow for very different reasons. "Anything you like, love. I think we deserve a snow day."

"I agree." Reyna pushed off the bed, offered a hand. "Shall we relax with a calming bath?"

"Just keep me from drowning, and I'll be good." Kianthe let her fiancée haul her off the bed, then staggered after her.

Later, they'd fiercely debate who won the game. But although

Kianthe put up a good fight—she couldn't argue that Reyna had been onto something.

And the next year, right before their anniversary, when Reyna drawled, "Want to play a game?" well . . .

Kianthe couldn't say "Fuck yes" fast enough.

Acknowledgments

Update: Summer 2024

Read below for the original acknowledgments—all of them still stand! But obviously, things have changed since this was an indie book, so let's expand accordingly.

To the amazing folks at Bramble, Tor US, and Tor UK: you guys are absolutely incredible. I have never felt so supported, appreciated, and seen as when working with you. Publishing is a tough industry, but your passion and empowerment makes everything seem a lot easier.

To the booksellers and librarians who tirelessly promote diverse books: we'd be nowhere without you. In a time of relentless book banning, you are the champions that will keep us moving in a positive direction.

Finally, to my literary agent, Taryn Fagerness: I'm not sure I can adequately thank you for the effort and time you've given my books. You are incredible, and I'm so fortunate we crossed paths! Here's to many more years and many more releases!

Original Acknowledgments (2023)

I've recently discovered that I experience mild panic when I'm forced to make a list, since I'm entirely convinced I'm going to forget someone important and they'll feel terrible about it and then

I'll be horrified that I forgot them because of course they're my favorite people and oh my god how could I—

So.

I'm going to keep this brief and vague, for my own sanity.

To Travis Baldree and the other cozy fantasy authors slowly making this space into a quiet retreat—thank you! I wrote a couple books, but a couple books does not a genre make. I'm so excited to be a part of this revolution into cozier literature, and I can't wait to read all the upcoming additions!

To my family: my ever-supportive, book-loving parents, my crocheting master of a sister, my grandparents (thanks for teaching Paige to crochet, Gaga!), my aunts and uncles and kick-ass cousins. You guys make my world go 'round. I could never do it without you!

To my dearest friends, the group of women with me through thick and thin . . . thank you for always supporting me, rallying around my accomplishments, and giving me the courage to try new things. And a special shout-out, as always, to my alpha reader, Audrey—none of this would exist without you, dear!

And finally, to the TikTok crowd. The influencers, the readers, the other indie authors. I literally would be nowhere without you guys. Thank you for giving cozy fantasy a home before the rest of the world noticed.

Thank you guys for helping make my dream come true. I hope to provide you with many more sapphic adventures in the future!

About the Author

Rebecca Thorne is an author of all things fantasy, sci-fi, and romance, such as the Tomes & Tea series. She thrives on deadlines, averages 2,700 words a day, and tries to write at least three books a year. (She also might be a *little* hyper-focused ADHD.)

After years in the traditional publishing space, Thorne pivoted into self-publishing. Now, she's found a happy medium as a hybrid author, and leans into her love of teaching by helping other authors find their perfect publication path.

When she's not writing (or avoiding writing), Thorne can be found traveling the country as a flight attendant, or doing her best impression of a granola-girl hermit with her two dogs. She's always scheming to move to a mountain town and open a bookshop that serves tea.